EASTER LILLY

Also by Tom Wicker

FICTION

The Kingpin

The Devil Must

The Judgment

Facing the Lions

Unto This Hour

Donovan's Wife

(under the name Paul Connolly)

Get Out of Town

So Fair, So Evil

Tears Are for Angels

NONFICTION

Kennedy Without Tears

JFK & LBJ: The Influence of Personality upon Politics

A Time to Die

On Press

One of Us: Richard Nixon and the American Dream

Tragic Failure: Racial Integration in America

TOM WICKER

WILLIAM MORROW
AND COMPANY, INC.
NEW YORK

Easter Lilly

A

NOVEL

OF

THE SOUTH

TODAY

None of the characters in this novel are intended to, nor do they, represent any actual persons, living or dead.
All places and events depicted are fictitious.

Copyright © 1998 by Tom Wicker

It is the policy of William Morrow and Company, Inc., and its imprints and affiliates, recognizing the importance of preserving what has been written, to print the books we publish on acid-free paper, and we exert our best efforts to that end.

Library of Congress Cataloging-in-Publication Data
Wicker, Tom.
Easter Lilly : a novel of the South today / Tom Wicker. —1st ed.
p.   cm.
ISBN 0-688-10628-5
1. Afro-American women—Southern States—Fiction.   I. Title.
PS3573.I25E2   1997
813'.54—DC21   97-31400
                                                    CIP

Printed in the United States of America

First Edition

1 2 3 4 5 6 7 8 9 10

BOOK DESIGN BY BERNARD KLEIN

www.williammorrow.com

The author deeply appreciates the generous help of those who advised him on courtroom tactics and legal procedures. They are unnamed, lest some blame should fall on them for errors that may remain—for which, the author takes sole responsibility.

EASTER LILLY

Book One

JASE

AT PRECISELY 6:55 A.M., JASON P. ALLMAN PARKED HIS TOYOTA
pickup at a 90-degree angle to the Stonewall County jail, his front
bumper just touching the cinder-block sidewall. He noticed immediately that Ben Neely's dent-fendered Fairlane was not in the
lot, so Jase checked his watch to make sure he wasn't late. Be just
like Ben, he thought, to take off and leave the jail unguarded if I'm
a minute late.

Jase was right on schedule, however. Vague worry stirred in his
mind. Usually, when he arrived for the daytime shift, he would be
irritated to find Ben's Fairlane catercorner across at least two parking spaces. Jase himself always parked carefully, not just in the jail
lot but everywhere—within the lined spaces, for instance, along
Waitsfield's single downtown street or on the blacktopped expanse
surrounding the Dixie Pride Shopping Mall.

Jase Allman even parked with care in his own driveway, watchful
of Ida Sue's flower beds either in spring or when the weather turned
so hot she let them go to weed. Jase never crossed the street against
Waitsfield's one stoplight; he saved grocery-store coupons from the
weekly *Stonewall News-Messenger,* and at bedtime he folded his blue
jeans neatly over the back of a chair.

"Maw'd whop one of us boys good if we'd of left our britches on the floor," Jase had explained to Ida Sue when in the first week of their marriage she'd asked him how come he was so neat. He knew by then that Ida Sue slept in the altogether her underwear in a pink heap by the bedside.

Jase got out of the Toyota, leaned back in past the steering wheel, and picked up a flimsy cardboard tray that held a bag of sugar-glazed doughnuts and two black coffees from the Krispy Kreme out at the mall. Holding one hand under the tray, he carefully closed the door with the other, admiring as always the ease with which the Toyota's latch caught.

Confound Japs had a way with fit'n finish. But American wheels gave a man more pickup on the interstates.

He carried the tray carefully around the corner of the jail, wondering again where Ben Neely's Fairlane might be. If Ben hadn't shown up the night before, Jase would've heard about it from Rob Moore at 11 P.M., asking where was his relief. As if Jase would know and Ida Sue wouldn't mind being woke up.

Living by his lonesome out at the Neely place, what was left of Ben's daddy's old farm, Ben Neely always drove in for the graveyard shift. Prob'ly what happened this time, Jase speculated, Ben let some girl drive'im—Ben's kind of girl, not too choosy who she rode with. Maybe let her use the Fairlane for the night, promise she'd pick up Ben in the morning.

Jase went up the two steps to the jail's front stoop, from which white pillars rose on either side. Like Mount Vernon. He pulled open a screen door that opened outward, and turned the knob on a heavy metal door that opened inward.

"Hot stuff!" he called out, stepping into the outer office, the cardboard tray held in front of him like an offering plate at the Neely Memorial Methodist Church. "Breakfast!"

Right away, even in the cheerful echoes of his voice, Jase knew something was wrong. Ben Neely should have been asleep or lounging with his feet up on the old wooden desk, Conway Twitty or Hank Williams, Jr., coming in from WCMH, We're Country Music Heaven, in Capital City. But the swivel chair behind the desk was empty and the tabletop radio was silent. The TV stared emptily down from the hospital mount that Ben Neely had cadged out of his big-shot brother Tyree—who was, among more important things, the county prosecutor. But that the TV was off didn't signify; TV would have gone off the air hours ago, after "The Star-Spangled Banner," and would not be available again until 7 A.M.

"Ben?"

The name rang back at Jase from the sheetrock that hid the inside of the cinder-block walls. He put the cardboard tray on the desk, leaned over and looked down at the floor, half expecting to find Ben Neely stretched out and sleeping it off. But Ben was not there.

Took off with the confound broad in the Fairlane, Jase figured. He did not know which woman, or even if there had been one, but the absence of both Ben and the car suggested the simple answer. Everybody knew Ben Neely was a chaser. Like Ida Sue said, Benjy had had wandering-hands trouble all the way back to high school—Ida Sue winking at Jase when she said it, good as telling him she had plenty of reason to know.

Anger flickered briefly in Jason P. Allman's usually placid heart—not about Ben Neely feeling up Ida Sue in high school, but because Jase Allman had been left to explain Ben's absence to Tyree Neely. Then anger was replaced by concern. Tyree, after all, had made it clear that he was leaving his brother Ben in Jase Allman's hands. So Jase regarded Ben Neely as a project, unwelcome maybe, but kind of like weaning Ida Sue off her usual can of Coors before bed, Ida Sue putting on a tad around the middle.

Ben Neely had seemed, moreover, to be coming along okay. Off the sauce, at work on time, staying out of trouble. Not even hanging out at Aiken's pool hall or the Purity Cafe. But now this.

Tyree Neely had dropped by the jailhouse the first morning after Ben had worked the eleven-to-seven:

"Jase, you recollect when old Sheriff Hobson decided he didn't need a deputy named Jase Allman that knew too much how a man could live like an English duke on seven thousand a year?"

"I thought Ida Sue'd leave me for sure," Jase had said. "She find out I'm outten a job."

"And you know who located the right man to whip Hobson's ass the next election, don't you?"

Jase was not sure how far he could go. "They tell me was the same man put up Tug Johnson's campaign money."

Everybody knew that when Tyree Neely caught a cold, Sheriff Tug Johnson sneezed, coughed, and went to bed. But even having said the obvious, Jase watched Tyree Neely's deceptively warm blue

5

eyes for a sign that it might have been too much or too little. He saw nothing and Tyree went on, in the quiet, almost hesitant way that always put Jase in mind of a cat stalking a bird in the weeds.

"And I reckon you wouldn't forget who put you in as jailer at a nice salary and got this new jailhouse built for you to run."

Jase had been glad Ida Sue was not there to see his nose being rubbed in it.

"Course not."

He tried to sound neither insulted nor weak-kneed—both of which he feared he was. There was no sign in Tyree Neely's lean, tanned face or the set of his thin lips or the near whisper of his voice that he knew what Jase knew: *I've got his balls in my pocket.* Tyree would never let on anyway; Tyree was seldom obvious; but of course he *did* know.

"Now you're honorable as the day is long, Jase. So maybe it's not too far out of line, one good turn deserving another, I ask you to kindly keep an eye on Benjy?"

Despite the deferential tone of the request, Jase Allman had been appalled. He wanted no responsibility for Ben Tillman Neely, the black sheep of the family that had been Stonewall County's most dominant since practically forever. And he wanted no responsibility at all for which he would be accountable to Tyree Neely, any more than he already was—Tyree, who called most of the shots in Stonewall from the county prosecutor's office and kept strict account of the balance sheet.

"When he's on duty, I mean. Talk to'im some. Kind of keep'im straight. Benjy's not a bad kid, you get to know'im."

Not sober he ain't, Jase thought. Not chained up around anybody that wears a skirt.

"I wouldn't ask it of you," Tyree said, almost humbly, "if I didn't know you for a Christian man."

Jase was not deceived by the warm eyes or the soft voice or the humility. He did not even put much stock in Tyree Neely's well-known devotion to bird-watching. A birder, Tyree liked to call himself. Prowling around the woods with a pair of spyglasses and a Nikon strung around his neck.

Personally, Jase Allman saw nothing about birds to like, especially the way they'd dirty up his Toyota as soon as he hosed it down. As for Tyree Neely, if *his* eye was on the sparrow, in Jase Allman's opinion it was only to figure out a new way to get somebody's balls in his pocket.

Jase said, "I'll do what I can, Tyree. Doubt if it'll be much."

Tyree Neely rose and waved an arm expansively. "My daddy use to tell me, 'You got to get up early in the morning you want to find a better man than that oldest Allman boy.' "

He turned to leave but stopped at the door, looking back at Jase sitting at the old wooden desk. "Kind of set 'im an example, is all. Maybe ever now'n then, let me know how he's doing."

For just a moment, Jase wanted to tell Tyree to shove it: *I ain't tattling on your little brother.* But for just another moment, Jase hesitated, thinking of Ida Sue, knowing exactly how Tyree Neely would react to defiance—not hastily, not angrily, but certainly. And in that moment, Tyree went on out and down the steps between the Mount Vernon columns.

Jase had watched him, that morning, through the front window as Tyree moved along the sidewalk—a slender, brisk, erect man, in neat banker's gray, bareheaded, hair a little longer on the back of his neck than was customary in Stonewall County, waving to people on the street, not letting on in any way what he and they and Jase Allman knew perfectly well—that Tyree Neely just about owned the earth under all their feet, not by title but by the control he exercised over Stonewall County.

Some birder, Jase thought.

"Up yours, Boss," he said aloud, knowing it was too late. "I ain't tattling on your little brother." He listened with shame to his own words, hollow against the sheetrock.

Now, weeks later, Ben Neely and the Fairlane had disappeared, the Fairlane probably parked in front of a flyspeck motel, Ben pissed out of his mind, snoring like a diesel truck on I-95, some bare-ass floozy snitching his wallet from his pants on the floor. Splitting in the Fairlane.

Jase Allman shook his head, sighing. Hard to see how Tyree could hold him responsible for Ben going off the track with a bottle and a girl. Except that men who had power tended to see what they wanted to see—even with Tyree Neely's mild blue eyes. Jase knew he could be off the county payroll by sundown. No job, and Ida Sue a girl who could sink a week's pay in one cruise through the Dixie Pride Mall.

7

Even in his distress, however, Jase Allman was a prudent man. If he was going to be thrown out in the street, no job, maybe no Ida Sue in bed anymore in her birthday suit, it was not going to be for any fault of his. He'd make his regular morning check on the prisoners—this morning, only the one prisoner—before sounding the alarm for Ben Neely.

Jase leaned over the desk to take the cellblock key from its usual place in the middle drawer. It wasn't there. He looked quickly over his shoulder at the metal door with its single small window that separated the front office from the cellblock. With a shudder of horror, he saw what he should have noticed the second he had walked in:

The cellblock door was slightly ajar.

He hurried to it, dread rising like bile in his throat, sure of what he'd find inside the cellblock. He hardly had to look to see that Easter Lilly Odum's cell door stood wide open. The sight seemed to cement his feet to the floor. Thoughts tumbled through his head like clothes awash in Ida Sue's Maytag:

Never lost a prisoner before . . . that bitch looking like she could bite thew the bars . . . but even Ben wouldn't . . .

Of course Ben Neely wouldn't. Jase knew it for sure—not that relief was in the knowledge. Was there still a Klan in Stonewall like in the old days, Ben Neely would have joined it sure as shooting, worn his robe down Main Street, grinning beneath the hood, maybe calling hisself a kleagle or some such crazy name. Made no bones how he disliked and distrusted the colored, Ben Neely didn't. Jase knew Ben'd sooner have took off with a billy goat beside him in the Fairlane than a woman black as the ace of spades. Even one with tits on her that'd stop a train. . . .

This certainty at least released Jase from paralysis. He took four quick steps to the open cell. Then he saw it on the concrete floor, just as he'd imagined:

Ben Tillman Neely on his back, one arm outflung, his head pointed toward the tumbled cot along one wall of Easter Lilly's open cell, his slack feet in blue and white Nikes forming a sprawling V near the toilet in the corner. His uniform trousers and his polka-dot shorts down around his knees, his privates limp on one thigh.

Hung like a Jersey bull, Jase couldn't help but notice.

Ben's open eyes were rolled-up egg white in his skull. A dark stain had spread across his denim shirt and streaked the floor past his outstretched bloody hand and an upended three-legged stool, into the metal drain sunk in the center of the cell. From Ben's chest protruded the handle of the Swiss Army knife he had always carried in his hip pocket.

In the dim red light that barely lit the cellblock at night, the red handle looked almost black. And to Jase Allman it still seemed to quiver with what once had been the throbbing of Ben Neely's heart.

SHEP

THE BRIEF STORY RAN WELL BACK IN *THE NEW YORK TIMES,* HALFWAY down the single column beside a Saks Fifth Avenue lingerie ad that occupied the rest of the page:

FLEEING WOMAN
CAUGHT, HELD
IN JAIL MURDER

The headline caught the eye but not the attention of W. Shepherd Riley as he sat at breakfast at the snack bar of the Little Giant convenience store in Otter Creek, Vermont. His attention was fastened on the Saks ad, which featured an unusually explicit drawing of a voluptuous woman with ample flesh about to spill out of a strapless bra.

Shep Riley sighed, recalling past delights, telling himself guiltily that he was getting to be a dirty old man. Just because in Vermont the so-called fair sex seemed to live mostly on fried foods and Fritos was no reason to work himself up over a mere drawing.

Still . . . the glories of New York women were a good reason to regret having left New York. Which, otherwise, he didn't.

Shep sipped tea from a cup advertising *Good Morning Amer-*

ica, a show on which he once had appeared. Since he had become a breakfast regular at the Little Giant, the cup was kept for him behind the counter. He put down the remnants of a day-old cake doughnut, the dried crumbs littering the front of his plaid shirt, turned the page hastily, and hoped the two other men at the counter had not noticed his focus on the bra ad.

"How they hold them things up?" Blue Denton asked.

Shep had thought Blue and the other man were too busy slurping coffee to have been looking over his shoulder. That they were drinking from Styrofoam cups would have told him, if he hadn't known it already, that they were not breakfast regulars at the Little Giant. Over the snack bar, a hand-lettered sign said: COFFEE 60C, BOTTOMLESS CUP.

"Uh . . . how the hell would I know?" Shep muttered, turning more pages rapidly. He flipped swiftly past the Washington news, which was of little interest to him anymore, to Editorial and Op-Ed, folding them back to back.

"How bout them Sox?" Blue Denton asked of no one in particular. Blue drove earth-moving equipment for Green Mountain Excavation and was Donkey King Video champion of the Eagle's Roost, Otter Creek's only bar.

"Come July they'll fold like a dish towel," the other man said. Shep knew him only as a pickup laborer called Shack. "Like always."

"Maybe not this year." Blue did not sound hopeful. "They added infield speed."

Shack held out his cup to Easy Ed Terrell, the counterman, who was leaning against the sandwich board. Above Ed's head a suspended poster demanded in large letters: ALL IN FAVOR OF GUN CONTROL RAISE YOUR RIGHT HAND.

The poster depicted Adolf Hitler giving the Nazi salute with his right hand. Hitler's image was superimposed on a target, with the familiar mustache at the bull's-eye.

Shack snorted: "The Lord knows they needed it. But they still got no pitching."

"Name of the game." Easy Ed moved without haste to refill Shack's cup. Easy Ed always moved without haste except, it was said in Otter Creek, when some deadbeat tried to get out of the Little Giant without paying.

Shack eyed Ed with the approval of one baseball man for another. "Got to be the Yanks," he said. "All that payroll."

Shep Riley had already taken his morning jog and had stopped later, as he always did, for breakfast at the Little Giant. He listened to Blue Denton and Shack—apparently Blue's helper for the day— without interest but with a warm sense of ease and pleasant boredom. Everything was as usual.

"Yeah, well," Blue said, "anything I hate, it's the goddam Yankees."

Things seldom changed in Otter Creek. No matter how often a new batch was brought in, the Little Giant's doughnuts never seemed fresh. Shep took another bite of his, sure that Shack was right—the Sox would fold when the weather got hot. That seemed ordained—everyone but Red Sox fans could take comfort from the certainty. And that nothing would happen in Otter Creek to make a man stir out of his usual track was why, women or no women, Shep Riley had left New York for Vermont.

"Steinbrenner." Easy Ed smiled as he spoke.

Blue Denton and Shack broke into derisive laughter, as if at a one-liner. Shep tapped his cup gently on the counter, not looking up from the *Times*. He was devoted to his morning perusal of the paper, which Easy Ed faithfully reserved for him. Other regulars had learned that it was of little use to interrupt Shep Riley while he read, though he was often the butt of their wisecracks:

"Look like he's mem'rizing that thing, don't it? Nose buried so deep in there. Reckon he's going on one-a them quiz shows?"

The only thing that remotely interested Shep on that morning's editorial page was an angry letter to the editor from one of New York City's most prominent businessmen, protesting the "herdlike conditions" he claimed to have been subjected to while serving two weeks of jury duty "like any good citizen."

Easy Ed refilled the *Good Morning America* cup, soaking the same limp Rosebud tea bag with hot water from the red-handled tap. Taped to the Little Giant's coffee maker was a bumper sticker: FIRST HILLARY, THEN GENNIFER, NOW US.

Ed set the refilled cup in front of Shep, who moved one hand inside the open neck of his shirt and began to finger—a habitual gesture with him—an inch-long streak of scar tissue under his right shoulder. Shep liked to joke, when anyone asked about the scar—

maybe when he was swimming in Otter Creek down behind the village, or playing pickup basketball with other middle-aged men at the high school gym—that the scar was the work of "a jilted husband."

Actually, the scar had been inflicted by the jilted husband's wife, a former home economics teacher from Alabama. She had thrown a sharp-heeled shoe at Shep when she discovered that she had given her all in a one-night stand rather than at the start of the romantic elopement she had wholly imagined, cautious Shep having promised nothing of the kind. He considered it dishonorable to deceive a woman in order to get her into bed, but if she insisted on deceiving herself, Shep regarded that as her problem, not his.

The shoe had been thrown a long time ago—so long ago Shep had actually started to believe the husband story. He looked up from the *Times* as Myrtie Barnes entered the Little Giant, in her usual hurry, making the place seem smaller and knocking over a life-sized cardboard cutout of Joe Camel.

"Hey, old-timer!" she called to Easy Ed. "How bout a little service over here?"

She bent, puffing, to pick up Joe Camel. Myrtie's heft would have registered on a highway truck-weight scale.

Not needing to ask what she wanted, Ed moved without haste to the lottery machine and peeled off a two-dollar Cash Explosion ticket. Myrtie set Joe Camel upright, fished in a shoulder bag not quite large enough to have carried a case of Gallo's Hearty Burgundy, and brought out a tiny coin purse.

"I give up buying them durn tickets." Blue Denton aimed his thumb over his shoulder at the Little Giant's unisex toilet, the door to which hung ajar when no one was in it. "I figure I got a better chance dropping my money down that john in there."

Shack drank his coffee noisily. "When I played one-a them punchboards the first time, over to Randolph there? Won a six-pack of Rolling Rock."

"Yeah, well . . ." Blue shook his head decisively. "I poured my last dollar down that kind of a drain."

"Wasn't so much the beer," Shack said. "I took it for a good-luck sign."

Shep read the letter to the editor slowly, remembering that he had once engaged in an acrimonious voir dire, perhaps with that very businessman—at any rate, one so much like him as to make no difference. Shep had a poor memory for names of people he did not wish to recall.

Myrtie paid for her Cash Explosion with a cascade of coins, scraped the cover paper off the ticket with a penny, and compared the revealed numbers carefully with those pasted on the counter. She threw up arms the size of fireplugs, and knocked over a sign braced against the cash register: $5 SERVICE CHARGE ON RETURNED CHECKS. THIS MEANS YOU.

Myrtie took no notice of the overturned sign. She went out, calling back cheerfully, "Got to get a winner one-a these days!"

She slammed the outer door behind her, knocking over Joe Camel again. Easy Ed went without haste around the counter and set the cutout back on its cardboard feet.

"Not that I had 'ny luck since," Shack said. "Good, I mean."

Shep recalled with satisfaction, as he choked down the last of his doughnut, that he had once dismissed button-down characters from jury panels almost at sight. In his courtroom days, he had preferred no one sitting on one of his cases with more than a high school education, and he had summarily rejected businessmen who were accustomed to getting their way in the endless meetings they thrived on. He had reasoned that they would get their way in the jury room, too; and in Shep Riley's experience, business types always favored getting tough on crime—except the white-collar crimes they regarded as capitalism.

Not, Shep reflected rather grimly as he sipped his lukewarm tea, that he had had all that many juries to pick in his unlamented New York years. Unlike the old days down South, he had had no need of Meg Whitman's psychological profiles of potential jurors. He had learned in New York, to his initial chagrin, that few litigants any longer needed a leftist lawyer, a lawyer with a reputation made in the days of segregation, campus revolt, and Vietnam protest. Having defended Black Panthers, ROTC building bombers, campus revolutionaries, lunch counter sit-inners, draft card burners, dope smokers, flower children, and Black Muslims with names like Jaybarr X apparently did not qualify even a cum laude Harvard Law graduate to be a rainmaker in the era of Ronald Reagan.

"Get a haircut, man," Appleton G. Lawrence, the managing

partner, had advised Shep the day he settled reluctantly into the New York office of his firm. "Your radical days are over."

A streak of practicality, which once had seen Shep through law school on his poker winnings, had never been quite extinguished by the Greening of America. Yet, years after that not-quite-fatherly conversation, years after he had tried to resign himself to life without litigation, as he listened with one ear to Blue Denton and Shack discussing baseball and luck, he was still ashamed that he had dutifully taken Appleton G. Lawrence's advice. When his prized ponytail of red hair and the sideburns that had curled below his prominent ears fell to the barber's sheet, they seemed to be drops of his own blood.

He had never really conceded the rest of the Lawrence dictum. Doggedly, futilely, Shep Riley continued to look for seeds planted at Woodstock and Kent State, in the Mobe and on the Edmund Pettus Bridge, to bear strange fruit among a generation enamored of Michael Milken. They never did, at least not to Shep's knowledge, and finally he had stopped expecting them to. He even threw into the wastebasket his remaining stock of pre-Appleton G. Lawrence business cards, his name and affiliation on one side, his once-fervent motto on the other:

I AM FOR ANY MOVEMENT WHENEVER THERE IS A GOOD CAUSE TO PROMOTE, A RIGHT TO ASSERT, A CHAIN TO BE BROKEN, A BURDEN TO BE REMOVED, OR A WRONG TO BE REDRESSED.
FREDERICK DOUGLASS, 1884

Surreptitiously, Shep still hoped—without *really* hoping—someday to celebrate a political coalition of the downtrodden, whether victorious or not, or just to see some bold person raise a fist again and shout, "Power to the people!"

"What I always say," Blue Denton said, "is a man makes his own luck. But not in no damn lottery."

Shep had had a dream once, shortly after moving to Otter Creek and starting to let his hair grow out again. In the dream, he was being hosed down by seg firemen during a civil rights march in Birmingham. He had awakened to find that some gremlin had set off the ceiling sprinklers in the Montpelier motel where he was staying while the house he had bought in Otter Creek was having its chain-pull toilets replaced.

"Onliest good luck I ever had," Shack said, "they sent me to Germany while them Commies in Washington lost the war in Vietnam."

Good luck indeed, Shep thought. He drank the rest of his tea and perused the op-ed page. Then—perhaps in search of an excuse not to get up from the snack bar and face the day, or perhaps with interest flickering faintly within him, as if he had glimpsed a half-familiar face in a blurred photograph—he turned back to the story of the fleeing woman charged with murder. This time, he did not even glance at the bolstered bosom in the Saks ad flanking the story: He read the short news account with interest rising like indigestion from his doughnut.

The woman accused of the jail murder turned out to be black.

Shep said out loud, "Might have known it."

Shack leaned forward, past the considerable bulk of Blue Denton, and looked at him curiously.

The woman had been captured after a high-speed chase along Interstate 95 and was being sent back to the town and the jail from which she had fled, to face the charge of murdering her jailer during her escape. The dead jailer, Shep read, was the brother of the county prosecutor.

Cornpone nepotism, as usual. Shep shook his head and muttered, "Burn, baby, burn."

That particular state not infrequently sent murder defendants to the gas chamber—or maybe by now, Shep thought, they used a "humane" method like lethal injection. Especially a black defendant accused of killing a white person. The state's well-known governor, someday to be a senator, perhaps a presidential candidate, had sought and won reelection twice, owing not least to the numerous death warrants he could boast of having signed.

"Who's gonna burn?" Shack's avid face leaned over Blue Denton's Styrofoam coffee cup.

As usual when reading the *Times*, Shep had not wanted to talk. This morning in particular, feeling an interest that seldom roused him anymore, he had wanted to drag from the *Times* story every ounce of information it contained, between the lines as well as in them. So he answered shortly, curtly, "Nobody you know."

In that state in the old days, Shep had represented an accused murderer, without fee but to no avail. The accused, when convicted, had been an eighteen-year-old black youth with an IQ of 84. Two years earlier, he had stolen two Snickers bars and a bag of Chee•tos from a service station. The owner had spotted, chased, and tackled him, whereupon the boy bashed in the owner's head with the first rock that came to hand. For his last meal, he ordered pork barbecue, coleslaw and hush puppies, and got all three from a merciful state.

"Do I detect, Counselor," Blue Denton said, "that you're in a more than usually shitty mood this morning?"

Shep realized at once that he had needlessly insulted an Otter Creeker, something he tried never to do. He not only had to live in Otter Creek; he *liked* to live in Otter Creek. In his decade of residency, he had come to like its people, its pace, its predictability. Though necessarily a flatlander forever, as all Vermonters considered anyone born elsewhere, he did not have to be an outsider. Nor did he want to be.

"Aw, hell, Shack," he said, "I was wrapped up in something here in the paper. What were you saying?"

Shack pretended to stir his coffee before muttering, "Just won'dring who was gonna burn, was all."

Shep was quickly as intent upon soothing Shack as earlier he had been upon studying the *Times*. Shep Riley was an easygoing man who had no wish, outside the courtroom, to force a confrontation or provoke an embarrassment; he knew it was advantageous to see himself as others saw him. And Shack, put off by a short answer to a reasonable question, undoubtedly was seeing what Shep Riley least wanted to be thought—a snotty carpetbagger.

"This black woman escaped jail down South and got caught," he explained. "They're going to try her for killing the jailer and I wouldn't bet a nickel on her chances."

Shack stood up, his work boots clumping on the floor, his big hard hands pushing himself away from the snack bar. As he turned away without another glance at Shep Riley, he looked as solid, as *permanent,* as Bucktail Mountain rising beyond the front windows of the Little Giant.

"Send'em all back to Affiker," he said. "If I had my way."

EASTER LILLY

THEY REACHED STONEWALL COUNTY SOONER THAN SHE HAD EX-
pected. Its familiar woods and fields, now looking alien and hostile,
fell away on either side of the speeding state police car. She was
almost accustomed, by then, to having her wrists handcuffed behind
her back. And anyway she would rather have felt her bones break
and her muscles dissolve than admit to the fat-necked whites in the
front seat that she was cramped and uncomfortable.

"Last time I had to transport one," the cracker driving said, "he
puked all over the car. Like to never got the stink out."

"Drunk?" the other one asked.

"Just sick. Claimed somebody poisoned the stew he et at the
county jail."

"Shit. Niggers always claim somebody trying to poison'em."

"He wa'nt no nigger," the driver said. "You'd of thought he
was, way his puke stunk up the car."

Through the green metal lattice that separated the top of the
front seat from the rear compartment, she could see only the backs
of their cropped heads and their thick necks, their massive uniformed shoulders. She let herself fantasize that the lattice was elastic
or maybe just rope she could pull apart enough to get her fists
through. She would put a hand on the outside of each stupid white

head, right over the red ears, and smash their heads together, hard enough to make even pig skulls crack. Then the car would run off the road and she would find a way to open the handleless doors, get away and go to Africa, or maybe even Paris.

The driver pointed at a clock on the dashboard. "Be there maybe a half hour." He called over his shoulder, "Hey, sweetheart, they give you brekfus?"

Powdered eggs, greaseball they called a sausage. She could feel them sitting on her stomach like wet cement. But she hadn't acknowledged these police assholes yet and didn't aim to start now. She stared out the window, neck stiff, body ramrod straight, back and shoulders aching, and recognized an old house from which Logan Clark used to sell stumphole liquor out the back window.

She had been a child then and Logan Clark a prosperous businessman—as prosperous, anyway, as niggers were allowed to be in Stonewall County. State whiskey stores then put Logan out of business and he wound up on relief.

She knew every road, every structure, every black household in Stonewall County—knew who lived in each unpainted house perched on its cinder-block legs, beyond its swept yard, under its chinaberry tree or beside its lilac bush. She knew how they made a living—if they did—who was whoring and who was stealing and who was working like a dog, sometimes two jobs day and night.

She knew all that and more—which of her neighbors, for instance, had been eager to vote when it still was possible to believe that voting would provide paved streets and drainage systems instead of the mud, dust, and ditches of what Whitey no longer had the gumption to call niggertown—at least not in front of those they now were careful not to call niggers to their faces. She made it her business to know which black kids were smart and hardworking enough in school maybe someday to get the hell out of Stonewall County for good. Like she ought to have done years ago.

"Cept you can't get away from the cracker," Fred Worthington, the black doctor who was sort of her boyfriend, had said the last time they'd discussed leaving Stonewall. "At least down here he's out there in plain sight. Up North, he can be hard to spot."

"If it's white," Easter Lilly had said, "it's cracker to me." But she'd made the mental exception she always did: except Mr. Timmons.

A pickup truck that had been following them, apparently reluctant to pass a police car, finally sped up and passed. A white boy she remembered from high school—he had a nose like a chicken's beak—was at the wheel. On the pickup's tailgate, a bumper sticker was plastered: HONK IF YOU LIKE RUSH!

The driver in the front seat hit his horn button twice. The one beside him was looking back at her, grinning. Bad teeth, whiskey nose, red neck. "Cat gotcha tongue back there?" he said to Easter Lilly.

She shifted her body stiffly on the seat, the handcuffs pinching her wrists, until she could look out the other window. They were just passing Nebo Church, with its graveyard and picnic grove, where—in what now seemed another world—her mother had been a leader of the choir, famous for singing "Will There Be Any Stars in My Crown?" The white folks would drive out at night to park along the road and listen to her mother and the rest of the choir singing at the August meetings.

That was before Mr. Timmons, her civics teacher in her senior year at the new consolidated, integrated Stonewall County High School—a shotgun wedding, if ever there was one—had started keeping her after class. She still thought of him as Mr. Timmons, because of the respect she'd had for a teacher, even a white teacher, and even after the first time he'd felt her up. She'd been only seventeen, too afraid to resist and didn't really know how—and anyway kind of liked to be treated special by a white man.

She'd *liked* Mr. Timmons. He was gentle and sweet to her, improved her homework papers, never got loud and bossy like other white men. Mr. Timmons would get tearful behind his thick glasses, like the bottoms of a pair of Coke bottles, when he'd tell her how much he loved her, and he almost always asked her permission before he did anything she knew her mother would say she ought not to let him do. For a while, they'd be alone almost every afternoon in his locked and secret classroom, Mr. Timmons crying while he did it to her. Then she realized her classmates knew what was going on.

She'd heard the whispers in the girls' room one day, whispers of white voices she was sure she was meant to hear. After that, she flaunted it in their faces, wearing tighter sweaters and shorter skirts, looking at Mr. Timmons in a certain way she'd learned from the movies, walking close to him between classes, letting her hand touch his if anyone was looking. She didn't much like it while he was doing it to her, but she liked to flaunt it at the white kids—especially stuck-up girls like Daisy Thorpe, who acted like she was Jackie Kennedy—that a white teacher was keeping *her* after school and not them.

Except one day in the spring of senior year, Mr. Timmons wasn't there—some old white sow of a substitute teacher was standing at his desk—and when the next day and the next and the one after that, the old sow was still there, fat as a hog and twice as mean, it was no longer possible to believe that Mr. Timmons was sick, or on a trip. *They*—she could never be sure but she could guess who—had sent him away, overnight, packed him out of town, no explanation to anyone. Easter Lilly Odum, of course, had needed no explanation. If she had, the sly looks of triumph on the white faces in her classroom, not to mention the way the old sow pointedly ignored her, would have served the purpose.

She had cried just once, sitting out in the clean, swept yard of her mother's house one night in a rocking chair she'd carried from the porch—her mom coming nervously to the front door once or twice and the moon shining mockingly. She missed Mr. Timmons's shy smile, the way he'd sometimes weep while he was doing it to her, and she was grieved that he had to slip out of town without a chance to say good-bye.

After her long, moonlight cry Easter Lilly never cried about it again, though she had thought often and sadly of Mr. Timmons. At Commencement, months later, she had walked across the stage in her white graduation robe and mortarboard, her back straight and stiff and proud, ignoring the whispers among the white parents.

"You really kill a white man?"

The cracker beside the driver had stopped grinning. She did not fail to catch the hint of awe in his voice.

You're mighty right she wanted to say *like I'd kill you I could get my hands on your cotton-pickin throat.*

But she only turned to watch Nebo Church fade into the distance. The old gray structure disappeared as they rounded a curve.

"Sho she did," the driver said. "Stole'is knife, let'im have it. Don't she look to you like she could of done it?"

The other one turned to look her over more closely. She was

used to that, crackers sizing her up, though usually it wasn't whether she could kill. She knew her skin was the rich chocolate color of a Mars bar. She knew she had long, slender legs and a big bosom over a skinny waist. She knew her eyes could dance, say *come here* or *get lost*. She knew her lips barely needed to form the words.

Even white men, who were *too* white to think any black woman could look as good as a Shirley Temple doll, looked twice and longingly at her. Of course, they believed she'd be twice as hot in bed *because* she was black. Much they knew about women. *Or* black people.

"She could've got'im back there all right," the driver said. "Built like she is."

Slow. That was the way she would throttle him. *Watching his fish eyes bulge out of his pig head.*

"But killing a white man? Not drunk or doped up or nothing?"

"How we know she wa'nt doped?" the driver said. "She could of come down off the dope time the boys picked'er up yestiddy."

Didn't need dope, she thought. Not with grab-ass Ben Neely, I didn't.

"If she was doped," the other one said, "I reckon maybe she might of done it." He had turned again to the front of the car, and she eyed the precise spot where, if she had had one, she would have stuck an ice pick into the back of his neck. At the hairline.

"Niggers didn't used to be so mean," the driver said. "Before all this dope, I mean. Makes'em crazy."

But, she almost cried out, she had not *needed* dope. Or booze. Or anything. Not even courage. When she had felt the knife handle hot in her palm, using it had been as easy as falling off a log. When Ben Neely had called her a stinking bitch, sticking the knife into him had been like using it on every white asshole who ever had leered at her, whispered obscene words in her ear, treated her like a whore waiting to be bought. But it had been more than that, too, more than woman and man, more even than black woman and white man.

Using the knife had been like sticking it in the hearts of all the slave-owning, nigger-killing, woman-raping Jeff Davises and Gene Talmadges and Tom-Tom Heflins and Jim Eastlands of history— into the heart of The Man. The blade going in, the strangled cry of surprise and disbelief, the spurting blood, the thud like a splitting watermelon when his head hit the concrete floor. Then, ah then! then! righteousness coming down like waters! She had avenged Malcolm and Martin, all the brothers wasted by the racists. She had paid off George Wallace, unmanned Reagan, finished Jesse Helms— wielded all at once and with her own hand the whole, hidden, irresistible force of Black Power. Wielded it literally to the hilt.

No. She definitely had not needed dope to kill Ben Neely. The knife going in had been enough of a high. She would never know another so wild, so free.

"They ex'cute women in this state?" the other one asked.

"They do. Law don't make no distinction like that." The driver showing off a little, acting like a lawyer instead of a jackleg trooper with a six-shooter in place of his manhood. "But it ain't so easy finding a jury that'll thow the switch on a woman."

"Speshly with boobs on'er like this'un." The one beside the driver made a circling motion with his hands.

"Course they don't actually thow no switch anymore," the driver said. "They got the gas chamber now."

"Ever man on that jury gonna be wishing he could get into something like that." The other one jerked his head toward the backseat. "Just once. You know they will."

"Don't crave dark meat myself. And look at it this way—"

Trying to sound judicious. Lawyerlike. But just a cracker.

"Thinking like *that,* maybe they'll remember that's exactly when she stuck that blade in'is heart. While he was getting in there. Could be they'll want to gas'er more'n ever, they think of that. And that prosecutor gonna remind'em ever time he gets on'is feet, him being blood kin."

She began to think seriously, for the first time, of going to the gas chamber. The driver was right—Tyree Neely would never settle for prison. And when he got her convicted, he'd go up to Arbor Hill himself, sit outside the window, watch them strap her down and the gas rise. He'd sit there and watch her choke, Tyree would, and be glad when she stopped breathing. Then go out with tears in his cracker blue eyes and tell the newspapers he hated to see a woman gassed but justice had to be done.

White justice. She had never known any other until she had driven the red-handled knife into Ben Neely's heart. She wished it could have been Tyree's; Ben was nothing but big talk, a kleagle without a sheet. Tyree was the mean one, under all that bird-watching talk. Tyree would have been worth killing.

Tyree Neely was not dead, however; his brother was. And it would be Tyree's court, Tyree's jury, Tyree's law that would try her. Ultimately, it wouldn't be just white justice she would suffer. It would be Tyree Neely's justice.

She tried to face this prospect without fear. To be afraid, she'd told Fred Worthington, was the worst thing that could happen to anybody, the only real shame. Fear was just another thing you had to fight, she'd insisted the morning she and Fred had taken seats in the Neely Memorial Methodist Church and all the cracker Christians moved to another pew.

Besides, there just might be one way to escape Tyree, she thought—though with little hope. Her fingerprints would be on the knife, and she did not aim to deny killing Ben Neely. Even to escape the gas chamber she was not going to give them the satisfaction of watching Easter Lilly Odum deny the best thing she had ever done. A Tyree Neely jury would never believe temporary insanity, either—not even to keep from sending a woman to the gas chamber. A nigger woman, anyway. But just possibly, maybe one chance out of a thousand . . .

"I was her lawyer," the driver said self-importantly, "I b'leeve I'd plead self-defense. Any old port inna storm."

The other one cackled, slapped a hand on the dash, and said, "Anybody'd buy that'd suck eggs."

24

TYREE

"OUT THE BINGO CREEK ROAD MAYBE FOUR MILES," TYREE NEELY was saying. "Just past Ma Clifton's hot dog place? This dirt road goes off to the left toward what used to be this old sawmill. Know where I mean?"

"Sure." Jase Allman was sitting on a windowsill in the jail office. "Us boys used to hunt rabbits back in there."

"Well, it was bout midafternoon when I parked by that old mill shed. The day before it happened—" Tyree nodded toward the cellblock. "In there."

Sitting at the office desk in a neat corduroy suit—the always courteous Jase having yielded him the best chair in the office—Tyree Neely could not bring himself to say any more than that about his younger brother's murder. It was too recent, too cruel, the wound too raw in his soul. He still didn't know what he'd do about the old family farm where Benjy had been living. And in only a few hours, they'd be lowering Benjy into the Neely family plot in Stonewall Memory Gardens.

Tyree talked on rapidly, to keep himself from thinking any more about that. "I got out of the car and walked on into the woods there, about as far as a football field is long. When I looked up . . ."

Sheriff Tug Johnson, overflowing a straight-backed chair, was watching *One Life to Live* on the office TV. The sound was turned down, not because Tyree Neely had asked for it to be lowered but because he hadn't had to. Even Tug Johnson knew better than to interfere when Tyree was talking about birds.

"I liked to drop my teeth," Tyree said. "There was this monster sitting up there on a limb of this old dead tree. Sassy as you please. About the size of a hound dog, looked to me like. Later I checked the book. Sure enough, those things go about two feet tall."

"How'd you know what it was?"

Jase, Tyree thought with gratitude, was trying hard to act interested.

"It had these two sort of tufts sticking up on top of its head." Tyree held up his index fingers beside his ears. "White throat bib, too. I never saw one in my life before but I could tell right away . . ." He lowered his voice respectfully, almost to a whisper. "A horned owl."

Jase Allman turned his head to watch a car swing into the jail parking lot.

"I never even *heard* of a horned owl around here before," Tyree said. "But I snapped the picture to prove it . . . with a close-up lens . . ."

"Scuse me," Jase said. "Looks like they're bringin Easter Lilly back already. They got here right quick."

Tyree Neely stood up immediately from behind the desk, thinking no more of the horned owl. He wanted to run out to the parking lot and strangle the woman with his own hands. But he restrained himself and asked quietly, "You see'er in the car?"

"Somebody in the backseat. Must of been her."

Tyree came around the desk and headed for the door. "I sort of half thought she'd get away again."

He really had. And he'd worried she'd maybe get blown to bits escaping before he could watch them strap her down.

Sheriff Johnson had not moved, but Jase rose from the windowsill and followed Tyree.

"Be along in a sec," the sheriff called after them. He did not look away from a man and a woman in a desperate clinch on the TV screen. "Gotta see how this turns out."

"Take your time." Tyree spoke pleasantly, but made a mark by the sheriff's name on his mental list.

He and Jase went between the Mount Vernon columns into a sunny but chill early spring day, and hurried around the cinder-block corner of the jail. Two booted and uniformed officers had got out on either side of a state police car.

They wore Smoky the Bear hats. Both held billy clubs and carried pistols holstered at their sides. One had a shotgun.

"Gotcha girlfriend here, Mac."

The one with the shotgun called across the top of the car; "Friggin ballbreaker, ain't she?"

He opened the door on his side and quickly stepped back, holding the shotgun at his side, aimed at the door. The other officer, his boots creaking, moved behind the car and put his hand on the butt of his pistol.

Tyree watched a tall black woman, hair hanging almost to her shoulders, shaped loose and easy about her head, get slowly out of the police car. She was graceful as an athlete, voluptuous as a movie star; her wrists were handcuffed incongruously behind her back. She stared for a moment at the officer with the shotgun; then her head snapped forward like a snake striking as she spat at him. The officer stepped back quickly and the blob of spittle fell just short.

Tyree Neely said to the other officer, "That's Easter Lilly, all right."

The officer with the shotgun moved its barrel a little as she walked slowly around behind the police car. Arrogant, Tyree thought. Shameless. He had had no use for Easter Lilly Odum—a troublemaker, rude and profane—even before she killed his brother. But even now, seeing her carriage and the regal set of her head on a heronlike neck, Tyree had to admit she was a damn fine-looking female. Except she was colored, she'd be a real beauty.

Easter Lilly ignored the officer with his hand on his pistol and walked purposefully past Jase Allman.

"Didn't figure to see you again this soon," Tyree said. He forced himself to sound as if discussing the weather. "But I knew I would some day." He clinched his fists in his pockets.

"Mothafucka." Easter Lilly strode past him without another word, without even looking at him.

Tyree turned to follow, one of the troopers on either side of him, Jase slightly in the rear. The trooper with the shotgun, now pointed loosely at Easter Lilly's back, said to Tyree, "First word out of'er all mornin. Had to be that'un."

Easter Lilly wore a pale blue dress, standard Stonewall County jail issue. Even so, Tyree noticed, his anger stirring again, her nails were painted pink, just as Jase said they'd been the day before she'd stabbed his . . . before she'd done it. The thin dress was tight and stretched above her waist, across her firm round bottom. Seeing which would persuade anybody, Tyree thought, of what had happened to his foolish, horny young brother. Easy for a woman built like a roadhouse stripper to mess around with Benjy, grab the knife from his hip pocket. Any red-blooded male would be aroused by Easter Lilly, even if she was a colored. And God knows, Benjy had been red-blooded about women. Got all the red blood in the family, in fact.

One of the troopers, apparently in appreciation of Easter Lilly's rear twisting under the denim, asked affably, "How come niggers got such high asses?"

Tyree was not surprised at the question. Men, white or black, tended to stare at Easter Lilly Odum—as, of course, poor Benjy must have, certainly after he found her in his keeping nights at the Stonewall County jail.

Easter Lilly turned the corner and the officer with the shotgun jumped out front to keep her in sight. Tyree and the others followed just as Tug Johnson squeezed massively past the door and out on the small front porch.

One of the troopers, eyeing Tug's uniform, whistled softly.

"That one sheriff or two?" he asked.

Tug Johnson was not fat; he was broad. His elephantine hips were no wider than his shoulders, from which a keglike neck rose to a cropped skull the size of the Civil War roundshot that one of Sherman's field pieces had imbedded in the Stonewall County courthouse steps more than a century earlier. Tug's pistol belt barely reached around his middle to an outsized brass buckle that displayed in two arcs the words WAITSFIELD WARRIORS. In smaller letters in between, a line read: STATE CHAMPS 1963.

Tug Johnson never let anyone forget that he had been a guard on Waitsfield High's one and only state championship (Class B) football team—a cherished distinction since Waitsfield High, having vanished, would never have another. At the instigation of the Supreme Court, Waitsfield High's all-white student body had been transferred to a new glass-and-stone, integrated institution—the Stonewall County Consolidated High School, known as SCCH, out near the Dixie Pride Mall. Even the old red-brick Waitsfield High building on Entwhistle Street had been torn down, a drive-in branch of the Bright Leaf National Bank taking over the site.

"See, Tyree?" the sheriff called. "I told you we'd get'er back for you."

"Seems like you had'er before," Tyree said. Tug Johnson's massive presence sometimes made him feel as he had when he was a child, sticking pins in balloons.

"This time for keeps." Tug came hugely down the steps and pointed at the jail door, eager to please and trying to sound mean. "Get on in there, woman."

"Mothafucka," Easter Lilly said again.

She detoured around Tug's bulk and went up the steps, defiant bottom swinging as if she knew it was being stared at. And of course she did, Tyree thought.

Tug Johnson said to Tyree, "She won't act so tough, she start sniffing that gas."

One of the troopers, sensing the sheriff's deference to the quiet man in the corduroy suit, asked; "You the mayor or something?"

"Prosecutor." Tyree saw at once that that told the trooper he was also the brother of the murdered man.

"Sorry bout your kin," the trooper said, ducking his head awkwardly. "Tur'ble way to go."

"I 'preciate that."

Though there's no good way, Tyree thought, if it's before your time. Somehow, seeing Easter Lilly back in custody had made it possible to think about Benjy again, even to talk about what had happened.

Tug Johnson squeezed through the door behind Easter Lilly and called over his shoulder to the troopers, "I'll take over, boys."

"How bout you guys give'im a hand, though," Tyree said mildly. "See she's locked up good?"

Both troopers went up the steps in their high, creaking boots.

"Not that Tug couldn't handle it, those cuffs on her," Tyree said to Jase, conscious that he shouldn't undermine the sheriff's authority. "But no use to take chances."

"Nossir. No use a-tall."

Tyree Neely did not fail to notice as they went up the steps that Jase followed a respectful pace behind—Jase still hoping not to be blamed for Benjy's death. Actually, Tyree mostly blamed Benjy himself, the young fool. And the Odum woman, of course. But let Jase sweat a little, he thought. Keep'im on his toes.

Tug Johnson and the troopers already had taken Easter Lilly into the cellblock. Tyree could hear the tramp of heavy boots on concrete, an iron sound of bars clanging against bars. Then the two troopers came back into the front office alone, the one with the shotgun letting it point at the floor. The other one was clipping a pair of handcuffs to his polished belt.

Tyree looked past them for the sheriff, and the troopers shuffled a little, their boots rasping on the floor. The one with the shotgun said, "He's kind of chewin'er out back there."

Tyree flinched at the thought, then shook hands with each of the troopers, briskly and cordially, squeezing their hands a little, the way he shook hands with everyone. He memorized as he did so the names on the tags over their breast pockets and made another entry on his mental list: Write a note to their commanding officer. Never hurt to give a man a pat on the back.

"Can't thank you boys enough," he said.

"Just doin our job, Chief. Who's gonna sign the receipt?"

"I will." Jase held out his hand. "Lessen you want the sheriff to do it."

"Do what?" Tug Johnson came out of the cellblock, trying to look important.

"Go ahead and sign it, Jase," Tyree Neely said.

On the whole, he liked the way his handpicked sheriff did what he was told, no questions asked. He might even have him reelected. But with Benjy gone and Easter Lilly acting like the Queen of Sheba, with these trooper characters taking it all in, the fat-ass was getting on his nerves. Prancing around like Mike Tyson.

Jase signed the receipt and with more thanks all around the troopers left. When the door closed behind them, Tug Johnson took a hitch in his belt, his massive shoulders rising even further around his ears.

"All right, Ty, let's get at it."

"At what?" Tyree Neely felt his nerves tighten further.

"Ain't we goin to squeeze the bitch?"

"I'm going to talk to her, if that's what you mean." Tyree did not like Tug's choice of words and emphasized the "I." He wished Jase were not standing by all ears.

"Well, then, tell you what, Ty. We better stay outside that cell. Talk thew the bars."

Tyree Neely hated to be called Ty. Benjy had known not to do it. So did Jase, who seldom first-named his betters, anyway. When Tug Johnson, who ought to know which side his bread was buttered on and who spread the butter, called him Ty it definitely showed a lack of deference. Tyree tried not to be too sensitive about the respect he knew was his due, much less to insist on it, but sometimes . . .

Besides, he was not like gullible Benjy, easily suckered by a woman's come-on. Which Tug Johnson ought to have known.

"I wouldn't give'er the satisfaction," he said shortly.

In fact, Tyree knew he still would have to restrain himself to keep from jerking Easter Lilly's hair loose from her arrogant head. *That* was how she aroused Tyree Neely. Most of the colored still knew their place; Martin Luther King hadn't really changed *that,* and most blacks and whites in Stonewall County got on pretty well, everything considered. But Easter Lilly Odum . . . you'd think she'd never heard of the Supreme Court or the Voting Rights Act or Jesse Jackson actually running for President.

"Anyway, she got no knife this time," Jase said. Which was another thing Tug Johnson ought to have realized.

Of course, it was true that Easter Lilly Odum just couldn't seem to quit stirring up trouble. Telling anybody who'd listen how she hated the white man—Whitey, she'd say. Agitating the decent colored. Even trying to talk the black kids out of playing football for SCCH, when now they had the chance to line up beside white boys.

Easter Lilly would raise some kind of hell every time the county commissioners met. Even ran for the board herself, without a Chinaman's chance to win. Spouting Black Power talk twenty years after nobody listened to it anymore. And those letters to the *News-Messenger*—at least they'd have to stop printing them now that Easter Lilly Odum was a known murderess.

Tyree Neely would see to *that*. In a roundabout way, of course. One thing he never did was threaten the press.

"I hope Ben boffed'er good," Tug said. "I mean before—"

"Benjy never had the chance." Tyree struggled to keep his voice low, level. He did not like dirty sex talk but he believed that to show anger was to betray weakness. A quiet manner was the more menacing, therefore the more convincing. "Not before she murdered him. Lissen, Tug, here's a coupla bucks—whyn't you go get us some coffee? No sugar in mine. Jase?"

"But we got to—"

"Two sugars," Jase said.

Jase might be a pushover in some ways but he was quick on the uptake when it mattered. Tyree said, calculating, "I like the coffee they got out at the Burger King."

It would take Tug a good half hour to get out there, buy the coffee, get back.

"Down the street here at the Purity, they let it sit in the pot too long. Tastes like blacktop."

"Why can't Jase go?" Incongruously, for a man so big, Tug looked and sounded as if he were about to cry. "I ought to help question that cunt. She don't—"

Tyree hated poolroom words as much as he hated to be called Ty. "Way I figure it, Tug, you might just scare her so bad she'd keep her mouth shut. Jase can be my witness if I need one."

Tug obviously did not know whether to be hurt at being sent away or proud to be told he'd scare even Easter Lilly Odum into keeping her mouth shut.

"Might be what she needs," he said hopefully. "Somebody scare the shit outten'er."

"Go get the coffee." Tyree turned abruptly toward the cellblock. "Come on, Jase."

SHEP

THE PROSECUTOR BROTHER HAD MADE A STATEMENT, WITH WHICH the wire service story in the *Times* ended:

> "There's not a doubt in the world that this woman lured Ben into her cell, stole his knife and murdered him. I intend to seek the death penalty, and I'm confident a Stonewall County jury will grant it."

I am too, Shep Riley thought.

He put his feet up on the old dining table he had bought at a secondhand store in Rutland. With both leaves inserted, the table served as his desk. It stood in the center of what once had been the dining room of a large bare house, the backyard of which ran down to Otter Creek, flowing behind the town. Sometimes in snow-melt season the water rose nearly to Shep's rear steps.

"Lured," he murmured, still studying the *Times* story.

The former dining room—in which Shep worked when the spirit moved him—was on the first floor, together with a kitchen, a large bedroom, and a sitting room he had furnished with a sofa and chairs from the same Rutland secondhand store. Uncarpeted steps led upstairs, but Shep seldom mounted them. He had left the second-floor rooms empty and had managed to shut off the heat registers in them, thus saving as much on imported oil as he usually earned from his desultory practice.

Lured how?

The prosecutor's statement intrigued him. The way a woman usually lured a man? There was nothing in the story about witnesses. How could the brother know what had happened in the jail without witnesses? And if there had been witnesses, how could the woman have got away in the murdered man's car?

Send'em all back to Affiker, Shack had suggested. And he wouldn't be the only one in favor of doing that. Particularly not down there in—Shep checked the name in the *Times*—down there in Waitsfield. So there was no official segregation anymore, the Klan was mostly underground, and the lynch types were afraid of the feds. So what? When there was a plausible charge, a black apparently having murdered a white with interracial sex in the background or maybe the foreground, a southern jury was likely to finish the case in an afternoon.

And not just a southern jury, Shep thought, trying characteristically to be fair. North as well as South, not to mention East and West, whites were too accustomed to thinking of blacks as shiftless, immoral, violent. Blacks were *expected* to be criminal. The burden of proof—even in the courtroom—was on them, not on the law.

How had a woman in jail come by a knife, anyway? Most likely it was the jailer's. Which the prosecutor brother would no doubt claim Easter Lilly Odum—was there some religious connotation in the name?—had taken away from him after she had "lured" him into her cell.

That might not stand up under tough questioning. Unless the jailer had been a ninety-pound weakling, which southern jailers seldom were, it wouldn't have been easy for a woman to take his knife away from him.

"And no witnesses," Shep said aloud. His words echoed from the dining room walls.

He threw the *Times* down on a set of documents he had typed on the Olivetti portable that sat on a green-metal table beside his rickety captain's chair. The Olivetti was one of Shep's few concessions to modernity, let alone technology. The dining table held a crookneck reading lamp whose 60-watt light he could direct to any spot he chose, a touch-tone telephone with which NYNEX had insisted on replacing the dial version that had seemed to him perfectly satisfactory, and a battered old hand-cranked adding machine that Shep had bought when the Otter Creek Credit Union, having been run out of business by a new branch bank with home offices in Brattleboro, auctioned off its own remains.

The typed papers on which he had thrown the *Times* had been prepared for a closing on the sale by B. D. Rogers—known publicly in Otter Creek as Beady and privately as Beady Eyes—of 3.2 acres of unimproved land to B. D.'s stepson Jerry. The old man had got rich in such deals—selling even his own daughter's husband just enough worthless land, at top dollar, for Jerry to set up his family in a mobile home without violating Vermont's acreage restraints.

His practice, Shep Riley knew well enough, was not what was expected of Harvard Law graduates, whether cum laude or not. Still, he preferred it to the cases that Appleton G. Lawrence had shunted off to him like foster children with records of delinquency: defending hapless criminals (the firm's limp gesture at pro bono work) too inept to get away with a mugging or a liquor store robbery, obtaining divorces for rich husbands from the women they'd married in their youth, and billing interminable hours of advice to Equal Opportunity Employers who wanted to hire no more blacks, women, Hispanics, or paraplegics than the law required.

Shep Riley had not been thrilled by these cases and he was excited even less by settled law. Shep had hankered to break ground, and still did. He wanted not just to cause justice to be done, rare as that was; he wanted to help *define* justice, to carve it from the inert mass of the world's injustice. And though he had no more chance to do it in Otter Creek than Appleton G. Lawrence had allowed him in New York, at least he now had plenty of time to salve his frustration with fishing in the summer and skiing in the winter. He could read the looks he once had had little time for, and could feel accepted in a community he liked. If there were just a few pretty women around . . . but best, he had learned, not to think about pretty women.

He reverted to the plight of Easter Lilly Odum in Waitsfield. Hard to make a murder case stick with no witnesses, he thought again, his feet on the table, Beady Eyes' closing—scheduled for 2 P.M.—momentarily forgotten. Unless, of course, the dead man was

35

white and the prosecutor's brother. And unless the accused was a black woman car thief in a boondocks county in what had been a legally segregated state in the good old days. And unless she had some drunken shyster for a court-appointed lawyer—not an expert practitioner, even if a little rusty, like W. Shepherd Riley.

The shiny black touch-tone rang, startling him. In Otter Creek, phone calls to the town's one law office were rare. He picked up the receiver warily, expecting it to bring him unwanted news—an overdue heating bill, an overdraft at North Country Trust, notice of an outdated inspection sticker on his rust-streaked Subaru.

"Trying to reach Shepherd Riley," said a brisk male voice.

In the languid pace of Otter Creek, Shep had become suspicious of urgency. "Speaking," he answered ungraciously.

"Oh . . . Mister Riley. Care to comment on the death of Jeffrey Fishbein?"

Or a new Olympic record? Or the latest Paris fashions? The tone, it seemed to Riley, would have been about the same.

"Who?" He could not remember anybody named Fishbein.

"Prob'ly knew him as Jeff the Joker. Famous for clowning it up back in—"

"The Joker's dead?"

He had forgotten, if he had ever known, that the Joker's real name was Fishbein. As many times as he had seen Jeff the Joker do his street theater, mock the segs, taunt the fuzz, outrage solid citizens with his irreverence. As often as they had sat late into the night with others just as confident that the Age of Aquarius was at hand, the room acrid with pot smoke, the beer cans piling up in the corner, the chicks happy to oblige, the good talk and the loud laughter seeming never to end, or even to have an ending . . .

"Heart attack," the brisk voice said with what to Shep Riley sounded like satisfaction. "They found'im dead in bed this morning in Phoenix."

"Phoenix." Shep could recall no connection between Jeff the Joker and Phoenix. Shep had never been in Phoenix, nor known anybody who had been. "Who is this, anyway?"

"McDougal of the *Post*. Your old law office in New York gave me this number." Shep decided on the spot to have it changed. "Lots of stories in the file linking you and Fishbein. So I thought if you'd care to comment—"

"The Joker was a good man," Shep Riley said. "Believed in ordinary people. Cared about freedom . . . compassion. Things like that. You could say he believed in the Sermon on the Mount."

"Believed in . . . hold it a sec . . . which sermon was that?"

"On the Mount. He acted like a clown but he wasn't really a clown. He just thought the best way to make his point was to—"

"Going too fast," McDougal said. "Let me get some of this down."

Riley tried to recall specific acts, times, places. The way the Joker had put on the National Guard kids at the Chicago convention with his water pistol. Mooned the police in Nashville when they went through that roadblock. Worn a clown suit and fake five o'clock shadow delivering a mock speech supporting Dick Nixon in Detroit.

"Just say the Joker always believed in America," Riley said. "That'll cover it."

He wondered if it still had been true in the last hours in Phoenix. He had not seen Jeff the Joker in years, or heard anything about him for almost as long. Had Jeffrey Fishbein continued to believe? To laugh even if he no longer believed? How had he wound up dead in bed in Phoenix?

"But listen," said McDougal of the *Post* in his eager young voice. "I'm doing a feature about the old days. Pegged to this guy's death, I mean. Desk thinks it's a great idea. Like lots of people have forgotten how things use to be, y'know?"

All too well, Shep thought.

"So the desk said you might could tell me some funny stuff about the sixties. Anecdotes. People stuff, y'know? Maybe about Fishbein. Or how they beat you guys up on that bridge. What bridge *was* that, anyway?"

Shep Riley hung up. He sat looking at the touch-tone, waiting for it to ring again. It did, eight times. Even after it stopped, the ringing seemed to go on inside his head, piercing in the quietness of the room.

Dead in bed. Had Jeffrey Fishbein lived to understand, as Shep Riley had, that the Age of Aquarius had never arrived in America? And probably never would. A great sadness filled Shep's breast, hurting him physically, a sadness not so much for Jeff the Joker— the Jeffrey Fishbein he probably never really had known, the stranger who had died alone in bed in Phoenix—but sadness for a past that he sometimes conceded, sometimes had no choice but to admit, still lived in him, dormant beneath dull contentment with dry doughnuts every morning at the Little Giant, with no expectation greater than the annual collapse of the Red Sox, in a town where little was likely to cause a man to stir himself.

In the past, Shep Riley had looked forward to whatever would happen, had *believed* in what would happen, and talked of it perhaps as eagerly as McDougal of the *Post* talked of people stuff. He had burned for the world not to be what it was, for change that had seemed then as near at hand, as tangible, as a flower in a National Guard rifle barrel. He stared at the touch-tone, which had brought unwanted news, all right, brought back a past that mocked him, a past in which Shep Riley, however deluded, however fatuous, had been alive, reaching, the future always just ahead.

Now—soon, someday—a touch-tone would ring on another table and another hand would pick up the receiver and McDougal of the *Post* in his eager, unknowing voice would ask, "Care to comment on the death of W. Shepherd Riley?"

Shep squared around to the old dining table, suddenly determined not to die in bed in Phoenix. Or in Otter Creek, for that matter. Forgotten, an artifact, a meaningless name from a bygone time, signifying not even sound and fury, to be commented on for some pimple-ass reporter seeking . . .

"People stuff," Shep muttered.

He scrabbled momentarily among the papers littering the dining table, shoving aside Beady Eyes' closure documents, retrieving finally a battered leather address book, stuffed and interleaved with business cards and torn bits of paper. He searched through it, in his haste scattering loose entries on the floor, until he found Meg Whitman's address and number.

Chattanooga, area code 615. He could not remember Meg's married name, only the picture she'd sent him from her wedding. Some rube house builder with a cueball head.

As Shep pulled the touch-tone toward him and punched in the digits, he hoped the number was still good. And his lawyer's mind began to stir, shake off the rust, work out a courtroom strategy for the defense of Easter Lilly Odum.

ALTON

ALTON MC KINNON GLANCED AT THE TIMEX ON HIS LEFT WRIST JUST as the phone rang. Nearly noon. Not long before Meg would come home for lunch. Already, he had done the chores. He had read the *Chattanooga Times* from cover to cover, too, except for the foreign news. The recession was not going away—not in housing starts anyway.

Alton had washed the breakfast dishes, swept the floors, made the beds, picked up the kids' room, hoping all the while that none of the neighbors would look in and catch him at woman's work. Or, God forbid, any of the boys from Smoky Joe's. Maybe, he thought, as he hurried across the kitchen to answer the wall phone, he could catch some sports on ESPN, even in the morning.

He had no real expectation that anyone would be calling about business, not the way things were going. Still . . . sooner or later someone would want a new house. Repair a roof. Aluminum siding. His voice almost trembled as he said hello.

"May I speak to Meg Whitman?"

The man's voice sounded to Alton like an insurance salesman's. Or somebody flacking something nobody needed. He was in no mood for a sales pitch, not with area housing starts in the pits. So he responded harshly, "You mean Meg McKinnon?"

"Uh . . . of course. McKinnon . . ."

To Alton McKinnon, his wife's name was more than a matter of pride; it was, or should be, her identity and a good part of his. He'd made short work of her talk about keeping her own name. Meg might be the one with the education, but *his* name by God was hers now and going to be for the duration. Like it was *his* money that put the roof over their heads, back when people were building. Food on the table. And when people started building again—

"May I speak to her?"

"Taking the kids to swimming class."

They could not afford swimming classes much longer. But Meg had insisted that the kids ought not to suffer just because business was bad. Alton loved his kids too much to argue with that, and, anyway, when Meg got the bit in her teeth . . .

"Call back in an hour or so," he said abruptly. "But we won't be buying anything today."

The voice on the line laughed. "I'm not selling anything, I'm glad to say. Could I leave a message for Miz McKinnon?"

Alton McKinnon did not take kindly to strange men who wanted to leave messages for his wife. When they didn't even know her real name. Too many men paid too much attention to Meg for his taste.

Nor did he care for this newfangled Ms. business. As if plain old Mrs. had become a dirty word. Men who used Ms., in Alton McKinnon's view, lacked balls.

The voice on the telephone began to leave the message: "Please tell Miz McKinnon that Shep Riley called and will call again, maybe . . ."

"The guy she used to work with?" Alton was shocked.

"Miz Whitman . . . I mean Miz McKinnon and I worked together years ago, yes."

"The lawyer?"

The voice laughed again. "Well, I *used* to be a lawyer, anyway. Tell Meg there's a case I thought might interest her."

The *nerve*. Alton wanted to hang up and had to restrain himself. He'd tell the guy off first. He'd waited a long time to tell off Shep Riley.

Alton liked to think about telling people off, to imagine how well he'd conduct himself toe-to-toe. In practice, he avoided confrontations when he could. He had the ingrained southern habit of civility—or perhaps, he sometimes feared, it was only diffidence. Except for that, he might actually have said what had been on his mind for years. Besides, just because the guy wanted to talk to Meg didn't mean she wanted to talk to him.

Unless they had been talking recently.

"She's not doing your kind of work anymore," Alton said. "Not in years."

The idea that Meg and Riley might be in touch again, talking, planning stuff behind his back, alarmed Alton. Had it gone so far he would call her up in broad daylight, bold as brass? Maybe, as he had long feared, a plain old construction man was not good enough for *Ms.* Meg McKinnon, with her college degrees. Maybe she secretly turned up her nose at a mere high school grad with dirt under his fingernails and no houses to build.

"I know she's not." The con man's voice he was hearing, Alton thought, wouldn't fool a jury of twelve Mongoloids. "I just thought maybe she might—"

"She's not doing your kind of work anymore," Alton said again, emphasizing each word. Nerving himself to the necessity, he put aside civility. "No use you calling again," he said. "She won't want to talk to you."

He cracked the receiver into its cradle, the abrupt gesture giving him, for the first time since he had answered the phone, a sense of control. Sometimes it paid to just come out with it—whatever you were feeling.

"Who won't I not want to talk to?"

Startled, Alton turned away from the wall phone to see Meg placing a large bag of groceries from the Price Chopper on the kitchen table. Even as he tried to think how to answer, he remembered with a sinking feeling that he had not given her any money for the supermarket.

"Some guy," he said vaguely, weakly. "Nobody."

Meg gave him the smile that never failed to soften Alton McKinnon's knees. He saw at once that his evasion would not be good enough.

"Why would you tell nobody not to call back?"

"Well . . . uh . . . nobody for you to bother about."

Meg pulled a light sweater over her head, dropped it on the back of a chair, and shook out her dark hair, fluffing it with her hands, a movement Alton always liked to see. He loved Meg's hair, even though she would no longer wear it long for him. She wasn't a girl anymore, she'd say. She was forty-two years old. But to Alton McKinnon, Meg looked just as she had when he'd fallen in love with her in high school, before she'd gone off to college and later to work with—

"Oh, I won't be bothered." Meg took plastic-wrapped iceberg lettuce from the top of the Price Chopper bag and went to the refrigerator. "Not unless you make some kind of a mystery out of it."

She opened the refrigerator and the crisper drawer and bent to arrange a place for the lettuce. Her skirt pulled tightly over slim hips and buttocks, rose above the backs of her knees, and Alton tortured himself with the thought of Shep Riley running his hands over those hips, between those legs . . .

"It must have been Clinton." Meg closed the refrigerator and turned to face him. "He wants to put me on the Supreme Court."

Alton wanted desperately to sustain the joke long enough for her to forget the call. "He's already named a woman," he said.

"I'm prettier than she is." Meg put a foot on a kitchen chair and ran her hands enticingly down her black stocking and up again. "Got better legs."

In fact, Meg's legs were somewhat thin—so she insisted, though Alton thought they were fine, like everything about her. Meg was one of those women who never put on weight, though she was a hearty eater and seldom exercised. She was tall—not the cuddly, bosomy cheerleader type that some people thought a woman ought to be. Not Alton McKinnon. He considered his wife's lean body, small breasts, and long legs just right, just what he wanted. Besides, he was uncomfortably aware that other men were invariably attracted to her. Not, he knew, that Meg did anything to lead them on; his wife was not that kind. There was just something about Meg, like a perfume touched behind her ears, that made them want to fetch her another drink and brag about their golf scores and swagger like juveniles.

"Best-looking lawyer in three states." Like all women, Meg loved to be flattered about her looks and Alton had often used this line to ease tensions. Anyway, it was probably true.

"Well, if it wasn't Clinton"—Meg put her foot down and straightened her skirt on her hips—"who was it?"

With her dark hair and eyes and contrasting skin so white it caused Alton to worry about the Tennessee sun, Meg made him think of a milkmaid, whatever a milkmaid was. Either she knew instinctively—Meg liked to say she'd learned to rely on her instincts—just how long she could stay out in the sun or she had a special kind of skin. In late summer she might pick up a freckle or two on her high cheekbones and on her neck and shoulders a veneer of tan so faint Alton imagined he could wipe it off with a Kleenex.

"Doesn't matter. You only do tax law now." Instantly, Alton realized his mistake.

"Was *that* what you were telling this nobody on the phone? That I only do tax law?"

"Well . . . I thought you *did*. I—"

"Who wanted to talk to me?" Impatience edged Meg's voice—which, Alton knew from experience, could turn quickly from agreement to demand. She tucked her plain, unruffled white blouse more tightly into her tubelike gray flannel skirt. To Alton McKinnon, the gesture resembled a man hitching up his trousers, turning serious, getting down to business—except that it was hard for him even to imagine Meg as a man.

"If that *was* someone that wanted to talk about a case—any case," Meg said, "we could use the fee." She slapped her hand against the Price Chopper bag. "I drew out of savings for these."

A slow rage started in the back of Alton's head. "Things'll turn up," he said. "I got enough in the bank to carry us."

"*My* savings, Alton. It's not the first time, either. It'll take every cent in *your* account to keep up the payments on your truck and backhoe."

The rage burned nearer his eyes. "I'll look after this family, Meg. No wife of mine needs to pay my bills."

Meg started to say something, thought better of it, and came across the kitchen. She put her thin hands softly on his cheeks.

"You *are* the man in this family . . . I know that. It's not your fault if people aren't building houses these days. When they start again, things will be like they used to be."

The soft touch on his cheeks—somehow Meg's hands were always soft—checked Alton's rage. He loved to be touched by Meg, to touch her; touching made things bearable. Only sometimes he was embarrassed by the way Meg liked to turn any little gesture—a peck on the cheek in greeting, a manly guiding hand on her elbow, a playful swat on the fanny—into an excuse for getting down and dirty. Alton never saw why touching had to lead to sex. He valued being *soothed,* like now, when Meg's hands were cooling, calming.

"If I just didn't feel like such a hopeless failure," he said. "I'm not used to making up the damn beds."

"You're *not* a failure . . . you're a victim of this economy. And I'm glad I can help out a little. If you'd just let me . . ."

Suddenly, her hands felt hot, accusing; rage at his inadequacy nearly blinded him. He seized her slender wrists and pulled them to her sides, speaking hotly into her face:

"It was your old sweetheart Riley on the phone. The son of a bitch's got a case I'm damn sure you'll be interested in."

TYREE

EASTER LILLY'S WAS THE ONLY OCCUPIED CELL. SHE SAT ON ITS COT, her long legs crossed, the hem of the blue jail dress just above her knees, her arms freed of the handcuffs. Her face, framed by the gentle fall of her black hair, was impassive.

Jase Allman unlocked the cell door and Tyree Neely went in and sat on a three-legged stool. Jase closed the door without locking it and leaned on the bars of the cell across the corridor.

"You probably don't think so," Tyree said, "but you've got rights and I'm going to read them to you." He did, from a card he took out of his pocket.

Easter Lilly did not appear to listen, her body language unchanging, reproving. She folded her arms, making her upright body seem accusing.

"You want a lawyer?"

Tyree longed to shake her into subservience. But though Easter Lilly's nostrils twitched as if in disdain, she said nothing.

All the formalities, Tyree thought. The niceties. No technicalities for her to beat the gas chamber with. He was proud that even though he was sitting not a yard from where his damnfool brother had let this woman cut him open like a cantaloupe, he was able to maintain his calm.

"Jase?" he said quietly. "Wasn't Cady representing her on the car thing?"

"Much as she'd let him."

Easter Lilly originally had been arrested while driving a pickup truck belonging to Southland Power and Light. When stopped by "Beetle" Bailey, an officer who thought it strange that a black woman was driving a Southland truck, she declared she had only "borrowed" it for a citizen's obligation—to get from Cognac, the colored community where she lived, to a county commissioners' meeting in Waitsfield.

"Better call him then," Tyree told Jase.

Easter Lilly had yelled at Beetle Bailey that she aimed to make Whitey explain why Cognac taxpayers couldn't get their streets paved, even if it was a niggertown.

That was so characteristic of Easter Lilly Odum that Tyree thought her story might even have been true. But Beetle Bailey had decided it was a car theft any way you looked at it—which was exactly how Southland Power *did* look at it, as did the outraged linesman who had been stranded on foot in Cognac. Of course, now that a murder rap hung over Easter Lilly, the original charge hardly mattered.

Jase went out to the front office to call Cady. Despite the faint sounds of *One Life to Live* or some other soap still playing on the television, the cellblock was quiet enough for Tyree to hear Jase's end of the conversation. Apparently, Cady—as usual in the afternoon—was not in. Jase left word for him to get over to the jail as soon as possible, came back into the cellblock, and leaned against the bars again.

"You call the Purity?"

Tyree knew Jase hadn't, but he wanted to remind him—Jase was a good fellow but a little sloppy about details—that attorney J. Preston Cadieux—pronounced Ka-ducks when anybody used the old lawyer's real name—read a lot of his briefs at a corner booth in the Purity Cafe ("Good Eats, Cold Beer") accompanied by a litter of Coors Silver Bullet cans.

"You can wait till Cady gets here if you want," Tyree told Easter Lilly. "But sooner or later you'll have to tell us what happened." As if we didn't know, he thought.

Easter Lilly sat unmoving on the cot, her slender legs crossed, her arms folded, seeming not to notice him or Jase. Tyree refused to look at her legs, exposed beneath the denim skirt. He did not like for women to flaunt their bodies at him—though he had to admit Easter Lilly Odum looked good even in jailhouse clothes. Which had brought Benjy nothing but trouble.

"I wish I had her lawyer here," he told Jase. "I don't want her claiming in court she didn't get her rights."

"Rights." Easter Lilly made the word sound like an oath. Her voice, after her long silence, surprised Tyree: "Only rights I ever saw round here had white skins."

After all we've done for them, Tyree thought. To have to listen to that kind of crap. He replied more emphatically than he had intended, "Christ, woman! When'll you start living in the twentieth century? Don't you know things've changed?"

"Oh yeah." Easter Lilly looked up at the ceiling. The movement drew attention to her graceful neck, her firm uplifted chin. "Like that peckerwood slob you call a lawyer coming in here smelling like a whiskey still."

Tyree was annoyed that she would trash an old man. Cady was a good lawyer, even if a little bad to drink. "You didn't have rights, you wouldn't get a lawyer at all."

The court always appointed Cady to represent indigent defendants, white as well as black, in Stonewall County. Tyree saw to that. Cady needed to make a living like anybody else.

"How'd you get Benjy to come back here where you could grab his knife, Lilly? Show'im a little something, did you?"

"My name's *Easter* Lilly, mothafucka. Easter . . . Lilly . . . Odum." She said the words slowly, distinctly. "And I didn't show that shitbird brother of yours *nothing*."

Tyree Neely stood up abruptly, his fists clenched at his sides. The movement was merely physical, like a chicken still flopping on the ground after its neck had been wrung; mentally, emotionally, he willed himself to keep control. Posed wide-legged in the middle of the cell, he leaned toward Easter Lilly where she sat motionless on the cot, her face still impassive, her brown eyes locked with his. Despite his efforts, Tyree's voice was louder than he meant it to be, echoing disconcertingly in the cellblock:

"Swiped that knife right out of his pocket, didn't you?"

"Yelling at me part of my rights?"

Take it easy, Tyree thought. Or she'll be telling some judge I brutalized her.

"Easter Lilly Odum," he said more quietly, "I'm asking you if on the night in question you didn't let Ben Neely think——"

"I didn't have to show no white-ass pussy-hound what he knows I got." Easter Lilly spoke as calmly as Tyree had tried to. "I didn't have to make'im think nothin he wasn't already thinking. He came tomcattin back here on'is own. Was *that* some of my rights, too?"

Her speech was getting slovenly, and this time she made "rights" sound like a joke. Stiffly as a marionette, Tyree went back to the stool, folded himself down on it, and stared at her again, wishing he could crack her skull against the cell bars. Especially the hairdo; what right did a murdering colored jailbird have to get herself looking so good?

Easter Lilly's calm voice, however, had the effect of calming Tyree Neely, too. His surge of anger passed and he was relieved not to have slapped her, as he had wanted, when she called Benjy a pussy-hound. Which the rascal may have been, but was that anything to get stabbed for?

"My brother didn't like colored people." Tyree was proud that he now kept his voice unexcited, too. "I heard him say he didn't, plenty of times. I'm not saying that's good or bad, the way he felt. I don't feel that way myself. I'm just saying my brother never in his life messed around with a colored woman."

"Just little white dollbabies," Easter Lilly said. "Just white as snow and at least ten years old and wearin a skirt he could lift up. Is all *he* ever mess with."

Tyree found himself chewing his lower lip at the idea that a Neely might have been a child molester. He made himself stop.

"I'm not claiming Benjy was an angel. I just say again, all I did say, my brother didn't mess around with black women."

"And I'm just sayin"—Easter Lilly's face now was drawn tight and her eyes were hot and hating—"he came back here that night with'is white dick in one hand and that knife in the other."

Silence fell on the cellblock, except for the murmur of soap opera in the front office. Can't believe what I'm hearing, Tyree thought, fury surging in him anew. She's going to claim rape.

The idea almost choked him. A colored woman accusing a Neely—a *Neely* of Stonewall County, the youngest son of John Bell

Neely himself—of being so hard up for sex he'd stoop to rape her at knifepoint. Tyree was glad old John Bell was not there to hear such garbage. Or their mother Gladys. Could they possibly be lying undisturbed in the Stonewall Memory Gardens when such foul lies were being told about the apple of their eyes?

Tyree Neely was not, however, the oldest son of John Bell Neely for nothing. He had not made himself, as he knew he was, the big mule in Stonewall County, bigger and richer than old John Bell had ever been, by losing his head or his cool. Not in that way would he be able to send Easter Lilly Odum to the gas chamber. John Bell Neely would have expected nothing less of his firstborn than to do right by the beloved child of his middle age. And Tyree Neely had never in his life, as boy or man, let his father down.

So he fought his fury as deliberately as a man might fight an attack of hiccups or a midnight cramp in his calf muscle. He did it by thinking again, forcing himself to think, of the horned owl in the old dead tree, the first horned owl anybody had ever seen in Stonewall County or anywhere nearby. And only when he knew he could speak without a quiver in his voice did Tyree Neely say to Easter Lilly, "You got any witnesses?"

She only stared at him for an answer. Easter Lilly knew, as he knew and Jase Allman knew—Jase leaning on the bars, hearing it all, a witness that she'd got her rights and never been touched—Easter Lilly knew that only she and Ben Neely had been in the cellblock the night Benjy was killed.

"Then nobody'll believe any of your lying rape talk."

Tyree knew *he* didn't believe it. Why should anyone else? About a Neely anyway, and Easter Lilly Odum, the colored girl who'd got the nigger-lover Timmons run out of town.

"What you did," he said, "you whispered in'is ear you'd give'im a little something, didn't you? If he'd bring you liquor or maybe dope. Leave the cell keys lying around. And when he was fool enough to believe you, like most anybody wearing pants would believe a woman like you—"

Easter Lilly interrupted, suddenly sounding tired—almost afraid, Tyree told himself. "Didn't you say yourself that brother of yours didn't like black skins?"

Tyree hated what he felt he had no choice but to say. "When a Jezebel like you"—how John Bell would have despised such words from a son of his to a colored woman!—"plays up to a man, he won't likely even think about the color of her skin."

Even in the line of duty, Tyree didn't like to dwell on what men and women did with and to one another. He was reluctant to think of a woman—white *or* colored—victimizing a man that way. Or *vice versa.*

Like you did Timmons, he almost said to Easter Lilly. But he forced himself to go on, his near-whisper clear in the silence of the cellblock:

"And when you got Benjy in here all hot and bothered, you stole his knife and stabbed'im, didn't you?"

Easter Lilly stood up and stepped away from the cot, pointing at it as if it were a threatening animal or a bomb about to explode. "I stabbed'im all right."

She did not sound tired anymore; she sounded like what Tyree knew she was—a colored barely a generation out of the fields.

"Jumped on top of me there'n yanked up my skirt. Nearbout tore my britches . . . you wanna see?"

She stooped and swiftly pulled the blue skirt up around her slim hips. Her white underpants, stark against her dark flesh, were ripped up one side, held together at the top with a safety pin.

"You could have torn'em yourself," Tyree said. "Later on."

Easter Lilly turned toward Jase, let him see her ripped underpants, then dropped her skirt.

"Tried to shove that bull pizzle of his where it got no business. Damn *right* I cut'im!"

Seeing the knife in his mind's eye, imagining the blade piercing the heart of John Bell Neely's youngest—eighteen years Tyree's junior—Tyree thought of what his parents' favorite might yet have done in the life so cruelly taken from him. The way Benjy was coming along lately, a smart young man beginning to wise up . . . till this foul-mouth vessel of sin took it from him. Stole the rest of Benjy's life and all of John Bell's high hopes for him.

"You won't ever steal another knife," Tyree said. "Guarantee you that." Suddenly he was not concerned for control, or for legal niceties. "Not after they turn on that gas."

He knew, looking into Easter Lilly's dark and furious eyes, that she wished she did have a knife, one in her hand right then. For a moment, he thought she really was going to make a move on him, even without a weapon. He almost wished she would; that would be as good as proof of what she'd done to Benjy.

Just at that moment, just when she might have trapped herself and made his job easy, and done it with Jase Allman watching— just then Tug Johnson came blundering into the cellblock carrying two plastic cups.

"I forget who gets the sugar," he said, as Easter Lilly Odum began to laugh in Tyree Neely's face.

MEG

MEG DID NOT HAVE TO ASK WHY ALTON SEEMED RELUCTANT TO
go to Smoky Joe's, even on the night when he usually met his pals
for beer and brooding about lack of work in the construction trade.
She did not have to ask because she knew he believed she would
be on the phone to Shep Riley as soon as he was out the door.

He was right, too. Except not as soon as he was out the door.

She gave him plenty of time to get to Smoky's and order his first
beer. Because when Alton was in one of his jealous moods, he was
perfectly capable of circling the block, sneaking up the driveway
and trying to catch her in whatever act he suspected. He'd done it
before.

Of course, Alton hardly expected to catch her doing anything
really shameful. Just perhaps to find her making a secret phone call,
or reading a letter she didn't want him to know she'd received, or
writing one. At worst, watching a rented porno movie, since he
thought rather unhappily that she was hipped on sex.

Alton not only knew she had never been unfaithful to him, and
she hadn't; he was incapable of imagining such an infidelity. That
is, he could imagine, in a jealous mood, *Meg* having a lover. When
Alton got into a jealous mood, he might think almost anything—

then forget all about it by the next morning. But he could never imagine, in any mood, *his wife* being unfaithful to him.

In fact, either as herself or as Alton's wife, Meg had never mustered up the courage to march into Blockbuster and rent a porno, though that might spice up a life that surely could use a little spice. But when it came to Shep Riley, Alton was *never* rational—which was why, if Meg could help it, that name was never mentioned in the McKinnon household.

On the other hand, as she'd told Alton, they could use a nice fat fee; and as she had *not* told him, she really would like to do something besides tax and estate work again—even with Shep Riley, even briefly. She was not, she told herself, actually bored with being a housewife. Done well, the way she wanted to do things, keeping house, raising kids, all of that was satisfying enough. For twelve years of marriage, she had loved and enjoyed her children—still did—and Alton most of the time, though he was not reacting well to hard times.

For the same twelve years, however, she had maintained a part-time law practice, not only for the extra income it provided, but for the good feeling of being strong and at least partially independent. So, from the moment she had learned of Shep Riley's call, she had known she would call him back.

Meg doubted she could take on whatever Riley might suggest, but she was bored with her undemanding practice. In deference to marriage and family, she had never developed her career to near its potential. She felt so wasted—as if her talents and education and experience were old documents, filed and forgotten—that talking to someone who had shared as much of her life as Shep Riley had, who had taught her much of what she knew, might make the past seem tangible again, and alive. Besides, something more could possibly come of it. She had been good at trial work. And she had loved the time she had spent with Shep Riley.

The *working* time, she insisted to herself, as she settled beside the bedside phone. In the old days, the cases had been hard, the opposition usually mean, the clients needy and sometimes noble, the rewards, when they came, worthwhile. Victory and vindication rather than money. Not that either Meg McKinnon or the former Meg Whitman despised money, or wished merely to wash the feet of the poor; but while working with Shep Riley she had come to value satisfaction more than dollars, the struggle for which in her later life with Alton and the children seemed unending and out of scale with . . . with *what?*

Meg picked up the phone by the bed that for so long she had shared with Alton. By then, she knew, he was well settled at Smoky Joe's, their little daughter Kate was safely in bed and asleep, and ten-year-old Hugh, had finished his homework and was being allowed to watch *The Secret Garden* on VCR.

. . . With *real life.*

The response came to her with a sense of shock. Her finger, poised over the phone buttons, hesitated. Could she actually look back upon her time roaming the South, working and sleeping with Shep Riley, as "real life," and her time with her family as something less? Alton would be enraged. Alton would demand to know what about their children? Were they not real life?

She knew she would not want or be able to deny it. She could not even deny it at that moment; but still she punched in the telephone number Shep Riley had sent on a postcard years before. She had written the number, with no name attached, on the rear flyleaf of her address book, then thrown away the card before Alton might come across it.

Shep answered on the third ring. Even by the word "hello," she knew his voice instantly, though she had not heard it for years. He had a deep courtroom voice, a practiced voice that once had caused her to believe in bliss as in justice. She had listened, then, with eager heart, as if hearing the voices of law and of love in one cherished cadence. Her whole being had resonated to its sound, as a dancer to a drum. But that had been years ago. Was it possible that he still could have that effect on her?

She told herself his hello seemed brisk, and she responded in kind. "I hear you've got a case," she said.

Silence echoed down the line. Then Shep said, "That husband of yours is a pistol."

"He'd use one on you if he could."

She wished immediately that she hadn't said it. She had not meant to remind him in any way that—

"Not because of anything I ever told him." Naturally, quick as

Shep was, he'd picked up the inference. Meg plainly heard the faint emphasis he had placed on the "I." She quickly tried to sound impersonal:

"Alton and I have no secrets from each other. What's it all about, you calling me after—"

"You mean this call's not a secret?" Shep Riley said. "He's maybe standing there listening to you?"

"Of course he's not." Then she said for effect, "But I'll tell him about it." She was not at all sure that she would.

"Frankly, my dear, I wouldn't. Mister Nice Guy sounded like he'd use a pistol on *you,* he caught you talking to me."

"He *is* a nice guy. I haven't got but a minute, Shep. What did you want with me?"

Another moment's silence fell on the line, as if he were studying his notes for a speech. Then, straightforwardly, without embellishment, he told her about Easter Lilly Odum.

Meg had read nothing about the case. "But you're still in Vermont," she said. "I called the Vermont area code."

"I'm going South tomorrow. I was hoping you'd join me."

"Oh, you were? Just drop everything?" She was annoyed, flattered. Excited? Only, she said to herself, at possibly getting back to work.

"As soon as you can get away," Shep said. "Meg, I haven't been so charged up about anything since the firm called me back to New York. I read that story in the *Times* this morning and it was like somebody shoved a red-hot poker up my rear end. I knew—"

"I thought you were through with this kind of thing. Hibernating up there with the polar bears."

"I was. Until I read about a bunch of rednecks trying to railroad a black woman into the gas chamber."

In his voice now, Meg could sense the old intensity that once had so captivated her. She could hear the conviction ringing in his words. She could almost see him striding up to a jury box, fists clenched, tie askew, red ponytail almost bristling, eyes as hot as embers in a grate.

She almost hung up, aghast at the clarity and ache of the memory. So she counterattacked: "But Shep . . . how do you know they're railroading her?"

"Because that's what they *do*. That's how things go down there. You know that; we learned it together. Meg, I'm just as sure of it as I am that . . . that there ain't no polar bears in Vermont!"

"You could look *that* up in a guidebook. But you haven't even talked to this woman yet. Or to anybody. You can't *know* if it was murder or not."

"I trust my instincts," Shep said. "I always have."

Like I trust mine, Meg thought. As I did once too often. With *you*.

"So you're just going to go down there following your instinct and defend some woman you never heard of before this morning. Who might be a murderer."

"Oh, she probably won't go to trial for months. I just want to get a sense of the case. A sense of *her*. And you could be a big help, so I thought I'd ask you to come, too."

"I can't," Meg said, almost automatically. But the words sounded too flat, so she added, "I can't leave the kids."

"But it'd only be for a few days."

"If you take on her case, it could be a lot longer."

"She'll already have an appointed lawyer," Shep said. "Some briefcase too young or too old to know his ass from third base. I aim to check *him* out. Or maybe it'll be a her. See that this woman has decent representation. I was hoping you'd help."

To her amazement, Meg suddenly realized that she just might do it. There was at least a chance Shep was right and the woman was being set up. Wouldn't be unusual in that part of the world. Or any other, for that matter. Exciting to think that if she *was* innocent, and if they *could* get her off . . . and exciting to think of working again with Shep Riley.

"You were always opposed to the death penalty, Meg. And that prosecutor prick has already said he's going to ask for it."

Same old Shep, she thought, quelling her excitement. Pushing my buttons. In fact, however, she did hate the death penalty.

"Right up your alley," Shep said. "That jury panel's sure to be full of the kind of people you've checked out a hundred times. Nobody's better at that than you were."

Another button pushed. But Alton would shriek and scream and suspect the worst. She'd have to pay someone to help him look after the kids. Respectable forty-something housewives just didn't drop everything and go off on some wild-goose chase into the past, looking for . . . what?

"It'll be like old times." Shep's eager voice seemed to vibrate all the way from Vermont.

"That's it, isn't it?" she said.

"What is?"

This time, it was Meg who let silence fall. She saw quite clearly that Shep *was* following his instinct—to get back into the old groove, ride the white charger again, kick the rascals in the balls. He had always savored the fight even more than the occasional victory, especially if he believed the cause worthwhile.

"Yeah." Shep finally broke the silence. "You got me pegged, all right." Meg had forgotten his sensitivity, his ability to see the world out of someone else's eyes, see *himself* as others saw him. Now he was doing it over hundreds of miles of humming wires. "I crawled in my hole up here and pulled it in after me. And now I want out."

Get a little publicity, too, Meg thought meanly.

"Tell you the bloody truth," Shep said, "I'm tired of being nobody. Forgotten, zilch, *nada*."

The words were as sincere as any she ever had heard from him. Then, in a rush, eagerly, he went on, "And I really do believe they'll railroad this woman if we don't stop it!"

Meg laughed. "Riley to the rescue. I'm afraid this time you'll have to ride that horse without me."

He sounded deflated. "Why's that?"

"Because I've got a husband and a family and a house to look after. I can't just drop everything and run off to fight windmills. Maybe you can, but I can't."

She meant what she said but still relished the idea of getting back into the arena. Not, she assured herself, of seeing Shep Riley again.

"Where are you?" he said.

"In Chattanooga. Where'd you think?"

"I mean right this minute."

Meg felt a vague sense of warning. "In the bedroom," she said. "Using the phone."

"What're you wearing?"

The warning bells were louder. But surely . . .

"Skirt and blouse," she said cautiously.

A brief silence. "Is it a pullover, or button up the front?"

"Button up," she said, and suddenly knew all too certainly where he was heading.

"With nothing under it? The way you used—"

"Listen to me, Shep," she said. "Even if I could come and help out, it wouldn't be like it was before."

Silence, longer this time. Then, "Meg, I wasn't trying . . . I was just remembering how you used to look those times when—"

"That was eighteen years ago, Shep. I don't look like you remember anymore." Though she knew that even at forty-two, she didn't look too dried up. "I'm sorry I can't take on your case but I'm afraid I—"

"Oh, I *know* what you're afraid of," Shep said. "You're afraid you'll fall in bed with me again."

"I am not!" Later, she realized, to her discomfort, that she actually had screeched the words.

"And you probably would, too."

Meg hung up, infuriated. To be treated like one of those pneumatic dollies in a man's fantasies! The arrogance of the bastard! If I do go down there, I'll show that conceited pig who's afraid. But of course, she wouldn't go at all.

When Alton came home, unsteady and smelling of beer, Meg was still angry, but not at him. In fact, he seemed so mellow that she amazed herself by telling him what she had not admitted to herself until that moment—that she was thinking of going away for a few days.

To silence Alton's bleats of protest, Meg hustled him into bed, and not until he was sweating and groaning above her did Meg realize that that son of a bitch Riley had pushed another one of her buttons.

IDA SUE

THE FROZEN CHICKEN POT PIES WOULD NOT HAVE BEEN HALF BAD,
Ida Sue told herself, if she had left them in the oven a few minutes
longer. They had defrosted all right but not enough to get rid of a
little chill at the center. But Jase wouldn't complain. Sometimes he
would go on and on about his mother's cooking, that old sourpuss
bitch, but he never said anything bad about hers. Jase was lucky
she put any kind of dinner on the table, little bit of money he
brought home. Besides, the way to Jase's heart was not through his
stomach alone.

To satisfy his sweet tooth, however, Ida Sue put a piece of Sara
Lee pound cake in front of him.

"All anybody could talk about at the Dinette today," she said,
"is y'all got that Easter Lilly back in jail."

While being courted by Jase and others, Ida Sue had never expected to work after getting married, but recently she had taken a
job as cashier at the Downhome Dinette out at the mall. She was
careful not to let anyone think that she was waitressing or wore a
uniform or anything common like that. She liked the extra money.
And all the talk in a popular spot like the Dinette kept her posted
on everything going on in Stonewall County. She could even meet
some new people.

"We sure-God do," Jase said, taking a bite of his Sara Lee. He went on with his mouth full, but Ida Sue was used to that and easily made out what he was saying: "Kind of like being in bed with a rattlesnake."

"I had a figure like that I wouldn't mind being called a snake." Not, she thought, looking down at herself, that anybody'd mistake me for Roseanne on TV.

"Is there some ice cream, Suedy? I crave some ice cream on this kind of a cake."

"You finished it up last night, and I didn't think to bring none home today."

"And toasted," Jase said. "This kind of cake toasts up real nice. When it's toasted, ice cream goes even better on it."

"Fixing it that way, you'd need chocolate sauce, too."

"I love chocolate sauce."

"But there ain't none. No ice cream, either. Eat it like it is and tell me what about a rattlesnake."

Jase chewed his Sara Lee, looking thoughtful. Finally, with his mouth full again, he said, "Just kind of feels like she's back there all coiled up."

Later, after watching *Melrose Place* on Fox, they got ready for bed. Ida Sue would have stayed up to watch Jay Leno on channel 4 but Jase had to be at the jail early and hated it when she didn't come to bed when he did. He always undressed quickly, hung up his clothes neatly, put on his pajamas, then lay with his hands behind his head to watch her undress.

Sometimes Ida Sue would give him a little show when she didn't aim to give him anything else. Ida Sue liked showing off. But it had been a long day. She stripped hurriedly and was down to her panties when Jase said, "Where'd you get that?"

"What?" She rubbed the red marks her bra had left on her rib cage.

"Around your neck."

Ida Sue's heart almost stopped. She had forgotten to take off the necklace and hide it somewhere.

"Oh, that." She was thinking fast as she stepped out of her panties and dropped them on the floor with the rest of her clothes. "Just a little something I bought myself at the Rockpile."

The Rockpile was a jewelry store at the mall, three stores down from the Dinette. It would be natural enough for her to do a little shopping there.

"What for?"

She unclasped the necklace and dropped it on the dresser, trying to seem unconcerned.

"Does a girl have to have a reason to buy herself something pretty?" She slipped into bed beside him. "Speshly when it hardly cost anything."

"I just meant was it something special like a birthday? Not that you had a birthday recently."

"And not that you'd of remembered it if I had."

Jase shifted uneasily and took his hands from behind his head. But the tone of her voice had made him too cautious to touch her. Jase had learned when not to get antsy with her.

"That ain't fair, Suedy. Your last birthday, I give you that birthstone ring you wanted."

Ida Sue knew then that she had turned the tables. He was now on the defensive. She pressed her advantage.

"Not till after I hinted and hinted. You'd of forgot all about it, I hadn't hinted all over the place."

She turned off the bedside lamp and settled herself under the sheet, turning her backside to Jase the way she always did when she wanted to go to sleep.

"You didn't tell me you wrote a check."

Jase's voice, in the dark, was maddeningly calm. She realized with faint alarm that he was still puzzling over the necklace. The way he could worry and worry a thing like a dog with a bone until a girl could just *scream*.

"I used some pocket money. I *told* you it didn't hardly cost a thing."

She kept her voice careless but she was afraid Jase might feel her heart pounding through the mattress. So before he could, she changed the subject. "You really think Easter Lilly Odum killed Ben Neely?"

"That ain't even a question, Suedy. She admits she killed'im. Question is . . ."

In the silence, she listened for her heartbeat, but it had slowed down and was natural again. That g.d. necklace, she thought. Whyn't I remember to get it off before he noticed?

"Question is"—Jase dragged it out, like the host of a quiz show—"did she do it on purpose or did she do it in self-defense?"

"You mean like he was trying to . . . to rape her or something?"

"That's what she's trying to make us believe. Person'ly, I ain't sure I do."

Given a moment to think about it, Ida Sue did. When it came to messing around, Benjy Neely had been like that battery in the TV ad. He just kept going and going.

"Ben was a right-down racist," Jase said. "I ain't exactly a lib'ral myself and I don't know anybody that is. But that Ben . . . I heard him say many a time how he just hated a nigger."

Ida Sue was not only glad to have the necklace safely out of his mind, if it was. She found the subject of rape quite interesting, in a horrifying sort of way.

"What's that got to do with it? That Benjy hated the colored." She was careful never to say and tried not even to think that other word Jase had used. He ought to be more careful, too, especially being a public servant. This day and time you could get into a lot of trouble saying that word.

"Just that Ben wouldn't . . ." Jase seemed to fumble for the word he wanted. "Ben wouldn't mess around . . . he wouldn't be in'trested in a black woman."

For a deputy sheriff with a badge and a gun, Jase could be real innocent sometimes. "Little you know," Ida Sue said.

"I'm only saying what Tyree said, and I reckon Tyree ought to know about his own brother."

"And if Tyree said spit, you'd chew tobacco."

"No, I wouldn't." Jase sounded injured. "I owe my job to Tyree and he could take me off the county payroll any time he wants, but I ain't chewing tobacco for him or nobody."

"But if he thinks Ben wouldn't go for a black woman, then you don't think he would, either. And I think you're both full of you know what."

Jase was silent for a long time, so long Ida Sue wondered if he was falling asleep. Unless he was feeling antsy, Jase usually dropped right off. And after she'd slapped him down about the birthday, he obviously wasn't feeling antsy tonight.

"You think Ben actually tried to rape her?" he said at last.

"I don't know nothing about that. It's just I went all twelve grades through school with Benjy Neely, I knew him practic'ly all my life, and I wouldn't put a thing like this past him."

Trying to seem casual, Jase said, "He ever mess with you?"

Did he ever, Ida Sue thought. "That's for me to know," she said, "and you to find out."

"Wouldn't blame'im if he tried."

Annoyed that he was not angry at the mere thought of Benjy Neely messing around with her, Ida Sue tried again: "I wouldn't put anything past that . . . that . . ."

"Now, now," Jase said, "speak no ill of the dead. But even a black girl?"

Ida Sue sat straight up, exasperated at his ignorance. "Jason All-man, you are a case! Maybe you don't know but I do! When a man's antsy—all hot and bothered, I mean—a man won't even *see* what color a girl's skin is."

She flounced down again and pulled up the sheets decisively. "Lessen it's purple," she said.

Jase had not moved. A long silence fell again. Then, pensively, he said, "Easter Lilly's a real looker, all right. To be colored."

In her mind's eye, Ida Sue could see Easter Lilly Odum striding contemptuously through the mall in one of her tight skirts. The way she pooched out her blouse. And she still remembered how when they were in high school, Easter Lilly had ruined poor Mr. Timmons that used to give all the girls As on their civics papers. And acting as if she was proud of it, even after she got him run out of town.

"I reckon Ben *could* have got hot'n bothered," Jase said.

Ida Sue was in no doubt of it. Alone with her in that old jail all night. Ida Sue had seen men turning to gawk when Easter Lilly passed. Not just black men, either. White men. Easter Lilly was one of the few coloreds that ever set foot in the Dinette. Perching at the counter with her legs crossed, looking like she'd spit in your eye, you even tried to be nice. Rearing back her shoulders to show off her top.

"Tyree figures she let Ben think he could . . . you know . . . have some fun," Jase said. "So he come back to the cell . . ."

Fear struck Ida Sue a startling blow. Ben Neely was dead but Jase was—

". . . rarin to go. Fore Ben knew it, she grabbed'is knife . . ."

63

Ida Sue sat bolt upright again, suddenly as angry as she was fearful. Benjy was dead but Jase would still be in that jail with that slut. Just the two of them sometimes.

". . . and let'im have it square in the heart."

"Jase Allman," Ida Sue said, "has that nigger ever even so much as cut her eyes at you?" She wanted to take him by the throat, wring the truth out of him. As usual, Jase did not perceive her agitation.

"Just to call me names."

"Because if she ever does and if you ever think for one minute *you're* going to have some fun with her . . ."

"Me?" Jase's voice squeaked in amazed protest. "I never . . ."

". . . I'll come down to that old jail and what I'll do, you'll wish somebody *had* stuck you with a knife!"

Alone all day with that rattlesnake. The idea of the two of them together so panicked Ida Sue that she balled up her fist to strike the only one within reach. Before she could, Jase said:

"Only woman ever gets me hot'n bothered, I already got."

Ida Sue slid back down in bed, feeling a little foolish but only partly mollified.

"Speshly," Jase said, "when she's sitting up in bed with her bare bazooms in my face."

The remark reminded Ida Sue not just that she was naked but that Jase Allman was not all *that* innocent. Jase was a man, after all, and men were always hot and bothered about women.

"I never knew you carried that much pocket money around," Jase said, "to buy yourself a necklace."

Book Two

CADY

IN HIS FAVORITE CORNER BOOTH AT THE PURITY CAFE, J. PRESTON Cadieux lifted his arm above his head, like a schoolboy asking to go to the bathroom. He knew this gesture would cause Pearl, the waitress, to bring him another Coors Silver Bullet, and he let his arm fall without looking up from the four-month-old copy of *Vanity Fair* that he had brought along from his office.

Cady had not troubled to brush off the dust the magazine had gathered in his waiting room before he began to read about a movie he-man, pictured in one of his many roles driving a speeding car. The he-man had developed a ruinous drug habit. But even so lurid an article was slow going for an elderly gentleman who had downed five beers since lunch; and Cady did not realize that he had read the first jump page three times.

A man of sensitivity and compassion, he was now feeling great sympathy for the he-man and great pride that he himself had never been tempted to swallow an upper or a downer or an in-betweener or whatever they called the damn things these days. Cady liked to say proudly, ''I just can't understand anybody delib'rately stickin a needle in their arm.''

Then, to whatever listeners he might have, he would add even more proudly, ''I'm a member of the *booze* generation.''

Which he certainly was, and proud of it, but in restrained circumstances only. Cady allowed himself six beers precisely, after lunch and before dinner. Six and no more. In his accustomed booth at the Purity, he would count the Silver Bullet cans before he raised his arm, and he almost never made a mistake.

Pearl came in after the lunch crowd left and handled the Purity's sparse afternoon clientele all by herself, counter and cash register both. She brought his sixth Silver Bullet glistening in her hand.

"You want anything to eat?" Pearl asked dutifully. She knew Cady never ate his dinner until he had put away his ritual half-dozen beers.

"Not a thing," Cady tapped the first jump page in *Vanity Fair*. "This poor fellow's screwed up his life."

"Which poor fellow?"

Pearl and Cady had engaged in the same exchange after she brought the fourth Silver Bullet. But she liked Cady and appreciated the wrinkled dollar bill he always left in the wet circles the beer cans made on the Formica table. In Pearl's experience, no one tipped better at the Purity Cafe than Cady after his beers.

"Forty grand a picture," he said to Pearl, as he had two Silver Bullets earlier. "Now he can't even get a part in a horror show."

"Oh," Pearl said, "that one."

She walked slowly back toward Earl Bullock, her only other customer. Earl was seated at the counter eating a piece of banana cream pie. Next to him, a bumper sticker pasted to the back of the cash register advocated KEVORKIAN FOR WHITE HOUSE PHYSICIAN.

"As for me," Cady called after her, "I'm a member of the *booze* generation."

He raised the new Silver Bullet, took a long sip, and refocused only a little blearily on the magazine. As he read the same jump page again, he was thankful that he could still charge the same sixty dollars a billable hour that he had been charging for years. Maybe not as many hours as in the good old days but that was only because he was getting on. Not because of . . . "Putting a needle in *my* arm," he said to no one.

Cady had almost finished the sixth Silver Bullet and had finally turned to the next page when a man slid down in the seat opposite him. This invasion of his privacy annoyed Cady a little, especially since the man barely looked familiar. But Cady knew, and was man enough to admit, that he was getting on. His memory was slipping, not badly but enough to notice, and maybe he *should* have known the intruder. Maybe he was even a client; better still, maybe he *wanted* to be a client.

"Sixty dollars an hour," Cady said. "And expenses."

The stranger looked judicious. "I used to get a hundred. In New York nowadays, they *start* at a hundred-fifty."

"This ain't New York," Cady said. "Thank God." So the man was evidently not a potential client.

"I'm Shep Riley." Seeming as if he expected Cady to recognize the name. Which was maybe, Cady thought, why he looked sort of familiar without really *being* familiar.

"And the waitress over there says you're Mister Caddoo."

Showing off his French. Cady did not like show-offs and had never learned French, though he knew the Stonewall County niggertown called Cog-nack should properly be pronounced Coneyock. "Around here," he said, "they call me Kadducks."

"Kadducks." The man nodded. "That's what the waitress said. And Cady for short."

"My friends call me Cady." To make things clear, he laid it on the line: "And I got a *lot* of friends."

Wiley or whoever he was nodded again. "I bet you do," he said. "How bout another beer? On me?"

"Had my limit," Cady said. "Never break it, either."

"Well, I'm parched." Wiley waved at Pearl, caught her eye, and pointed at the Silver Bullet cans.

"I understand"—he turned back to Cady—"you're defending Easter Lilly Odum."

"Who?" Cady said.

"The black woman they've—"

"Oh, her. That stole the power comp'ny's truck."

Pearl brought two beers, placing one in front of each of them.

"Had my limit," Cady told her. "He only meant to order one."

"Sorry." Pearl reached for his can. Cady pulled it away.

"Changed my mind."

The stranger, Smiley or somebody, chuckled as Pearl walked away. "I knew you for a sport the minute I saw you."

"Yeah, well . . ." Cady raised his can and found his seventh even better than his sixth. "I don't know you from Adam, Mister . . ."

"Riley. I thought you might pick up the name. I used to defend a lot of folks down in these parts."

Something came dimly back to Cady. "Used to?"

"Like, for instance, Joe Nathan Hampton, over in Beaslee County. They had it in for Joe over there and he was looking at fifteen to twenty for B and E before I took his case. Got him off on a lesser included with six."

"You sure did." Over his limit or not, J. Preston Cadieux was still a lawyer. He knew all he needed to know about Joe Nathan Hampton, hence about the stranger in his booth. "And the damn-fool parole board let'im walk in three."

"Joe Nathan hadn't had much chance."

By now, the conversation had focused Cady's mind.

"That three-spot Hampton pulled on account of you got'im off on the B and E. . . ." Cady sipped Coors, measuring his words. "Not two years later he raped a teenage girl right here in Stonewall. Doin life at Arbor Hill now, I'm glad to say."

"Did Joe confess the rape?"

"Not him. But the gal picked'im out right off, on account while he was ramming it in, she left a fingernail scar on'is face four inches long."

Shep Riley looked contemplatively at his beer can.

These do-gooders, Cady thought. I wouldn't be surprised this one sticks a needle in his arm. "So you're the Good Samaritan . . ." He was feeling oratorical. "Got that ape turned loose on an unsuspecting public."

Riley nodded. "I guess that's me, Cady."

Cady wondered briefly whether he should make the valid point that Shep Riley was not his friend, probably never would be, and therefore had no right to call him Cady. Another swig of Coors and his natural courtesy persuaded him to mind his manners.

"Fact is"—Riley waved a hand as if to dismiss something unpleasant, maybe Joe Nathan Hampton—"I came down here hoping to help defend Easter Lilly Odum."

Cady was amazed at the man's sheer brass. Just having heard that one of the animals he'd so eagerly pled for in the name of civil rights had turned out to be a rapist that belonged *under* the jail, not just in it, now the damn do-gooder was falling over himself to let another one loose to do it again.

"I am not aware . . ." Cady was outraged. And even after nearly seven beers, he could still summon up his courtroom voice. "That anybody asked you."

"No one did. But it's not just a car theft anymore, Cady. It's Murder One."

This jarred Cady momentarily. Then it all came back to him. Ben Neely gettin'is dick caught in'is zipper.

"I've litigated a lot of murder cases." Riley spoke with the kind of assurance Cady mistrusted, particularly in do-gooders. "My hunch is we could plead manslaughter. Maybe self-defense."

Cady finished his seventh, his outrage enhanced. Talking to *me*, a Wake Forest Law grad, born and bred in the South, nearbout forty years in practice, like I don't know my own business. "Who said anything about *we*?" he demanded.

Riley grinned. "Just one lawyer to another."

Cady's anger turned to apprehension. Do-gooders were bad news in more ways than one, and it came clear to him that Riley's arrival in Waitsfield meant trouble. Just calmly walking into the Purity Cafe, sitting down at a man's table, buying him a Coors, then trying to take over his case. Prob'ly planning some kind of racial circus to boot.

"I read in the paper what happened down here, Cady. The way it looked to me, Miss Odum's going to need the best defense she can get and I'd like to help out."

"*Miss* Odum," Cady repeated, remembering Simmons. Or maybe it was Timmons. Whichever, Shep Riley had just confirmed his worst fears.

"Don't seem to be any witnesses," Riley went on. "So I'd—"

"You talked to that jungle bunny yet?"

Riley finished his own beer and said quietly, "I'm going to see her later. How're you going to defend somebody you're already calling names like that?"

Buying that beer definitely had been just a come-on. This Riley was going to be big trouble. "You been to see Tyree?"

"Who's Tyree?" Riley said.

Cady sat up and began to arrange six empty Silver Bullets in a diamond, as he did every afternoon before he left his booth at the Purity. This time, he had a seventh can left over. He placed it squarely in the center, then took Riley's can and put it against a corner of the diamond, like the tail of a kite. Over this arrangement, he looked as steadily as he could at his unwelcome visitor.

"Mister Riley," Cady said, wishing sadly that he had never accepted a beer that breached his limit, "you don't know your ass from a hole in the ground."

SHEP

DESPITE HIS EVASIVE RESPONSE, SHEP RILEY HAD KNOWN VERY WELL that "Tyree" was not only the county prosecutor but the brother of the dead Ben Neely. Actually, he had arrived in Waitsfield under no illusion about the man. In the Pittsburgh airport where he had had ninety minutes to kill between planes that morning, Shep had got out his battered address book and found the name and number he wanted. He glanced at his watch, decided it was late enough for even a journalist to be at work, then punched in the digits and his calling-card number.

"You have reached the offices of the *Capital Times*," a theatrically precise voice informed him. "If you are using a touch-tone phone, press One now."

"Oh, shit," Shep said aloud, to the discomfort of a woman using the next phone. He pressed 1 obediently, though he hated voice mail, frequently getting lost in the lengthy "menu" recited by a remorseless, user-friendly voice.

"If you know the extension of the party you want to reach, please enter it *now*."

"How the hell would I?" he demanded of the phone.

"If you wish to place a classified ad"—voice mail sounded more cheerful at this possibility—"press Two *now*."

"Up yours," Shep replied, and the woman at the next phone turned her back.

Voice mail proceeded maddeningly through directions for reaching Subscriptions, Weather Information, News Desk, Obituaries, Sports Scores, ad infinitum. Finally, "If you would like to speak to an operator personally, press Zero, followed by the Pound key *now*."

Shep stabbed viciously at the two buttons. "Your call is very important to us . . ." voice mail cooed. "You will be connected to the first available operator. So please don't hang up."

After several minutes of Muzak had oozed along the line, an obsequious southern accent broke in: "And how may I help you today?"

"Why couldn't you have answered in the first place?" Shep demanded. "I've been listening to that recorded schlock for the last two hours."

The southern accent said in a hushed whisper, "I agree with you, sir. But the management . . ."

"In the coming electronic world," Shep said, "on the communications highway, will there be a rest stop for romance? For soul mates like you and me?"

A giggle. "Oh, sir . . . things won't ever get *that* bad."

"Don't bet on it, Scarlett. Can you connect me with Larry Knight?"

"Yes sir, if he's in. And in the future you may dial Mister Knight direct on four six six four."

He scrawled the extension number in his address book while 4664 rang five times.

"Knight here. You're on the air."

Shep was taken aback. "Are you running a talk show now?"

"If I were, would I still be answering my own phone?"

"Well, I'm glad you're at the same old stand," Shep said. "Larry, this is Shep Riley. Maybe you'll recall . . . some years ago I defended Matthew Barlow in that rape trial you covered."

"Oh, yeah," Knight said. "The nigger-lover lawyer."

Knight was one of his state's most respected reporters and had covered the Barlow trial ably. Someone had told Shep Riley then that Larry Knight covered the *Capital Times*'s circulation area "like AstroTurf." Shep—who never forgot potentially useful information—had recalled, these many years later, that Stonewall County was part of that circulation area.

"I thought that kind of talk went out with George Wallace," he said, not angrily. "It did. I'd only use it to describe a bleeding-heart liberal that got Matthew Barlow off a lifetime rap."

"But Matthew was *innocent*. You covered the trial; you ought to remember."

"You mean they didn't prove Barlow did the rape he was charged with," Knight said. "I concede that. But last I heard, he's doing five to ten for a carjack."

No use arguing, Shep thought. "Anyway, I didn't call about Matthew Barlow."

"I know damn well you didn't," Knight said. "We read *The New York Times* even down here in the boondocks. Some kid at the AP filed that story on Easter Lilly Odum and of course the *Times* printed it like they print anything makes us cornpones look evil. So am I likely to be surprised that before the ink's dry a famous civil rights lawyer is on the line hoping for a nice fat headline?"

"Not so famous anymore, Larry. Over the hill, you might even say. I just thought a black woman accused of killing a white man in your part of the world might need a little legal help."

"Listen, Counselor . . ." Knight's voice softened into something remotely like sympathy. "I know you mean well; your kind usually do. But you'd better keep your head out of this particular noose. Tyree Neely tells me it's open-and-shut Murder One, and I've never known him to bullshit the press. Besides, that woman's always been a troublemaker down there in Stonewall. Even in high school, something about a white teacher she was banging. Tyree said they had to, ah, ask him to leave town."

"The prosecutor? The dead man's brother?"

"More than that." Shep took fast notes on the back of an envelope that had been folded into his address book. "Tyree runs that county and runs it clean. Drive down to Stonewall, spit on the sidewalk, you might do a little hard time."

"I'll be careful where I spit," Shep said. "Do you know if Miss Odum has a lawyer?"

"If a defendant down there needs help, court usually appoints a guy they call Cady. Don't remember his real name. I doubt"—

Knight paused for emphasis—"*Miss* Odum's got a pot to piss in, so Cady's probably it."

All of which—after another flight, an hour's ride in a bus smelling of a toilet compartment at the rear, and a quick call to the *Stonewell News-Messenger*—Shep had found to be true. He left the Purity Cafe after talking to Cady and crossed a once-busy street— Waitsfield Avenue—now almost empty of cars and people. The street was lined with retail stores struggling to survive in "downtown," fly-specked window displays of cheap crockery and tinny vacuum cleaners and plastic-looking shoes reflecting a losing battle against being "malled."

Shep spotted the county courthouse by its clock tower and headed toward the national and state flags above its entrance. The old stone building sat in the middle of a square around which streets ran on all four sides. Numerous shade trees and stands of grass struggled to survive in the square's sandy soil. A few shrubs were beginning to show spots of green, heralding a new spring, and scattered under the trees were green-painted benches on which a few old men took their ease—blacks as well as whites, on separate but equal benches.

Fronting the courthouse steps, from a pedestal slimed green with age, a stone Confederate soldier leapt forward forever, slouch-hatted, his blanket roll sashed across one shoulder, his rifle at the ready, in timeless assertion of southern machismo.

Shep remembered entering the capitol building of another southern state years earlier. A sweet-faced receptionist in a lace collar had picked up his unsouthern voice immediately. "Y'all must have brought this weather with you," she exclaimed sincerely, holding out a soft, damp hand, and clearly suggesting that the rainy day outside could not possibly be blamed on the South.

Rounding the statue, going up the granite steps, in one of which a Civil War cannonball remained embedded, Shep wondered how those southerners who had sprung to arms in 1861 would evaluate their fabled Confederacy today, with its interstates and its skyscrapers and its country clubs and its federal military bases, its banks and golf resorts and direct flights to Europe, its faux plantation houses flanked by swimming pools and tennis courts and two-car garages.

The county prosecutor's office was at the end of a third-floor corridor reached by an ancient elevator that rattled and creaked alarmingly. The corridor was tainted with familiar courthouse odors—disinfectant and tobacco smoke and floor polish, perspiration, urine, and years. Tyree Neely's name was painted in a half circle on the upper, pebbled-glass half of the last door on the right. The circle was completed with letters spelling PROSECUTOR.

Shep entered without knocking, to find a secretary who seemed improbably gorgeous for the outer office of a county bureaucrat—tacitly confirming that in Stonewall County, Tyree Neely was a good deal more than a prosecutor. Cady had been about as expected, but a beautiful young woman where a political hanger-on or maybe an elderly, deserving cousin should have been seated, was a pleasant surprise.

"Way-ell . . ." the secretary greeted him in an exaggerated accent. "Ah don't b'leeve Ah've seen *you* around befoah."

She smiled devastatingly. Her dark hair hung about her face in artful curls; her blue eyes were warm—Shep loved blue eyes and black hair—and her perfect teeth were dazzling against the subdued red of her lips. Her shoulders were surprisingly bare.

"I haven't *been* around, Miss . . . ah . . . ma'am. Is Mister Neely in?"

"I juss *knew* you were fum out of tow-un," the receptionist drawled, standing to disclose a body tightly swathed in slinky black, below its snowy shoulders. She extended a red-nailed hand across her desk. "Ah'm Daisy Thorpe." As she pronounced it, her last name sounded like "Thaw-up."

"Shep Riley," he replied. "Are all the girls in this town named after flowers?"

"Why . . . I don't b'leeve I know any *otha* flowah gulls."

Shep hated to break the magnolia mood but believed in shock tactics: "I was thinking of Easter Lilly Odum."

Daisy Thorpe dropped his hand as if it had been a toad-frog. Her smile vanished abruptly. She sat down quickly, tossing back her dark hair with a decisive sweep.

"Did you have an appointment, Mister Riley?" Most of the southern accent, like the inviting smile, had disappeared.

"Well, no, I'm afraid not. But if he's busy, I can—"

"Mister Neely," Daisy Thorpe interrupted, "is not in. I have no idea when he'll be back."

"Maybe, then, you'd tell me where I could find him."

Try as he might, appreciative of women as he was—even one as suddenly hostile as Daisy Thorpe—Shep could not help letting his eyes fall to her low neckline.

Miss Thorpe promptly rose, took a jacket from the back of her chair, swung it around her shoulders, and ostentatiously held it together in front of her.

"Mister Neely did not say where he was going. Or when he might return."

Shep cursed himself for trying to startle her with Easter Lilly's name.

"Now look, Miss Thorpe . . ." He shifted gears. "If I offended you in some way, I certainly didn't mean to and I sincerely apologize."

Daisy Thorpe sat down again, looking only slightly mollified, still holding the jacket together. Before she could reply, the phone rang. Daisy picked it up and said, "Mister Neely's office." She listened a moment, then swung her chair around to present her back. She murmured a few words Shep could not hear, listened again, then hung up as she turned to face him.

"That was Cady calling from the Purity." The resentment in her voice only faintly echoed the vanished southern accent.

Shep shrugged. "I thought maybe he'd wait until tomorrow."

He had at least, he thought, put the wind up in the old drunk. Daisy let go the edges of her jacket and leaned forward a little, as if daring him to stare. Shep carefully kept his eyes on hers.

"Let me give you some good advice, Mister Riley. If you try any of that self-defense foolishness you mentioned to Cady, Tyree Neely will hang you up in little strips on the courtroom wall."

So Cady was expecting him to be in court with Easter Lilly, and worrying about the prospect. Daisy Thorpe was worried, too. Shep wondered if she slept with her boss. He always wondered if a beautiful secretary slept with her boss, and believed most did.

"Hang me up with the help of the appointed defense attorney?" he asked.

"Mister Neely won't need any help." Both pride and protectiveness sounded in Daisy Thorpe's voice. "That black slut murdered his brother Benjy and Mister Neely's going to prove it."

"With a Stonewall County jury and Cady for the defense," Shep said, "you just might be right. Tell Mister Neely I'll be in for a chat in the morning, will you?"

Just then, the door opened behind him. A touch of chagrin darkened Daisy Thorpe's beautiful face. A man of medium stature, wearing a dark suit and a blue shirt with a white collar, entered the office and closed the door behind him.

"Daisy," he said in greeting, and looked inquiringly at Shep.

"Mister Neely, this gentleman—"

Shep interrupted before she could say anything prejudicial. "I'm Shep Riley," he said, holding out his hand.

"My God." Tyree Neely shook hands heartily. "It's an honor to have you in this office. Where've you been keeping yourself all these years?"

Shep was both flattered that the prosecutor had recognized his name and surprised to be so warmly welcomed, particularly after the open hostility of Cady and Daisy Thorpe.

"Here and there," he said. "Trying to keep my hand in."

"That case you brought in Georgia for that innocent guy doing life for murder? What was his name?"

"Mordecai Jones."

"I've got a copy of your closing argument in my files. It was a classic."

"Well, thanks," Shep said. "I haven't thought of Mordecai in years." Since the case itself, to be exact. He hoped Jones had not turned out to be another Joe Nathan Hampton or Matthew Barlow.

"Mister Neely?" Daisy said.

"Why're you standing out here, Mister Riley? Let's go in the office and—"

"Shep. Call me Shep, please."

"Mister Neely?" Daisy said again.

"Come on in, Shep, let's see if we can't find a little bourbon and branch to ease the pain."

"Mister Neely, Cady called," Daisy Thorpe said. She had replaced her jacket on the back of her chair and above the strapless black dress her white shoulders stood out startlingly. "He said Mister Riley is here to take part in the Odum defense."

Tyree Neely nodded, and led Shep toward the inner office.

"I figgered *that* out the minute I heard his name. You drink bourbon, Shep?"

"Actually," Shep Riley said, before the inner-office door closed and left Daisy Thorpe in silence, "if you maybe had a little vodka, I'd rather . . ."

EASTER LILLY

IN THE CELLBLOCK WITH ITS HIGH SLITS FOR WINDOWS AND ITS fluorescent tubes constantly burning behind metal grillwork, the time of day was hard to tell. Easter Lilly had worn a battery-powered Casio when she was first jailed for car theft, but it had been taken away, along with her shoulder-strap pocketbook, dress, keys, earrings, and high heels. When stopped for speeding in Ben Neely's Fairlane, she had been barefoot, had no money, and had eaten nothing but half a moldy Mounds bar she had found in the glove compartment.

The license plate had been quickly traced, the jail killing was all over local radio, and she was soon on her way back to Stonewall County. Now, her few brief hours of freedom seemed fleeting, unreal. She could not even remember how it had felt to be speeding along back roads and then I-95.

Why, she wondered—shielding her eyes from the fluorescents—had she even tried to run? Why hadn't she melted into the familiar surroundings of Cognac, where she'd spent her life and people would have helped and hidden her—some anyway, because they, too, knew that Whitey would send her to the gas chamber no matter what she said had happened in her cell. Why hadn't she lain low for a while, even slept in the woods if necessary? Then, when they'd maybe stopped looking for her, if they ever did, she could have borrowed a car or boarded a bus and got far away from Stonewall County and Tyree Neely.

She knew why she hadn't done that, why she had sped in terror through the night toward an imaginary escape. She knew why, but she didn't like to admit it, even to herself. But as she lay on the cot in her cell, the harsh fluorescents glaring like truth in her face, she could not deny to herself that she had panicked.

Not at first. At first, there in the silence of the jail, she had been proud, exhilarated, high as a kite. Not thinking straight but not panicked. She seemed to have walked a foot or two above the concrete floor as she left the cell with hardly a backward glance at the thing on the floor and almost danced along the corridor into the outer office. Floating as she was, when she had seen the telephone on the desk, it had seemed natural, the most sensible thing in the world, to pick it up, call someone and share her joy. Without hesitation, she dialed the number of Dr. Fred D. Worthington, the only black practitioner in Stonewall County.

He had come on the line grumbling and almost inaudible, at that hour of the morning.

"How y'all doing?" Easter Lilly had said cheerily, as if calling a girlfriend for a chat. If she had had a girlfriend.

Dr. Worthington was not just the county's only black doctor. He was the head of what passed for the local NAACP; he and Easter Lilly had organized several protests and demonstrations—embarrassing failures, mostly, in a black community that wanted primarily to be left alone—and he had become as familiar and obstreperous and futile an attendant at monthly county commissioners' meetings as was Easter Lilly herself. Afterward, they would drink together and laugh bitterly at white certainties. They were not yet engaged or even lovers, but Easter Lilly could tell that Fred wanted both. He was nicer than most men but still male, sometimes aggressively so.

"What?" She could tell by the sharper tone of his voice that Fred had come fully awake as soon as he recognized her voice.

"Just wanted to say . . ." She was still proud, still exhilarated, still swept up in the exaltation that had flooded through her as the knife in her hand plunged at last into her hatred. "Just let you know I feel as spotless as a lamb."

"You feel . . . what'd you say? Easter, where are you?"

"In jail." She happily turned her head to see the door that led outside, to freedom. "But I'll be out in a minute."

"In a minute!" Fred shouted. "Good *God,* girl! That stunt with the truck; they'll *bury* you if they can. They'll—"

"Truck, shit," Easter Lilly said, "just wait'll they see."

Fred fell silent. She could hear him breathing hard along the miles of wire from Waitsfield to Cognac. Why was Fred breathing so hard?

"How come you on the phone?" he said at last. "If you still in jail?"

She had relished little in her life as she relished the words that tripped off her tongue.

"Cut Ben Neely. Cut'is heart out."

"You cut . . ." Fred's voice dropped off again, then came back in a sudden shout: "Jee-zuz, girl! You *crazy?*"

She had panicked then, yanked by that word back to reality, to the sheetrock walls of the jail office, back to the silence and the thing on the floor of the cell. *Crazy!* She had gone crazy. She slammed the phone into its cradle and ran for the door, forgetting to look for her clothes, forgetting her purse, keys, shoes, forgetting everything but the need to run—everything but that and Fred's voice shouting *crazy!*

Easter Lilly threw open the door, ran past the Mount Vernon columns in her bare feet, down the steps and around the corner into the parking lot. She ran hard, ignoring the burning and pricking in the soles of her feet, ran hard toward the single car in the blacktopped lot, ran hard to get as far away as she could before Jase Allman came in and found all she'd left of Ben Neely.

Before they told Tyree.

She was startled from her shamed remembrance of fear and flight by Jase Allman saying through the bars, "You awake in there?"

For a moment, she was almost as panicked as if Jase *had* come in that morning and found her standing over Ben Neely's bleeding body. She sat up quickly, dropping her arm from her eyes, briefly terrified into thinking it *was* that morning. But Jase was only staring quizzically at her as she lay on the cot in her cell—not at a dead man sprawled on the floor.

Easter Lilly had no idea what time it was except that it had been maybe an hour or two since Jase had brought the plate of hot dogs and gummy rice, half eaten now beside her cot. "No way to sleep in *this* place," she said.

In fact, she had slept some the night before, even after Tyree Neely, quiet as a moccasin, had threatened her with the gas chamber. She had slept the sleep of exhaustion.

"Man out here to see you," Jase said.

Somebody from Cognac, Easter Lilly thought. Maybe Fred with a food basket. Her stomach knotted in harsh memory of the lunchtime fare. Not even any ketchup to put on the weenies.

"White guy," Jase said.

Easter Lilly was disappointed that there would be no lunch basket. But she was curious, too.

"That prosecutor pig?"

"Never seen'im before," Jase said. "Says he's a lawyer."

"Tell'im I got a lawyer. What that old sot calls himself."

"Oh, Cady'll sober up time court takes in. Like he usually does. Guy out here says he aims to help Cady handle your case."

Easter Lilly was immediately suspicious. Tyree Neely planting a stooge. Hoping I'll say something he can use. As if he needs anything but one of his tame juries.

Then it occurred to her that maybe she could turn a stooge back against Tyree. It was possible. She had spent a lifetime dealing with Stonewall County whites and even though the cards had been stacked against her most of that time—and certainly were now—she had confidence in herself. Except for Tyree, crackers weren't as smart or as tough as they believed they were. Her life had taught her that. Her brain began to calculate how she might send whoever this gumshoe was back to Tyree with a story he'd have a hard time keeping out of the trial.

"Send'im on in," she said. "I better not catch you listening at that door, though."

"I ain't gonna listen. But if I was"—at the cell door, Jase looked back at her and almost allowed himself to smile—"you wouldn't catch me."

She should have told Jase about Ben hitting on her, she thought. As white skins went, Jase wasn't the worst, even if he'd married an airhead like Ida Sue Medlin. If she'd told Jase that Ben Neely was trying to mess around when they were alone in the jailhouse at night, maybe things would have turned out different. Not that she wanted Ben alive again, but she had started to worry—really worry—about the gas chamber.

Easter Lilly was standing at the bars of her cell when the white man came in from the office and stopped, looking at her. He was not young but he was tall, though a little stooped. He did not have broad shoulders but something about his carriage suggested strength, if not physical power. A tight jawline and a jutting chin distinguished a face neither handsome nor ugly. His ears stood out a little too far from his skull, and what once had been red hair was salted here and there with gray and needed a trim. Something in his eyes intrigued her.

"I'm Shep Riley," he said.

Easter Lilly believed right away that he was not, after all, a stooge for Tyree Neely. Not even from Stonewall County, because she knew most of the local crackers, but not this one. His voice was not southern, either. More telling than any of that, he had an air of independence—square stance, strong face, that puzzling but direct gaze—that could not have survived subservience to Tyree Neely, or anybody else.

Not moving beyond the threshold of the cellblock, he said, "You heard of me?"

White, all right. White arrogance, to ask that.

"No." Easter Lilly did not ask why she should have heard of him. She knew he would tell her, anyway.

"How about Joe Nathan Hampton?"

"That girl that scratched'im lied in'er teeth," Easter Lilly said. "She put out for any pair of pants had five dollars. Joe Nathan wouldn't pay."

Riley took a step or two toward her cell. "I defended Joe Nathan . . ." She still couldn't fathom what she was seeing in his greenish eyes. "Before that happened. In another case. How about Mordecai Jones in Georgia?"

"I ain't studyin Georgia," Easter Lilly said.

"Mordecai was doing life for a murder he didn't commit. I got him out. I used to help a lot of your people, all over the South. Like in Louisiana one time . . ."

Easter Lilly listened without paying much attention. One of those white assholes hot for what they called justice. Thinking you could get justice for niggers in a white courtroom. Get a brother off here, a sentence cut there, nail some crooked whitey sheriff—bingo! you had justice. But what whites cared about was power, not justice. Some nigger beat the rap; another got the chair. Whites still had the power.

The lawyer finished his recital of courtroom triumphs—Easter Lilly did not fail to notice that they all had been years ago—as if she should kiss his hand. She watched warily as he moved close to her cell.

"Now your case," he said. "I just talked to Tyree Neely and I guess you know people around here, they hear his name, they just about get down on their knees. I hate to tell you this, but Neely says there's not a doubt in the world you're going to the gas chamber."

"I ain't studyin no gas chamber." Easter Lilly spoke more bravely than she felt. She'd heard it before and from the horse's mouth, but the fear renewed itself, and she was ashamed of it.

Shep Riley, nearly a head taller than she, took hold of the bars, his white hands on either side of his head, and stared down at her.

"Neely's dangerous," he said. "The quiet ones are always the worst. But I think we can beat him because you acted in self-defense when Neely's brother tried to rape you. Am I right?"

Easter Lilly's heart skipped a beat. *Self-defense.* What she had been thinking herself. Hoping to set up. Still, she had to be careful. It was downright unnatural for a cracker to think like she did, when another cracker had been killed. She said, cautiously, "I'm not saying a word without my lawyer."

"I *am* your lawyer," the man said. "If you say I am."

Easter Lilly looked into his eyes again. Could it be . . . ?

"What about the beerhead?" she said, hardly daring to believe what, at such close range, she thought she had seen.

"You don't have to get rid of him. Just make me part of your defense team, too."

He seemed almost to be pleading with her. And just then, as if a light bulb had come on in her head, Easter Lilly knew what she was seeing in the white man's eyes.

Mr. Timmons.

What she had seen all those years ago in the white teacher's eyes, she had not since seen in the eyes of any man, white or black, that had stared at her hotly. Not in bull-hung Ben Neely's, for sure. None of those eyes had been tearful or sweet, like Mr. Timmons's. This lawyer's weren't, either. But close enough, she knew without a doubt. And knowing that, she understood what to do.

"White man . . ." She heard the words come out just as she had intended, husky and inviting. "I *need* a lawyer. Bad."

She opened her mouth a little and saw him swallow. She let her breasts rest against the cell bars, where he'd think he could just move his hands a little, and feel her up. His eyes moved, barely a flicker, and she could tell that he wanted to, like they all did.

Gas chamber, shit she thought.

"Your kind of lawyer." She watched his smile rise toward the fever in his eyes.

JASE

"IS THIS MOVIE TOM CRUISE OR TOM HANKS?" IDA SUE ASKED AS
Jase pulled out of the driveway.

When the Allmans went anywhere at night, they always took Ida
Sue's Bronco. Jase liked his Toyota better but Ida Sue thought it
was kind of like poor white trash going to the picture show in a
truck. Jase could do what he wanted, she said, but she didn't aim
to drive anything but American wheels.

"Cruise." Jase was the movie buff in the family.

They lived in a mobile home in an area called Green Oaks,
though most of the oaks had been cut down by Southern States
Realty, the landlord, to make room for more mobile homes. Tyree
Neely had been one of the organizers of Southern States, and Jase
believed he still had an interest. So even at home, he thought,
sometimes resentfully, Tyree had a grip on him. Jase religiously
paid the rent on time, every first of the month at the Bright Leaf
National Bank.

"They ought to call one of'em Rock or Richard or something,"
Ida Sue said. "I get'em mixed up, both being Toms like that."

Ida Sue did not like living in a mobile home and usually wanted
to go out to the movies or somewhere at night. Jase kind of liked
not having siding or shingles to worry about. He had installed a

cinder-block foundation all the way around and was proud that it was the only one under a mobile home in Green Oaks.

"Glad to get out of that dump for once," Ida Sue said. "Makes me feel kind of scrooched up."

They had been to the movies twice and had eaten at the Orange Bowl on the other side of Waitsfield twice more, in the last week. But Jase only said, "We won't always be living in a mobile home, Suedy. I got my eye on a place in town that you'd just love."

Though he doubted the county would ever raise his jailer's salary enough to buy a real house. Or to have kids, which he wanted and Ida Sue said she was on the fence about.

"Your eye ain't the same as a down payment," she said. "Let me know when you put *that* on some place I'd just love."

They were going to see *A Few Good Men* at the Cinemaplex Plaza out at the Dixie Pride Mall. Jase did not really care which Tom was in it. He was wondering instead if Dimmy Moore would show her knockers bare. He hadn't been able to tell from the previews if it was that kind of a movie.

"I'm gonna have a jumbo popcorn," Ida Sue said. "I feel like a lot of popcorn tonight."

Jase knew that Ida Sue would say he ought to be ashamed, wanting to see Dimmy Moore's boobs. He *was* a little ashamed, like the time Ben Neely had sneaked a copy of *Penthouse* magazine into the jail and insisted that Jase look at what Ben called snatchshots. Jase had never in his life expected to see any such thing between the covers of a magazine. He wondered what a man would do if his wife or his daughter or even his sister ever showed it off like that.

"With melted butter," Ida Sue said. "I skipped lunch so I could have melted butter on my jumbo and not worry about the calories."

Those girls in *Penthouse* were strangers, however, not *real*. Dimmy Moore he had seen often enough in the movies, she was like somebody you *knew*. And somehow it was more exciting to think of somebody you knew with nothing on than to look at snatchshots of strangers. Like if you could sneak a peek at some good-looking woman undressed that you saw all the time. Maybe Daisy Thorpe.

"They was saying at the Dinette that some out-of-town lawyer was in to see Cady at the Purity this afternoon," Ida Sue said.

Jase was a little scared to think dirty about Daisy Thorpe because she worked for Tyree Neely. As far as Jase was concerned, that meant Daisy might as well be closed up in a barbwire fence. Not that he'd ever try anything with another woman, anyway.

He swung out to pass an old Dodge Dart and the Bronco leapt under his feet.

"He come in to see Easter Lilly, too," Jase said, liking the Bronco's pickup but not really the steering. A little heavy, seemed to him.

"You got to admit this car leaves that old truck of yours in the dust," Ida Sue said. "Wha'd he want with *her?*"

"I din't listen. But they was back there yackin a long time."

"Who's he, anyway?" Ida Sue asked. "Stop sign up ahead."

"I see it, Suedy."

Jase dutifully stopped at the intersection, let two cars pass, then turned carefully on to the highway leading to the Dixie Pride Mall. He gunned the Bronco a little, though he did not like to drive fast.

"I don't really know *who* he is. But on the way home tonight, I run into ol Cady comin out of the Purity. Drunk as a skunk. I give'im a lift; he said the guy was some big lib'ral from up North."

"S'what I heard at the Dinette, too. They said he aims to stir up trouble about that Odum floozy."

"Sounds like you know more'n I do. Who said that?"

Ida Sue waved her hands airily in the greenish light from the dashboard. "Just some of them at the Dinette."

Jase was never sure who Ida Sue talked to at the Dinette. He did not like to go in there while she was working, maybe embarrass her. He enjoyed the town talk she brought home, but he sometimes wished he knew more about who was saying what.

"If that *is* what he's up to, he better watch'is step," Ida Sue said.

Jase thought so, too. But he was reasonably sure that this Riley couldn't stir up trouble that Tyree Neely wouldn't know how to handle. Even when Tyree went on too long about horned owls or chickadees or such like, Jase had a healthy respect for his landlord and employer.

"I bet he never heard of what happened to Mister Timmons that time."

"Yeah, well . . ." Jase passed an old Chrysler Imperial with only one taillight, and that one blinking. As he had expected, the Imperial was full of colored, like clowns in the Volkswagen at the Clyde Beatty Circus that came through every year. "That's got nothing to do with Ben Neely."

As if shocked or bee-stung, Ida Sue flung herself against the far door of the Bronco.

"Sometimes I want to shake some sense into you, Jase Allman! If she would mess around with Mister Timmons like that, stands to reason she was messin around with Benjy Neely."

Jase understood the connection Ida Sue was making but did not believe in it. Two and two didn't always make four except in arithmetic. Once Rob Moore had found a ten-dollar bill in front of the jail and naturally assumed finders keepers. But it turned out, after Rob had spent the ten-spot at the Waitsfield Bowladrome, that Tug Johnson had lost it. Tug *said* he did, anyway, and made Rob pay it back.

"That Timmons business was a long time ago, Suedy."

"Well, she *could* have been, just the same."

Jase drove on awhile, not wanting to argue the point. Suddenly, it seemed a good idea to speak up before they got to the Cinemaplex Plaza, instead of afterward as he had planned, because if Dimmy Moore *did* show them off, that might put Ida Sue in a bad mood. She said female nudity in the movies made her squirm.

He wondered how to ask it, then plunged right in. "Why didden you wear your new necklace?"

"What?" Ida Sue said.

"The one you bought yourself at the Rockpile."

Ida Sue said nothing while a pickup truck roared out of the night toward them. Jase automatically registered it as a Chevy "like a rock." The truck bed was full of kids, white kids. As it sped past them, Jase could hear young voices shouting and laughing.

"Sounds like they're having a good time." Ida Sue's voice was a little resentful. "I decided I didn't love that necklace all that much. Kind of clashed with my eyes. I may take it back."

"They could all be dead by morning," Jase said. "Burning up the road like that, prob'ly half drunk. They might not let you."

"Might not what?" Ida Sue said.

"Let you take your necklace back."

"Sure they will. I paid cash."

Jase turned into the huge parking expanse of the Dixie Pride Mall and drove carefully in the designated lanes toward the brilliantly lit marquee of the Cinemaplex Plaza. A scattering of cars was parked in front of it.

"I forgot," he said. "Out of your pocket money."

He parked between the Spotless Cleaners van from Waitsfield and a Subaru Brat that he knew was Betty McKenzie's by the two bales of hay in the open bed. Betty was spending her father's insurance money raising horses. She always wore riding britches with leather in the seat and crotch and the inside of the knees and Ida Sue said it *had* to mean something—she wasn't saying what—for a woman to call attention to those parts of herself.

"That's Mister Johns's," Ida Sue said now, across the roof, as they got out on either side of the Bronco.

"What is?"

"The Monte Carlo. It's Mister Johns's."

"Oh," Jase said. "I forgot he drives a Caddy."

Fielding D. Johns had been imported by Stonewall County—which everybody knew meant Tyree Neely—to supervise the big new sewage treatment plant that had been built near the outskirts of Waitsfield with money Tyree's congressman had squeezed out of Washington. Johns had been managing a sewage plant in wintry Massachusetts and was eager to move to the Sunbelt when Tyree found him through a national association of sanitation engineers.

"Ever time I see that man," Ida Sue said, "I almost laugh in his face."

Tyree's import from Massachusetts had no sooner arrived in Stonewall County than irreverent locals began to mock the way he said "lawer" instead of "law" and "toMoTTo" instead of "toMAYto"—like he was imitating JFK. But Fielding D. Johns had not become a real figure of local fun until some wag—many claimed credit that none could prove—referred to him as "Flushing" D. Johns.

"You got to admit," Worth Bagwell, the undertaker, had said to Tyree Neely in Jase Allman's hearing, "him running the sewage plant and all, it kind of fits. Like calling a bus driver Speedy."

"But the man's an engineer," Tyree had protested. "A technician. A man that's got a degree from MIT's not somebody to make fun of."

That was one thing, however, that Tyree Neely could not control. The nickname stuck and inevitably it got back to Fielding Johns, or maybe somebody forgot and called him "Flushing" to his face. He had drawn more and more into himself, rarely speaking to anyone and going straight home from the sewage plant after work. His wife Nellie was said to be bad to drink. If true, people whispered, you could hardly blame their college-age son for not having come to Waitsfield at Christmas.

"I bet she's at home passed-out drunk and he's at the movies all alone." Ida Sue took Jase's arm as they walked across the parking lot toward the theater.

"I never seen her drunk."

"Well, you wouldn't," Ida Sue said, "if she just guzzles at home, like they say."

"But when he's alone, he usually drives his Cherokee like he does to work." Jase added, as they walked on, "Confound shame. Educated fella like that, all this talkin and sniggerin behind his back."

Ida Sue took Jase's hand. A half-moon had risen in the sky beyond the Cinemaplex Plaza but it was hard to see through the yellow glow of the neon lights on the marquee. She let her hip rub against his as they walked, and put her lips close to his ear.

"Le's sit in the back row," she whispered. "Case we feel like . . . doin anything."

Jase shivered. How he'd known Ida Sue had fallen for him was what had happened one night in the back row of the old downtown Waitsfield Grand, before they'd ripped out the seats and turned it into a flea market. He'd been cautiously feeling her thigh through her thin skirt, ready for her to knock his hand away any second, when in the dark, the hazy beam of the projector throwing Arnold Schwarzenegger monstrously on the screen above them, Ida Sue's fingers, light as a butterfly, swift as a hummingbird, fluttered for the briefest of seconds against his hard-on.

As she withdrew her hand and let it rest on his, he knew everything was settled. Jase Allman believed devoutly that when a nice girl like Ida Sue Medlin let on in any way that she knew what a man had between his legs, she must be willing to marry him.

As they came close enough to read the posters at the Cinemaplex Plaza's entrance—four other movies were playing, including *The*

Piano, which Ida Sue refused to see because they said some male actor showed his business—she suddenly dropped Jase's hand and pulled away, sounding angry: "I thought you told me it was Tom Hanks."

Jase had stopped wondering if Dimmy Moore would show anything and was thinking instead that Ida Sue seemed like maybe she was in the mood. He wanted to keep her that way.

"If I did," he said, "I sure am sorry."

Like he would be again, he told himself, as he reached for his wallet at the ticket window, if he said anything more about the necklace from the Rockpile.

SHEP

PROMPTLY AT 10 P.M., SHEP RILEY TURNED OFF THE TV IN ROOM 22
at the New South/Best Western Motel, phoned the front desk, and
asked to be connected to Miss Whitman.

"Meg Whitman," he said. "She may be registered under
McKinnon, Meg McKinnon."

"Just a moment, sir," the clerk said. After perhaps thirty seconds
of silence, he came on the line again. "We have a Miz Margaret
McKinnon in room fourteen, sir."

"That's the one," Shep said. "Put me through, will you?"

The phone rang twice, during which time Shep wondered if he
had guessed wrong. Even if he had, he needed to talk to her. After
the third ring, Meg answered; he'd have known her voice even if
he hadn't spoken to her the day before.

"Welcome to Dixieland." Shep had given much thought to how
he would greet her, and had decided to play it light.

Silence fell on the line before Meg said, "You sneaky bastard . . ." She did not sound, he told himself, as if she really meant
it. "How'd you know I was here?"

"Easy. It's the only motel in town."

"I mean, how'd you know I was coming at all?"

He had not guessed wrong, Shep told himself. There was no

indignation in her voice, as low and whispery as he remembered it.

"Because I knew you wouldn't be able to stay away. Not from a good case. And a chance to get back in business."

"With you?"

"And maybe a chance to get away from that tough guy of yours."

"You *are* a son of a bitch," Meg said. "I haven't even been here ten minutes and you're already calling."

"I checked the Trailways station for the last bus in. Listen, we need to talk. I'm in room twenty-two."

Meg spoke with spirit. "Shep, I am *not* coming to your room. Put it out of your mind."

"But it's close by. You won't even need to call a taxi."

"I told you. I'm not going anywhere near room twenty-two. We can talk at breakfast."

With women, Shep Riley believed in taking charge. And the more Meg protested, the more he was sure he had not guessed wrong.

"If you aren't here in five minutes," he said, "I'll be knocking on the door of room fourteen."

"There'll be no answer." Meg hung up.

Shep turned on the TV again and watched a few minutes of Barbara Walters interviewing an underage Hollywood star with a pout and a beard stubble. Then he turned off the set again, put on his jacket—he had shed his tie upon returning to the New South/Best Western after his conference with Easter Lilly Odum—and walked through the buggy night, under the motel's frontal arcade, toward room 14.

Lined-off parking spaces on a blacktop drive separated the New South/Best Western from a lighted swimming pool slightly larger than a billiard table. The pool was enclosed by a chain-link fence, on the locked gate of which hung a sign reading: CLOSED WHEN NO LIFE GUARD IS PRESENT.

Beyond the fenced-in pool and its bordering lawn, cars sped ceaselessly both ways along a three-lane highway, their lights illuminating on the other side what once had been a drive-in hamburger joint. The kind where you ordered from a girl carhop in hot pants and a tight blouse, then ate from a little tray she hooked in the window of your car. They had been put out of business by McDonald's, Hardee's, and other fast-food "restaurants."

He had eaten at many a drive-in with Meg in the old days and he was looking forward to seeing her again. The mere sound of her voice on the phone had provoked some of the old flare in his groin. Meg always had been attractive beyond her looks—smart as a whip, eager, warm, her cool reserve quickly dispelled.

He had known few women as exciting—the Alabama home ec teacher who had put the shoe-heel scar on his chest maybe, and a real estate writer for a New York newspaper who as they rode the elevator to his twentieth-floor apartment had gone down on him before they reached the fifth. Neither had had Meg's ladylike air of allowing herself to do things she'd never done before and would never do again. But of all the women he'd known, including Meg, none had had the sheer physical beauty of Easter Lilly Odum.

Shep had not expected anything like Easter Lilly. He was conditioned to accept conventional white standards of feminine beauty. He knew, of course, that black women's bodies were *women's* bodies, as provocative as any white woman's, often more so. But he had not been prepared to find genuine beauty—beauty transcending race, that could have been of any race—in a black woman who made no attempt to look white, or to meet white conceptions. No painted mouth, no painted lids, just what nature had arranged, the dark hair falling loosely about her head and framing a classic face, cheekbones from mythology, eyes a man could sink into.

Easter Lilly's physical beauty was in bone structure, carriage, attitude, the graceful hands and arms, the long legs, the perfect round of hips, the womanly breasts Shep was ashamed to remember he had wanted to fondle like a teenager on a date. While her beauty had a dimension more than physical, Shep Riley was not a man to overlook a woman's appearance. Like most men, he usually took that as his first standard of judgment.

Shep was acutely aware, however, of the long, brutal history of white men preying on black women's bodies—Ben Neely most recently. So he tried not to dwell on Easter Lilly's obvious sexual attractions. He told himself he was not that kind of man. And anyway, the lawyer's code of ethics would not allow him to take a woman who was a client for his own pleasures.

Easter Lilly held as much sexual promise as any woman Shep had ever coveted. A lot of women over the years—all white. What he was remembering, however, as he strode toward room 14, was mostly the sense of presence she gave off, like a powerfully alluring scent. To be with Easter Lilly would be to know pride and strength and purpose combined with beauty—or perhaps beauty's essence.

So it was that Shep actually was thinking of Easter Lilly Odum, and of the red tongue that had wetted her sensuous mouth, when he tapped on the door of room 14.

MEG

BEFORE SHE HEARD THE EXPECTED KNOCK AT HER DOOR, MEG HAD
hooked it to the safety chain that would prevent it from opening
more than an inch or two. Not that she feared Shep would try to
force his way in. Shep Riley was not a rapist, whatever else he
might be. But the chain was a good way to end, if necessary, the
argument she fully expected, even anticipated, but that she feared
he would otherwise find a way to win. Shep usually won arguments.
Especially, Meg remembered glumly, with me.

Though she was tired from a long day of travel, Meg had remained fully dressed. When she heard the knock, she took her time
crossing the room, then opened the door until it was halted by the
chain. Through the gap between door and jamb, after all those long
years, she saw Shep's face, a little thinner than she remembered,
under red hair going noticeably gray. The hair had been sharply cut
back, too; the ponytail and the sideburns that once had flared below
the prominent ears were gone.

Better the old way. Sexier.

"Your nose," Shep said, "has not changed."

Why was he talking about her nose? Which she thought her worst
feature, too bony, too often red. Then she remembered that
through the narrow opening he could only see the middle of her

face; and what seemed the perfect retort came to her as if in one of those little clouds over a character's head in the funny papers:

"Wrong, Riley. It now smells more acutely."

"Smells what?"

"A fucking liar."

She had not said the word since she had seen him last—it would shock Alton—and the feel of it on her lips gave her a guilty thrill. But the description seemed just right for Shep Riley.

"You always could sniff out one of those." Shep trying, as usual, to sound cool and witty, like Cary Grant.

"Not the kind"—she took great pleasure in saying what for so long she had wished to have the chance to say to his face—"that talk about love when what they mean is *making* love."

"I see," Shep said. "You hated making love, didn't you?"

Touché. Shep had been her first—not counting mostly forgettable college-girl experiments—and so far her only lover, hence the best. Making love with Shep . . . she shivered and quelled the memory. Maybe it had only been youth. The truncated recollection nevertheless caused her to think guiltily of Alton at home with the children. What would the children think of their mother if they knew . . . ?

"I didn't hate the sex," she conceded to him—an understatement, she conceded to herself. "Just the lies that went with it. Let's talk about this case of yours. Unless we can talk over breakfast?"

Through the gap above the chain, Meg could almost see Shep wondering if she was playing hard to get. Of course, he'd resist the idea that she could possibly be serious. She knew Shep's face so well, even without all the red hair that used to surround it— the way the eyes blinked and the lips pursed a little as he thought. Once that face, every line and bone of it, each of those small gestures, had been dear to her. Now it seemed strange to watch it reflect his calculations.

"You've cut your hair," she said, without intending to. Why should I give a damn, she asked herself angrily, how Shep Riley wears his hair?

"Not only that," he said. "What if I told you that living in Vermont, I've given up sex for fly-fishing?"

Meg laughed out loud. "Does a bear give up honey?"

"Unhook the goddam door and I'll show you."

She knew with satisfaction, almost a sense of triumph, that he was a little baffled. As usual, she thought, he had been confident of getting his way with a woman.

"Meg, goddammit . . . I just want to tell you what we're in for here in God's little acre. And I'm planning to sleep in tomorrow."

Meg was not fooled. Genius, she thought, putting the chain on the door. The mere thought of being in bed with Shep had caused that telltale ripple to goosebump along her spine. So she said, "I can hear you okay from right where you're standing."

"Then did you ever hear of Tina Turner?"

The question puzzled her and she wondered briefly and in faint dismay if he had given up so easily what she had had no doubt—had hoped, in fact—was his real purpose. She wanted to enjoy thwarting it, as for years she had thought of doing, as she had planned on doing all through her dreary day's travel. But she had not wished for it to be so easy. She had wanted to twist the knife.

"Saw that movie," she said.

"That was Angela Bassett playing the role."

"What kind of game is this, Shep?"

"Our client is right up there. I don't mean she looks *like* them or like anybody else. Easter Lilly's unique. But she's an incredible beauty, too."

Might have known.

"No wonder you decided to take her case, then. But she's not *my* client yet."

"I never saw the lady before today," Shep said. "I just figured anybody in her position would need a lot of help."

In some detail, then, he told her what he had learned about Tyree Neely from Larry Wright and J. Preston Cadieux and Daisy Thorpe. He told her that Easter Lilly Odum had asked him to join her defense team and had confirmed and strengthened his belief that she had stabbed Ben Neely in self-defense.

"Not, of course," Meg interrupted his flow to say, "that looking as good as Tina Turner had anything to do with your considered professional judgment."

She thought she noticed a faint hesitation, as if her question had startled him.

"Not a thing," he finally said. "But this Neely—he's like a cat you can hardly see its claws. You know the last thing he said to me, as I was leaving his office?"

Meg was listening intently, not just to the facts he was giving her but to the old familiar passion in his voice, the conviction, the confidence to dare the odds. That hadn't changed even if he was older—ten years older than she was, which made him fifty-two. He had cut his hair and claimed to have given up sex—fat chance!— but he seemed in other respects the same Shep Riley, even frustrated as she hoped he was by the unexpected door-chain on room 14 in a backwoods motel.

"He said, and I'm not kidding . . ."

A strange conversation to have through an inch of space, Meg thought, particularly when the New South/Best Western was little different from dozens of other motels in which she and Shep Riley had lit up many a lusty night with the colored lights of sex. More often, she thought wryly, again shivering a little, and certainly lustier, than Alton McKinnon's wife and her children's mother should let herself remember.

"He actually said, 'Did you ever see a horned owl?' The guy's a bird-watcher! But underneath all that, he aims to send our client to the gas chamber. Makes no bones about it. Which is why I'm counting on you to do your thing again."

Meg's specialty in their old collaboration had been checking out prospective jurors, trying to learn which ones, if any, might be susceptible to whatever argument Shep intended to put up for the defense—and which ones probably would be implacably hostile. With her background in psychology as well as law, she had become expert at it, and consequently Shep often had been able to seat jurors he wanted and dismiss many he didn't. He had even "won" cases with a hung jury—Meg's one or two selected pigeons holding out, as she had predicted they would, for acquittal.

"They've got a panel list already?"

"You'll have to see Tyree Neely to find out," Shep said. "You want to make a right turn on red around here, you have to see Tyree."

Meg peered around the edge of the door at Shep only an inch or two away on the other side. His shirt was open at the neck, and he wore no tie, just the way he had usually appeared in her reveries. Except for the shorter, graying hair.

"On the way from the bus station," she said, "the taxi driver said Waitsfield got along for two hundred years without a motel, before somebody named Neely built this place. You suppose it was the same Neely?"

"I wouldn't doubt it. You'll find him in an office on the third floor of the courthouse, with Miss America guarding the door."

Meg put off thinking lawyerly thoughts about the jury panel. Time enough for that in the morning, after she'd seen Tyree Neely. Shep had suggested something more interesting.

"You really think she sleeps with him?"

Shep looked knowing. He had always professed to know women. When in fact all he really knew was what women could do in bed. Or would. Meg had believed fatuously that she was an exception, until the moment she discovered she wasn't.

"Bet my last dollar on it," Shep said. "It's my instinct."

Meg believed in instinct, too, but made a face of disagreement on this point.

"Secretaries don't generally sleep with their bosses, Shep. It'd be too uncomfortable for both, cooped up in the same office every day. Especially since feminists like me started raising hell about sexual harassment."

Besides, she thought, even if *you'd* never believe it, women don't generally sleep around. "And anyway, if he's the kind of person you say, he wouldn't risk any kind of a scandal."

She watched Shep think this over, saw his face change, and heard him say exactly what she'd expected.

"Since when were *you* a feminist?"

Meg wanted to say, "Since you." But she believed she'd made that point. If not, no words would.

"Since the Clarence Thomas hearing."

Shep nodded. "It was after that weekend," he said gravely, "that I gave up sex."

His face was practically in the gap at the edge of the door. So was hers. They could almost rub noses, Meg thought. His tone was so solemn, his face so serious, his words so laughable, their deadlock at the door so ridiculous, that she could not help laughing. A slow grin spread over the part of Shep's face that she could see.

"So feminism must be the reason," she said when she had

stopped laughing, "that you think this woman that looks as good as Angela What's-her-name acted in self-defense."

Shep's smile vanished. "No doubt about it. That night Easter Lilly was all alone back there, asleep in this empty cellblock. Way after midnight, she wakes up with a knife at her throat and this jailer creep pulling off her underpants."

Shep suddenly turned his head until she could see around the edge of the door only the right side of his face, where a red sideburn once had been, and the way he swallowed hard, his Adam's apple moving in his thin throat.

"Made my blood boil"—he faced her again—"just to hear her tell it."

"Poor girl."

Meg did feel a woman's inevitable horror of rape, but she was moved, too, by Shep's obvious emotion. He always had been one to let his feelings show, always had bordered on sentimentality, particularly about injustice and helplessness.

He shook his head vigorously, the middle of his face jerking left and right of the narrow opening through which she saw him.

"Believe me . . . after you meet Easter Lilly, you'll never think 'poor girl' again. She isn't just beautiful. She's tough, she's proud. She's survived a hard life. That's how she could . . ." He stopped, searching for words. "That bastard jailer didn't know what he was getting into. No pun intended."

Meg's curiosity was frankly prurient. "Did he actually . . ."

"I didn't push her to tell."

Had he really been that sensitive to a woman's feelings? Not many men would have been. Especially a lawyer seeking the facts. Behind the door, she lifted her hand to the security chain, just to be certain it was tightly fastened.

"But Shep, how *can* you be sure what happened that night if there weren't any witnesses?"

Through the gap she watched him nod once, jerkily. "Because that's the way things happen in this shitty world. Because that's the kind of vultures some men are. And because down here nobody else is going to listen to her story. *I* listened, and I believe her. And I'm not going to let them"—he swallowed hard again—"strap her down for fighting back."

That was what—Meg discovered anew in his words—she re-

membered most, had remembered best for eighteen years: Shep
Riley's fundamental quality, what made him a rarity. A Harvard
cum laude could have made a fortune as a Wall Street lawyer, been
a partner in a big, rich downtown firm. But Shep cared little for
carpeted offices, fat bonuses at the end of the year. He had been
willing to sacrifice all that in the belief that the big fish would always
eat the little fish; Shep Riley had never doubted that, and had
aligned himself long ago with the little fish. For his conviction, he
had spurned money and power; he had lived his faith.

Which, Meg knew, shivering again, was how he could be sure,
even without witnesses, of what had happened in the jail that night.
He could be sure because of the willingness his faith gave him to
believe Easter Lilly Odum.

"Why she ran after she did it," Shep said, "she panicked. That's
another reason I believe her. She admitted it to me. Because what
black woman in Stonewall County wouldn't have panicked and run?
That white son of a bitch lying on the floor with his pants down
and a knife in his heart where she stuck it?"

Meg once had loved Shep Riley for his faith. She had been certain, and still was, that it was more than mere compassion. But she
had loved him, too, for what they had been together in those motel
rooms odorous with stale tobacco, disinfectant, and sex. Together,
in those days of daring and accomplishment, they had been something she had never known before, or since. She was faintly surprised to find herself again shivering at the memory.

"If you won't help," Shep said, "I'll just have to take it on
alone."

Meg was only a little more surprised to realize that she had
slipped the chain out of its hook. She wondered, but only for a
moment, whether his conviction or her shivering body had guided
her hand. Then she knew it didn't matter. She stepped aside and
swung back the door, feeling the kind of relief she sometimes had
felt when finally bringing herself to do something she had told herself she never could.

"The reason I came when you called"—with the unabashed joy
of feeling herself desired, she watched pleasure transform Shep's
face—"is I always wanted to learn about fly-fishing from an
expert."

TYREE

TYREE NEELY WAS AT HIS DESK EARLY, CATCHING UP ON ENTRIES into his bird book in the precise Zaner-Blosser hand he had learned at Waitsfield Elementary in the good old days before integration. During field trips, he kept ample notes, scratched on any available piece of paper, and—when he could—took photos of his sightings. Periodically, he transcribed his notes into a big, ruled ledger, one bird to a page, if possible with a photo to validate the sighting. Sometimes, unfortunately, the light had been dim or the sighting had moved too quickly or he had fumbled too long with the close-up lens and he would have no picture for proof. Tyree kept such detailed notes, however, that he entered the bird anyway, confident the entry would never be challenged.

A few minutes after nine, Daisy Thorpe came in with the morning mail and the small milk-glass vase of fresh flowers she put on Tyree's desk every day. Daisy waited while he made an entry:

> Big-headed, big-billed, about 1' from tip of dagger bill to tail tip, uneven crest. Evidently a female, owing to rusty streak on breast-band.

With plastic photo corners, Tyree fixed a picture of a belted kingfisher beneath these notes, then sat back in the cushioned desk

chair that Tug Johnson, Jase Allman, and Rob Moore—all of whom
he had placed on the Stonewall County payroll—had chipped in to
buy him for Christmas the year before.

"Morning, Daisy. What's the bad news today?"

"Just the usual sort of stuff in the mail, Mister Neely. Nothing
you need to worry about."

She wore a quite plain dress, dark blue with a high neckline, the
skirt stopping fashionably just above her knees, a single strand of
pearls encircling her white neck. Tyree noted with approval that
the dress covered her shoulders and upper arms.

"A Miz McKinnon called before you came in," he told Daisy.
"Says she's a colleague of Mister Riley, that Yankee was in yesterday, remember? I told her to stop by at nine-thirty."

Daisy picked at the flowers, arranging them prettily on the corner
of Tyree's desk.

"I declare . . . anybody'd think Easter Lilly Odum was Queen
Elizabeth. Fuss over her everybody's making all of a sudden."

"Won't be too much of a fuss," Tyree said.

He had been, however, more upset than he let on to find Shep
Riley of all people—Tyree had not heard of the man in years—
moving in on Cady. But it would never have done to show his
dismay, and it had not taken long for him to learn that Riley knew
little more about the case than he'd read in *The New York Times*.
Tyree had expected a lot from a man who'd been on TV and
featured in *Time* magazine, but as they had chatted in his office, he
realized that Shep Riley had not yet even interviewed Easter Lilly.

"It's just . . . all that talk to Cady about pleading self-defense,"
Daisy said.

The mere mention of that caused Tyree to get a little hot under
the collar all over again. The very idea!

"I'll bet he thinks he can walk into a little old town like this
and get her off just like that." Daisy snapped her fingers. "He
doesn't know the kind of a lawyer *you* are."

Tyree was accustomed to Daisy's flattery and he did count himself a pretty good country prosecutor. He also knew that even a
resourceful lawyer like Riley had no real idea of the opposition he
faced. The man had been out of circulation for a long time. Maybe
over the hill.

Still, Tyree replied to Daisy's compliment with his usual calculated self-deprecation. "I don't reckon I'm in Riley's league, Daisy."

She frowned and turned to leave his office. Tyree saw his moment and called after her, "That a new dress you're wearing?"

She turned back to him, flaring her skirt a little, looking down at herself, a hint of puzzlement on the carefully made-up face beneath her dark curls.

"This old thing? I've had it for ages, Mister Neely. Maybe I never wore it to the office before."

"Don't think you have. I'd have noticed . . . like I noticed that outfit you had on yesterday. What there was of it."

Daisy's snowy neck and face colored. "I meant to explain about that, Mister Neely. You see, I had to go to Judy Pearce's bridal shower yesterday evening, and I just *knew* I wouldn't have time to go home and change, so I—"

"It's all right." Tyree congratulated himself on his tact. "I just thought it might be a little chilly, nothing on your shoulders like that."

"—so I changed in the ladies' room, thinking you weren't coming back," Daisy said. "But when I was about to close the office, that Riley person came in and . . ."

Satisfied that he had made his point, Tyree said, "I just wouldn't want you catching cold."

He realized immediately that Daisy would take these words to mean even more than he intended. She obviously did, still blushing but looking at him archly over her shoulder as she went out.

"I *never* catch cold," she said in tones just above a whisper, an intimate implication that Tyree Neely needn't worry about anything like that—not with Daisy Thorpe. The door closed behind her.

"Shoot," Tyree muttered. He had wound up letting her think he was concerned about her well-being. Which he was, but not as Daisy hoped. Daisy had determined to marry him; in fact, Daisy seldom thought about anything else, Tyree believed, except maybe clothes. Her determination was relentless—and got on his nerves, even though she was pretty as a ruby-throated hummingbird. He doubted Daisy coveted only his male charms, such as they were.

Besides, he was just not the marrying kind. Having managed to get through his fifty years without taking on a woman to share his life and trappings, he saw no reason to do so at such a late date.

The sooner Daisy got *that* through her pretty, rather empty head, the better off they'd both be.

RING-BILLED GULL
Dovelike, smaller than herring gull, distinct black ring encircling bill, pale green legs. 20" approx.

He'd spotted that one sitting still—giving him plenty of time to fit the close-up lens—on a rotting old pier slanting out of the ocean, the last weekend he'd been able to walk the winter beach.

Daisy opened the door again and looked at him fondly, her blue eyes warm under her coifed hair.

"Miz McKinnon is here a few minutes early."

Tyree walked around his desk to greet his visitor. For Daisy's benefit, he appeared more eager than he felt. The woman who entered his office with springy step was taller than average. She was not exactly thin but carried no excess weight. She had dark hair, worn short, and lively brown eyes, unshadowed and not as come-hither as Daisy's large blue ones. Her only makeup was a faint touch of lipstick. She wore no jewelry but a plain wedding band, of which he approved. Tyree believed women should be married.

"I'm Meg McKinnon," she said. "Nice of you to see me so early, Mister Neely."

His visitor was not, Tyree was relieved to see, a raving beauty like Daisy Thorpe, and she was not a young girl. He would not have to act like a man bowled over. But her long stride, her out-stretched hand, the openness of her face, made him almost like her—though, in general, Tyree Neely did not like women, particularly women he knew nothing about. They seemed to him an imposition on things as they ought to be.

"Never too early to start the day." That had been a favorite maxim of John Bell's, drummed into Tyree at a young age.

He placed a leather-cushioned chair for his visitor, and had scarcely returned to his desk before she got down to business. "I'm acting as co-counsel for Easter Lilly Odum and I—"

"Whoa," Tyree said good-humoredly. "Yesterday morning Easter Lilly only had Cady. Yesterday afternoon she got Shep Riley. And today she's got you. Tomorrow maybe Thurgood Marshall?"

Meg McKinnon laughed, the sound of it soft, unforced. Most women—Daisy, for instance—tried to laugh like a bell pealing.

"If Justice Marshall hadn't already gone to his reward," Meg McKinnon said, "we'd be mighty glad to have him on the team."

Tyree laughed, too, but lifted a finger. "But not Cady?"

She stopped laughing. "I haven't met Mister Kadducks but my colleague, Mister Riley, doesn't expect any . . . ah . . . friction."

"Won't be any," Tyree agreed. "Cady'll prob'ly quit, he finds out for sure what you and I know. That the famous Mister Riley is taking over the case."

"With Miss Odum's consent."

Tyree nodded pleasantly. Meg McKinnon appeared to know what she was doing. He liked that, though he cared for women lawyers even less than for women in general. Women lawyers usually looked as if they were wearing boiled shirts too tight in the collar.

Not this one. The McKinnon woman had small breasts, hardly noticeable under a white blouse. Otherwise, Tyree would have managed not to notice them at all. He deplored ostentation of all kinds, including showboats up front. As on the repellent Easter Lilly Odum. Tyree would not have allowed the silly Mount Vernon columns in front of the new jail if he hadn't feared that, without such obeisance to tradition, the voters would have disapproved the bond issue.

"With or without Cady," the woman said, "we expect Miss Odum to be found not guilty."

"Then I expect you'd be better off without him. I guess you mean not guilty of Murder One?"

"Of anything. It's not a crime to defend yourself."

"Not"—Tyree smiled with some difficulty—"if you can prove that's what she did, Miz McKinnon."

He expected her to tell him, in the effusive southern manner (her voice telling him she was not a Yankee) to call her Meg. Instead, she said pointedly, "We don't have to prove innocence, Mister Neely. It's your job to prove guilt."

A woman lawyer, all right.

"I don't expect to have much trouble." Not wanting to offend, he added hastily, "But I reckon you and Mister Riley might cause me right smart of it."

"It'll be up to a jury to decide."

A Stonewall County jury, Tyree thought. But let them find out for themselves.

"Which is why I'm here. When will you pick a jury panel?"

Tyree lifted his eyebrows, though he was not displeased by the implication. "Me? I don't pick anybody, ma'am."

"I didn't mean *you* personally." Though he was quite sure that that was exactly what, in her mannerly way, she *had* meant. "I mean the county, whatever your procedure is."

"Since the suspect admitted the deed"—Tyree wanted to sound lawyerlike in front of a smart lady—"no need for a magistrate's hearing. Her confession is probable cause."

He ticked off the process on his fingers. "Next week, prob'ly, week after at the latest, she goes before county court downstairs, and I'm right sure Judge Brigman'll bind'er over to superior court for trial. I'll write up an indictment and take it to the grand jury we already got sitting. I expect they'll vote it out right away."

"Of course," Meg said. "Grand juries usually rubber-stamp whatever a prosecutor wants."

Tyree smiled amiably. "Some do, some don't. Next August, superior court's in session here. Judge Ottis Reeves sitting. A hard man, but fair."

"She'll be tried right here in Waitsfield?"

"Next reg'lar session of superior court."

"With a Waitsfield jury?"

"Well . . . Stonewall County."

"Chosen at random?"

"Like anywhere else," Tyree said. "County clerk draws names out of a box, from taxpayer and voter lists."

He did not point out that Bobby Isham, the clerk, worked at the pleasure of the Stonewall County commissioners, all of whom got elected at the pleasure of Tyree Neely.

"And who conducts the voir dire in this jurisdiction, Mister Neely?"

"Opposing counsel, like anywhere else."

"Well, some courts nowadays," Meg McKinnon said, "the judge does it."

"Afraid we're not that up-to-date around here." Tyree did not like to admit this. He made a mental note to look into the voir dire process, though he doubted he would ever want to entrust it to the inspirations of Ottis P. Reeves.

"Actually," Meg McKinnon rather surprised him by saying, "I prefer the lawyers to do it. Unless you just want to save time."

Tyree spread his hands generously. "I've got all the time in the world, Miz McKinnon."

A right nice lady, he thought. A kind of odd, quiet way of making a man feel in charge. Might be pleasant to have her on *my* side— maybe in the office here instead of Daisy mooning around, showing off her shape.

He walked with Meg McKinnon to the door of the outer office, making a show of gallantry, mostly because he felt that way toward this subdued and mannerly lady, but again partly for Daisy Thorpe to notice. Daisy apparently did, frowning down at her desk and looking a bit teed off. Tyree went happily back to his private office and his bird book.

COMMON GALLINULE
Red bill and forehead, white flank band, white undertail. Loud, repeated henlike sound. Seen swimming in old Picket millpond.

Tyree was not really thinking about the common gallinule as he affixed a rather fuzzy picture of it to the page. He was thinking about Meg McKinnon. Something about her, no doubt about it. So prim and controlled, nothing obvious or flashy. The kind of woman, he was surprised to realize, a man might like to find out more about.

The phone rang, and Daisy said on the speaker, a little abruptly, "Carl Hoover from the motel."

Really teed off, Tyree noted with satisfaction.

"Okay," he said, and Daisy put Carl Hoover on the line.

"Sorry to bother you, Tyree. But you said I should let you know anything bout this Riley."

"No bother a-tall."

When Tyree had sold his majority interest in the New South to Best Western, he had their lawyers write into the deal that Carl Hoover would stay on as manager as long as Tyree Neely wanted. He had let Carl know about that part of the contract, of course—

not exactly calling a due bill, just believing a man's loyalty was bound to be greater when reinforced by gratitude. And Carl was *already* grateful, since before handing him the motel job in the first place, Tyree had got him off the hook on a rubber-check charge.

"So I thought you might like to know . . ."

Carl Hoover kept Tyree well up on matters like who was sleeping off a drunk in the motel, or who was sneaking what woman not his wife into the New South/Best Western, and how often. Of course, Carl's reports covered scarcely a tithe of Waitsfield sexual goings-on, since the locals were less likely to be spotted and recognized if they shacked up at the Howard Johnson or the Shady Rest, not too many miles across the line in Beaslee County. Besides, almost anywhere in Stonewall, plenty of dark places could be found to get at it in the backseat of a car.

"Him and the broad that come in later . . ."

Tyree's interest perked up. He'd never acted on any of Carl Hoover's reports, though some were savory. He'd never had to. But Tyree always tried to take the long view. He'd known that sooner or later his handpicked motel manager would have some useful info.

". . . spent the night in her room together."

Tyree's first reaction was a flick of satisfaction to have got a little stroke on Shep Riley. Next he felt faint annoyance that Carl Hoover had called a lady like Meg McKinnon a "broad." Then the news hit him like a mule kick in the stomach.

Until he felt it, Tyree had not realized how much he had liked the McKinnon woman, looked forward to seeing her again even on the other side of a courtroom. Now Carl Hoover was telling him that Meg McKinnon was Shep Riley's shack job. And her wearing a wedding ring. Which just went to prove that they were all cheats.

"She ain't hardly been registered half an hour," Carl said, "he was over there with his dick hangin out."

Tyree closed his eyes against the image. He had found out more than he wanted to know. But Tyree prided himself that he could take it as well as dish it out, and he had no difficulty concealing his distress from Carl Hoover.

"Oh, well, Carl," he said, "what can you expect from strangers these days?"

He did not feel philosophical about it, however. He felt cheated, humiliated, and—most disagreeable of all—badly surprised. Tyree considered himself a good judge of people and Meg McKinnon had seemed such a nice lady, not at all the common run.

"I reckon it takes all kinds," Carl Hoover said.

DAISY

BY THE TIME TYREE HAD FINISHED HIS CONVERSATION WITH CARL Hoover, Daisy Thorpe was no longer teed off. *Three cheers* she was thinking *for old Carl. Even if he is a tattletale.*

She listened carefully for the click of Tyree's receiver being replaced, then hung up her own and sat back in her office chair, happily remembering a phrase picked up from Tyree Neely's prosecutor practice: in flagrante delicto.

Daisy had taken a dislike to Shep Riley the instant he compared her name with Easter Lilly Odum's. Daisy remembered Easter Lilly, from their days as forced classmates at the newly integrated SCCH, as not only uppity but making a disgraceful show of herself with that insipid white teacher.

Named after flowers.

Indeed! As if a similar name made Daisy Thorpe anything like that cheap black twit that had run around with one white man and murdered another.

Daisy had welcomed Carl Hoover's news for another reason, too. Her perceptions were keen when it came to Tyree Neely, and she had not failed to observe in his manner that the lady lawyer had favorably impressed him. Though God knows *why*. Daisy lumped women lawyers in with schoolteachers and librarians: dried-up, superannuated crones. And this particular woman lawyer was not only *ancient* but skinny.

Daisy had worked hard to get and keep the kind of figure men gawked at. And since she believed looks and sex were all men really cared about in a woman, she decided that Meg McKinnon must somehow have let Tyree know she could be had. Why else would he have been so interested?

This insight had turned out to be correct, certified by Carl Hoover. Even so, Daisy found it hard to see why any man, even the insolent Riley, would look twice at an anorexic bag of bones like Meg McKinnon. But whatever reason there might have been for Tyree to be attracted surely had come to a screeching halt with Carl Hoover's phone call, praise be.

Tyree came out of the inner office. "Going down to the snack bar, Daisy. Can I get you anything?" As always, Daisy was pleased that Tyree was too gentlemanly to order *her* to go to the snack bar for *him*.

"Black coffee, thanks," she said.

At the corridor door, he looked back, shaking his head. "Got to get back in the woods soon. This town life is too complicated for me."

Wanting to sympathize, Daisy stopped herself, just in time, from giving away her telephone trick. Carl Hoover's news had pleased but not surprised her, since she had few illusions about women *or* men. If she ever had had any, they had been lost years before, when a TV crew had come to Waitsfield to film the old frame birthplace of Clint Collingwood, a big money-winner on the NASCAR racing circuit.

Collingwood, nationally known as the "Lead-footed Country Boy," by then had fled Waitsfield for a mansion near Daytona Beach with a swimming pool shaped like a Chevy logo. When the TV crew finished the Waitsfield shoot and left town, Daisy Thorpe, aged seventeen and newly deflowered, was riding in the front seat of soundman Vic Buckley's Firebird, Vic driving with one arm around Daisy's shoulders, a six-pack of Miller High Life between them, the smell of pot rank in the car.

"Just think," she'd told Vic as they passed the city limits, "I'll never spend another day in this shitty burg again."

A week later, Daisy called her father collect from the police station in Orlando, Florida, then slipped back into Waitsfield on a midnight bus with a ticket the old man had sent her by FedEx. Widowed for a decade, Randolph Thorpe met her with stern composure and a fierce glare at anyone looking on. The next day, Daisy was privately examined by his old fishing companion, Dr. Jacob A. Huntington, retired. Daisy was found to suffer neither pregnancy nor venereal disease, and Doc Huntington gave both of them ample reason never again to mention the occasion.

"If you tell your daddy about this," he said, pulling up his zipper as he peered down at her frightened face, "you'll be in reform school faster'n you can say Jack Robinson."

Daisy soon appeared at the C&W Pharmacy soda fountain, inventing fulsome reports on her week at Camp Nawakwa for girls, out in the western part of the state. She never smoked marijuana again, always dressed conventionally, presented herself at the Stonewall Presbyterian Church every time its doors opened, sang each Sunday in its choir, and became well-known in the romantic wasteland that was Waitsfield for keeping herself as sexually pristine as a rose in the morning dew. Daisy thus retained her social standing and polished a spotless reputation within Waitsfield's female establishment. When she read in *People* magazine that a television technician named Vic Buckley had overdosed and died in a Chicago hotel, her only regret was for old time's sake.

The truth of her "misfortune," as she taught herself to think of it, went to their graves with Randolph Thorpe, who eventually died a stoic death from prostate cancer, and with Doc Huntington, who expired in a wheeze of emphysema and whose funeral Daisy feigned illness to avoid. After her father's death, she had been pressed by sympathetic Waitsfield women into the employ of Tyree Neely and, unsuspected by her permed and corseted sponsors, into a second education at his feet.

"Must be *won*derful workin for a man that's into *ever*'thing," Helen Hudson, the postmaster's sister and housekeeper, once had enthused at a Garden Club party on Confederate Memorial Day.

"More than you'd believe," Daisy replied fervently.

By then, not least because of Vic Buckley and Jake Huntington, Daisy had shed all illusions. Owing to her father, she knew life was hard and unforgiving, and owing to the pedagogy of Tyree Neely, she had few scruples about what she wanted. She listened in on his phone calls without a qualm and routinely kept open the squawk-box line to his desk whenever she thought anything interesting might be overheard. Reading his mail and poring over his files, of course, were among her duties.

The only one of Tyree's activities she was never able to penetrate, even by stealth, was his bird-watching rituals—an unfair and typically male exclusion that made Daisy grit her perfect teeth. But she liked to remind herself, "All in good time."

She had no doubt that Tyree Neely would not forever be able to go rambling off by himself at whim, in search of orioles and warblers. And though Daisy Thorpe had no interest whatsoever in any feathered creature (she preferred even the Thanksgiving turkey to be frozen, with a pop-up tube to signal when it was done), she was entirely confident that when the inevitable moment came for Tyree Neely to place a golden ring on her exquisitely shaped third finger, left hand, she could quickly learn all she would need to know about underbodies and swallowtails and wing linings.

Everything else necessary, Daisy already had learned.

SHEP

SHEP RILEY HAD RETURNED TO HIS OWN ROOM JUST AFTER DAWN—
though before he was fully dressed and about to leave, Meg had
pulled him back into bed for a last embrace. Or round of combat,
Shep thought. He had been surprised at her ardor, though he remembered her as a pretty hot number under her ladylike
demeanor—white gloves and a little black hat for church on
Sundays. After her hard words to him at the door of room 14,
however, he had had no reason to expect such an athletic night.

As he crept exhausted along the arcade toward room 22—getting
too old for the game, he thought ruefully—he resented again Meg's
accusation that, eighteen years earlier, he had lied to her about love.
He had no recollection of violating his rule never to tell a woman
he loved her in order to get her into bed. It *was* true, though, that
for a time he had been avid for Meg's hard little breasts and aggressive hands.

A fat man, yawning and scratching his balls, came out of room
19 in pin-striped underwear and squinted at the sky. Shep hated
encountering anyone at such an early hour. It was too much like
being caught coming out of a harlot's room. But the man looked
at him without interest.

"Might get some rain later on," he muttered, still scratching.

"Hope so." Not caring, Shep hurried past, relieved that the man in shorts obviously thought him just another early riser. He heard the door to room 19 close behind him, unlocked room 22, and hurriedly undressed. Meg had not let him have much of the sleep he badly needed. Besides, he felt somehow besmirched. He did not let himself think about that as he fell across the bed and into unconsciousness.

Shep awoke to someone knocking on his door. With one eye, he peered mistily at his wristwatch. Five after noon.

"Housekeepin."

"Wait a minute." Shep yawned and sat up. "Can you come back in a half hour."

"Well, awright." Housekeeping sounded disgruntled.

Shep shaved, showered, dressed, and walked out to the front desk. He asked the man at the desk to call a taxi to take him to the Purity Cafe.

"Comin right up."

The man at the desk was a cadaverous individual with foul breath, wearing a Hawaiian shirt. He checked a number penciled on the sheetrock next to the wall phone. A nameplate on the motel desk said CARL HOOVER, MGR.

"You want to use the extension in your room next time, Mister Riley, it's Beeline. B-E-E-line."

While he waited for the taxi, Shep again was disturbed about his night with Meg. Not that it hadn't been memorable, as if they had been making up for years of lost time and opportunity. But he felt uneasily that somehow, this time, he really had misled Meg, been untrue in that sense to himself.

The cadaverous manager seemed to be looking him over with something more than curiosity.

"Get a good night's sleep?" The man's sallow face was blank. An unlit cigarette seemed glued in the right-hand corner of his nearly lipless mouth.

"Fine," Shep said.

He looked out over the parking lot toward the empty pool. It was too early in the year for swimming; but past a neon sign in the picture window fronting the office—reading backward, he made out FREE TV—he could see the man from room 19 sitting in a plastic lawn chair that seemed about to buckle under his weight.

"All new mattresses last month," the manager said, his cigarette bobbing with the words.

"Well, I slept well, thank you."

"That's Best Western for you. They really know how to look after the guest."

The same cab and the same driver that had brought Shep to the New South/Best Western pulled up in front. Shep got in just as the driver turned off a radio voice that was saying, ". . . cashing welfare checks made out to six different . . ."

"Sorry damn trash." The driver turned to ask, "Purity Cafe, right?" He sounded as if he were mixing concrete in his throat.

"Right."

The driver turned on to the three-lane highway. Cars sped past as he picked up speed. His eyes, reflected in the mirror, seemed to peer into the backseat.

"You really here to defend that Odum woman?"

"How'd you know that?"

"News spreads round here. I reckon you know the prosecutor's the brother of the guy she kilt."

"Tyree Neely. I talked to him yesterday."

The driver made a left turn. "Wha'd you think?"

Forewarned how news spread, Shep answered carefully, "I wouldn't take him lightly. Even if he weren't Ben Neely's brother."

"You got that right." The driver slowed for a stop sign.

"Well, I'll make out, I guess. Unless Neely knows how to fix a jury."

"Tyree wouldn't do that." The driver sounded offended. "Tyree's honest as the day is long. Him and me was in high school together."

"I was just joking," Shep said. "I didn't—"

"Wouldn't need to fix no jury, anyway. Not in Stonewall County."

He drove on into downtown. "See," he said in his concrete-mixer voice, "round here, ever'body'n his brother owes Tyree a little something."

This did not surprise Shep Riley.

"You take my license there . . ." The driver pointed a dirty-nailed finger at the dashboard and a plastic-covered image of a sagging moon face above bold letters: QUENTIN HODGES, HACK LICENSE

NO. 2. "I was to cross Tyree somehow, that could be pulled fore I could turn round."

"Even if you went to school together?"

"Oh, I got better sense'n to do something like that. Tyree wouldn't either, us being classmates'n all. Point is . . . he *could*."

Which is why, Shep thought, nobody crosses Tyree. Afraid of what he might do. Or could. Whether he would or not.

"They don't owe him, then they owed his daddy," the driver said. "Comes down pretty near to the same thing, don't it?"

"A family thing, huh?"

"Onliest trouble the Neelys ever had was when the old man got Tyree outten the draft that time."

"Vietnam?"

The driver's head nodded on his massive neck.

"Course it blowed over. Even me, two good buddies kilt in my outfit . . . if I could of got out of goin, I sure would've too."

The cab pulled up in front of the Purity Cafe. Waitsfield Avenue was empty except for a few people hurrying past the forlorn storefronts and a Mountain Dew delivery truck parked at the curb.

"Two bucks." The Beeline Cab had no meter. "Plus a quarter for the call."

Shep took a five from his wallet and handed it to the driver, who gave him back two ones, and clicked three quarters out of a changemaker at his belt. Shep waved away the quarters and got out of the cab. Bending to the window, he said, "I figured it'd be a tough jury, Mister Hodges, but thanks for the warning. I thought yours was the only cab in town."

"It is." Quentin Hodges clicked the quarters back into his changemaker. "Oh, you mean why I'm number two? Bill Creech use to have number one but when he kick the bucket . . . Bill had this cancer that just ate'im all up down in here . . ." Quentin Hodges rubbed his hand over his ample belly with a certain relish. "They never got round to changin my number."

He tipped an Atlanta Braves baseball cap and drove off. Shep hurried into the Purity and took Cady's corner booth. The rest of the place was busy with people who worked, Shep surmised, in other downtown establishments. Most were elderly and looked sad—probably hangers-on that some suburban mall had left behind.

"What kin I git you?" a waitress said.

She wore an imitation-lace tiara, dingily white atop a massive pile of ginger-colored hair pulled at the back of her head into a bun the size of a softball. She thrust a bony hip against his table and looked down at him indifferently, from eyes old with hardship.

Shep ordered a ham and Swiss sandwich and iced tea, stifling his impulse to talk to the waitress, learn her story. He ate in silence and more quickly than usual, telling himself he wanted to get away from the waitress's tired face. Only when she brought him his check and turned disinterestedly away did he admit to himself that he really was hurrying to see Easter Lilly Odum again.

Shep stared at his empty tea glass—as always in the South, the tea came already sweetened—loathing himself as well as the residue of sugar under the melting ice. He wondered if age was making him a dirty old man, if he had become the kind of mindless, hard-on woman chaser he despised. Like President Kennedy—as he had learned to his shock and disgust, long after the murder of a man who had been the idol of his college years.

The inescapable fact—Shep slapped down an overgenerous tip for the sad-eyed waitress and rose from Cady's booth—was that all the time he had been making love to Meg he had been thinking about Easter Lilly Odum. All night long, he had transposed the slim white body straining against his into the black flesh he could never have—was not *supposed* to covet, did not *want* to lust after. Even in his shuddering moments of release, when consciousness should have fled into ecstasy, he had fancied it was Easter Lilly into whom he was pouring his essence, from whom he was absorbing renewal.

What a betrayal! Of Meg, of Easter Lilly, most of all of himself. Like ol Massa prowling the slave quarters. Shep slammed the door of the Purity Cafe and strode down Waitsfield Avenue, telling himself earnestly that he had to put Easter Lilly out of his mind in every way except as the victim he was defending. He must not think of her in any more personal way. As a white man and as a lawyer, he had to control his impulses. He *had* to see her as a client, nothing else.

He cut across the courthouse square, paying no attention to the old men on the benches under the trees, and walked a block down a side street to the jail. He trotted up the steps, between the Mount Vernon columns, and into the jail office.

Jase Allman sat behind the desk, reading *Popular Mechanics*. "The lady's already been in," he said.

"Good. But I need to see Miss Odum, too."

"Seem to me like," Jase offered mild but unmistakable reproof, "y'all going to handle her case together, maybe you ought to talk to her together."

Shep took off his jacket, hung it on the back of a visitors chair, and loosened his tie.

"From now on, that's what we'll do."

This was easy for Shep to say because he had already sworn to himself that after today he would not see Easter Lilly alone. Jase sighed, got up, and turned a key in the heavy door leading to the cellblock.

"She ain't ate'er lunch."

He stood aside to let Shep enter the cellblock. As the door closed behind him, Shep could see Easter Lilly lying on her cot, apparently asleep and naked to the waist. He turned in panic to leave. But Easter Lilly sat up just then and he saw that the top of the blue jail dress was down around her hips but that a black bra partially concealed her high breasts. Easter Lilly saw him, too, but made no effort to cover herself further. For a moment they stared at each other through the bars of her cell. He could not take his eyes from her rich chocolate flesh, the ribboned catch that fastened the bra in front.

"Hot in here." Easter Lilly's voice was lazy and unconcerned. "Whitey's too cheap to put in a cooler."

He was glad he was not inside the cell because he feared he would have fumbled at the ribbon. *Like Ben Neely*. He felt nauseous. *As sick as Ben Neely*.

"Hey, man. How bout you call my mom, ask her to bring me some food fore I starve in here?"

She nodded at an untouched plate of what looked like creamed chipped beef on toast. "My brother in the Army call that stuff shit on a shingle. You in the Army, man?"

"Navy," he said. "That's what we called it, too."

"You must not ever seen a woman cooling herself."

The lazy voice, the indolent eyes, the way Easter Lilly slowly pulled the jail dress up, the heat in the cellblock . . .

"Way you're staring, I mean."

She knows he thought *she knows what I'm thinking.* He felt as he had when as a teenager, he had peeped through a knothole into the girls' dressing room at Henderson's Pond. Some girl pushed her finger through from the other side, and he'd barely avoided being stuck in the eye. Would have served him right.

Nobody then had known his shame. Now *she knows.* Shep shook his head and took a step forward, grasping the bars of Easter Lilly's cell.

"Let's get down to business." He stared determinedly just above her head. *Show her I'm not Ben Neely.* "You got anything to back up your story of what happened that night?"

Easter Lilly reached under her pillow, pulled out a piece of white cloth, and tossed it at him. He caught the cloth through the bars: a pair of panties. They were torn down one side, held together with a safety pin.

"What he did, trying to get what he wanted." *What you want too,* he could see her thinking. But she only said, "While he could still want it."

Finally lowering his gaze, Shep saw that Easter Lilly's feet were bare. That surprised him somehow. He saw that they were well shaped, with pink soles and long, elegant toes. He had never before really *noticed* a woman's feet. My God, he thought again, I'm in real trouble.

"You think we can prove Ben Neely did this?" He waved the panties. "Or that you were even wearing them when he . . . at the time of the attack?" There *had* been an attack, he was sure.

"You're the lawyer, man. But I don't reckon they'll think I go around ripping up my own britches."

"Time Tyree Neely gets through with'em, that's exactly what they might think."

"And time I get through tellin'em bout that brother of his, Tyree'll wish he never heard of Easter Lilly Odum."

Shep was trying to think how the torn panties could be used in evidence. Why hadn't the prosecutor taken custody of them?

"Neelys all think they walk on water." Easter Lilly put her bare feet on the cement floor. "But I get through telling what *I* know, that water'll look like mud."

With the distraction of her dark flesh now covered by the blue jail dress, Easter Lilly was still desirable, but less stunning. Shep could marvel at the shape of her face, the way her hair fell, the smooth skin, the dark, slender legs, even the arch of her foot. But she was no longer a sexual goddess luring him into unknown depths, from which he might not be able to return.

"We're still going to have to *prove* what you say, you know," he told her, and set about finding out if that would be possible, questioning her in detail about Ben Neely's death. Even with all his latent lawyer's skills gradually coming back, Shep was unable to extract from her anything more definite than the firm assertion—not real proof—that Ben Neely had ripped her panties while trying to rape her, and that while fighting him off she had stabbed him with his own knife.

"Called me a stinking bitch," she said. "I made sure it was the last thing he ever said. Swung that blade as hard as I could."

Shep believed her, the more so as in response to his questions she repeated her story without change. He wondered if . . . feared that . . . her visceral impact on him (he longed to stroke her lovely feet, take the strands of her hair between his fingers) would influence his judgment. Ultimately, though, he believed her implicitly. Her story had the ring of conviction. Above all, it matched his idea of the way things happened, particularly to black women at the hands of white men.

"I don't see how we can introduce the panties," he said. "Tyree'll just use'em to claim you're lying."

"You're the lawyer," Easter Lilly said. "But even Tyree can't make me say anything but the truth."

She did not know, he thought, what a tough lawyer could do to a woman who claimed to have been raped. Especially a black woman accusing a white man. Her willingness to face Tyree impressed him, but he knew truth was not in itself an adequate defense. Even truth had to be believed.

After a half hour, Jase Allman opened the cellblock door to announce that visiting time was over. Shep doubted that hard-and-fast visitors rules existed in the Stonewall County jail, but he didn't argue. His interrogation of Easter Lilly was by no means done—and he was developing serious doubts about how to proceed—but he was anxious to leave, anyway. Easter Lilly's presence, physical and personal, was squeezing breath from his lungs.

"Well," he said, "I have to go meet my partner."

On the cot, Easter Lilly leaned back on her elbows, her breasts pointing at him through the jailhouse dress. Again, he found himself unable to look away, and felt dread as well as desire. He had read of obsession in books, and possibly had seen it in other men, with other women. Was this obsession with Easter Lilly? Or something less phenomenal, more vulgar? He had imagined himself making love to her while actually entwined with Meg, hadn't he? God knows *that* was vulgar.

"Your partner," Easter Lilly said. "Got something going with her, man?"

Did she know that, too? But how could she? He shook his head weakly.

"You like your ladies better stacked up than she is, huh?"

Shep mustered what dignity he could. "I don't talk about my partner," he said. "And what I really like is a lady who can prove what she says."

Easter Lilly laughed—*at* him, he thought, as he turned to leave the cellblock, desperate to escape something he did not understand and could not control. He wanted to look at Easter Lilly again, at her lush body, and was afraid to. He wanted to slap the mocking smile off her face and he wanted to take her in his arms, and he hated himself for both impulses.

"White man," she called after him. "You get me turned loose, how'm I gonna pay you off?"

Feeling not unlike Lot's wife, he looked back. The mocking smile was still on Easter Lilly's face, above her insistent breasts. He called up his last reserve of dignity, feeling it threadbare and forlorn. "I'm not in this for money," he said.

Easter Lilly folded her arms and lay back on the cot. "I didn't think you were."

Then, as he hurried again toward the cellblock door, toward escape, she called out, "Don't forget to call my mom."

JASE

JASE ALLMAN HAD GONE OUT ON THE PORCH AND WAS LEANING against one of the Mount Vernon columns, trying to think what to do. Inside, he saw Shep Riley come back into the office from the cellblock, retrieve his jacket, and stand for a moment looking at the floor.

Jase wanted to warn Riley. The man seemed like a decent enough chap, pleasant-spoken, courteous. Jase valued good manners. On the other hand, it was none of his business.

He still had not made up his mind what to do when Riley came out on the porch and leaned against the other column.

"That's a lot of woman." Riley spoke as if to thin air.

Easter Lilly, Jase thought, had that effect on some men. Even some that would hardly even notice colored people. But he took Riley's remark as a sign. It more or less opened up the subject.

"Something I sort of wanted to say, Mister Riley."

The red-haired lawyer's face seemed to light up. "Listen," he said, "if you've got any reason whatever to think she could be telling the truth . . . ."

"About Benjy?"

Riley just looked at him without speaking. Privately, knowing Ben Neely the way he had, Jase figured it at maybe fifty-fifty that

Easter Lilly's story *was* somewhere near the truth. But he was not about to say that to *anybody,* not even Ida Sue. If Tyree Neely didn't believe it, Jase Allman was not fool enough to say he maybe did.

"That ain't what I had in mind," he said.

He was again overcome by doubt. Jase Allman was not going to risk his job or anything else, if he could help it. But he hated low-down gossip. He would feel like killing anybody that spread dirt on Ida Sue.

"You got to try Easter Lilly's case before a jury of what they call her peers. That right, Mister Riley?"

"How well I know it." Riley sounded dispirited.

"That means Stonewall County voters." Jase added cautiously, "It ain't gonna help you, is it, they don't like you person'ly?"

"Or if they're all beholden to the prosecutor."

The man was learning fast. Prob'ly how he got to be a big-shot lawyer in the first place.

"Which is how come you want to stay on the good side of anybody that ain't."

Riley stood away from the column. "What're you getting at, Mister Allman?"

"Jase. Ever'body calls me Jase." But he appreciated Riley calling him Mister. Real polite.

"Jase. What do you mean?"

Tyree had not come right out and said it himself, so Jase Allman had no intention of doing so. What Tyree *had* said that morning— just dropping by the jail to chat, not making anything special of it, in that easygoing but pointed way of his—was that if folks knew what was going on at the New South/Best Western they'd see the kind of immoral, depraved people that would defend Easter Lilly Odum.

Then the good-looking lady—Ms. McKinnon—had come in, saying she was working with Mr. Riley on Easter Lilly's case. When it came out she was staying at the New South, too, a looker like her, even a little past prime, Jase had not had to be a brain surgeon to figure out what Tyree was hinting at.

"They give you a nice room out there at the New South, Mister Riley?"

In finally making up his mind to speak, two things weighed heavily with Jase: his disdain for common gossip and his dislike for Carl

Hoover—Tyree's spy at the motel—who in Jase's opinion never had been worth the powder to blow him to hell. It took Tyree just to keep Carl out of jail.

"It's okay," Riley said. "A little skimpy on the towels."

He looked puzzled and Jase didn't blame him. He tried to make things a little clearer, without coming right out with the facts. He said, "Folks round here wouldn't want a distinguish vis'tor from up North to be in the wrong kind of a room."

He watched Riley working his way through this, lawyerlike, his face slowly closing into a frown. Jase had felt sure a smart lawyer could decipher the message, but just to make sure he added a clue: "I bet they give you one with a telephone, din't they?"

That, he vowed to himself, was as far as he was going to go. Any damn fool would know that motel-room phones went through a switchboard at the front desk. Jase heaved himself away from the Mount Vernon column and nodded casually at Riley.

"Better get back to my paperwork."

Which was true enough. He had not even got started good on *Popular Mechanics*.

EASTER LILLY

THEY TURNED OFF THE FLUORESCENTS IN THE CELLBLOCK AT 9 P.M.
Then a red bulb over the entrance door would cast a dim glow
over Easter Lilly's cell and she might be able to sleep, even in the
close jailhouse air. It was in that same bloody light from the red
bulb—the way she hazily remembered it—that she had fled in panic
from Ben Neely's sprawled body and the knife sticking out of his
no longer lusting heart.

She lay on the cot just as she had that other night, and just as
then, before trying to sleep, she spent a long time washing herself
at the lavatory. With the toilet, the lavatory offered the only sanitary amenities in the Stonewall County jail. Jase Allman had told
her the only good thing she knew about Tyree Neely: that the
prosecutor had refused to allow installation of a closed-circuit TV
surveillance system because jailers could use it to watch women
prisoners bathing or changing clothes.

"I wouldn't of done it, anyway," Jase had told her, sometime
before the night of Ben Neely. "But . . ."

He stopped abruptly; and even then Easter Lilly had known he
was about to say that Ben might have.

If men were in jail at the same time as women, they would be
put in cells across the corridor, and for that possibility, Tyree Neely

and his handpicked county commissioners, parsimonious as well as prudish, had provided a plastic curtain—like a divider in a hotel ballroom—that could be drawn along tracks in the floor and ceiling.

Easter Lilly had washed herself thoroughly, as she always did. If there was any one thing she despised, it was the mean white belief that black people smelled bad *because* they were black. Since it had first dawned on her that Whitey believed such lies, Easter Lilly always washed herself hard enough to peel the skin right off her bones. But getting rid of her skin was never in her mind. A black skin was the only kind she wanted. A white skin, in Easter Lilly's experience, was a sure sigh of hatefulness. Except for Mr. Timmons.

So she washed herself vigorously, as hard and as often as she could, not because she feared smelling bad but because she was determined never to give *them* the slightest reason to think maybe their nasty white notions were right. Lying on the hard cot, waiting for the fluorescent to go off and the red bulb to come on, she felt the cool of the wash water lingering on her skin. But Easter Lilly was not easy in her mind, even though the redheaded lawyer with Mr. Timmons's eyes *said* he believed her.

"You're going to walk," he'd promised.

It was the other lawyer that troubled Easter Lilly. The woman with the long legs and smoky voice, in the Peter Pan collar that made her look younger than Easter Lilly believed she was. The woman didn't like her, didn't trust her, most likely didn't believe her. Easter Lilly saw all that in her snooty white face. And she'd hardly even looked at the torn panties.

"They'll think you did this yourself."

Which was almost exactly what Tyree Neely had said, when she'd shown *him* what his shit-licking brother did. What the red-haired lawyer said a jury might believe.

"Can't help what they think," Easter Lilly had replied. "I'm telling you what happen."

She was used to women not liking her—even her mom, sort of, after Mr. Timmons; but her mom would stand by her because your mom had to. Her mom would bring meatloaf sandwiches and fried chicken and believe whatever Easter Lilly said. Sort of, anyway.

The Peter Pan collar might finally have to stand by her, too, since she was the Timmons-eyed lawyer's partner. But that first afternoon she'd tossed the panties back to Easter Lilly, looking skeptical and like not wanting to get her hands dirty. Then she asked, "When you were trying to fight him off, did he . . . I mean . . . how far did he go?"

Easter Lilly seized the opportunity to shock her mistrustful visitor right out of her sweet little collar. "Like to tore me wide open." She had enjoyed the way the face above the Peter Pan flinched and flushed. She wanted to see more: "Cock thicker'n your arm."

After a while, a squeak in her husky voice, Peter Pan managed to say, "Did you see a doctor?"

"A doctor?" Easter Lilly had been genuinely incredulous. "Po- 'leece crackers gonna call me a *doctor*?"

"So there's no proof of that, either?"

"That he rape me?"

"That he injured you."

"Only proof I got is I can't hardly sit down. I don't reckon you'd want me to show'em why. In court, I mean."

That was when the Peter Pan collar stood up to leave, not look- ing so young anymore, hard-eyed the way most women looked at Easter Lilly Odum. But it made more difference with one that was supposed to be on her side.

"*I'll* send a doctor, Miz Odum." Her voice again was low and smooth.

Nothing else but a barely civil good-bye. So what worried Easter Lilly, as she lay no longer feeling the cool of the wash water on her skin, was that the sweet-faced bitch in her little-girl collar might go straight to the red-haired lawyer and tell him she didn't believe a word she'd heard.

Cooter Rollins, the substitute jailer they'd brought in to replace Ben Neely on the night shift, opened the cellblock door and looked around its edge at Easter Lilly.

"Time for lighth out."

Cooter hadn't wanted to work the after-midnight shift and had swapped hours with Rob Moore. Easter Lilly was glad of it. Rob wasn't anywhere near as bad as Ben Neely, but Rob was all eyes all the time.

"So maybe I can get some sleep."

Cooter stood carefully behind the cellblock door, with nothing in his eyes like Mr. Timmons or the red-haired lawyer. Certainly not like Bigdick Neely. Cooter looked more like he maybe expected Easter Lilly to pull another knife.

"Well, lithen . . ." He sounded anxious but she knew he was just scared of her. "I don't make the rulth around here."

When they both had been at SCCH, the white boys had given Cooter his nickname. She had had no idea where it came from, and she had none now. Nobody called him anything but Cooter.

"You did . . ." Easter Lilly could not resist teasing him. "I bet you'd have me chained up like a crazy woman. Tough guy like you use to be in school."

"Naw." But Cooter clearly was pleased at the description. "I can handle prithners 'thout chainin'em up. Thpethly women."

He closed the cellblock door heavily. In a moment the fluorescents went out and the red light came on. In its dim glow, the near darkness, Easter Lilly stopped worrying about the Peter Pan collar. The redhead was the one that counted. As long as he believed her, she had a chance, and she had never expected any more than that— usually not that much.

Men were funny, she thought. Men would do almost anything for what hardly mattered to a woman, as long as she didn't get beat up for it. Except maybe the kind of woman who thought she had one of the crown jewels between her legs. Which, come to think of it, Peter Pan probably was that kind. Though all any woman really had down there was a key that if she knew how to use it could even unlock a cellblock door.

The last thing Easter Lilly remembered before she slept in the red glow was what the do-gooder lawyer said just before he left. *I'm not in this for money.* As if I couldn't tell, she thought, and drifted into a dream in which it was not Ben but Tyree Neely into whose heart she stuck the knife.

Tyree was trying to choke rather than rape her. She took the knife from Mr. Timmons's hand, and when the blade went in, she felt the same satisfaction she had felt actually doing it—that she had felt before, in a hundred dreams of settling the ancient score.

ALTON

TWO DAYS AFTER MEG'S DEPARTURE FOR WAITSFIELD, ALTON McKinnon had been able to put a crew to work tearing down a garage in the backyard of Arthur Bledsoe, the druggist. Bledsoe's wife wanted more room for her rock garden.

"Art can park his smelly old German car in the street," she told Alton. "That diesel exhaust killed my impatiens last summer."

Demolishing a garage was not much more than kid stuff but Alton was grateful for anything that kept his boys—not to mention himself—off welfare and his mind off Meg and Riley. But no matter with what fury he swung a sledge or yanked at a crowbar, he still in mind's eye saw them making love, probably in some sleazebag motel, sometimes in the backseat of a car, even standing up.

"Something eating you?" Bubba Shelton, a young carpenter who slicked his hair straight back, asked over their lunchtime bologna.

"Good people having to do a shitty job like this."

Actually, the dry taste of the sandwich Alton had made for himself that morning after getting the kids off to school angered him all over again. Meg should have been at home making his sandwiches.

"I don't mind with that Miz Bledsoe hanging around," Bubba said. "Worth an hour's pay to watch her swing that thing."

Unmarried Bubba had sex on his mind morning, noon, and night. Alton usually ignored his youthful enthusiasm. This time, in his bitterness sharing Bubba's lascivious fantasies—though not about Betty Bledsoe—Alton egged him on.

"Old Arthur," he said, "working his ass off mixing headache powders. And his wife shaking it at you."

As no doubt, *his* wife was shaking it for Shep Riley. Though slender Meg did not have as much to shake as Betty did.

Bubba's voice turned confidential. "Al . . . you think I could maybe get in there?"

When Alton got home after the second day on the garage job, the rotting old timbers and siding hauled away and nothing else to do but jackhammer the concrete floor, to his surprise Meg was waiting for him in the kitchen. Alton was glad he was wearing his sweat-stained overalls.

"You're working," she said.

"Just a little old piece of a job. I din't expect you back this soon."

"I *told* you I wouldn't be gone long."

He did not want to tell her that he had been worried about her and Riley—had even feared during one sleepless night that she wouldn't come back at all. Why would she, with a husband who hadn't brought home decent money in months? But he only said, "I figured you'd get interested in that case. After not working for so long and all."

"Oh, I did." Meg put her arms around the sweaty overalls, looking up into his face with an aggressiveness that almost embarrassed him. "But I was *more* interested in getting home."

Alton looked down into her eyes, wondering giddily—to *me*? He wanted to shout, strut, throw her over his shoulder. But he was not, he reminded himself sternly, that kind of an ape.

"To see the kids," he said.

"The kids, sure." Meg slid her hands down his overalls to his buttocks. Alton was taken aback but not too much to let her pull him close. He put his arms loosely around her. Meg made a saucy face up at him and whispered, "Are you packing a gun or just glad to see me?"

After dinner and the usual study hour for Kate and Hugh, Alton and Meg were finally able to get away to their bedroom. Even then, of course, they had to be careful. Hugh's room was separated from theirs only by a thin wall, and Alton thought him too young to find out what his mother and father occasionally did at night.

"So what if he does?" Meg kicked off her flat-heeled shoes. "Everybody finds out sooner or later. Like about Santa Claus."

"Well, it'd be one thing to *tell* him." In fact, Alton McKinnon dreaded the day when he would have to enlighten his son about the birds and the bees. "Something else again if he was to hear us doing it through the wall."

"We have *never* done it through the wall," Meg said. "But it sounds kind of kicky."

As Alton began to unbutton the Hawaiian shirt he'd put on for dinner, Meg, in panties and bra, unbuckled his belt. She zipped down his fly and pushed his slacks and shorts below his hips.

"Look at *that*," she said. "Maybe you *could* do it through the wall."

"He'll *hear* you, Meg." Alton actually was thinking how silly he must look with his britches falling down around his ankles.

"Shush, or he'll hear *you*. Unhook this thing for me."

Obediently, while trying to step out of his pants, he reached around her.

"Alton, you looney," Meg said. "This one opens in front."

After a while, when they were lying quietly in the dark, Meg's head on his shoulder, his arm around her slender body, no sound anywhere but an occasional car passing on the street, Alton thought gratefully, *Hugh couldn't possibly have heard.*

Even if once or twice, he'd thought maybe he'd actually have to put his hand over Meg's mouth. He could not remember her being like that since their honeymoon on St. Simons Island. Then, on the first two nights, he had been too sunburned to do anything. After that, Meg had shown him stuff he'd never even imagined a man and a woman could do. Or a nice girl would.

Which was okay until he began to wonder where she'd learned the kind of things that weren't in any of the sex manuals *he'd* ever read and certainly hadn't been mentioned by old Dr. Mudgett, whom Alton had insisted they consult before their wedding.

Maybe, he told himself after St. Simons, women just *knew* about lovemaking. Though that went against everything he'd been told growing up. He felt a certain pride that his ladylike, quiet, college-educated bride that nobody would ever accuse of looking or acting like a sexpot knew so much.

Over the years, however, Alton also had come to feel a sneaking shame that Meg could be so wanton in bed. Sometimes, like tonight, he worried that he yielded too easily. But he couldn't help feeling a little chesty that she'd come back to him from Riley. Riley could stick *that* up his kazoo.

"The trial won't start till summer," Meg said abruptly, her whispery voice startling in the darkness. "Maybe not till fall."

"You're not going back?" The idea had not occurred to him until she mentioned the trial.

"I don't know. But it *is* an interesting case. And I doubt if it would take more than a few days if I did go."

"Why would you?" But Alton had a sudden, sinking feeling that he knew.

MEG

SURELY NOT BECAUSE OF THAT REDHEADED SON OF A BITCH, MEG thought, damning herself as well as Shep Riley at the thought.

"Maybe to see if I can still be a good lawyer," she said to Alton.

Of all the things she did *not* intend, she told herself, going to bed again with Shep Riley was first and foremost. Of course, she had not intended to the last time, either. That knowledge only reinforced her determination.

"*I've* never doubted you're a good lawyer," Alton said.

She had learned all over again exactly what kind of a womanizing, unconscionable liar Shep Riley was. As he had proved again, running out on her in Waitsfield the way he had. Mortifying! And after he had caused the restraints and decencies of a civilized wife and mother to fall away from her like a whore's underwear.

Not a bad analogy.

"But I haven't done my specialty in years," she said. "Checking out a jury panel. Picking out jurors we'd have the best chance with."

"That's what you'd do if you went back? For Riley?"

"For the client," she said. "That's who a lawyer really works for. In this case, the defendant."

"But that's how you used to divide up the work?"

In the daytime, Meg thought bitterly—amazed and angered that in one night and against her resolute intentions Shep Riley had aroused in her all the lusts that must have been accumulating in her placid years with Alton McKinnon, lurking in her like intestinal parasites. And then to have him brush her off like that. The bastard.

"Riley tried the cases and you provided a sympathetic jury?"

Not entirely, she thought bitterly. He ran the show and I gave him what he wanted. Then and now.

"Something like that," she said, feeling deep shame. She'd only been pretending, maybe indulging in a little wishful thinking, when she'd blurted out that old Mae West wisecrack about packing a gun. Now she wished she hadn't; it had only embarrassed Alton.

It was not his fault that he was a dull thud in bed. His boondocks Gothic parents probably claimed they'd found him in the cabbage patch, so Alton's idea of being a man didn't have much to do with sex. A good provider was his idea of a good husband. And it was ridiculous to worry about Hugh listening at the wall, when children nowadays knew everything about making love and probably had done it themselves as soon as they could pull down a zipper. His or hers.

Meg had known all about Alton when she'd married him for the stability she'd never had and the family responsibility Shep Riley would have derided. It certainly wasn't for romance. Romance tapped on your motel-room door at night and left before breakfast. She'd known exactly what she was doing when she married Alton, a decent, honorable man who loved her in his own limited way. A better love than romance. And a better man than—

"And the defendant is this Easter Lilly Something?" Alton said. "The black woman charged with murder?"

Shep Riley.

In the quiet of the house, broken only by Alton's low voice— mustn't let Hugh hear—remembering Alton's clumsy grapplings of a few moments before, aware of Alton's merely dutiful interest, Meg suddenly longed for Shep Riley. Under whose lean straddled body she would writhe and moan into gorgeous oblivion. See the colored lights again, the bombs bursting in air.

In the shock of recognition, Meg heard herself stammering—as if she had been caught fingering herself in the bathroom—"Yes, but . . . she . . . she claims self-defense. She says he was raping her. I mean . . . he was when she stabbed him.''

I *hate* Shep, she told herself, and the memory of the way he'd dismissed her in Waitsfield kindled her anger all over again. She certainly did not want the son of a bitch for hearth or home or children or church on Sunday—in any way that she valued Alton McKinnon. With shame, however, and a thrill of recklessness, she confessed to herself what she did want: what Shep had reawakened in her in one night at the New South/Best Western.

"No wonder this case interests you," Alton murmured. "If you think you can prove the woman was raped."

Meg seized on his words, grateful for any respite. "That's not it. I don't believe a word of her story."

This was not precisely true. On balance, Meg doubted Easter Lilly's version of events. Still, neither as lawyer nor woman could she dismiss it entirely. Something bothered her. Something about the knife, maybe?

"Hardly a word, anyway."

On the long trip from Waitsfield, when she wasn't thinking furiously of Shep Riley's desertion, Meg had gone over in her mind every word, every shade of attitude on Easter Lilly Odum's face, as she exhibited the torn panties—triumphantly, Meg decided—and exulted in the details of her alleged injuries.

Trying to embarrass me, Meg thought. Not knowing I'd heard rape stories before. Uglier than hers.

"Then why"—Alton logical was more maddening than Alton occasionally irrational—"why would you even *think* of going back?"

Meg had asked herself that insistently, doggedly seeking a convincing answer. Why go back to Waitsfield to help defend a woman who might well be a liar and a murderer? When, anyway, she had little of Shep Riley's passionate feelings for victims? She hoped Alton would not think her next words as hollow as she knew them to be: "Because lawyers believe everybody deserves a defense."

"Even Hitler?" He sounded merely incredulous.

That lying Riley had thrown her aside like a used condom. And the next day, when she'd called his room he'd said—he'd actually said—in that calm and hateful voice, as if he expected her to believe him, "Can't stop by tonight, sweetheart. Too much to do."

And after her protestations, which she soon would have given much to be able to take back, he'd said, "I'm out of here tomorrow, Meg. You might as well go, too."

"Hitler wasn't an American," she said, marveling at her agility. She was lying like a whore, to conceal a whore's guilt. "But in this country, the Constitution says every accused person deserves a defense."

"Well, *I* wouldn't do it," Alton said. "If I didn't believe her story. I guess I'm just not as generous as you are."

Alton thought her generous. Alton loved her, even if he didn't know how to show it. She wanted to turn her face into the pillow and weep for him. Or for herself.

"I've been thinking things over," he said. "Maybe I was wrong to try to stop you from working."

When she had betrayed him, betrayed Kate and Hugh, betrayed everything a decent wife and mother ought to stand for. Betrayed them all. And dying to do it again, would help defend maybe a lying murderer so she could do it again. With a man I . . . ought to hate.

"I just got it in my head that you working would make me sort of . . . you know . . . less of a man."

She turned toward Alton, raised herself on an elbow, and leaned to kiss him. "You're a man," she whispered.

In your own good way.

Book Three

IDA SUE

TOOTIE BLYLOCK PUT HIS BREAKFAST CHECK ON THE FORMICA counter of the Downhome Dinette and laid a five-dollar bill on top of it. Ida Sue did not even have to look at the check. Tootie had breakfast at the Dinette every morning, same order every time— cup of coffee, refill, toasted white with sausage.

"Fixed like a sandwich," Tootie would say to Sharlene Landis, the counter girl. As if Sharlene didn't know. Sharlene sometimes put in Tootie's order as soon as she saw him coming.

"You expect to hear from the movie folks today?"

Tootie had asked that of Ida Sue, ever since her first day behind the register. Then, he looked her up and down with hot unwinking eyes and said, "Shape on you like Betty Grable."

"Like who?"

Ida Sue spoke sharply, though she could tell from the old goat's look that he thought he was complimenting her.

"You wasn't even born then," Tootie had said. "Use to be a hot number in the movies."

Conscious that it was her first day behind the register, Ida Sue believed she'd better lay down some rules with bug-eyed types like Tootie Blylock. Even if he was older than God. So she said, "I'll thank you not to be calling *me* no hot number."

Tootie was not offended. "Any of them movie folks ever tried to sign you up?"

Sometimes geezers were the worst, Ida Sue thought. With their leaky old eyes. "No," she said, "and if they had, my husband Jase would of give'em a fat lip."

She laid out $2.35 in change from Tootie's fiver.

"I know who your husband is." Tootie stared at Ida Sue's chest. "Me'n his daddy was in the war together."

The only war Ida Sue knew anything about was in Vietnam, and Tootie Blylock, eyes and all, was too old for that one by about a million years. But she quickly remembered that Jase's daddy had been a decorated hero in some war a long time ago. Jase thought the sun rose and set on his daddy, a tobacco farmer before he dropped dead of a heart attack during a Ronald Reagan rally.

"Jase's daddy like to wet'is pants first time he seen Betty Grable." Tootie Blylock picked up his change and carefully separated out the two quarters he would leave on the counter for Sharlene. "So'd I. In the movies at Fort Benning."

Ida Sue had a hard time picturing Jase's daddy getting antsy over a woman, even a movie star, considering he'd married Jase's dough-faced mother. "I'll tell Jase we talked about his daddy," she said, with respect, accompanied by her most ingratiating smile. But not about Betty Grable, she thought.

Every morning since that first one, after eating his sausage sandwich and bringing his check to the register, Tootie asked her if she'd heard yet from the movie folks.

"Still waiting," she said now, hating—as she always did—this morning ritual with a liver-spotted old codger.

"Don't know what they missin," Tootie said, eyeing Ida Sue's blouse. Then he turned to put the two quarters for Sharlene in front of the stool where she'd served him. Sharlene said Tootie like to broke his neck sometimes, trying to see down her front.

Ida Sue watched Tootie leave the Dinette and turn toward the Rite Aid Pharmacy, where Sharlene said he looked for dirty books in the paperback rack. She hoped Jase would never get that old, with hair growing out of his ears.

Tootie was hardly out the door when Mr. Johns hurried in and took a seat at the counter. The Dinette was always bustling with people, which was why Ida Sue liked working there.

I'm sort of a people person, she told Tyree Neely when he asked her why in the Sam Hill she had gone to work when Jase had a perfectly good county job. I just *love* finding out what makes people tick, Ida Sue said.

"And I get plenty of practice at the Dinette," she later told Jase. "Seem like sooner or later, ever'body shows up at the Dinette."

Located between Penney's and the Thom McAn shoe store, about midway of the main corridor in the biggest building of the Dixie Pride Mall, the Dinette was right in the middle of things. Rockpile Jewelry was just beyond Penney's. Then came a Sears mail-orders-only store.

Ida Sue worked the register on the seven-to-three shift. To her knowledge, someone was sitting at the Formica counter every minute of every one of those hours, if only to drink coffee and eat home-baked pie that actually was delivered by truck out of Capital City. Everybody that worked in the mall came to the Dinette on their break, and practically everybody that shopped in the mall stopped in for a bite or maybe a Diet Pepsi.

"A gold mine," Sharlene complained, "and Woody don't pay us pea-turkey."

Most breakfasters—like Tootie Blylock—had left, and the Dinette was quiet enough that Ida Sue could hear Mr. Johns ordering coffee from Sharlene. Sharlene was wearing the green blouse that Ida Sue thought made her face look kind of yellow. Ida Sue was always careful about her colors, constantly on view behind the register like she was. And never too tight a blouse or sweater like Sharlene, men getting antsy a woman gave them the least excuse.

Sheriff Tug Johnson heaved himself off a stool at the far end of the counter and lumbered along to the register like a truck with broken shocks. He put his check on the counter and Ida Sue was not surprised to see all that he had eaten—the strawberry Belgian waffle, two fried eggs, what the Dinette billed as country ham, grits, red-eye gravy, and coffee light with sugar.

"Gettin on toward summer, sweetie pie," the sheriff said as Ida Sue punched up his breakfast charge.

"Be here fore we know it," she replied with deliberate indifference. Ida Sue did not like Tug Johnson because it seemed to her unfair that such an unattractive bucket of slops should be Jase's boss. Tug was the biggest man Ida Sue had ever seen and the ugliest.

147

In Ida Sue's opinion, Jase ought to be sheriff, lean as he was and twice as good-looking. Besides, Tug Johnson always looked at her like she was some kind of a bimbo.

"Bathin suit time," Tug said. "What I like about summer, it's bathin suit time for you gals."

Which was a typical kind of common thing Tug Johnson liked to say. Ida Sue did not have a dirty mind like Sharlene and some other people she could name, but she did sometimes wonder how it would feel to have a repulsive elephant like the sheriff flop down on top of you at night. Which Mrs. Johnson must have to put up with at least ever so often, men being what they were.

"Reckon ol Jase'll be glad to get that trial over with next month," the sheriff said. "I sure will be. Get that black widda outten our hair."

She did not need to ask who he meant. It had been April, nearly three months ago, that Easter Lilly Odum had been taken back to the Stonewall County jail.

"Is it gonna be next month?"

"Next s'perior court term, sugar." Tug Johnson took a toothpick from the holder beside the register. His huge brass belt buckle clunked against the metal edge of the counter. "Judge Ottis P. Reeves presidin."

Ida Sue laid out his change on the rubber mat beside the register. "The same Reeves that use to be prosecutor right here in Stonewall County?"

"The same." The toothpick went up and down in Sheriff Johnson's mouth. He took a small stack of cards from his shirt pocket and put the cards on the counter. "Don't mind if I leave a few of these here, do you, sugar?"

Ida Sue picked up a card: SHERIFF TUG JOHNSON it read on the top line. Below that: Y'ALL KNOW ME.

"I don't mind," Ida Sue said, "but I better not speak for Mister Richardson."

She had no doubt that Woody Richardson, who owned both the Dinette and the Purity downtown, would sweep the sheriff's election cards off the counter. "Beggars'n politicians," he was fond of saying, "ain't shakin their cups in *my* rest'rants."

She didn't want to annoy Sheriff Johnson, however, him being Jase's boss—although if he called her sweetie or sugar one more time or kept looking at her with bedroom eyes, she might have to kick him in the shin. Or somewhere else.

"Much oblige," Tug Johnson said, and went ponderously out.

Dreading Woody Richardson's wrath, Ida Sue promptly picked up the SHERIFF TUG JOHNSON cards and put them under the counter, just as Fielding D. Johns placed his check and a dollar bill on the rubber mat. As usual, he said nothing. Mr. Johns was always in a hurry, never drank more than one cup of coffee despite the Dinette's "bottomless cup" policy of free refills, and never kidded around with Sharlene or Ida Sue, the way most of the Dinette's male customers and even some of the women did.

Ida Sue supposed that was because Mr. Johns was a Yankee. But at least he never called her sugar.

"Have a nice day." She smiled brightly, restraining herself from laughing. Every time she thought of his nickname, "Flushing" D. Johns, it about broke her up.

After he left, the Dinette was almost empty, for a change. Sharlene was carrying dirty cups and plates to the serving window between the kitchen and the counter by the time Porter McDowell finished his coffee and pineapple Danish and brought his check to the register. Ida Sue had been well aware of Porter's presence in the last banquette, but she pretended to be busier than she was, leafing through the paid checks impaled on a spike.

"Lookin good," Porter crooned when he reached the register. "Lookin re-e-el good today."

"You hush." Ida Sue did not look up from the checks.

Porter knocked softly on the counter.

"How bout a little service round here," he said.

Ida Sue took his check and money and made his change, still not looking up. She liked the way Porter was always comical, but she was wary of arousing Sharlene's attention.

"Good enough to eat."

Ida Sue looked up then and saw him waggling his eyebrows, which she suspected he plucked.

Porter was young, slender, swarthy, brown-eyed, constantly smiling. His dark hair was cut in what he hated to hear anybody call the Bill Clinton style, and he had a slight gap between his front teeth that he thought made him look like David Letterman. Even in the summer heat, Ida Sue noticed with admiration that he wore a tie and a U.S. flag stickpin with his short-sleeved button-down white shirt. A black plastic penholder and two ballpoints protruded from his breast pocket.

"You make it today?" Porter murmured.

Ida Sue cast a wary glance at Sharlene, who was too far away to notice anything going on at the cash register. Betts Holden, who usually waited on the banquettes, was out in the kitchen folding paper napkins.

"You're awful," Ida Sue whispered to Porter McDowell.

"No, I ain't. It's just I'm bout to croak."

"Hah!" Ida Sue tried to look skeptical and knowing, like Julia Roberts in *Pretty Woman*.

"Broken heart," Porter said, his face and voice mournful. "Fraid I ain't long for this world. With my broken heart."

Ida Sue knew it was a line, but she liked it, anyway. Porter was a hoot and not too grabby.

"Break's at eleven," she said. "Half hour as usual."

Porter swept up his change, waggled his eyebrows again, and his briefly mournful face broke into a grin that showed the Letterman gap in his pearl-white teeth. His freshly shaven jaw glistened and Ida Sue caught a whiff of Old Spice. Porter always smelled divine.

"Reckon I can hold out *that* long," he leaned forward to whisper, and added, "Behind the Kmart at leven."

Ida Sue stuck his check on the spike, not looking up to watch Porter stroll out of the Dinette. She was a little short of breath, but the risk was like not taking a dare in high school. You had to do whatever it was or be a nerd.

She felt deliciously wicked, not because anything was going to happen—she was sure Porter McDowell was all bark and no bite, which was part of his charm—but because Porter was *fun*. Forbidden at that. And the one thing you could never say about Jase Allman was that he was a barrel of laughs.

SHEP

SHEP RILEY'S LIFELONG BELIEF—INSTILLED IN HIM BY HIS FATHER, who had had it from *his* father—had been that fish started biting at dusk. He had therefore stayed on the river until he could hardly see where he was casting, although, as usual, there had been no more bites than in the day's earlier sunshine. So as Shep drove his elderly Subaru into the driveway of his house in Otter Creek, only two small brownies—just big enough for keepers—lay in the deep pocket of his fishing vest.

"As a fisherman," he said aloud, "you're a good lawyer."

Shep had learned to be reasonably proficient in casting a fly upstream into a ripple, then letting it float in a long arc downstream and across the current. But he would never, he feared, have the skill or the patience to "read" the water. And if a fisherman couldn't tell what trout were feeding on—mayflies, midges, whatever—he wouldn't know what kind of a fly to offer the crafty bastards. He would catch one only by luck.

Of which, Shep thought, he never had had much when fishing. He chuckled at the irony of having told Meg McKinnon he had given up sex for fly-fishing.

Reading the water oughtn't to be harder, the thought of Meg reminded him, than figuring out a jury panel—a puzzle she had been adept at solving. But reading water, catching trout, *was* more difficult; because Meg had had only other human beings to analyze, while a fisherman actually had to *think* like a trout—a cannier species than man, and equally deceptive.

He cut the engine of the Subaru and flicked off the headlights he had scarcely needed. It was nearly 9 P.M. but, in Vermont in July, twilight still lingered on roads Shep knew like the lines beginning to crease his face. He stepped out, still in his heavy wading boots, and stripped off his fishing vest. Leaning against a front fender, he shrugged the straps of the overall-like waders off his shoulders and began to pull the clinging rubber down along his legs and feet. He finally got the waders off and stood bare-legged and shivering in white tube socks, a pair of plaid undershorts, and a denim workshirt with rolled-up sleeves.

"Getting a little chilly," he said to the night.

Studying the skies with his city man's limited understanding of weather—little sharpened by his years in Vermont—Shep decided to gamble against rain and leave his two fly-rods with their delicate reels in the cartop ski rack. He was not worried about theft, not in Otter Creek.

He slung the wading boots over the backyard clothesline that sagged between two sugar maples, ambled in his feet to a faucet protruding from the stone underpinnings of his house, and turned a hose on the mud sliming the waders on the clothesline.

Abruptly, the phone inside the house began to ring. Shep's immediate instinct, a relic of his New York days, was to run to answer it. But in laid-back Vermont he had developed resistance to such knee jerks. Whoever wanted him could call back, and would, probably tomorrow.

Holding the hose with one hand as he played its spray on his waders, he opened his plaid shorts with the other and urinated on the ground—reflecting that this pleasure was the highest privilege of being male. Had to be some compensation.

The phone kept ringing. "I gave at the office," Shep said to the unknown caller.

He shut off the faucet and put himself back inside his shorts.

The phone rang on. "The check's in the mail!" he shouted.

After two more rings, the night silence descended, as abruptly as the phone had broken it.

"Good riddance," Shep said.

He went to the Subaru, retrieved his fishing vest from the hood, then entered the house by the back door he never hesitated to leave unlocked. The plate on which he had eaten his luncheon tuna-on-white gaped at him from a round table standing in the middle of the linoleum floor. A thin ring of water from melted ice in a sweating glass surrounded what had been his cranberry juice.

Shep put plate and glass in the sink, wiped the table with a paper towel, groped in the pocket of his fishing vest, and took out the two slippery little brownies. He had gutted and beheaded them on a rock at riverside, intending to fry them in cornmeal for his dinner. But as he rinsed his hands and gazed in distaste at the small fish on the sideboard, he shook his head sadly.

"They don't make one good one," he muttered.

The phone rang again. Somebody really wants to talk, Shep thought. Which suggested, even before he could amble to his make-shift desk in the dining room, the caller's identity. He picked up on the fourth ring and asked, "How'd you know I was home?"

"I was sitting on the front porch when your car went by," Penny Booker said. She ran the Olde Tyme Antique and Junque Shoppe in what had been the garage of her house on the outskirts of Otter Creek. "Whyn't you answer the first time I called?"

"I was in the backyard pissing."

Penny paused only infinitesimally. "What I like about you, Riley, you're so refined."

Shep sat down in his old swivel chair and put his feet on the dining table.

"I wasted nearly four hours this afternoon damn near breaking my neck on all the rocks in that ice-cold creek you Vermonters call a river. And I came home with nothing to show for it but a pair of minnows I could put in my watch pocket. I'm so goddam refined I might just throw'em out and go to bed hungry."

Penny clucked in feigned sympathy. "I could come over and fry'em up for you."

She had inherited the Junque Shoppe one foggy morning when a speeding truck from Bagel 'n Bread of Albany ran over her husband Gus. A little hung over, Gus had been jogging on the wrong side of the highway. Penny affected mourning dress for a year, but after the first month betrayed no other sign of grief.

"You can't come over," Shep said. "I haven't got my pants on."

He estimated that the Junque Shoppe's trade, without Gus's skin-flint management, would hardly support Penny, much less her son, a fifteen-year-old hulk incongruously called Gussie. Penny and Gussie lived quite well, however, owing to the damage award Shep had won by persuading a jury to believe that Gus had *not* been on the wrong side of the road on the fatal morning, and swearing in a radio weatherman to testify that there had been no fog, either.

"So much the better," Penny said. "You're expecting me."

Shep had fruitfully invested his one third of the take from Bagel 'n Bread; but he was not so grateful for the most remunerative case he had handled since coming to Vermont that he harbored the least desire to marry the widow, much less take on Gussie.

Having herself no more than necessary motherly concern for Gussie, Penny knew and even understood his attitude. She continued to pursue Shep, anyway—"just to help me remember the one thing a man's got that I miss," she confided to him.

"If I were expecting you," Shep said, "I'm so refined I'd have put on my pants."

"Then you must have been going around since last spring with your weenie hanging out. Cause it seems to me you haven't been expecting me for at least that long."

Shep *had* been avoiding Penny since his quick trip to Waitsfield. He felt lingering regret about what he was sure Meg thought was his callous behavior, and he had spent too much time mooning over Easter Lilly Odum to think much about any other woman. Not that he had been pondering Easter Lilly's defense; he had been day- and sometimes night-dreaming about the woman herself.

"I've been busy, Pen." At that very moment, he envisioned Easter Lilly's chocolate flesh.

"Balls," Penny said. "To my certain knowledge, you haven't been busy for years."

"Since I won your case, you mean?"

"Which a law school freshman could have done. In front of a Vermont jury against a million-dollar out-of-state business run by a guy with a foreign name."

"Do I detect a whiff of anti-Semitism here?"

"Anti-Rileyism. I called to tell you Gussie's spending the night at some friend's house. So I could, too."

Shep sighed. He was in no mood for Penny. His mind was on Easter Lilly—even though she was unreachable, a dozen states away to the south and a client at that, in jail accused of murder. But he did not want to offend Penny, who had been generous with her substantial charms. Besides, the day might come when those charms would be the best he could hope for.

On the other hand, he doubted Penny could be insulted deeply enough to alienate her for good. Otter Creek was too small and she was as hard up for affection as he was.

"I've got a headache," he said.

Penny snorted. "I told that to Gus so many times I even got to believing it. You want me to come over or not?"

"Ah, hell, Pen—I'm bushed. I really was out on the river for four hours, and I think I'll just fall in bed."

"You idiot," Penny said. "Sooner or later you're gonna want somebody warm and cuddly . . ."

"Which, my dear, you certainly are."

". . . and *I'll* be the one who won't answer the phone."

"You're probably right." Shep tried to sound humble. "I'll call you soon, anyway."

"Don't think I'm holding my breath." Penny hung up. An unmistakable bitterness had inflected her final words, but Shep was relieved, anyway. Out of it again, he thought ungraciously, never doubting that Penny would answer if he ever did call. And, as she'd suggested, sooner or later he would.

Later, probably. He fumbled through the litter on his dining-table desk and found a lined sheet of paper torn from a dime-store notebook. In pencil, in a round schoolgirl hand, Easter Lilly had written in evident haste:

Lawyer Man –
Come on back down here soon
and handle my case. That
old sot not worth killing.
Tyree's man besides. Counting
on you to get me off. No money
to pay but you know I'll make
it worth it to you.
                        Yours sincerely,
                            E. L.
P.S. The white
lady don't like me. So how
come we need her.

Shep pondered again why Easter Lilly had underlined the word
"*case*." He came to the same conclusion he always did: The word
had to be a substitute for something Easter only wanted to suggest.

"Handle *me*," Shep murmured. But in the stillness of the dining
room, he feared that was not only wishful thinking but too subtle
for Easter. But "get me off" surely spoke for itself and was not
subtle at all. Finally, by underlining *"sincerely,"* she'd obviously
meant she'd really make it "worth it" for him to defend her even
if she had no money.

He threw the note down in exasperation with himself. No better
than a teenager wondering why a girl who'd written him a note
had put the stamp on upside down. Easter's underlinings probably
meant no more than the enthusiasm of the hand that had set down
the hasty words. That he read double meanings into them didn't
mean those meanings were there. And even if they were, Easter
Lilly—sensing, as women did, a man's vulnerability—probably was
trying only to ensure his return to Waitsfield.

No Shep thought, yielding to instinct and desire. The scrawled,
hurried words on the lined notepaper were like a whisper sibilant
in his ear. Easter Lilly's suggestive mouth, the bold cast of her
head, her insolent legs and promising body—in his fervid memory,
all seemed to offer indescribable pleasures. He closed his eyes and
imagined Easter in his embrace, her eyes enraptured, her ebony face
transfigured. He had never wanted a woman so much. So . . . car-
nally.

He faced, then, the truth that—as the summer had worn on—had become undeniable. *Obsession.*

He said the word aloud, tasting it foreign and strange on his tongue. Could Shep Riley, the great liberal lawyer—the description rang mockingly in his head—be guilty of the ineluctable white male fantasy that black women, because they were black, were voraciously sexual? Worse—had he fallen into the parallel conviction that black women, like black males, were of a subordinate race fit for white dominance? Was he in his rage to possess Easter Lilly Odum assuming a white man's right to a black woman's exotic body?

"No way," he said to the note on his desk.

Even in the stillness of his barren house, even to himself, he sounded uncertain, insincere. *Obsession.* The real possibility of what he could not believe commanded him to cut this foul growth out of himself, as a surgeon would excise a tumor lest it prove malignant. He determined to do the same, no matter the pain, like a thorn from his heel or a knife in . . . but *that* simile only turned him back to craving Easter Lilly, as Ben Neely must have.

Desperately, as if to do the necessary surgery immediately, Shep pulled the telephone toward him, picked up the receiver, and from memory punched in a number. Far to the south, he heard a phone ringing, then the affected voice of Jase Allman's wife.

"Could I speak to Jase?"

"He's watching the Braves on WTSB."

"This is Shep Riley, Miz Allman. Calling on court business."

He could hear a sigh, followed by a long, deliberate silence.

"Jase don't love to be innerrupted watching the Braves."

"And I hate to do it. But I won't take more than a minute of his time."

More silence. Then, dimly, "Jase! That Yankee lawyer again!"

Not until he heard her call did he realize that he had no idea what he wanted to say to Jase Allman, or maybe wanted Jase to say to Easter Lilly, or what he *could* say that would put an end to his obsession. Whatever might do that could only be said to himself.

"What can I do for you, Counselor?" Braves or no Braves, Jase spoke as politely as always.

"Sorry to get you up from the set." Shep groped for something suitably impressive to say. "Who's winning?"

"The Cards. You wanted something?"

Shep seized the first remotely plausible idea that came to him. "They set a trial date yet for my client?"

"Next term. In August. Startin the fifth, I b'leeve."

"Fifth of August. In Waitsfield, I suppose."

"Right here," Jase said. "Your case'll come first, bein the most important we got."

"Well . . . thanks, Jase. I just wanted to know."

"You'll get official notice, I b'leeve." Jase's tone suggested there had been little need to call him away from the Braves.

"Oh, sure, sure." Trying to sound casual, Shep asked, "How's Easter Lilly doing?"

"Fit's a fiddle. Twice as sassy."

"Feeding her anything decent?"

"Just jail chow. But that boyfriend brings her stuff."

"Boyfriend?" Astounded, Shep took his feet off the dining room table. "I didn't know she had one."

"The black doctor. Fred Something."

"He comes to see her?"

"Worthington. Fred Worthington."

"How often?"

"Ev'ry other day or so. Sort of polite in person, but Tyree says he's a troublemaker, too."

"I didn't meet him." Of course he'd be a troublemaker, Shep thought. Easter wouldn't give any other kind the time of day.

"I expect you will at the trial."

"If he's her boyfriend, I guess so." Maybe gives him more than the time of day, Shep thought. Or did, before Ben Neely. A woman like that.

"Braves got the bases full, Counselor. Was there anything else you wanted?"

"No, no, you get on back to the game, Jase, and many thanks."

Shep hung up and sat still in the old swivel chair, staring at the lighted doorway into the kitchen, something constricting and burning in his chest. A boyfriend. A black doctor. Bringing her stuff to eat.

"God *damn* it!"

His shout bounced back from the dining room walls. Aghast at the echo of his own words, alarmed by the jealous anger flaming in him—*jealous! by what right?*—Shep stood up, kicked the chair away, seized the note, and balled it up in his hand. He stalked through the kitchen, threw the note in the trash basket, and hurried down the back steps into the starlit quiet of the Vermont night.

Beyond his yard and the old twin maples, beyond the wading boots swinging from the clothesline and the Subaru parked nearby, he could hear from the foot of his lot the loud whisper of Otter Creek sweeping over its rocky bed, rushing mindless to the river.

Shep bent, groped, felt the cold metal of the faucet in his hand. A spurt of water erupted from the hose that suddenly whipped like a snake at his feet.

"You hard-on son of a bitch," Shep snarled at himself, grabbing the hose by its nozzle.

He leaned forward and thrust the nozzle against the back of his head. The jetting water, cold as the fast-flowing creek, beat forcefully against his skull, streamed from his hair, slopped between his shoulder blades, soaked his shirt, and spattered around him in a chill white mist. But it did not clear his brain of angry visions or soothe the fear it could not reach.

TUG

"I SEEN THIS GREAT BUMPER STICKER YESTERDAY," TUG JOHNSON said to Tyree Neely. "Who you reckon thinks them things up?"

Tyree did not take his eyes off the goddam bird book he was always scribbling in, but Tug plunged on. He had spent a long time figuring his approach, and he was not one to change plans in the middle of a stream.

"On this old Impala. Cruising along out near Cognac."

Tyree scribbled some more, but finally said, "I bet you never saw a tufted titmouse."

"I bet I never did, either." The sheriff laughed, suddenly, nervously, and took a chance. "Less you mean Easter Lilly."

Tyree stopped writing and looked up, frowning. "Don't get your point, Tug."

"*Tit* mouse." The sheriff cupped his spadelike hands in front of his chest. "Sort of fits Easter, that name. Titmouse."

Not bothering to reply, Tyree returned to his bird book.

"Cept Easter ain't no mouse." The sheriff knew he had lost his gamble. Tyree Neely seldom liked any kind of sex talk. But Tug resolved not to be put off by any of Tyree's birdshit.

"This bumper sticker. It said: CLINTON AND GORE—GONE IN FOUR. Ain't that a howl?"

Not smiling, still not looking up, Tyree said, "We should be so lucky."

"Them two softheads. Gone in four is right."

Tyree looked up then, still not smiling. "Oldest rule of politics, Tug. You can't beat a horse with no horse. You tell me who's our horse, I'll tell you it's a howl or not."

Tug Johnson did not personally know anyone in Stonewall County who planned to vote Democrat. But Tyree not only knew more about politics than anybody in the county; he did not like to be disputed on the subject any more than he liked to talk about tail.

"Anyway . . ." Tug doggedly tried to stick to his plan. "That bumper sticker wan't the only thing funny bout that Impala."

They were in Tyree's office in the courthouse, where Tug Johnson always felt a little out of place, as if he had blundered into a ladies' room—a possibility that terrified him even to think of.

"That made me take notice, I mean."

The sheriff had his own office on the ground floor, with a long counter separating his desk from the taxpayers who dropped in during the day. Two women on the county payroll waited on such visitors and sometimes a deputy hung around the office waiting to make himself useful. Tug felt more comfortable there, in his own digs.

"What was that?" Tyree said.

Tug liked to sit at his own desk, playing with the computer terminal he had almost learned how to use, his sausage fingers punching awkwardly at the keyboard. Or maybe studying wanted posters. Paying no attention to the people that came in to be waited on by the women at the counter. A busy man, the sheriff of Stonewall County. In his own office, in charge of things.

"See . . ." Tug shifted cautiously in a chair too frail for his mass. "I could tell by the license plate . . ."

In Tyree Neely's smaller, quieter quarters, Tug always felt like an intruder on the goddam birds. Or the important deals he supposed Tyree to make over the two telephones on his desk—the regular county prosecutor's black touch-tone, the red Princess on a private line, to which the sheriff did not have the number, or know anyone who did.

"It was the Impala Porter McDowell drives."

Those phones and the fucking bird book Tyree always had his nose in made Tug feel like the hired hand that, down deep, he knew he was. Though he had to admit that Tyree Neely was too much the gent to rub it in who was boss.

"Who?" Tyree said.

Tug noticed Tyree's impatience. He often noticed more than Tyree thought he did. Like the way Tyree had been annoyed by the titmouse thing. But the sheriff had come to Tyree's office because he believed it his duty to let the prosecutor know what was going on. Tug Johnson prided himself on doing his duty. Despite Tyree's indifference up to now, Tug knew he eventually would get Tyree's attention, say something more important than Tyree's bird book.

He'll see, Tug thought, and said, "Smart-ass kid brings in new movies ever week. To Video Variety out at the mall." Not every law officer would have recognized that car, Tug knew, congratulating himself on his alertness.

Tyree nodded, but kept working on the goddam bird book. "The one we stopped from bringing in X-rated?"

"That's the one." Got Tyree's attention now, Tug thought. Tyree hated smut. "Drives down here ever week in that Impala."

"Still trying to push dirty movies."

"Not that I know of. Billy Wright at the Variety, he says he wouldn't carry'em anyway, not in a family bidness. Ever seen one of them things, Ty?"

Tyree threw down his ballpoint pen, sharply enough to startle Tug Johnson, and stared at the sheriff.

"Of course not. But I know what X-rated means, and I won't have it in Stonewall County."

"Like you told'im that time you wouldn't," Tug said. "I don't reckon Porter's likely to forget what you told'im that time."

Porter McDowell had later tried to bribe Tug Johnson with a couple of X-rateds for his private viewing. Didn't get him anywhere, of course—not with Tyree hating porno. But the sheriff had watched both films one night after Mrs. Johnson had gone to bed.

What shocked him most was the size of the dongs on the men. Wilson Gifford, the blocking back for the old Waitsfield High state champs, had been hung so long the guys had called'im "Rodney" when no girls were around. But even Gifford, now a mortician in Newport News, wasn't in the same class with the guys in those X-rateds.

"So get to the point," Tyree said.

Tug cleared his throat again, stretching it out.

"They was a woman with Porter. Comin up behind the Impala, I could make out the back of her head." He gestured with his hands around his head. "Had this long hair." The little twat out at the Dinette that had practic'ly spit'n his eye.

Tyree made a so-what face and Tug hurried on. "In the middle of the front seat. Sittin right up against ol Porter real cozy." Bare-faced little bitch could of at least waited till he was out of sight before she dumped his cards.

"I never heard sitting close was against the law," Tyree said. "Long as they're not on the wrong side of the road."

"I din't say it was." Tug felt faintly aggrieved. "Somethin bout that long hair . . . made me curious." He did not tell Tyree he had recognized the hair right away. "So I swung out'n passed'em. They wasn't speedin or nothin and, like you say, scroochin up ain't a violation. So I went on by, nonch'lant, mindin my own bidness."

"But you managed to get a look at this woman," Tyree said. "Didn't sprain your neck or anything, did you?"

Tug resented this sarcasm. Sullenly, he unloaded the import of his news sooner than he had planned. "Was Ida Sue Allman."

Tyree blinked.

Encouraged, Tug Johnson poured it on. "Jase's wife."

"I know who the hell Ida Sue is."

Tyree stood up abruptly, turned his back, and gazed out his office window, down the dusty, empty length of Waitsfield Avenue. Past his slender form, Tug could see a wrecker truck from Eddie's Exxon moving aimlessly along the street. He felt triumphant. Teach that snotty little trick a lesson, he thought. Many times as I tried to be nice to her.

"Law officer's got to know how to follow folks thout bein spotted. So I kind of loaf along back to the mall, keepin ahead of'em. With the Impala in the mirror, y'know? They never made out it was me."

"You sure it was Ida Sue?"

The hint of doubt in Tyree's voice caused Tug hastily to produce his clincher. "Porter drove round behind the Kmart. So I park at the corner. Sure-nuff, maybe thirty seconds later, here come Ida Sue trottin toward the Dinette. Was her, all right."

"Well, damn it all," Tyree said. "She must not have the brains God gave a brass billy goat."

Brains, Tug thought, was not what a man would joyride with Ida Sue for.

"I just hate like the very devil to be a tattletale," he told Tyree, "but I thought you needed to know. After what's already been goin on at the jail."

Tyree turned and spoke sharply. "What's going on at the jail?"

Tug was surprised. He folded his large hands over his championship belt buckle, covering it, taking strength from its solid feel.

"I just meant"—he had no idea what had got Tyree's pecker up—"Ben gettin cut."

"That's all you meant?"

"Just we don't need no more trouble down at the jail."

Tyree stared at him and demanded, "What's Ida Sue got to do with the jail?"

"She's Jase's *wife*. Jase *works* there." Tug could not see what further explanation was needed.

The office door opened and Daisy Thorpe came in with a sheaf of papers in her hand. She saw Tyree standing by the window and seemed to catch the tension in the room. "Oh . . . I should've knocked. But I thought . . ."

"No, no." Tyree sat down and waved her to his desk. "Let's see what you've got for me."

Tug watched Daisy cross the room on her slender legs. She wore a mannish-looking suit with a tight blue jacket that did nothing to hide the goodies under it. A better-looking woman than Ida Sue Allman, the sheriff thought. He had the sinking feeling that Tyree had welcomed her interruption.

"Just the afternoon mail," Daisy said.

Tyree'd quit fussin with his damn birds, Tug thought, studying her hips and bottom, he got better stuff right here'n'is office.

"Okay," Tyree said. "Give me and Tug just a minute more."

She left the office. Sensing that he was about to be dismissed, wondering why, Tug heaved himself out of his chair.

"I were you," Tyree said, "I wouldn't say anything about this to anybody else."

Tug was insulted that Tyree would think he might blab. "I ain't goin to. But if Jase Allman's wife keeps carryin on with Porter McDowell . . . whole county's bound to hear bout it fore long."

Tyree nodded unhappily. "You leave that to me."

"And after that nigger cut Ben, it'll look—"

"I *said* leave it to me, Sheriff. Just leave it to me."

Tug walked out of the room, hearing his feet thud heavily on Tyree's fancy-pants carpet, feeling the way he used to feel in school when some teacher picked on him. He had not expected Tyree to get mad, and he had no idea what caused his anger. Tug had thought he'd maybe have a kind of chuckle with Tyree over Jase's wife carryin on with the dirty-movie man. Then they'd decide together what to do about it. Kind of like partners. He could not figure why things hadn't worked out that way.

In the outer office, Daisy Thorpe was standing in front of a filing cabinet, her back turned to him.

"So long, Daisy," Tug called, eyeing the rounded bottom smooth under Daisy's short skirt. But he went quickly on out into the corridor. Tug didn't mess around even with women in his own office, though Connie Shelton once had made come-on eyes over the fax machine. These days a man just *looked* at a woman, she'd haul his ass into court. Besides, Tug assumed Daisy Thorpe was Tyree's woman, so doubly off limits.

"See you around," Daisy called. Tug could tell from her voice that it was an afterthought.

He lumbered toward the elevator, thinking of Jase Allman in bed with his little cheat of a wife, of Tyree seeing Daisy Thorpe's breast-works ever time he looked up from his friggin birds.

While he, the sheriff of Stonewall County, star guard on the only championship football team Waitsfield would ever have, went home at night to a titless old bag that snored like a ten-horse outboard.

CADY

J. PRESTON CADIEUX WAS BADLY IN NEED OF A SILVER BULLET. HE had lunched unwisely on the hickory-smoked barbecue special at the Purity Cafe, washing it down with iced tea and topping off with sweet potato pie. He had allowed himself no stimulants before or after, however, owing to his rigorous self-discipline and to his belief that he ought to be cold stone sober when he interviewed a client. The last time he had gone to see the snotty bitch, she had apparently detected something on his breath and called him ''an old rumdum'' to his face. Which he definitely was not, Cady told himself, even if he did like a few beers every now and then.

''Yesterday afternoon was the last drop I touched,'' he had replied, truly aggrieved.

''Better chew you some Dentyne gum, anyway,'' Easter Lilly said.

A week later, in the hot and airless cellblock of the Stonewall County jail, the barbecue special a greasy softball in his stomach, the luncheon remnants of Easter Lilly's corned beef hash glazed on a tin plate by her cot, Cady devoutly wished he had lined his innards with an ice-cold Coors. Cool down the barbecue special, and the hell with her darkie nose.

''What you got to understand''—he stood in the corridor clutching the bars of her cell, trying not to see the corned beef—"they can't be two lawyers tellin a jury diff'rent stories bout the same homicide. Know what I'm sayin?"

"Yeah. You want me to plead guilty."

"Well, goddammit . . . you *are* guilty. You say so yourself."

"Of sticking him. Not of murder."

Easter Lilly was lying on her cot, her hands behind her head, sweat on her forehead and damp in half-moons under her arms. Her hair lay in a dark fan around her head. The blue jailhouse dress fell over her knees and was tucked neatly under her slender thighs. The top buttons of the dress were open.

Niggerish, Cady thought, showing so much. But he was a widower and too old any longer to mess around with women, or even want to.

"Killin a man with a knife *is* murder," he said.

"Not if he's trying to rape you."

"Which you can't prove and nobody's likely to believe, anyway." In Cady's experience, women who yelled rape usually had been asking for it. Like this one with her dress half open. "So I say throw yourself on the mercy of the court. That way—"

"What mercy is that?" Easter Lilly asked.

Cady ignored the question. "You might get off with no more'n a few years. Maybe eight for Murder Two."

"Don' b'leeve 'at shit!" A man's voice rang from behind the plastic curtain pulled along the middle of the corridor.

"This state," Cady pushed on, anxious to make his point. "They don't—"

"Spit'n'is eye, babe!" The indignant voice from behind the curtain dropped abruptly into a mutter. "Whoever you are."

"Shut your mouth back there!" Cady had had enough, and let his courtroom voice ring through the cellblock. "Fore I charge you innerfeerin an off'cer of the court."

Mollified by his own threat, he turned back to Easter Lilly and lowered his voice. "I say this state don't treat women like ord'nary criminals; they—"

"Treat'em like dirt," Easter Lilly said. "Black women, anyway."

Cady shook his head strenuously. As the lunch special in his belly seemed to move in synch, he wished he hadn't.

"You got civil rights now, Easter. The law——"

"I wouldn't mind you call me Miz Odum."

"Oh, Christ!" shouted the man behind the curtain.

"The law"—Cady tried to speak majestically—"is color-blind."

"Uh-huh," Easter Lilly said. "All white."

"I'd-a reelize it uz that killer bitch over there," the hidden voice called. "I'd-a kept my mouth shut."

Cady was encouraged to renew his argument. "Now you just listen to me, Eas . . . uh . . . woman . . ."

"I'm listening. You just ain't saying anything worth hearing."

"Best advice you ever had! An I been practicin law since fore you were born!"

Easter Lilly's smile, Cady thought, was mocking. That annoyed him, coming from a colored, but Cady had to admit that she was a good-looking piece, damn her jigaboo eyes. Like those high-yaller gals use to come to town in the Silas Green from New Orleans tent show. All leg and chest. He could still remember wond'rin what it'd be like with one of those Silas Green gals.

"Trouble is . . ." Primly keeping her knees together under the denim skirt, Easter Lilly sat up on the cot.

Which, come to think of it, was prob'ly why a whippersnapper like the damnfool Neely boy got'is dingus up over this'un. Wond'rin what it'd be like in there.

"Trouble is, this other lawyer thinks I got a case."

Cady tried to snort. The effort made his stomach heave. "Self-defense against rape? No Stonewall County jury'd believe that kind-a crap for a minute!"

"Hell, no!" called the unseen man.

"But you just said . . ." Easter Lilly looked at the ceiling as if trying to remember what Cady had just said. "You said the law was color-blind."

"I'm talkin bout the *evidence* now."

She stood up swiftly, easily, the smile gone from a hardened face, and took a step toward him. Soft and silent. Catlike, Cady thought. He shrank back but kept hold of the bars.

"Only evidence," she said, "is a dead cracker that come back here'n the middle of the night tryin to get what I got. And nobody can prove he didn't."

"Tyree Neely can."

Easter Lilly made a spitting sound, again like that of a cat, and moved closer to the bars. If Cady hadn't felt it would be weak tactics, he would have retreated to the middle of the corridor and put his back to the curtain that separated the men's and women's cells. But you couldn't let'em see you back off. He forced himself to hold still, even though he suddenly thought he could smell her.

"And you better not make"—Cady's voice cracked on the prosecutor's name—"Tyree mad."

"Don' make *that* sumbitch mad!" echoed the man behind the curtain.

Easter Lilly came closer to Cady, the smile he thought mocking again touching her dark lips. They parted just enough to show teeth even and white as grains of hominy but sharp as a cat's. She took hold of the bars with red-nailed hands, just outside of Cady's, and looked straight into Cady's eyes.

Something in their glands, Cady thought. Makes'em smell.

"Tyree's got no evidence, either," she whispered.

"Goldurn draft-dodger," the hidden man whined.

What right did a colored bitch have to look into a white man's eyes? Cady shifted his gaze to avoid the insult. It fell on the remains of the corned beef hash and an image flashed nauseously in his mind—a haunch of skinned squirrel.

Nigger food.

Cady's stomach clinched. In sudden fury he spat words at her: "You stink!"

Easter Lilly's eyes flashed, her lips pulled swiftly back from her feline teeth, and her hands darted through the bars, stabbing at Cady's throat. Their long nails, incongruously painted, looked to him like bloody blades. He leaped back against the mid-corridor curtain, another image, of something he had not even seen but could easily imagine, lurid in his brain—the knife sticking out of Ben Neely's heart. Cady edged along the curtain toward the door into the jail office. He had no thought of tactics now—only of getting away from Easter Lilly, from those stabbing blades.

"Don't come back!" she yelled. "Shitface bastard!"

Cady hastened into the jail office and slammed the metal door. Jase Allman had all the office windows open. An electric fan barely stirred the air. Cady wiped his brow with a sodden handkerchief, the barbecue roiling his stomach. He was sure that black cat of a woman would have killed him if she could. His relief at his escape mingled nauseously with fear and pork.

Even so, he thought longingly of an ice-cold Coors and the cooling idea comforted him. Jase looked up from a magazine.

"Something wrong, Cady?"

Cady sat down on a hard chair, his knees weak. "I think I just got fired." He was shocked at his own words. Fired by a blackbird murderess.

"That Riley takin over the case?"

"Yankee son of a bitch butted in where he wasn't ask."

"I don't doubt you done your best," Jase said.

Cady nodded unhappily. He was not so sure.

"You wouldn't have a cold beer round here, would you, Jase?"

"Not in a county building. I got a couple Doctor Peppers in a cooler, though."

Cady's barbecue lunch shuddered.

"She thinks she's gonna walk," he said. "That prick put it'n'er head Ben tried to rape her."

"Nothin but her word for that."

Suddenly, Cady was not sure of that, either. It seemed to him that he could not be as sure of anything as he had been before eating that damn pork. Before things got out of hand in the cellblock.

"Not like Ben Neely to go for a black girl," Jase said.

Which was Tyree's line, too. But the fearful sight of those red-tipped blades coming through the bars was fading into Cady's memory of Easter Lilly long and lean on the cot with her top buttons open and those legs that could squeeze a man to death. . . .

Tyree be damned. Fact was, you couldn't hardly blame Ben Neely all alone with a piece like that, if he . . . "Tween you'n me and the gatepost, Jase," Cady was shocked to hear himself saying, "I wouldn' be surprise if that's what happen that night."

Jase put down his magazine.

Horrified at his own words, Cady added hurriedly, "Not that anybody could ever prove it."

A strange, ruminative look darkened the jailer's eyes. "Matter of fact," Jase said, "Ben Neely was hornier'n a mountain goat."

Cady jumped up, his legs barely functioning, his heart cold with foreboding. He headed for the door and the Purity Cafe.

"Couldn't talk about anything but women." Jase's voice followed Cady to the door.

Cady didn't pause. Things were *really* going to hell now, he thought. All out of control. He needed a beer as badly as he ever had. As he reached the door, he said with desperate urgency, "Neither of us better remember what the other'n just said!"

His momentum carried him out on the porch and between the Mount Vernon columns. Tyree Neely in an ice cream suit was walking toward the jail. Like a biblical apparition, it seemed to Cady.

Like retribution. Spotless as a lamb and coming for me.

He turned and leaned back through the doorway.

"Jase!" he whispered fiercely. "I didn't even *say* what you might've thought you heard me say!"

TYREE

BY THE TIME TYREE NEELY REACHED THE JAILHOUSE STEPS, J. PRESton Cadieux was coming down again. Tyree glanced at the gold Movado on his wrist and saw that it was well past Cady's accustomed arrival hour at the Purity Cafe. He tried to sound jovial, though he was dreading confrontation with Jase Allman.

"Seeing you here makes me nervous, Cady. You and that client of yours cooking up some surprise?"

Cady was sweating profusely. Missing the beer, Tyree thought. Then, more generously, he remembered it was midsummer and the sun was flaming down from a malevolent southern sky, bouncing off the concrete sidewalk in soupy waves. Must be like Shadrach's furnace back in the cellblock, where Cady undoubtedly had been visiting Easter Lilly Odum.

"Surprise?" Cady looked blank.

"To spring on me at the trial."

"Hah! She can take'er trial and shove it, for all I care."

Tyree was startled. He knew Easter Lilly Odum was hard to get along with, and Cady had been over the hill ten years ago. Still . . .

"Don't much care for her myself," Tyree said. "But then I'm not her attorney."

"I ain't, either. Just been fired. Listen, I got to meet another client down at the Purity."

Named Coors, Tyree thought. Then, with a sinking feeling, he focused on Cady's news. "Fired? What for?"

"She's goin with that Yankee know-it-all. I reely got to meet this guy at the Purity, I—"

Tyree seized Cady's arm, fury swelling like an inflating balloon in his head. "She's decided to plead rape?"

"I *told*'er that was a loser. I said that big mouth Riley don't know what he's talkin bout."

"Not if the son of a bitch aims to prove my brother tried to rape that . . . that . . ." Even in his anger, Tyree was careful not to use a racial epithet, and finished lamely, "That woman."

"I *told*'er all that."

The full implications of Cady's words hit Tyree Neely then. No more Cady to plead Easter Lilly guilty. No weak defense. Shep Riley instead. Looking for headlines. Dragging the Neely name into the mud. John Bell's favorite accused of a felony no white man should ever have to face: raping a colored girl.

"So she fired me." Cady pulled his arm free. "I can't be late. Got to make tracks."

Tyree's anger faded as he watched the old man shamble hurriedly toward the Purity Cafe. Pathetic old boozer. But a good lawyer in his prime. A loyal friend. Whose father had served six terms in the state senate, of course with John Bell Neely's help on Election Day.

In recent years, Tyree had tried to look after Cady, as John Bell would have wanted—throw some business his way, overlook his problems. Now Tyree couldn't help feeling a little let down. Surely the old sot could have played along with Easter Lilly at least long enough to keep her from firing him off her case.

Tyree went on up the jail steps and strode between the Mount Vernon columns into the office. It was not noticeably cooler than the sidewalk had been, though a big floor fan was whirling and rattling in the middle of the room. Jase Allman sat behind the desk, reading *Sports Illustrated*. When Tyree came in, Jase—not hurrying—closed the magazine and put it in a drawer.

Tyree, almost himself again, was further soothed by this expectable performance. Nothing wrong with a man reading on the job on a slow day—the usual kind at the Stonewall County jail. Jase Allman was too much of a straight arrow to act as if he'd been caught goofing off. Which didn't make Tyree's task any easier, but at least conformed to the way things should go.

"Here to see Easter Lilly?" Jase took out the cellblock key ring and swung it around his forefinger. The keys clinked and rang like a New Year's noisemaker.

"Not right now."

Tyree wiped his forehead with his ironed linen handkerchief. Even at the height of summer, he believed his position required him to dress properly, in linen or poplin, seersucker in a pinch, though that wrinkled too easily for his taste. Today, with his white linen suit he was wearing a starched blue button-down shirt and a red-and-blue rep tie knotted neatly at his neck. His oxblood tasseled Weejuns were brightly shined by one of the colored hangers-on at the courthouse.

"Cady was just in," Jase said. "Had some kind of a row with'er."

Tyree ignored Jase's remark and proceeded as he'd planned. "Jase . . ." He mopped his forehead again, to add credibility to his statement, and said, "We got to break down and put in an air conditioner for you boys."

"Be right nice to have." The key ring jangling from his finger, Jase pointed toward the cellblock door. "But they need it worse back there."

Just like Jase to worry about drunks and loafers doing county time. Plus one lying black whore.

"Voters'd never stand for it," Tyree said.

He immediately regretted thinking of Easter Lilly as a whore, even in his private thoughts. Unfair. Whatever else, Easter Lilly had never put out for money. No evidence of that. The Timmons fool had been getting it free, until the town finally called his number.

"Reckon not." Jase's face appeared mournful at the thought of the voters.

Tyree realized then that his planning had gone no further than the air-conditioner opening. And that old fool Cady walking away from the case had diverted his thoughts from Jase and the thing he had come to do.

"But I be dog if I see how anybody can sleep in that oven back there." Jase returned the cellblock key ring to the drawer.

It would have been a lot easier, Tyree thought, if Jase were a blowhard like Tug Johnson. Instead of a decent fellow.

"Speshly," Jase went on, "with Kenny Rice in for D and D again. Kenny back there with a female, we got to run the partition down the middle. Closes off what circulation they is."

Tyree took off his linen jacket, sat down in a straight chair by the desk, and folded the jacket carefully over his lap.

"I was you, Jase, I wouldn't lose much sleep over Easter Lilly Odum sweating a little."

"Oh, I ain't losin sleep over *her*. Even less bout Kenny. I had a ten-dollar bill for ever night Kenny's slept it off back there, I'd be rich as Rockefeller."

"Trouble is . . . ." Tyree was not really thinking about the heat in the cellblock, or in the office for that matter. He was wondering how to get around to the point of his visit. "Kenny never does anything we could send him up to Arbor Hill. Fistfight in the pool hall, is about all Kenny's good for."

"I wouldn't want to see Kenny do no state time, anyway," Jase said. "Kenny's all right sober, and he wouldn't last a week, all them Arbor Hill thugs with homemade shivs looking for punks."

There he goes again, Tyree thought. Worrying about the likes of Kenny Rice that never drew a sober breath since he got home from Vietnam.

"Listen, Jase . . . ." Tyree ran the handkerchief over the back of his neck. Might's well get it over with, he thought. "I know the county don't pay you a whole lot."

Jase looked interested. "I sure-God could use a raise, Chief. Ida Sue don't love livin in a mobile home."

"Can't say I'd care for it myself."

"So I'm savin to buy a reg'lar house in town." Then, as if remembering to whom he paid his rent, Jase added, "Not that they's a whole lot wrong with Green Oaks."

Tyree appreciated Jase's delicacy but bored in, anyway. "I hear Ida Sue's working out at the mall."

"Not cause we *need* the money. Comes in kind of handy, though."

"I bet it does." Tyree seized what he thought was likely to be as good an opening as he'd get. "You folks getting on all right otherwise?"

"Can't complain." Jase looked a little puzzled. "It's just . . . you know women. Grass is always greener somewheres else."

Tyree was not sure he did know women, or if he wanted to. He thought he knew enough *about* them. "Never satisfied with what they got?"

It came out as a question, though he'd tried to make it sound confident, knowing. Ida Sue Allman, he thought irritably, must be off her cotton-picking rocker. Running around with a porn salesman when she already had a good man with a county job.

Which was one of the reasons Tyree Neely aimed to stay single— the way they'd cheat on a man. He wouldn't trust Daisy Thorpe, for instance, in a nunnery. And not just because of her history, either. Twisting it around the office like she did.

As if he'd read Tyree's mind, Jase Allman said, "Not reely like that with Ida Sue. I never buy that house in town, I doubt she'd fuss at me too much."

How could a man live with one and not know her better than that? Tyree wondered. Whatever else, Jase obviously was a fathead about Ida Sue. "One thing about this jail job, Jase. I reckon you get home in good time every night."

"Reg'lar as the sun goes down."

"Ida Sue, too?"

Jase tensed, and leaned forward, his hands clasping together on the desk. "You wasn't who you are, Chief, I might have to take that amiss."

At that instant, Tyree Neely decided to go no further. No matter how he tiptoed around the facts, he saw, he would only make Jase Allman mad. Ida Sue obviously had Jase pussy-whipped—a phrase Tyree hated, as he hated any off-color reference to the female body or the reproductive act. He would not even have *thought* it except that there was just no getting around the fact—which he hated worse than the word or the idea. Great God! That an empty-head of a girl could have a good man like Jase Allman—honest as the day is long, reliable as the rising sun—eating out of her cheating hand. Like a spavined old horse munching a rotten apple. Loving it, to boot.

Ida Sue, Tyree thought bitterly, could work the Dinette cash register in her birthday suit, like Lady Godiva on the horse, and Jase would knock down anybody that gawked. There was just no getting around it. Women had what men wanted—most men, anyway—and knew how to make the fools pay for what they got.

Well, it was not going to happen to Tyree Neely. He was not even going to risk Jase Allman's wrath, challenging the way of the world. Tyree held up his hands, palms out. "If that was out of line, I apologize, Jase. Most sincerely."

"I know you didn't mean nuthin, Chief."

"Of course not. I just worry bout Ida Sue in that cramped-up mobile home."

"No need." Jase wiped the thought out of the hothouse air with a dismissing gesture of his hand, as if whipping away cigar smoke. "Green Oaks is okeydoke, Chief. Better than some folks're doin."

Clearly, Tyree thought, he would have to find some other way to get Porter McDowell out of Jase's hair. Since, clearly, Jase would refuse to admit that McDowell or anyone else was *in* his hair. Much less that saintly Ida Sue could be doing the two-time on him.

"Next time the commissioners meet, maybe I could—"

Later, Tyree wasn't at all sure what he was going to suggest he might do, for at that moment Dr. Fred Worthington came barging into the jail office in a suit as white as Tyree's. In the doctor's case, the suit made him look blacker than a spade flush, even with a couple of food stains down the front of the jacket. Or maybe, Tyree thought, they were emergency room smears from Stonewall General, where Worthington sometimes worked on coloreds bad off from knife or gunshot wounds.

"Come to see Easter."

"Yo." Jase took the cellblock key ring out of the desk drawer. "Who else? She just had some kind of go-round with Cady. Might need some coolin off."

Worthington took the key ring. Grinning, he held up a basket with a napkin draped over the top. "Got a pistol and a file in here. You want to check it out?"

"Last time it was just fried chicken. But bein's the boss is sittin here watchin, I better take a look."

Worthington held out the basket; Jase flipped off the napkin, looked inside, laid the napkin back, and said to Tyree, "You reckon she can saw thew the bars with spareribs?"

Tyree was unhappy with Worthington's white suit and with the clear suggestion that county food was not good enough even for a knife-wielding black killer. Nor did he care for the obviously easy relationship between a rabble-rouser like Fred Worthington and a white man on the county payroll. That he'd put there. Tyree had no intention, however, of making a fuss on either score. He avoided confrontations when he could, and he knew better than to provide the least ammunition to a man like Worthington. Or his mistress. Which Tyree had no doubt Easter Lilly was, the doctor getting it for free like crazy little Timmons. At least Worthington and Easter were the same race.

"She's not going anywhere, Jase," Tyree said. "Not this time. I think she even may have learned her lesson."

Fred Worthington stared at Tyree—insolently, Tyree thought.

"Was your brother got the lesson," Worthington said. "Just didn't live to learn it."

Tyree controlled himself against renewed fury, not just at the suggestion that Benjy had deserved what he got, but that a black man dared to speak so brazenly to the Stonewall County prosecutor. Which is the kind of thing we get, Tyree thought, we give these monkeys equality. But he only said mildly, "We'll see about *that* at the trial."

Carrying the basket and the key ring, looking neither at Jase nor Tyree, Worthington strode to the cellblock door. Tyree knew he ought to say nothing further, ignore the white suit and the insolence. Let the score be settled in superior court before twelve good men and true, as well as reliable Judge Ottis P. Reeves. But the way the black man walked, the flaunted suit, the defiant body language, the flourish with which Worthington inserted the key in the door, said plainly and openly to Tyree Neely:

Up yours, white man.

Four words too many, even if unspoken. Tyree could not stop himself from speaking and managed only to maintain a conversational tone, as if he and Jase still were discussing an air conditioner for the cellblock. He hoped that made his words the more insulting: "Too bad there's no place around here for conjugal visits."

FRED

"THAT CRACKER BASTARD."

Fred Worthington stood outside Easter Lilly Odum's cell, and spoke through the bars.

"Which one?"

"Neely. The prosecutor."

"He's pissed," Easter Lilly said. "He thinks that family of his hung the moon. Even little brother Ben with his zipper down."

Fred shook his head ruefully. "And you had to pick out Ben Neely to stick a knife in."

"What *really* pissed Tyree," Easter Lilly said, "I aim to say little brother tried to rape me. What's in the basket?"

Fred held it closer to the bars. Easter Lilly reached through and removed the napkin.

"That don't give him the right," Fred said. "He just now as good as said you and me . . . you know. Were gettin it on."

Easter Lilly laughed. "Don't he wish. Then he could say I'm a roundheels, don't have to be raped. Fred, honey, I don't much love spareribs."

Easter Lilly, Fred had learned, always spoke her mind. Whether about an unfair tax rate or sanitary conditions in Cognac or any number of white stupidities. He was long used to this trait, generally admired it, but recognized it also as Easter's gravest weakness. Like there were times it would be better to keep her big mouth shut. Or even say something nice. Like now, about the food he'd brought.

"Best they could do at Good Jelly's."

If he'd gone to the Purity Cafe or the Dinette or some other white place, he thought, instead of to the best café in Cognac—in fact, the only café—she'd have been lucky to get stale biscuits and cold greens.

"Ribs too greasy," Easter Lilly said. "Even like Good Jelly fixes'em. But if that's all there is." She took a rack of ribs, wrapped it in the napkin, and laid it on her cot.

"That ain't all there is." Fred took a pair of scissors from his jacket pocket. "They just looked in the basket. I could of had a hand grenade in my pocket. But these're not for you to cut anybody with."

"My hair." Easter Lilly smiled at him. "How'd you know I wanted to trim it."

Fred looked pained. "You don't even remember you told me the last time I was here? I thought I could give you a hand."

"Surgeon's hands. Just what I need."

She picked up a three-legged stool, took a thin piece of cloth from above the washbasin, and put the stool down near the bars. Spreading the jailhouse towel over her shoulders, she sat down with her back to Fred.

"Just a little off the ends," she said. "And try to keep it straight all the way around."

Obediently, reaching past the bars, Fred began to trim Easter Lilly's hair. Locks of it fell limply from the scissors and lay blackly on the towel about her shoulders.

"You know what?" Fred touched the nape of Easter Lilly's neck and let his fingers linger there.

"What?"

"I wish, too."

"Wish what?"

He knew she knew. They had discussed it often enough, got close a time or two, but he had always struck out. Once, driving home from a commissioners' meeting at which they'd jointly made a fuss about Cognac not being connected to the new sewage plant being run by Fielding D. Johns, who was paid from taxpayers' funds, he'd talked her into going late at night to his place. When they got there, she'd yacked away about how sweet Mr. Timmons had treated her—never mind what the rest of the world might think. Only she knew the truth.

Which had made Fred Worthington so mad—Timmons's mere name infuriated him—that he'd driven her to her mother's house without once trying to feel her up.

"We were gettin it on like Neely thinks."

Easter Lilly looked at him archly. She did it well, he thought. Easter Lilly knew the tricks.

"Right here in jail?"

"Wherever. Whenever."

She leaned forward to touch the mattress on her cot.

"Thin as a dime-store blanket. You wouldn't like it."

"I wouldn't give a shit," Fred Worthington said. "Even if there wasn't no mattress."

Nor had she, he thought, when she was doing it with Timmons.

"You'd be on top," Easter Lilly said. "But I'd have the springs sticking in my back. Woman's always got the springs sticking in her back."

"Goddammit, Easter, I'm serious." He hated himself for *being* serious.

Easter Lilly stood up, turned to the bars, and looked up into his eyes. She did that well, too. He tried not to let himself be fooled.

"Ah, baby," she said. "No good wishing for what can't be."

"You'll be out of here someday. You sayin it can't be then, either?"

Easter Lilly laughed. But she could not, Fred thought in unwelcome triumph, keep the strain out of the sound.

"We won't hardly be gettin it on when I'm six feet under, will we? Damp down there."

"I thought that new lawyer said . . ."

"He did. But Tyree gonna pick the jury. And like you just said, Tyree's *pissed*."

Fred Worthington wanted to turn and leave, taking the scissors and the spurned ribs with him. Show her she didn't really . . . but she held her face up to the bars and instead of walking out, Fred kissed her soft wet lips. Helplessly, telling himself not to, he tried to run his tongue between them. She pulled away.

"Baby," she whispered, "you got to understand I don't feel much like that kind of stuff. Not locked up in a cage."

Fred stepped back. "You never felt much like that kind of stuff *before* you were in this cage."

She held her hands through the bars. Almost reluctantly, he let her grip his free hand.

"I just told old rumdum Cady to get lost, baby. I'm goin with the new lawyer and maybe . . . don't make any bets . . . maybe I'll be out of here someday."

Fred Worthington believed, but did not say, that her freedom, if it came, would change nothing between them. He knew in his gut that his love—he didn't like to call it that, even in his head, as if to do so were an admission of defeat—was hopeless as justice. But he knew nothing to do except to pursue both. Deny the inevitability of defeat. Keep on.

"Maybe you will," he said. "With the new lawyer."

"Yeah. That old sot Cady couldn't . . ."

"Not just that. The new lawyer's gonna tell the truth of what happened."

Easter Lilly put her face up to the bars, as if to be kissed again.

"Won't he?" Fred asked, instead of kissing her.

"Ah, Fred, baby . . ." She turned her back again and sat on the little stool. "Just finish my hair."

DAISY

TIME TO ACT, DAISY THORPE HAD DECIDED. SHE WOULD MAKE HIM an offer he couldn't refuse. Like in *The Godfather*.

So when Tyree Neely entered the office, neat in his summer poplin and blue oxford cloth, gold hummingbirds emblazoned on his dark tie, tasseled Weejuns gleaming on his small feet, Daisy waited only a minute or two before taking the mail in to him.

He did not look up from thumbing through the briefcase that stood open on the floor but said, "Thanks, Daisy," into its maw.

On the corner of his desk, she fluffed the morning flowers she had brought in the customary vase, until Tyree stopped rifling the briefcase and picked up a letter. It was an invitation, Daisy knew, to speak to the Rotary Club in nearby Whitesboro on Labor Day. He studied the letter as if it were the Declaration of Independence, obviously expecting Daisy to go away.

Like a good little girl, she thought rebelliously. Instead, "I've got this idea," she said.

Tyree finished reading the Rotary Club letter before looking up. She could tell that he did not even notice the lace kerchief with which she had modestly masked her V-neckline. Daisy had learned early that her boss noticed the absence of modesty more than its presence.

"An idea?"

He imagines it's about clothes, Daisy thought. Or hairdos. As if a pretty woman never thinks about anything else.

"The Community Concert in Capital City."

Tyree looked down at the next letter, a bread-and-butter note from O. K. Dixon, a land developer, thanking Tyree for having persuaded the county commissioners to pave a stretch of road running past one of O. K.'s remoter properties.

Instructed, Daisy thought, would have been a more precise word, and O.K. would not learn until later how he would be called upon to respond.

Staring at the note, Tyree said, "What about the Community Concert?"

"They've got this opera company Saturday night. Doing *La Bohème*."

"Out in the sticks," Tyree said, "touring opera companies always do *Bohème*. May be the only opera they know."

Daisy was embarrassed to hear him pronounce it *Bo-aim* when she had said *Bo-heem*. Sensitive also to a note of impatience in his voice, she hastened to the point. "Knowing how you love opera, I ordered two tickets."

Capital City was only about two hours away by car, but since *La Bohème—Bo-aim, Bo-aim—*wouldn't start until 8 P.M., they'd be unable to get back to Waitsfield at any decent hour. Daisy had not actually made reservations at the Walter B. George Hotel in Capital City, knowing that that would be going too far. Tyree would want to do that much for himself. She had no doubt of what then would happen at the Walter B. George. After dinner, wine, opera, and the little black dress she had reserved for a romantic occasion.

"Two?"

Tyree laid aside O. K. Dixon's letter, picked up the next piece of mail, and appeared to study it.

That could hardly be, since it was only an offer from AT&T to provide some wizard new service that, as far as Daisy could see, no one needed. Surely he couldn't be interested in *that*.

Daisy said, "I haven't been to the opera for *ages*."

In fact, Daisy Thorpe never had been to an opera. But Jukebox Saturday Night on Waitsfield Avenue kept, along with its rock, pop, rap, and soul inventory, a small shelf of classical tapes for the odd egghead who might wander in. Rather surreptitiously, Daisy had searched out and bought a dusty cassette of *La Bohème* starring Luciano Pavarotti, whom she had heard on *Three Tenors*. She intended to study the cover notes, if not actually listen to the music, in case Tyree wanted to talk about the opera on the drive to Capital City. *Bo-aim*, she said to herself again. *Bo-aim*.

Tyree dropped the AT&T brochure and asked, "Who's going with you?"

For a smart lawyer, Daisy thought, he could be thicker than blackstrap molasses. "It's my birthday present. To *you*."

Tyree stared up at Daisy, his lips parted to show his even, carefully flossed white teeth. Actually, his fifty-first birthday was almost a week off, but congratulatory cards already had come in from numerous county employees and were displayed on the credenza between his desk and the window overlooking Waitsfield Avenue.

"Oh," Tyree said. "Are you asking *me* to go with you?"

Daisy was too exasperated to be careful. "I'm not *asking* . . . it's my birthday present."

"But I can't go, Daisy. Not this weekend."

That was the one response Daisy had not expected. She knew Tyree's calendar was clear of appointments until the next Tuesday, and that he was always caught up on his paperwork. His desk, except for the flowers and the morning mail, was clear as a classroom blackboard in summer.

Shouldn't mix work and play, he might have said sternly and typically. Too far to drive, he could have whined. Eventually, however, Daisy was sure that whatever protest Tyree might make would come down to: What will people think if you and I spend a night together in Capital City?

Tyree was as sensitive to his reputation as a virgin keeping her knees closed, so Daisy—knowing his anxieties—had been nerving herself for days to tell him that most of Waitsfield probably would never know. And that some large part of its population probably already thought that they slept together. At least, she hoped they did, since that might eventually bring pressure on him to legitimate their relationship.

"You can't go?"

You turkey she said to herself, feeling unexpectedly, fatally, thwarted.

"Wish you'd told me sooner, Daisy." Tyree's eyes blinked—a sure sign, she had learned, that he was lying.

"But I checked your calendar." She was, she feared, in one of her father's less hateful phrases, shouting down a rain barrel.

"Just last night"—Tyree blinked rapidly—"I called Lawrenceville and made reservations at the Clio."

He often stayed at the Clio Motel in Lawrenceville, a town near the coast where on his bird-watching jaunts he might see beach, wetlands, or water birds. But his blinking eyes were a dead giveaway; it was as if he sought to prevent truth from being read in them. Besides, always before, he had asked Daisy to call the Clio *for* him. She had the number memorized and knew to ask for 16, a no-smoking room without a water bed.

"You're going *birding*?" Her sarcasm was heavy. Instead of for a night with me? she wanted him to understand.

"If I'd only known," Tyree said. "I'd have—"

"You can't change your plans?" In fact, you won't, she thought.

"Cady's going with me. Can't back out now."

His eyelids fluttered. Daisy Thorpe doubted that J. Preston Cadieux had ever looked at a bird in his life, nor had been sober enough at any time in his old age to tell a sparrow from a hawk. But Cady, of course, would confirm Tyree's hasty excuse if Daisy asked him point-blank. Which she was too proud to do, anyway.

"Somebody'll want that extra ticket, Daisy. I doubt you'll have any trouble getting rid of it."

"Of course not." Daisy controlled her anger with difficulty, and spoke as coldly as she could, letting disdain drip from her words. "I'll find *someone* to take me."

Leaving her icy words hanging in the air, pointed as a stalagmite, she stalked out of Tyree's office, her back and neck stiff, her hips rigid, trying to convey her anger in body language—but also hoping Tyree would think she meant some *man*.

Only he wouldn't, because, he probably knew as well as she did that there was not another unmarried male in Stonewall County with whom Daisy Thorpe would condescend or could bear to converse all the way to Capital City and back. Only a bunch of clods in white socks.

Much less sit through *La Bo-aim* with. Or shack up—she considered the word deliberately, feeling freed by the crudity—at the

Walter B. George. Nor would Daisy Thorpe be fool enough to seek out a *married* man, even if there was one remotely qualified and willing to risk scandal and divorce.

But *God,* Daisy thought, flouncing down in her desk chair, anger turning to a sort of assertive arrogance, I'd make it worth some son of a bitch's while. And I do mean *in bed.*

As she would have made it worth Tyree Neely's, she thought meanly, if in his nerdish, hyperrespectable way—why was he so tough about most things and so mealymouthed about love?—he had not chosen a bunch of god damned birds in the bush over one in the hand.

Over *me*! The idiot!

Despite these angry reflections, Daisy Thorpe well knew that idiocy was not one of Tyree Neely's problems. And for the first time in her intimate study of the man, her subtle but determined pursuit, Daisy wondered seriously if Tyree was homosexual.

The thought had of course occurred to her before—when he ignored, as he usually did, her frequent hints about coming to dinner at the old Thorpe house on Aiken Street, or looked askance, if at all, when she had displayed even discreet cleavage or a silkily clad thigh. She had always dismissed these suspicions. After all, that Tyree studiously showed no personal or sexual interest in his secretary was not sufficient ground for such a repulsive idea. Nor was his bachelor status, which she had been so confident that eventually she would alter. Tyree, she had concluded when unworthy doubts arose, just was not "ready"—for what, she had never quite decided. Nor had she been able to calculate when he *would* be ready for whatever it was.

This time, the ugly question would not go away. Tyree could not have missed the clear implication that she was ready to spend the night with him at the Walter B. George Hotel. *Screwing,* she thought with relish, his brains out. Somehow, despite his rebuff, the idea excited her still. But instead of grabbing the offer, and maybe *her,* right there in the office, as a real man certainly would have done (on Tyree's desk, like Kevin Costner did to Susan Sarandon on that kitchen table in *Bull Durham*), Tyree had concocted on the spot and in something as near panic as she ever had seen in an ordinarily levelheaded person, an excuse far flimsier than her own about his birthday and his supposed love for opera.

"Chickened out," she said aloud. No doubt about it.

Daisy was familiar with rejection, having practiced it happily and effectively on Waitsfield's ham-handed Lotharios, as over the years they groped clumsily at her blouse buttons and under her skirt, blubbering wet attempted kisses near her averted lips. Daisy had gloried in her lovers'-lane reputation for untouchability, since no would-be swain's fumbling eagerness could blot out for one moment her single-minded intent to become Mrs. Tyree Neely—an ambition she knew would be destroyed if the mere rumor of erotic goings-on should reach Tyree's sensitive ears.

Now, however, *he* had turned against *her* the piercing arrow of rejection. For the first time since that ancient misfortune with Vic Buckley had stained the clean sheet of her life, Daisy had risked too much, laid herself too open. She had incautiously disclosed (less openly, thank god, than that other foolish time) the restless but usually controlled urges gnawing like mice at her roots.

Fuming and humiliated, her carefully devised plan in tatters, the secret scheming of years suddenly vulnerable, Daisy confronted the stark fact that he hadn't been able to face even one night of abandon at the Walter B. George Hotel. With the best-looking, sexiest woman in Stonewall County. What did that tell her about the possibility of someday taking him to the altar?

The blunt truth was that Tyree had slapped her in the face— almost literally—with her two tickets to *La Bo-aim*. If only there *were,* she thought viciously, some other man she could take to Capital City, screw his brains out, she'd do it in a flash. Would she ever! Rejection had made her feel bold and wanton.

But there was no such man and, anyway, that would be like cutting off her nose to spite her face. She only needed to get even— not to do something foolish that would kill any remaining chance of bringing insufferable Tyree to heel. If she still wanted him, if he wasn't really a . . .

Tyree came out of the inner office just then and strode past her desk without speaking. At the door, apparently thinking better of his chilly demeanor, he turned and smiled at her, and said as he had a hundred times, "Going to the snack bar, Daisy. Can I bring you anything?"

Daisy tried to shift the ice from her heart to her eyes and her voice. She thought of Old Stoneface, her father, and of his slimy so-called friend the doctor making her squeeze his wormlike white old shriveled-up thing. Ancient hatreds boiled in her, and she was on the verge of telling Tyree to commit the same anatomical gymnastic that had been her parting suggestion to Vic Buckley, one long-ago night in Orlando, Florida.

Instead, with a mighty effort at self-control, she said slowly and pointedly, "I don't believe there's a thing you can do for me."

You bird-brained fag she wanted to add.

She could not yet be sure about Tyree, however. Maybe he was only neuter or bisexual—she had heard of such creatures. In which case, there still was a chance. But even as she bit back her words, she knew she would get even. Daisy Thorpe rejected men, not the other way around. Self-respect demanded that she settle the score with Tyree Neely.

EASTER LILLY

KENNY RICE WAS BLOWING BREATHILY INTO HIS HARMONICA AND Easter Lilly Odum, naked from the waist up, was giving herself a sponge bath, when Jase Allman rapped on the cellblock door to let them know he was about to enter.

"Just a minute," she called, and reached for the limp napless cloth Stonewall County called a towel.

"Take your time." Jase held the door open no more than an inch. "I just want to talk to Kenny."

Kenny Rice's strained version of "Bury Me Not on the Lone Prairie" was interrupted by a long groan and an irate voice from behind the plastic curtain that split the cellblock corridor. "I don't need no lectures, Allman. Not from a Christer like you."

Easter Lilly had dried herself and buttoned her denim jail dress up the front.

"I got my shirt on now," she called.

"Sumbitch wudden of notice if you hadden," Kenny Rice said.

Sure enough and despite Easter Lilly's assurance, Jase looked away from her cell as he pushed open the cellblock door.

"You ready to eat, Kenny?"

Another groan, this one louder, came from behind the curtain.

"*I* am," Easter Lilly said. "Long's it's not that Egg Beaters shit."

"Oatmeal today." Jase advanced into the cellblock, a tray in each hand. Holding them on either side of the plastic curtain, he pushed it with his chest a few feet along its track. "From the Purity."

"Better than nothing," Easter Lilly said. "Maybe."

She considered it her civic duty to complain about the county food, but Jase never seemed to mind her criticisms. She watched him disappear on Kenny Rice's side of the plastic curtain.

"You guys ever heard of biscuits?" Kenny asked. "Toast maybe? Jelly?"

"Cuppa coffee here'll drown that poison in your belly," Jase said. "Sloe gin again?"

Kenny Rice made a retching sound, then said, "Switched to Southern Comfort."

Kenny sounded so wretched that Easter Lilly was glad she drank little or nothing. Half a can of beer sometimes. A woman was vulnerable enough, a black woman more so—a drunk black woman was a sitting duck. As for men like Kenny Rice and most of the brothers she knew, except Fred, she had never understood why they slurped it down, staggered around, fell, picked fights, usually threw it all up, sometimes on themselves.

"That'll pickle your liver, too." Jase's voice was caring, almost gentle.

Jase was a cut above most crackers, Easter Lilly thought again. Which wasn't saying much. Prob'ly not a drinker, either.

Mr. Timmons never touched booze. If he had, Easter Lilly believed, she might have started, too. Back then, she might have done anything for Mr. Timmons with his sad smile and soft hands.

"I tole you I din't need no lectures, Allman, so shut your fuckin face."

"Bad news is the oatmeal, Kenny. You ready for the good news?"

"I'm ready for Tylenol. My kingdom for a coupla Tylenols."

"Your kingdom don't rate Carter's Little Liver Pills," Jase said. "Good news is, Tyree says turn you loose."

Turning Kenny Rice loose didn't match her idea of the vindictive Tyree Neely she feared. But then Kenny was white. If he'd been one of the brothers, Tyree would have thrown away the key.

"That draft-dodgin prick," Kenny Rice said. "I know what he's up to."

Jase reappeared from behind the plastic curtain, carrying only one tray, and looked back.

"Says it'd cost the county more'n it's worth to haul your sorry ass into court."

"Hah!" Kenny Rice's laugh was short, sharp, unfunny as a pistol shot. "Tyree don't want me tellin some judge how his ol daddy pulled strings, kept *his* sorry ass outta the Nam."

Jase came along Easter Lilly's side of the plastic curtain, saying, "Ever'body in town knows that story."

"I'd of tolt it again, anyway," Kenny Rice muttered. "Just to watch'is fuckin face when I did."

She watched Jase stop in front of her cell and wink, his usually solemn face screwing up comically around his right eye.

"More power to'im, I say. Any man that can beat the draft."

Easter Lilly agreed wholeheartedly. Dragged off to foreign lands, shot dead for white-ass Uncle Sam, blown to bits, home in a body bag. Girlfriends left alone. Who needed it? Not even a cracker like Tyree Neely.

She reached between the bars, took her bowl of oatmeal from Jase's tray, and eyed the gray stuff without enthusiasm. Some kind of skin on top.

"If this the bad news, Jase, what good you got for me?"

"Tyree ain't turnin *you* loose," Kenny Rice yelled.

"Kenny's bent outta shape this mornin." Jase shook his head mournfully.

Easter Lilly put the oatmeal back on the tray. "I ain't *that* hungry, man." She picked up instead a Styrofoam cup of muddy-looking coffee.

"Maybe one thing." Jase watched her sip warily at the coffee, Easter Lilly eyeing him over the rim of Styrofoam. "Readin the coroner's report last night," Jase said. "On Ben Neely."

She was instantly on guard. Jase might be a cut above most crackers, but he still was one of Tyree's boys. Had to be, on the county payroll. If Jase Allman wanted to talk about the coroner's report, Tyree Neely had put him up to it.

"Said they was this cut inside Ben's hand."

Easter Lilly tried to remember from the flash-by jumble of that night in her mind. Seemed so long ago, almost like it had happened to somebody else.

"I had my way," she said, "it'd been'is throat." *Or his balls.* She waited, alert for whatever move Tyree was trying to make through trusting Jase Allman.

"Your new lawyer seen that?"

"He will." Easter Lilly did not know if Shep Riley had even read the coroner's report. Maybe jealous old Cady had never shown it to him. But she decided to send Tyree a message by his own messenger boy.

"I got me a smart lawyer now, stead of old Shitface. This one ain't gonna miss a trick."

She sipped coffee—too weak, too cool, too sweet, as usual.

"I doubt he will," Jase said. "How come that cut on Ben's hand?"

For all Easter Lilly knew, Jase was wearing some kind of hidden tape recorder. Or maybe had planted one on Kenny Rice across the corridor. Kenny was cracker all the way, and Tyree Neely was low-down enough for any kind of trickery. One smart son of a bitch, she had to admit.

"How come *you* think?" she finally demanded.

Jase, holding the tray with her rejected oatmeal, shrugging, looked innocent as a puppy dog that had peed on the floor. "A smart lawyer, which I ain't but you got, might tell a jury it shows they was a fight over Ben's knife."

Didn't sound much like a plant from Tyree.

"And Ben cut'is hand in the fight," Jase said. "That what happened?"

"You crazy, man? Wasn't Chinese checkers back here that night. I'm too busy staying alive to know it even if he'd cut his damn hand all the way off."

Jase's eyes narrowed. "You ain't said before that Ben was tryin to *kill* you."

So that was it. Tyree trying to get her to tell conflicting stories. One to Jase, another to the jury, raise enough doubt about both so nobody believed either one. But it took Easter Lilly only a second to see how to evade the trap.

"Not at first. Come in here, wake me up, pussy on'is so-call mind. How'm I gonna know *what* he aims to do, I don't give'im what he wants?"

Jase was studying her too closely, she thought, uncomfortable under his steady gaze. See if I'm lying. *Break me down.*

"I hadn't thought about it," Jase said, "till I read that coroner's report."

"Thought about what?"

"The blood on'is hand. Seem like I recollect blood on Ben's hand. That mornin I found'im."

Easter Lilly began to wonder then—cautiously, hesitantly—if maybe Jase Allman was *not* just a mouthpiece for Tyree Neely. Because Jase seemed to be trying to figure things out, not plant something on her.

"Man," she said, "you seen blood on his hand?"

"Like to not notice," Jase said. "Not sure I did. All the rest of it so confusin, y'know?"

Easter Lilly did know. It had all happened so long ago, so quickly, so violently, in a dim red dreamlike light. Ben Neely *could* have cut himself. If the coroner's report said there was a cut inside his hand and if Jase Allman maybe remembered blood on that same hand, Ben *must* have cut himself. She wished she could remember everything that had happened. Maybe they had struggled over the knife, just like she'd been telling them. Maybe Ben Neely *had* tried to rape her at knifepoint, she'd fought him, then cut him to the heart with his own knife. Maybe it *was* self-defense.

She felt a momentary elation. The new lawyer would have something to go on. He could get her acquitted. He'd—

From the jail office, a ringing telephone shattered the silence that had fallen on the cellblock. It seemed startlingly loud. It jarred Easter Lilly's teeth, pounded her eardrums. Her elation faded into resentment of the unknown caller, interrupting Jase's memory, maybe purging from his sluggish mind the facts that might save her from Tyree Neely.

"Scuse me." Jase hurried out of the cellblock, carrying her breakfast tray.

After a moment, the phone stopped ringing. Silence descended again, to be broken by the renewed wail of Kenny Rice's harmonica, this time a slowpoke version of "Oh, Susannah."

Easter Lilly lobbed her Styrofoam cup through the bars against the plastic divider. Coffee dribbled down the curtain's stiff folds. She wished it had hit Kenny Rice in the face.

"If you can't carry the damn tune," she called angrily, "whyn't you shove that thing up your ass?"

"Oh, Susannah" broke off in mid-note.

"How bout yours?" Kenny launched off-key into "Yankee Doodle."

Jase came back without the breakfast tray.

"Tyree wants me up at the courthouse." He pulled the coffee-stained curtain on its track back along the corridor. "Got to get over there right away."

His master's voice, Easter Lilly thought meanly, before remembering that Jase might actually be *her* ally. She wanted to scream in frustration. Just when it was all beginning to come out the way she'd been saying it happened.

She was good at masking her emotions, however; had had to be good at putting on a face for gullible crackers. She said, "Better put on your necktie, man. Tyree likes a sharp dresser."

Jase looked upset and she was surprised to see that he had taken her mocking counsel seriously—Jase frowning as he went out of the cellblock, seeming almost to be talking to himself. "Didn't wear no tie. Ida Sue said it was too hot today."

JASE

MAYBE THE REASON TYREE WANTED TO SEE HIM, JASE ALLMAN hoped, was so important he wouldn't notice about the necktie. Like Easter Lilly said, Tyree was a bear about proper dress. But even he could hardly expect the county jailer to wear a tie with his deputy's uniform while working indoors in the middle of the summer. Just a day or so before, Tyree himself had suggested that an air conditioner was needed in the jail office.

Jase was nevertheless apprehensive as he turned the jail duty over to Edgar Powers, the deputy Tyree's office had sent over to relieve him. And he could not help but worry as he trotted across the courthouse grounds in the withering heat. What could Tyree want with him?

Daisy Thorpe's summons sounded urgent but Jase could think of nothing that had gone wrong at the jail. The only offense he himself had conceivably given was that time he had suggested that he and Ida Sue might someday move out of Green Oaks. Surely Tyree wouldn't evict them just for that; and even if he would, he'd only be cheating himself out of the rent Jase paid religiously on the first of every month. Not every tenant was so reliable.

Still . . . there was no telling. Besides, the necktie business could be serious, Tyree being Tyree. Maybe, Jase thought in a grim stab at cheering himself up, as he hurried up the courthouse steps and into the air-conditioned interior, *he wants to ask me about some bird. Maybe a jailbird!*

The joke didn't make Jase feel a lot better, and he wished he'd ignored Ida Sue and worn a necktie, heat or no heat. He rode the creaking elevator to the third floor and walked with some reluctance down the corridor toward the prosecutor's office.

Got my balls in his pocket, all right. Jase knew he could be out on the street by sundown. And hardly enough in the bank account to pay next month's rent.

As he opened Tyree's door, Jase was briefly glad that Ida Sue had a steady job. But as he saw Daisy Thorpe busy at her desk, he was ashamed of himself. A grown man ought not to have to depend on the little woman to bring home the bacon.

"Got here as fast as I could." Panting as he spoke, a little more obviously than necessary.

Daisy placed papers in a squared stack on her desk blotter.

"You didn't have to run, Jase. Not in this heat."

He nodded at the closed door to Tyree's inner office and said, honestly, but also to impress Tyree's secretary, "He calls, I don't let no grass grow."

Daisy looked thoughtful. Not for the first time, Jase thought how beautiful she was—the long dark hair framing a cool white face, the faintly disdainful nose, the delicate brows arching over sky-blue eyes, the swanlike neck rising from a prim blouse that picked up the color of her eyes, the slender figure that Ida Sue said a woman would kill for but Daisy Thorpe didn't get by dieting.

"Used to bring lunches to school that'd choke a horse," Ida Sue said enviously.

Jase Allman never let himself think of Daisy as anything but Tyree Neely's girl. Everybody in Waitsfield believed that's what she was. In a nice way, of course, Daisy being known as a devoted virgin.

Besides, Jase had replied truthfully when Ida Sue demanded to know if he thought Daisy Thorpe was sexy. "I'm monogamous," he said.

"What's that mean—nogamus?"

"*Mo*-nog-a-mous. It means . . . like when you and me got married, I meant what I answered the preacher."

Ida Sue's frown disappeared. "Forsaking all others?"

Jase nodded and Ida Sue kissed him triumphantly. "I meant it, too," she declared.

Jase had not told her that he had forsaken all others—not always voluntarily—*before* as well as after they had taken their vows in the Neely Memorial Methodist Church. On their wedding night at Pawleys Island, he had known *what* to do and Ida Sue had not questioned why she had had to show him *how*. Nor he how she knew.

"Jase." Daisy Thorpe peered down at the papers on the blotter. "It was me that called."

"Yeah. Said Tyree wanted to see me right away."

Daisy moved the stack of papers an inch to the left, murmuring as if it hardly mattered. "Tyree's not here, Jase."

"Not here?" Jase's first reaction was relief about the necktie. "But you said in his office."

"He's in Lawrenceville." Daisy looked him in the face at last, her voice edged as Jase had never heard it. "Bird-watching."

He heard himself say stupidly, "But I thought—"

"With Cady." The same strangely whetted voice.

"Cady don't know no more bout birds than I do."

By then, Jase was puzzled, not only about why he had been summoned to Tyree's office if Tyree wasn't there, but why Tyree had taken an old drunk to Lawrenceville to spy on unsuspecting birds.

"Probably not as much." Daisy's voluptuous mouth straightened into a thin line. "But I thought *I* ought to talk to you before Tyree gets back."

"You did?"

Jase resolved at once to stop sounding stupid. He did not want to seem stupid to Daisy Thorpe, who was not only a pretty woman but who certainly talked often to the man who was their boss.

"Because Ida Sue and I were in the same class at SCCH."

"I seen the graduation picture."

Jase remembered Daisy and Ida Sue standing one in front of the other among the thirty-odd graduates—the taller Daisy in the rear—with Easter Lilly Odum at the end of the third line, one of the dozen black faces in the picture. Easter stood a little farther from the next cap-and-gowned senior—a white girl—than was necessary.

"Terrible likeness of me," Daisy said. "Good of Ida Sue. I

thought it'd be better coming from one of her old friends than from . . ." She hesitated. "Tyree can be . . . ah . . . pretty blunt."

Jase thought Tyree was rather soft-spoken, and he had never heard Ida Sue mention Daisy Thorpe as an old friend or in any way but enviously of Daisy's figure. He was vaguely discomfitted by what he was hearing.

"*What* would be better?"

"He'd tell you himself when he gets back. Probably make it sound worse than an old friend would."

Jase leaned down and put his big hands on Daisy Thorpe's desk. Whatever was coming, he suddenly was sure, would be worse than anything he had imagined as he hurried to the courthouse. Nor would it have anything to do with wearing a necktie.

"Worse than it *is*," Daisy said.

Jase's natural gentleness, far more than his deference to Tyree or his respect for women, stopped him from reaching across Daisy's desk, bunching her thin blouse in his hand—even if she was Tyree's girl—and jerking her to her feet. He wanted to shake it out of her. At the same time, he dreaded hearing it. Whatever it was going to be.

"About Ida Sue?"

Was she maybe dead in a robbery shoot-out at the Dinette? Or a wreck on I-95? But Tyree wouldn't have gone off to Lawrenceville without telling him anything like that.

Jase watched Daisy draw a deep breath and square herself in her desk chair.

"Jase," she said, "there's this rumor."

DAISY

SHE FEARED FOR A MOMENT THAT HE WOULD HIT HER, AND SHE watched the massive hands braced on her desk for the first sign that she should duck. Then Daisy remembered she was talking to Jase Allman, who might have been dumb enough to marry a flibberti-gibbet like Ida Sue Medlin but who was well-known in Waitsfield never to have hurt a fly, much less a woman. In the echo of her words, Jase's face was unchanged—Jase leaning on her desk as stiff and still as a department store dummy.

At last, his eyes steady, he said, "What rumor is that, Miss Thorpe?"

The formal address was a bad sign. For years, Jase had called her "Daisy." But it was too late to turn back, though Daisy suddenly wished she had not started down this road. Not even to get square with Tyree Neely.

"About Ida Sue." Hardly daring to move her lips, Daisy was ashamed—despite herself—of what she was saying.

"It ain't true," Jase said.

Daisy had been eavesdropping only routinely, via the squawk box, when Tug Johnson had told Tyree about Ida Sue Allman joy-riding—if that was what it was—with Porter Somebody. Daisy was uninterested. In her view, Ida Sue always had been a fool, Jase

Allman was a nobody, and the Porter character sounded crude. So Tug's story had little meaning for Daisy until a day later, when Tyree called Bert Wagram in Capital City.

Daisy had had no idea who Wagram was and might not even have bothered to monitor the call, except that some girl answered, "Statewide Videos," in the perky secretarial tone Daisy herself tried to avoid. Daisy hated being just a secretary and believed her IQ was as high as Tyree's and at least double Tug Johnson's.

Sure enough, Bert Wagram of Statewide Videos turned out to be Porter Thingamabob's boss.

"Ty!" Wagram had blared. "How they hangin, Ty?"

Daisy knew by then to expect the moment of silence with which her boss expressed—at least to himself—his displeasure at this double transgression. Then, under control as always, Tyree answered jovially enough, "Doing fine, Bert. Yourself?"

After minimal ensuing pleasantries, Tyree got right down to it—direct and tough, the way Daisy liked to think of him.

"One of the best route men I got!" Wagram sounded wimpy.

"I don't care if he's Billy Graham, Bert. Don't send'im back down here."

Wagram was not ready to give up. But he would, Daisy thought, he would.

"A rainmaker, Ty. Got that route going great guns."

Tyree smoothly shifted gears. "Well, I guess you know your own business, Bert. Just this week I told a guy from Piedmont Flix we already had a video distributor for Stonewall County. I—"

"Piedmont Flix?" Wagram whined. "Chickenshit thieves!"

Tyree seemed almost to agree. "If I didn't have to put up with this sleazy kid of yours trying to peddle dirty movies in our county, Bert, I wouldn't give Piedmont Flix the time of day."

That did it. After listening carefully for the click of Tyree's receiver going down in the inner office, Daisy hung up with a sense of pride in her man, as she then had had no doubt he someday would be. Tyree Neely got things done. Tyree understood *how* to get things done.

"A rumor about Ida Sue?" Jase said. "Don't you believe it."

Daisy's shame turned quickly to contempt. The stupid lunk not only had married a simpering little fool who had never made an A in her life, not even in home ec. He was actually refusing to believe a word against her. Tyree Neely was not the only idiot wearing men's pants in Waitsfield. She heard her own voice firming up, "It's a little more than a rumor, Jase."

The hands spread on the edge of her desk closed into white-knuckled fists.

"Who's spreadin this lyin damn rumor?"

Daisy seized on any alternative to the mucky details. "Nobody's spreading it. Tyree was going to talk to you about it, maybe next week. But he wouldn't *spread* a rumor."

"Somebody must be spreadin it."

Quickly, rushing her words, tumbling them out with as little expression as possible, Daisy told him that Sheriff Tug Johnson had seen Ida Sue in Porter McDowell's car, Ida Sue obviously having met McDowell's during her morning break from the Dinette's cash register. As she talked, Daisy could identify no reaction on Jase Allman's face.

But when she was finished, he spoke as quickly as she had; "Tug Johnson's a bald-face liar."

"Well . . . that's what Tug told Tyree he *saw*." Daisy gestured with a white, graceful hand at the inner office door. "He was talking so loud I couldn't help but overhear. You know how Sheriff Johnson talks."

"He talks bullshit," Jase said. "Pardon my French, Miss Thorpe. Did Tyree b'leeve that pussle-gut liar?"

Daisy shrugged. The gesture emphasized her artfully uplifted bosom, and she supposed that could do no harm. Jase might be a moron about Ida Sue but he was, after all, a man. Not, she thought sadly, like Tyree Neely with no red blood in his veins.

"What reason would he have not to? Why would Tug Johnson lie about a thing like that?"

Jase's voice was even, measured. "Because he's a no-count heap of you-know-what that's got a thing for Ida Sue. Always has had. But you b'leeve him, too, don't you?"

"Jase . . . Tug *saw* them together. He *saw* Ida Sue and this Porter person. Tug couldn't have just made that all up."

Jase stood away from her desk, and Daisy was surprised to see that the jailer was not as tall as he somehow seemed to be. Jase only *seemed* to loom above her desk and everything else in the room.

Including me, Daisy thought, her earlier fear that Jase might hit her again prickling on her skin.

"If he told Tyree that lie about Ida Sue, he *did* make it up."

"But why would he *do* that?"

Daisy felt called upon to defend—not Tug Johnson, whom she despised—but the story she had repeated. Now that she had chosen this way to get even with Tyree, she had to make it stick. Besides, Daisy did not think harshly even of Tug Johnson for using what he knew to whatever he'd thought was his advantage—only that he had not done it conclusively. Tyree did that kind of thing successfully, and she knew she would have done it, too. In fact, she acknowledged to herself, she *was* doing it, right at the moment.

It just happened that she also believed Ida Sue Medlin capable of any foolishness, as she always had been, right back to grade school when she'd let boys tickle her during recess. Ida Sue might even have run off with a TV soundman, Daisy thought with sudden malice, but she'd never have had the good sense to throw him overboard before it was too late.

"Ever time Tug Johnson gets anywheres near Ida Sue," Jase said, "he thinks I don't notice him lookin, but I ain't blind. He's just payin her back cause she don't give'im the time of day."

Jase raised a hamlike hand and Daisy flinched involuntarily. But he only pulled off his deputy's badge and threw it on the desk. It rang tinnily and bounced into Daisy's lap.

"Don't do *that!*" she cried.

Suddenly, Daisy knew why Tyree had not repeated Tug Johnson's story to Jase, why he had told Tug to keep it to himself. And she saw immediately that when Tyree returned from bird-watching to find Jase Allman's discarded badge, he would know who had done what. Maybe even why, smart as he was. She snatched the badge from her lap and held it out with her prettiest plea on her face.

"I'm done with that," Jase said.

Daisy was abject. She forgot her contempt for a man who could be duped by the likes of Ida Sue Medlin, and she was terrified to think of Tyree's return.

"*Please* don't, Jase."

Surely even Jase Allman would not quit a good county job over a thing like this. Over brainless Ida Sue Medlin, who would let certain boys feel inside her sweater when she was fifteen. So the certain boys liked to brag, anyway.

"The only reason I opened my mouth . . ." Daisy despised the plea in her voice. She consoled herself that it was only necessary. "I thought if you said just one word to Ida Sue—"

"I wouldn't stoop that low, Miss Thorpe."

"—Tyree'd never have to mention—"

"And I ain't workin for scum like Tug Johnson that muddies up a girl's good name."

Daisy saw the opportunity to turn tough.

"You don't work for Tug Johnson, Jase. You work for Tyree."

The charge renewed Daisy's disdain for lumpish Jase. He had no more practical common sense than the silly little baggage he'd married. A Stonewall County wage earner should not have had to be reminded of the facts of life.

"Not no more, Miss Thorpe. Tyree's been good to me, but I ain't workin for somebody that b'leeves Tug Johnson's dirty rumor."

"I didn't *say* he believed it. I don't *know* if—"

"You didn't say he didn't. You didn't say he told Johnson to shut'is dirty mouth like he ought to've."

She was a Stonewall County wage earner, too, Daisy remembered. At least until Tyree Neely found out what she'd done. She wondered, as she fingered the deputy's badge, if she had shown any more common sense than mule-headed Jase. She held out the badge again, knowing it was no use.

"Is your mind made up, Jase?"

"Comes to Ida Sue"—Jase turned toward the door—"my mind was made up a long time ago."

Book Four

MEG

MEG PARKED HER RENTED HONDA CIVIC ON THE SUN-BAKED BLACK-top near the Cinemaplex Plaza, left the front windows cracked open to admit outside air, and braved the blazing summer heat to go in search of Jase Allman.

In the enormous expanse of the Dixie Pride Mall, she knew, it could take the afternoon to find him. As it happened, in the teeming central corridor of the first building she entered, Jase was standing, stern and military-looking, at a sort of faux parade rest in front of a Sears, Roebuck mail-order store facing a display of bras and panties in a shop called Patty 'n Peg's.

Jase looked at Meg without recognition. He wore field-green trousers, a bit too large, a cap with a black bill webbed with cracks, and a white short-sleeved shirt whose collar points flared up like long albino eyelashes. A patch over the breast pocket read "Security." A heavy belt holding up the overlarge trousers suspended a ring of keys on one side; a leather holster on the other, she supposed, concealed a pistol within.

"Mister Allman!" she cried, more confidently than she felt. "I didn't expect to find you way out here."

Jase looked at her with polite incomprehension.

"You don't remember me, but last time I was here, we met at the jail. Where I thought you'd—"

"The lady lawyer," Jase said—polite but unsmiling. "I ain't at the jail no more."

"That's what they told me."

Meg guessed from his solemn face that he was wondering what else they might have told her. Which was only that he and the sheriff had had a falling out—about what, no one seemed to know.

"Man can't hang around a jail too long," Jase said. "Gets to feelin shut in hisself."

"Probably a lot more interesting here." He could use some reassurance, she sensed. "All these places to watch out for."

"No'm," Jase said. "Mostly old folks fallin down ever now'n then. An ladies lookin for the rest room."

Meg had looked for Jase Allman as soon as she returned to Waitsfield, thinking he was still a deputy sheriff. Based on her long-ago experience as a lawyer in the South, she had a special regard for deputies, though most were as hostile to "carpetbaggers," as racist and sometimes as brutal as the general run of southern lawmen. A deputy, however, usually knew a lot about the high and low life of the county where he worked. He was likely to know something, perhaps a lot, about any voter or taxpayer drawn for a jury list, and, unless he was readying himself to run for sheriff, often would be willing to share his knowledge, thus boosting his ego. Which made him a potential source of vital information that Meg could use to advise Shep Riley which jury panelists to accept and which to eliminate.

"Does he like dogs?" she once had been inspired to ask a Deep South deputy of a potential juror.

"Sooner pi'sen than feed'em," the deputy said.

The prosecutor had held out to the end to seat the dog poisoner but, on Meg's advice, Shep had used a peremptory challenge to get rid of him.

Brain-picking deputies was nevertheless chancy. Lawmen themselves, they tended to be partial to potential jurors who probably would vote guilty. Meg had an intuitive sense, however, that Jase Allman was a fair-minded man, and Meg Whitman usually followed her instincts.

"Well, maybe you could help me," she said to stone-faced Jase.

Big, dumb men usually wanted to help a woman. It made them feel more manly, which they all needed, and less dumb, which some did.

"Yes'm." Jase pointed to his left. "It's down here a-ways. Hang a left at the first—"

"No, I mean . . . I'm looking for a Coke or a shake or something cold and I thought maybe you'd know where."

"The Dinette, ma'am. You just passed it." He nodded over her shoulder, his face still solemn. Jase Allman, Meg saw clearly, was not happy being a mall security guard.

"Guess I was too busy looking for you." She watched for his face to register the flattery. It didn't. "Can I buy *you* something?"

"I thank you kindly," Jase said, "but I better stay on duty."

Had duty caused the trouble with the sheriff? Jase Allman did not strike Meg as a man to neglect his duty, whether to Stonewall County or the Dixie Pride Mall. Nor, she concluded, was he likely to fall all over himself just to please a woman—certainly not a woman who looked as if she had spent much of the day behind the wheel of a rented car with no air-conditioning.

"Mister Allman," she said, "I'm going to be frank."

His heavy, sand-colored eyebrows, above rather sad blue eyes, might have risen a centimeter, or maybe she only imagined this faint reaction. She hurried on. "I need to talk to you about Easter Lilly Odum."

She might have informed him that he had just won thousands of dollars in the Pick One state lottery. His shoulders relaxed; his arms sprang from their parade-rest pose; his face with its vast precipice of forehead and its Olmec chin broke like a child's kaleidoscope into a swift, crooked grin. He took her arm and twirled her toward the Dinette as gaily as if she had been his partner in a high school dance.

"Dinette makes a chock'lit shake would fill a water bucket, ma'am."

Had it been the mention of Easter Lilly or her declared candor that had effected his meltdown? Probably both, Meg thought, as she was swept like driftwood down the crowded mall corridor, among tides of short-sleeved summer shoppers trolling their bags of consumer goods, past ranks of mall-rat girls on the lookout for shoplift options and troops of boys wearing baseball caps backward above vacant faces. Jase's guiding hand steered her through these obstacles and around oncoming strollers impelled by young women aggressive with motherhood, until at last he held open for her the frosted door of the Dinette. Its chilled air, rushing out to the mall, babbled with the midafternoon snack trade. Its hidden Muzak wailed a Garth Brooks lament.

"Booth open back there," Jase said. Still holding her arm, he maneuvered them past tables of eaters and drinkers and handed her with a gallant flourish into a Naugahyde banquette. Hamburgers sputtering on the grill, Meg thought, smelled like prosperity.

Jase sat across from her, took off his crack-billed cap, and rested his elbows on the Formica table. He was, she saw by his uncovered head—what she had not noticed in his jailer's incarnation—still young, with the fundamentally untroubled face of inexperience.

"Where's the other one, ma'am?"

"Mister Riley? Coming soon, maybe even today."

That Shep *was* coming, she could be sure of, if little else about him. In numerous phone calls grumpily accepted by Alton McKinnon, Shep had made it clear that he was convinced Easter Lilly Odum was innocent of calculated murder and that he intended to defend her in court. He had insisted on it to the point that Meg wondered if he were letting Easter Lilly subvert his judgment. But Shep Riley was an advocate above all. Shep *believed*.

"You're at the New South again?" Jase asked.

"In Waitsfield, where else?"

Jase looked down at the tabletop. "Mister Riley'll be there, too?"

He looked up, his fair, open face reddening. But his eyes would not meet hers, and he quickly looked down again. So, Meg's instinct told her, he knows or at least suspects . . . or maybe that redheaded so-and-so had boasted about his conquest. Reconquest.

"Separately." She pronounced the word deliberately.

"Oh, I didn't mean . . . I just thought . . ."

Jase lifted his red face again, this time with an air of decision. "Y'all watch out for the guy that runs the place. Tyree's got'im by the short hairs."

Meg was not surprised to hear it, but she was not immediately sure what she should watch out for.

"Tyree seems to have a grip on everybody around here," she said. "Except maybe you."

She hoped the compliment would extract from Jase the story of why he was no longer a deputy sheriff. But he seemed only to want to change the subject.

"You think Mister Riley can win the Easter Lilly case?"

"If anybody can." And he just might, she thought.

"He called me a coupla times this summer. Want'n to know about Easter Lilly."

Jase looked at her a little strangely. But having made something of a breakthrough with him, she was anxious to exploit it, and pursued her own track.

"I stopped by the county clerk's office before I went to the jail, Mister Allman. Picked up the jury list."

"Jase. Down here, ever'body calls me Jase."

"Jase, then. Have you seen the jury list?"

"No'm." He leaned across the Formica table. "Tha's my wife there, ma'am. Ida Sue. Pretty one just come to the cash register."

Meg turned. From a distance too great to read the facial expression of the woman at the register, she seemed exactly what Meg would have expected in Jase Allman's wife—huge, gold-colored earrings dangling beneath high, tightly wound blond hair, busty, hippy, not quite dumpy, not quite chic, not quite casual, and of course chewing gum—a girl, Meg thought snidely, who only a few years before would have been traipsing through the mall in a miniskirted pack of too-tight T-shirts printed with suggestive slogans.

"Lucky you," she said, turning back to Jase.

He was grinning vacuously in the direction of the cash register. The glad light in his eyes unexpectedly filled Meg with sadness. She had seen a similar light in Alton's eyes, and had betrayed what it reflected. She knew instinctively that the girl at the register would betray Jase Allman, too, maybe already had, and go her way secure in the knowledge that, no matter what, he would keep on looking at her with his trusting eyes. Some men were born to be betrayed, some women to betray them.

It was a new way of thinking of herself, and the woman at the register was new company in which to find herself. Meg wondered if she should be wearing tacky earrings, too.

"Lucky is right," Jase said.

Ida Sue must have looked their way just then, because Jase began to wave, his boulderlike face breaking again into a fatuous grin, like a child's on Christmas morning, before the wheels come off the toy truck. Meg turned again and saw Ida Sue making her way between tables in their direction. Seen at closer range, her face was pouty, her crimson lips curved like an archer's bow. Before she could reach their booth, Jase was standing up.

"Wancha t'meet the better half," he gushed to Meg. "Ida Sue, this here's . . ." A look of dismay spread over his face as he realized he did not remember his companion's name. He went on lamely, "One-a the lawyers defendin Easter Lilly."

Meg put out her hand. "Meg Whitman."

Ida Sue, earrings dangling like yellow exclamation points, took the proffered hand gingerly, as if to avoid germs. She popped gum and her eyes faintly narrowed in what Meg took to be challenge.

Alertly, Meg picked up the cue. "I hope you don't mind your husband showing me where to get something cold to drink."

"Oh, Jase's got plenty of time these days." The bowed lips fell again into a scarlet pout. "Just standin around out here."

Jase either didn't notice or ignored the wifely barb.

"Honey . . . why'n'cha sit down with us, take a little break?"

"I already had my break," Ida Sue said. "Got to get back to the grind. Y'all forgive me?"

"Listen . . ." Jase's voice was, Meg thought, a little too unctuous. "Can you order us a coupla them chock'lit shakes?" He made swirling motions with his hands, indicating the size of the shakes he had in mind.

"Sure can." Ida Sue, chewing her gum, eyed Meg without enthusiasm. "Don't eat fat'nin things myself but I see it can't do you no harm." She put a slight emphasis on the *you*. But Meg knew how to be catty, too.

"Oh, I can eat anything, Miz Allman. Never put on an ounce."

Ida Sue turned away, then whirled back, as if having made up her mind to say something. "I wouldn'a thought a lady lawyer would want anything to do with Easter Lilly Odum."

"We don't think she's all that bad," Meg said. "She maybe just had to defend herself."

"You been around here awhile," Ida Sue said, "know'er like local folks do, maybe you'll think diff'rent."

She swept off toward the cash register, jaws working. Meg was watching her go when Jase said, "You got it right already. Ben Neely tried to rape Easter that night."

Meg was stunned. Nothing in any of the documents she had seen or in any conversations she or Shep had had with Jase had suggested that he, too, thought Easter Lilly had been fighting off a rape. No wonder, she suddenly thought with certainty, Jase was now a mall security guard. Tyree Neely would have kicked him off the county payroll for far less.

"Can you prove it?" Maybe—she suddenly hoped—when Shep arrived she could present him with a tidy case, all wrapped up for his approval. Take him down a peg.

Having delivered his bombshell, however, Jase turned eagerly to the defense of his wife. "Ida Sue's kind of opinionated bout Easter. They were in school together."

"Your wife looks a lot younger." And not half as smashing, Meg thought.

"Don't she?" Jase looked proud. "But it's like she said, folks that know Easter Odum don't think much of her. They think . . ." He hesitated. "Well, when they were in school . . ."

Meg had done her homework. "I know about that schoolteacher story. It doesn't prove a thing about this case here and now."

Jase nodded. "But folks *think* it does. I mean, like Ida Sue said to me, if it was one white man back then, it could be another'n now. Is what folks think."

"But *you* think she was fighting off a rape when she stabbed Ben Neely? If you've got evidence we can . . ."

"I knew Ben pretty good. You don't mind my saying this kind of thing, any woman he could put his hands on, he would."

Probably, Meg thought maliciously, including Ida Sue.

"But, Jase . . . everybody says Ben *hated* blacks. Made no bones about it."

"Yeah, well, you see . . ." Jase paused again. "I don't love talkin bout such things in mixed comp'ny, ma'am. But the way I figger it . . ." He stopped. Then, in a sudden rush, his words tumbled at her across the Formica surface. "Any man'll thow a woman down and do bad things, he's got to hate'er guts."

He looked at Meg anxiously, as if for forgiveness. "That's the way I figger it, anyhow."

Meg felt new respect for Jase Allman. He was clearly a fool for Ida Sue but otherwise not so dumb.

"But I don't think I hear you saying you *know* what happened in the jail that night."

"Oh, I know, all right. Just took me a while to figger it out."

Slowly, as if speaking to a first-grade class, he told her what he believed, concluding almost triumphantly, "That's the only way it *could* of happen."

He had the confidence, Meg saw, of a man who could not conceive that his word could be doubted, because *he* knew his word was good. Unfortunately, a jury might not take it at the value Jase placed on it—not a Tyree Neely jury, not after Tyree presented *his* argument.

"That makes a lot of sense," she said. "But I'm not sure it *proves* anything the jury will believe. Will you say all that on the stand?"

Jase lifted his right hand, as if to take the oath then and there. "I never cared a whole lot for Ben Neely anyhow."

"Well, don't say *that* to the jury. And listen Jase—right now I need a different kind of help."

A waitress brought the chocolate shakes. Jase thanked her, familiarly calling her "Sharlene."

"What kind of help?" Jase asked, when they were alone again.

"With the jury list." With her spoon, Meg stirred the thick shake. Jase lifted his to his mouth.

Meg pulled the pages of the jury list from her purse and put them in front of him. She explained what she wanted and he nodded. But after quickly scanning the list, he shook his head rather sadly.

"Tyree could've dictated it, ma'am."

And maybe did, Meg thought sarcastically. She wanted him to study the list uninterrupted, however, and let him read on. He occasionally took a slurp from his chocolate shake.

"This'un here . . . Ray Meachum." He put a forefinger on the list. "Tyree set'im up in business, y'know. Luminum siding."

"That's just the kind of thing I need to know."

On the second page, Jase pointed out another name, Monroe F.

Jeffries. "Went to State with Tyree. Class of sixty-five, maybe six. In there somewheres."

And a moment later, "Now this-un, Grady Cole, maybe . . . Tyree sent'is daddy to Arbor Hill for beatin up Grady's mother. But I don't know. Grady's kind of scairt of his shadder." Jase looked mournful and ran his finger farther down the list of names. "Ol lady Cole took Grady's daddy back, anyway."

He got to the end of the list and flipped the pages together, tapping them into a neat stack, pushing them across the table.

"Onliest name on here I don't hardly know at all," he said, "he ain't orig'n'ly from Stonewall County."

"Which one is that?"

He showed her with a blunt finger.

"Then I might as well start right there." Meg put the jury list in her purse. "Where can I find him?"

SHEP

AT ABOUT THE SAME TIME MEG WAS TALKING TO JASE ALLMAN IN the Dinette, Quentin Hodges's Beeline Cab, hack license number 2, pulled up in front of the New South/Best Western Motel. Shep Riley got out, carrying a briefcase, and followed by Quentin Hodges, who opened the trunk lid.

Shep paid and tipped him and took his suitcase out of the trunk.

"Wait for me while I get checked in," he said.

"Welcome back." The usual cigarette was pasted to Carl Hoover's lower lip—maybe, Shep thought, the same cigarette that had hung there months earlier. Hoover's angular face was gaunt and beard-shadowed, like an actor's in a horror movie.

"Thanks. Miz McKinnon checked in yet?"

"Just today. Room fourteen again. But this time she signed in 'Whitman.' "

Shep put down his suitcase and filled out a reception form. "I don't know my departure date."

The motel manager turned the form around and checked it over. "No car?"

"I'll probably rent one later."

Carl Hoover looked at him with sly, up-cut eyes. "You want room twelve?"

You son of a bitch Shep thought, but said only, "Put me down at the other end if you got a room down there. Maybe twenty-two like the last time."

The manager shrugged his thin shoulders. "This time-a year, I got more rooms than Clinton's got broads. Twenty-two it is."

"Makes your job easy then. You like your job, Mister Hoover?"

The cadaverous face looked up at him. Yellow-tinged fingers pried the cigarette loose from the lower lip. "Beats workin nights in a steam laundry."

"Sure it does," Shep said. "Good perks, good company to keep. Best Western tells me they only hire managers with solid reputations." *Take that* he thought *and this.* "No criminal records or bad credit."

Carl Hoover put the cigarette in a tin ashtray from Waitsfield Ice and Fuel. His hand seemed to shake a little. "You talked to the comp'ny?"

"I was so impressed with this place the last time I was here, I called to say so. Can you cash a check, Mister Hoover?"

The shadowed face turned wary. "How much?"

"Walking-around money. Say fifty?"

Carl Hoover pulled open a drawer and gloomily examined its contents. "Twenty-five do you?"

"For the time being." Shep took a checkbook and a ballpoint from his jacket pocket; on the ballpoint, yellow letters spelled OTTER CREEK CREDIT UNION. "I can promise you this won't bounce."

"Oh, I ain't worried about that," the manager said. "Just I can't spare more'n twenty-five right now."

Shep signed the check with a flourish and ripped it out.

"Reason I said that about bouncing, I was talking with the State Bureau of Investigation. They told me one time they had a lot of trouble around here with rubber checks."

He held out his own check above the reception desk. Carl Hoover made no move to take it.

"The SBI," he said, "told you that?"

And plenty more Shep thought.

Carl Hoover slowly reached for the cigarette and put it in his mouth again, his hand now shaking visibly.

"Regular epidemic, they said." Shep dropped his check on the counter, where it lay like an oversized calling card. "Checks bouncing like tennis balls. Two tens and a five'd be great."

He had a hard time not smiling, as he thought to himself *No more phone calls to Tyree Neely, Scumbag. Not from you.*

The manager handed Shep the money and a key attached to a wooden block. "Twenty-two," he almost growled. "On the end."

"Mind if I leave my bag with you for an hour or two?"

Carl Hoover eyed Shep's suitcase with plain loathing. "I'll have somebody put it in your room."

"Great." Shep touched the wooden block to his forehead in a mock salute. He turned—only then allowing himself a smile—toward the entrance and Beeline Cab waiting outside.

The motor was already running as Shep climbed into the backseat. Quentin Hodges in his Atlanta Braves cap looked back at him quizzically.

"County jail," Shep said. Then, as if unable to stop himself, he asked, "You ever kicked somebody in the balls, Mister Hodges? Somebody that had it coming?"

Quentin Hodges had turned back to the steering wheel and the gearshift. The cab began to move.

"Not since Vietnam," he said.

IDA SUE

WHEN THE LAWYER PAID FOR THE TWO CHOCOLATE SHAKES, IDA Sue tried hard to be nice.

"Hope y'all enjoy yourself while you're here."

The woman took her change without counting it. In Ida Sue's experience at the cash register, most women counted their change. Maybe this one was more lawyer than woman.

The lawyer smiled pleasantly. "I don't suppose that trial will be a lot of fun, Miz Allman."

Sure-God won't, Ida Sue thought, noticing stubby, chewed nails. Like she's almost *trying* not to be attractive.

Ida Sue said, "And I reck'n we must seem kind of country down here to you. But lots of good folks here in Stonewall."

"Oh, I'm sure of that. Good folks everywhere."

Which seemed to Ida Sue a sneaky sort of put-down of Stonewall County. She watched the lady lawyer leave the Dinette. Hardly any butt on her, skirt falling straight in back. Ida Sue was thankful to be curvy like a woman was meant to be. But not sloppy like Shar-lene.

She took her handbag from under the counter and walked back to the booth where Jase still sat, twisting his long spoon in the bottom of his glass. He looked glum, as he usually did since he quit the county. Or whatever happened.

Ida Sue wondered what had become of Porter. Such fun, but then he suddenly wasn't around anymore. Not that she missed *him* a whole lot. She never actually cared much for Porter. Too pushy. But he'd been fun. Porter could make anybody laugh. She did miss that, Jase not being what you'd call a scream.

Porter hadn't even sent her a postcard, care of the Dinette, to say where he was and how sorry he was not to be seeing her anymore. Which made her glad that she'd taken his necklace back to the Rockpile. Besides, when she'd found out how little the cheapskate had paid for it, Porter had gone way down in her estimation.

The Dinette was quiet and nearly empty as she slipped into the Naugahyde seat opposite her husband.

"She paid for your shake."

"I told'er not to." Jase clinked the spoon in the empty glass in exasperation. "I told'er I'd pay for'em."

"Prob'ly thinks you can't afford it anymore." Ida Sue took the spoon out of his thick hand. "Anything I hate it's somebody fiddlin with an empty glass. Or a plate."

"She said *she* invited me, so she'd pay. She . . ."

Ida Sue put his spoon down with a crack. "She must of known you ain't with the county no more."

"She knows *that*. She went by the jail lookin for me. But that don't mean—"

"Sure it does. She's got a brain in her head; she could figger it out that you're hardly makin half what you use to make from the county. Little as it was."

Jase picked up the spoon. "Oh, she's got a brain, all right. That lady's *smart*."

"Bein a lawyer, I guess so."

Ida Sue took a mirror from her bag and inspected her face. Though generally satisfied with what she saw, she resolved to pluck her eyebrows that very night. And though she knew Jase was faithful as a bird dog, she could not resist putting him on notice. "She makin eyes at you?"

Jase looked crushed and put the spoon in the glass again. "Aw, Suedy . . . she's just down here for the Odum trial. She ain't in'trested in—"

"Well, even if she is, I guess I don't need to worry bout *her*." Ida Sue pushed back a lock of blond hair from her white forehead. "I guess you wouldn't mess around with a toothpick like that."

Jase clinked the spoon. "Mess a*round?* Suedy . . . the only reason I'm helpin that lady is she wants to know bout folks that might get on the jury."

"Cause you like'em stacked up, don't you?" Still looking in her mirror, Ida Sue spoke with practiced sarcasm. "Like ever man I ever knew."

"Damn right. Stacked like the little girl I married."

Ida Sue touched her hair again and put away the mirror. Then, as if suddenly recalling earlier words, she said, "You're *helpin* that bitch?"

Jase let the spoon fall in the glass and sat back from the table. "I don't like you usin words like that."

"Oh, you don't, don't you?" Ida Sue snapped shut her handbag. "Let me tell you something, Jase Allman. Some strange woman comes round makin eyes at *my* husband, I reckon I got a right to call a spade a spade!"

"But she wasn't—"

"And as for you lec'trin *me,* Mister High'n Mighty, I'll thank you to remember who's payin most of the bills these days!"

Jase looked crushed. "I *know* who's payin," he said. "But I promise you, honey . . . it ain't gonna be like that much longer."

"Well, I'm sure I don't know why it won't. I ain't seen folks knockin the door down, that dump we live in, off'rin you big money."

"But I got some lines out. I think maybe—"

"Jase Allman, the only line you got to put out is a big fat one to Tyree Neely."

Jase's face hardened. "No way. I ain't goin back to Tyree."

Softening suddenly, as if fearing she had pushed Jase across some real if invisible line, Ida Sue took one of his hands in both of hers. "Aw, honey . . . you don't think you'd be workin out here if . . . listen, if Tyree didn't want you out here at the mall, they'd *never* of hired you!"

Jase put his other hand on top of her white ones. "I know Tyree's got some kind of in'trest in the mall." Quiet anger echoed briefly in his voice. "Like ever'where else in Stonewall."

"But you with your stupid pride . . . you're gonna help that . . . that . . ." Ida Sue quickly thought better of whatever word she'd had in mind. "That *woman* . . . instead of makin things up with Tyree."

A new thought struck her and she pulled her hands free of his. "Help her how?"

"She wants to know bout folks that might be on the jury, that's all. So I said I'd tell her what I know."

"But ain't she and that other one tryin to prove Easter Lilly didn't really . . . that Benjy was . . ."

"Tryin to rape her. That's what they think."

"So if you help them, it's like you think so, too. You'll be goin against Tyree again."

"Suedy . . . it was him went against *me*." That was as near as he'd come to telling Ida Sue why he had quit the county.

"Jase Allman, if you know which side your bread's buttered on, you'll get your everlovin fanny down to that courthouse an make it up with Tyree! Whatever it was."

"It ain't that simple," Jase mumbled.

"Well, if Tyree didn't stop the mall people hiring you, it's got to mean he'd be willing to take you back on the county if you'd just go down there and—"

"No way," Jase said. "I ain't gonna do that, Suedy. No matter what."

EASTER LILLY

EASTER LILLY WAS ROUSED RUDELY FROM AN AFTERNOON NAP BY Cooter Rollins's shout: "Your lawyer's here!"

At that moment in her sleep, she had been seeing herself in a long white dress running hand in hand with Mr. Timmons through a field of wildflowers toward a cool green edge of trees. In her waking confusion, she expected to see old Shitface Kadducks come wobbling along the corridor, so it took a moment for her to comprehend that the red-haired figure carrying a briefcase was someone else.

"Sorry to wake you up." The redhead peered through the bars.

"Wha . . . whad you say?" Easter Lilly heard her sleep-slurred voice echoing stupidly from the cellblock concrete.

There was little to do in the Stonewall County jail but sleep, so Easter Lilly often dreamed of Mr. Timmons in the afternoons. At night, although no tiring daytime chores had been required of her—she had only to tidy up the dime-store sheets on her thin mattress—she usually slept as deeply as if worn down by a hard day's hoeing in the cotton fields at Parchman. Then, in her nightly dreams, crackers with whips and rifles drove long lines of convicts like so many mules, like the beasts of burden—the black man's burden—they were. In those savage jailhouse dreams, she would hear the clip-

clippping of hoes chopping the uncaring earth, the clank of their chains, sonorous doomed voices responding to the caller in convict chant:

> Oh wasn't I lucky
> When I got my time,
> Babe, I didn't get a hundred,
> Got a ninety-nine.

Sometimes the convict voices would be strangely overlain with her mother's remembered soprano, bell-like in old Nebo Church:

> Alas and did my Savior bleed,
> And did my Sov'reign die?
> Would he devote that sacred head
> For such a worm as I?

"I told you I'd be back," the redhead said.

Easter Lilly, slowly coming awake, remembered the do-good lawyer Riley. Who believed in justice. Who said he'd win her case, set her free. "I didn't ever doubt it," she managed to say, her tongue still thick with interrupted sleep.

"And I still think you're going to walk."

Blearily, she remembered that her trial was about to open. Riley sounded more confident than Easter Lilly ever allowed herself to be.

"Not if Tyree can help it," she said.

She swung her legs off the cot and sat up. In the long nights when she was not dreaming of her black heritage of woe and rejection, Easter Lilly had sometimes writhed in a redly lit personal nightmare—*Ben Neely's hard wet hands tearing at her, his swollen penis thick and rearing, his vile whispered words scalding*—until in the blood-tinted darkness she would bound upright like a released spring, sweating and afraid, at once relieved by reality's return and shaken again by the rage that had driven the knife.

"Maybe this is one time Tyree won't have his way," the redhead said.

As Easter Lilly came more fully awake, she remembered Riley's

Timmons eyes, how he'd said of her case *I'm not in this for money.*

"So you can talk the talk," she said, "but . . ."

She was vaguely contemptuous, even of a man who promised to be a savior. Easter Lilly held most men in contempt. Their pathetic fantasies, their fatuous yearnings. For what? she sometimes wondered. What kind of magic did they somehow expect out of what was just friction, flesh moving on flesh.

". . . how do I know you can walk the walk?"

Right that minute, she guessed, Riley was trying to peer through her denim dress to whatever he fancied underneath. She'd seen that look many times, even—different, of course, less greedy, less predatory—in Mr. Timmons's eyes. He was male, too, and all males looked with longing at females. But that didn't mean this one was like Mr. Timmons. No one was.

"You *don't* know it," Riley said. "I hope you *do* know I'll do my damnedest."

The words sounded throaty, as if he were trying to swallow them. Again she was reminded of Mr. Timmons. Waking in the afternoons, in silence dripping past her cell like water torture, she would have time, all the time in the world, to think and remember. It was not surprising, she had come to believe, that with his sad eyes and gentle voice and his hands like caresses, Mr. Timmons so occupied her daytime dreams. It had been, after all, in those quiet afternoons behind the locked door of his classroom at SCCH that he had made her feel included, for once—rather than frustrated and angry, set apart from most of the world around her.

In those long-ago afternoons, too, she believed, she had given Mr. Timmons not just her willing woman's body, the mysterious power of which she comprehended neither then nor now, but an occasional and temporary peace. She had known that their time, her inclusion, could not last, and that for Mr. Timmons their merged world was as much torment as ecstasy.

"We're going to prove," Riley said, "that it was self-defense. Not murder."

He put his briefcase on the corridor floor, stooped to open it, and took out a sheaf of stapled papers.

Even as a schoolgirl at SCCH, Easter Lilly had been bitterly aware of a gulf that seemed unbridgeable between her world and the white world. So it was miraculous that Mr. Timmons would hold her close, even in the isolation of a locked classroom, that he could stand so far aside from his race, from any race, from the *idea* of race, and accept her so completely—risk his standing, his very existence, among his own kind, for the poor reward, as it seemed to her, of those secret hours and secret acts that, in the end, could not even be secret.

"You were a woman fighting back . . ." Riley's words, in the echoing cellblock, rang like oratory. "And we're going to make people see that!"

In the brevity of her experience, Easter Lilly had not been able then to understand how such a love could exist with the anxiety and regret that produced the salt tears that sometimes streaked her body as she lay in his arms. She had grown to be a woman before she realized that those tears had been for *her*, too, and for the escape they could only briefly make from a violated order.

"I only wanted to be seen for what I am." Her murmured words were all but lost in the fading echoes of the redhead's speech.

Mr. Timmons's tears, she would tell herself in the hours following her afternoon dreams, had been shed in vain. For she had never wanted or treasured anything, then or later, as much as she wanted and treasured what he already had given her: as much acceptance, inclusion, as she would ever have.

Riley was looking puzzled and she stirred herself from reverie. "I'm innocent, Lawyer. Of murder, I mean."

He nodded and held up the sheaf of stapled papers. "Coroner's report. Have you read it?"

"No, but Jase Allman told me about that cut on Ben's hand. Before Jase quit."

"Jase's not here anymore?"

"Some kind of falling out with the sheriff. Didn't you see Jase wasn't here?"

"I thought it was his day off or something."

Easter Lilly, by then fully awake, was no longer thinking of Mr. Timmons or of anything but her impending ordeal in court.

"You think it's important, Mister Riley? The cut on Ben's hand?"

He held up the coroner's report again. The feel of it in his hand seemed to have focused him on the case, she thought, instead of on *her*. Rather have'im working than breathing hard. She could always turn him on again. With men like him, with any man, it never took much.

"That cut suggests he must have had the knife in his hand . . ."

"At my throat," Easter Lilly suggested.

"Which means you wouldn't have had to grab it out of his pocket."

"He had it out already." Easter Lilly stood up. "And Jase saw blood on Ben's hand. The morning he found'im down there dead." She pointed toward the drain in the cell floor.

Riley sounded excited. "Will Jase testify to that?"

Close up, she thought, the lawyer's face was not unattractive—not freckled all over like some of these red-haired crackers. And his eyes, now that they were no longer undressing her, were eager and intelligent.

Easter Lilly shrugged. "Haven't even seen Jase since he told me about the hand."

"Where can I find Jase now?"

She shrugged again. "Maybe old Cooter in the office might know. I told you, I ain't even seen Jase. Must of quit or maybe got fired the same day he told me."

Riley's eyes showed interest. "You think Tyree found out what Jase remembered."

"Could be," Easter Lilly said. "Jase got a call that day that Tyree wanted to see'im. And Tyree don't put people on the payroll to testify against'im."

Riley picked up his briefcase and put the coroner's report back in it.

"I better talk to Jase as soon as I can. If he'd testify for us"— he closed the case with a decisive snap—"could make the difference."

"I were you," Easter Lilly said, "I wouldn't count on Jase being willing to do anything like that. He's always been one of Tyree's men."

"Struck me as fair-minded, though. When I was here before."

As if crackers knew fair from fuck-you, she thought, watching Riley turn toward the cellblock door. Halfway there, abruptly, as if remembering something he'd forgot, he swung around and said, "Who's this Fred Worthington?"

Easter Lilly was at first too startled to reply. She had not even known he knew Fred's name, much less wondered who he was. Then she realized Riley had betrayed himself in a way that even his eyes hadn't.

Hooked she thought.

"My boyfriend," she said.

She was amused at the consternation that broke through the controlled lawyer's mask that had been Shep Riley's face. But he was important to her, far more so than Fred Worthington. Fred could bring ribs and chicken; he couldn't set her free.

Easter Lilly spoke again, quickly, softly, "But what I need is a *lawyer*."

She made it sound like a promise. And was amused again to see the relief in his Timmons eyes.

MEG

THE STONEWALL COUNTY EFFLUENT CENTER LOOKED, MEG thought, like a sanitized death camp. The late afternoon sun burned down on an apron of pavement underlying a squat structure in the shape of an overturned bowl, and a saddle-roofed office building, both of white cement. At one side a long, rotating arm spraying clear liquid swept round the surface of a glittering pool. Acres of well-mowed grass surrounded the pavement, the pool, and the buildings but failed to soften the harsh, sun-baked glare of the Stonewall County Effluent Center.

Meg drove slowly through an open entryway in heavy wire fencing and entered a black-striped parking lot. She stopped the Civic in front of a small VISITORS sign, next to a slot with a wheelchair symbol, and reluctantly emerged into blistering southern air that seemed to rise in waves from the pavement. She could detect a faint chemical odor, perhaps from the open pool, but the expected, fetid smells of even a euphemized sewage plant were not detectable in the antiseptic atmosphere.

She hurried past a Cherokee wagon and other parked cars, one of which displayed a red and white bumper sticker: JESUS IS MY FRIEND. The air-conditioning inside the office building slapped her like a moist, purposeful hand, and an elderly woman looked up inquiringly from a computer terminal.

"To see Mister Johns," Meg said. "I called a half hour ago."

"Oh . . . Miz Whitman?"

Meg had given her maiden name instead of Alton's, partly because she was working again, but also in an effort to lessen her irrational sense of betraying Alton and the children—irrational because being back in Waitsfield was not in itself any kind of perfidy. Even Alton had conceded she had a right to follow her profession.

The elderly woman spoke quietly into an intercom box, then smiled at Meg. "You can go right in, Miz Whitman."

Fielding D. Johns awaited her behind a desk bearing a prominent nameplate—SANITATION ENGINEER—in a large office bloodless as the rest of the Stonewall County Effluent Center. As she entered, he turned to a smaller table behind him and switched off a small radio. Silence fell in the chilled room with the force of the sunlight outside. A picture window offered a view over the pool and its sweeping sprinkler arm.

Looking all day at a pool of sewage, Meg thought, was not how she would choose to spend her time.

"Would you have a cup of coffee, Miz Whitman?"

In the frosted air, coffee might have been good, but Meg could not quite reconcile the idea with the scenery. She had the impulse to shock the large, academic-looking man smoking a pipe behind the desk, so she did.

"What's the difference," she heard herself asking, with a kind of horror, "between effluent and shit?"

Fielding D. Johns did not flinch. He pointed with his pipe to the nameplate. "I am."

She had shocked herself, not Fielding Johns. "I don't know why I said that, Mister Johns. Please forgive me."

He shrugged. "Actually, it's a good question that people don't usually ask. I could give you a fuller answer if you want."

"I'm a lawyer, not a scientist. I'll take the explanation you've already given." She found a chair and sat down. "Did you know you're on the jury panel for the Odum trial?"

He sat down, too. "I'm supposed to report to the courthouse Monday morning."

"Which doesn't mean you'll actually be picked for the jury."

"I'd rather not be. I've got plenty to do right here."

"If that's the way you feel, my colleague Mister Riley might be willing to excuse you. He's defending Miss Odum, you know."

"I didn't know *anybody* was defending her."

"What made you think that?"

Fielding Johns leaned forward and fixed an intense gaze on her. Meg tried to return it, but again almost broke into a smile—Flushing Johns, she thought—and steeled herself not to think it again.

"I bet he hates that nickname," Jase had told her. "I would if I was him."

"I didn't think anybody'd have the nerve," Fielding Johns said. "Not in this county."

She felt a faint stirring deep in her consciousness, an instinct that she thought must be like whatever it was that told hunters game was near—though she had never fired a gun. The feeling caused her to pick her way more carefully.

"Mister Riley is a very experienced attorney. Why wouldn't he defend Miss Odum?"

"He's an out-of-town guy, and they don't much care for out-of-town types around here." His eyes narrowed hardly enough to cause their lids to move. "I know something about that."

Meg sensed resentment in his words and her instinct stirred more insistently. But, like a hunter near game, she was anxious not to startle the quarry.

"Mister Riley knows something about that kind of thing, too, Mister Johns. He's often been an outsider and he's not afraid of being one again."

In spite of herself, she felt a swelling of pride in Shep. He would go into the lion's den, she thought, in pursuit of his idea of justice. He had done it before.

"I didn't mean to suggest he'd be *afraid,* Miz Whitman. It's just that he probably can't win the Odum case. Not in Stonewall County."

"Why not?" She could sense the coming kill.

"Oh, come on." Fielding Johns smiled a little stiffly. "Easter Lilly Odum killed a white man, they say in cold blood. Tyree Neely's brother. In a county where they think the Neelys are next to the Man Upstairs."

Meg stared at him, wide-eyed—a trick she had learned long

231

before, which sometimes helped to convert honest cynicism to reluctant truth.

"Maybe not sitting at the right hand," Fielding Johns conceded,
"but at least in the same room."

"So because it's a Neely that's dead, you think they'll convict
her whether she's guilty or not?"

In the quiet office, Fielding Johns's voice had dropped in volume,
and was uninflected, as if he were reciting something memorized.

"His brother has a lot of clout around here."

"I know about Tyree Neely's clout. I just don't believe an American jury—"

"A Stonewall County jury," Fielding Johns interrupted.

"I don't believe *any* jury will convict an innocent woman for
that kind of reason."

He looked faintly surprised. "Innocent? She admits she did it,
doesn't she?"

Outside, in the brilliant sunshine reflected from the concrete, the
sweeping sprinkler endlessly circled the pool, an oddly cooling sight.
She waited while the sweep completed a slow circuit.

"The way Easter Lilly tells it, Mister Johns—and Mister Riley's
going to show it in court—she acted in self-defense."

Fielding Johns stared at her, his face impassive.

"I didn't mean to be offensive earlier," Meg went on, "and I
hope I'm not now. But a woman's life is at stake, and I'll be blunt.
Why do you think, when they found Ben Neely dead, his pants and
shorts were down around his ankles?"

Fielding Johns's expression still did not change. Again, he spoke
as if reciting a lesson learned.

"In the *News-Messenger* Tyree said she must have promised him
sex, got him back to her cell, stabbed him with his own knife, then
used his car to escape."

Meg could not tell if he actually accepted this, or if he had been
in Stonewall County long enough to be wary of disagreeing with
Tyree Neely.

"That's what *he'll* try to prove," Meg said. "But Easter Lilly
says Ben was trying to rape her. At knifepoint. *That's* what Mister
Riley's going to argue."

Fielding Johns sat still as a stone, looking at her, while the sweep
circled the effluent pool. Then, in his careful monotone, he said,

"In a Stonewall County court? An outsider defending a black woman charging rape? Against a white man?"

He shook his head—in emphasis or anger? Meg wondered—stood up abruptly, stalked to the picture window, and stared out at the pool and the white desolation around it.

"Your man's not that good," he said. "I doubt anybody is."

"He's got some evidence." She was not certain Shep did. She was sure only that he believed. "And he's good with juries."

"With a Stonewall County jury . . ." Fielding Johns swung around to face her. "He'll have to be better than good." His voice had become intense, anger palpable in it at last. "Rape's hard to prove, anyway. I know something about *that,* too."

Meg's instinct suddenly was sure and warm, like a blanket on a cold night. She felt a familiar excitement, and hoped it did not show in her face.

"Tell me what you know, Mister Johns."

Fielding Johns grinned at her mirthlessly—she thought wolfishly—his large teeth suddenly yellow and predatory.

"Call me Flushing," he said. "Everybody around here does."

TYREE

TYREE NEELY LISTENED WITH INTEREST WHILE CARL HOOVER INformed him that Shep Riley also had returned to the New South/ Best Western. Earlier in the day, the motel manager had reported that the woman lawyer had checked in.

"Adjoining rooms?"

"Funny thing," Carl Hoover said. "I offered him the one next to hers but he wanted to go down the other end."

Tyree was glad to hear it. Not that it necessarily meant anything. Riley still would be only a short walk away from his lady love, but at least he and she were being careful of appearances. That spoke well for her, partially justifying the favorable first impression she had made on him. "He's just being careful, Carl. Keep me posted."

Carl Hoover seemed to hesitate before answering, "I'll do my best."

As Tyree hung up, he heard Daisy Thorpe's delicate rap at his door. She had been tiptoeing around lately, as if fearful of disturbing him. He called out pleasantly, "Come on in, Daisy."

She entered slowly and stood before his desk with her hands clasped in front of her, like a schoolgirl summoned to the principal's office, or a choirgirl about to sing "Jesus Loves Me." She wore a cream-colored linen dress, high in the neck, long in the skirt, sleeveless to reveal well-shaped white arms. Daisy was not a sun worshiper, unlike the typical Waitsfield woman who tanned herself melanomic in the lethal southern sun. Not a freckle spotted Daisy Thorpe's perfect nose or marred her smooth white brow.

"I've been thinking, Mister Neely . . ." She was looking just over his left shoulder. It had been weeks, he realized, since Daisy had looked him in the eye. "Maybe I ought to resign."

Tyree was startled, even though she *had* been acting strangely.

"Why on earth would you do that?"

Suddenly her eyes were boring into his. After so long, the impact was startling. As if for the first time, though Daisy had been around the office for years, he saw how blue her eyes were—blue as the indigo bunting he had sighted in an old cow pasture just the week before—and how striking beneath the dark hair that framed her face.

"Because I just can't take it anymore—the way you've been treating me since—"

"That *I've* been treating you?"

"Oh, I know it's all my fault! That you're always so cold and stern to me now. Since Jase Allman quit, you're acting like I committed a crime or something! And you *know* I didn't mean for things to turn out the way they did."

Tyree saw with alarm that Daisy was about to cry. He was willing to do anything to keep a woman from crying. He always felt baffled, helpless, *unmanned,* when a woman started crying. Especially if her tears appeared in any way to be his fault.

"Oh, come on, Daisy, don't . . . listen, I *don't* . . . blame you." He hated to hear himself stammering, but not as much as he would have hated to see Daisy crying. "If Tug Johnson had kept his mouth shut the way I told him . . . and I *haven't* been cold and stern, that I know of . . . not on purpose, anyway."

"But I just can't *stand* it, Mister Neely . . . that I've made a man I admire so much mad at me, I mean. I used to just *love* working for you . . . but now . . ."

Tears, horrifying Tyree, finally spilled from her large, despairing eyes, slid glistening through a faint line of eye-shadow and across the smooth cheeks she never rouged toward the quivering chin that rose from a neck as white and graceful as an egret's.

Bubulcus ibis he said desperately to himself. Anything not to think about Daisy crying.

From somewhere, she produced a handkerchief hardly larger than a postage stamp.

"Daisy, there's *nothing* to cry about!"

Daisy cried on, further demoralizing Tyree. But even as he spoke, he worried that he was being too hasty. "I don't blame you about Jase. I blame that fat clown. Now, please, Daisy . . . don't cry anymore. Daisy, please?"

He needed to get hold of himself, he thought. No good to let a woman's tears affect your good judgment. The Jase business had been bad enough without this kind of a scene.

"I'm *sorry*," Daisy murmured through the handkerchief dabbing daintily at her soft red lips. "*So* sorry."

That birding trip to Lawrenceville—that fool trip, Tyree thought—Cady had spoiled with his drunken complaints. Besides, he'd spotted no birds worth an entry, only a few lousy killdeers, the kind he'd seen a hundred times. Then, on his return, Tyree had found a deputy sheriff's badge on his desk, atop a neatly typed note from Daisy Thorpe saying that Jase Allman had resigned and she would explain.

On top of a wasted weekend in the field, that had been too much. Fingering the badge irately, Tyree demanded the explanation. At first, Daisy answered defiantly, "Sheriff Johnson came in and told me what he'd seen . . . I mean about Ida Sue and—"

Tyree had exploded. "I told that idiot not to tell a soul!"

"Well, you weren't even good and out of town before he came in hemming and hawing and the next thing I knew he was spilling it all out. The whole story. I could hardly believe it, Jase bein so nice. How could Ida Sue *do* that?"

She's a woman, Tyree wanted to say. That's how. But he kept silent and thought about getting a new sheriff elected.

Daisy, still calm, went on, "He said you were going to talk to Jase when you got back. But I went to SCCH with Ida Sue, I've known her all my life, and I thought maybe if I . . ."

Under Tyree's icy glare, she started to look doubtful and her voice quavered a little. "I thought maybe it'd be better if I spoke to Jase, as an old friend of hers. You know . . . a friend could maybe put a better face on things than . . . I mean . . ."

"Than I would have."

In fact, Tyree thought as he spoke, I'd decided I wouldn't even mention it to Jase. Stick my nose into somebody's marriage like that. But the damage was done. By that fat-ass and this nosy little chatterbox. He wondered sadly why good intentions so often produced bad results.

"I couldn't be*lieve* Jase'd get that upset! To quit a good county job the way he did."

"I'd have believed it," Tyree said. "Why I wanted Tug to keep his big mouth buttoned up." Prudently, he did not add that Daisy should have kept her prettier red lips closed, too. "Jase Allman's all wool and a yard wide. I knew he'd stand by his wife."

As soon as he'd seen the badge on his desk, in fact, and read Daisy's note, he'd understood what had been for months vaguely on his mind, not decided, not settled, only floating around, like an appealing but impractical urge to own a flashy car or live on an island in the Caribbean. He'd been fiddling with the notion of ditching Tug Johnson and putting in Jase Allman. Even young as Jase was and with a flighty wife that could lose him votes.

"Well," he'd finally told Daisy that first day back from Lawrenceville, "let's don't sweat it too hard." Turning the page, closing the book. As John Bell had taught him to do when there was no help for it. Never cry over the bird you didn't sight, Tyree had told himself a hundred times. Look for the next one.

After that, things had seemed to go on well enough, though Daisy was not quite as loosy-goosy in the office as before. He'd thought that had been the end of it. Until now.

"I'm not crying." Daisy masked a hiccup with her tiny handkerchief. "I know you don't *like* crying."

Maybe, he thought as she stood before him in her cool linen dress, maybe I have acted a little chilly. And over the weeks, the atmosphere in the office *had* been a little charged. He'd been angry at Tug Johnson and maybe some of his feelings had spilled over on Daisy. Who had, after all, blundered in where she'd had no business. Daisy should have had sense enough to keep quiet, no matter what big mouth Tug Johnson told her.

"You meant well . . ." Hoping she really had, hoping to shush her crying. "And if I've acted as if I thought anything else, I haven't meant to and I'm sorry. But, Daisy . . . no need for you to quit. No need at all.''

Daisy looked at him with mournful blue eyes. She was pretty as a marsh hen, Tyree had to admit. Nice to have around the office, looking the way she always did, bringing him flowers.

Tyree had rigorously never allowed himself to think bedroom thoughts about Daisy Thorpe. He did not like to think about any woman in such a common way. Such trashy thinking struck him as demeaning—to him, maybe more than to some woman. Weakness. Tyree Neely hated weakness, in himself most of all.

From the day newly orphaned Daisy had asked him for a job— which some of the older women in Waitsfield already had called to urge him to bestow—Tyree had steeled himself against Daisy's obvious attractions. For one thing, he had been a dedicated puritan since once in New Orleans when he had visited, in a fit of curiosity he still regretted, what he then knew only as a party house. He had quickly departed, his curiosity turned to nausea and in panicky fear of disease.

For another thing, one or two of the Waitsfield ladies who called to ''recommend'' Daisy had told him in strictest confidence that the poor little thing had done her dead level best to live down that foolishness with the TV man. She'd been a motherless teenager, they said, with no one but that hard old man to turn to, and the Lord himself wouldn't find a blot on her notebook since.

''Besides,'' as Mrs. Erskine Cole put it, ''the Bible tells us to let him who is without sin cast the first stone.''

Or her, Tyree thought. Durward Springs, who read meters for Southland Power and Light, had confided to Tyree while seeking his help in beating a shoplifting rap brought by the former Clark Department Store—put out of business by the Dixie Pride Mall— that in earlier years he had enjoyed regular trysts with Mary Belle Cole herself.

''Mary Belle liked it dog fashion,'' handsome Durward had boasted, to Tyree's disgust (which had not prevented him from filing the story in his copious memory, even though it cast disrespect on his mother's generation).

So alerted to Daisy's misfortune, Tyree had never found it necessary even to hint that he knew more about her than he let on. He even rather enjoyed his unaccustomed forbearance—but was prepared to act if it became necessary. He had no trouble, therefore, in remaining neutral about his decorative secretary, especially after it became clear to him that Daisy had targeted him for her little female games, ultimately for matrimony. Like that crazy idea of going off to *La Bohème* together.

"You really mean it, Mister Neely?" Daisy responded eagerly to his charitable words. "You're not mad at me?"

Tyree had the feeling that he was about to say something he would come to regret. Yet, knowing she had set out more traps for him than a boy hunting rabbits, he still could not stop himself. Strangely but definitely, he heard himself say, "I do not want you to quit your job. Why"—he tried to lighten the moment—"what would I do without fresh flowers on my desk every day?"

Daisy's eyes glowed through traces of tears. "You won't be cold and stern anymore?"

"I never was," Tyree insisted, though he suspected he might have been. He rose and reached his hand across the desk. "Are we friends again?" He put slight, but he hoped noticeable, emphasis on "friends."

If Daisy did notice, she didn't let on. But she took his proffered hand, hers warm in his palm.

"I'm *so* glad, Mister Neely."

For just a moment, he feared she was going to kiss his hand. But she only squeezed it and hurried toward the door.

Twisting a little more than usual, Tyree allowed himself to think—and two other ideas flashed in his mind like geese following a leader. One was that Vic What's-his-name had had a sexy toy to play with, since he apparently had liked that sort of thing. The other was that Tyree Neely had no need of it, and thank the Good Lord for that.

The door closed behind Daisy's undulant form. Tyree was immediately ashamed of himself, not only for thinking lascivious thoughts about Daisy and Vic but for letting the sight of Daisy's bottom inspire them.

But his discomfort soon was interrupted by Daisy's voice on the squawk box, "Judge Reeves on the line."

His thoughts turning gratefully to the trial coming up, Tyree picked up the phone. He knew he was as ready to go to court as he'd ever be. The jury list was just about what he'd expected. He had a little stroke on practically every name on it, and they knew it as well as he did. Any he didn't, he could keep off with per-emptories. He'd even prepared a few phrases for his summation, and he was exhilarated to think that at last Easter Lilly Odum was going to get hers. In the gas chamber at Arbor Hill.

The way John Bell would want.

"Ty?" said Ottis P. Reeves.

Tyree Neely silently ground his teeth. But Ot Reeves, after all, would be presiding. And Ot was reliable, which was why Tyree had pulled the necessary strings to get Ottis Reeves appointed to the bench, despite his reputation for drinking and messing around with women.

"How about that Tyree?" Tug Johnson had said at the time, when Tug thought Tyree was out of earshot. "Ot Reeves ain't hardly out the door before Tyree's in Ot's old office."

This overheard remark did not displease Tyree. Never hurt, he thought, to let the troops know where the power lay.

"Judge." Tyree tried to sound pleasant, despite Ot Reeves's greeting.

"Just thought I'd let you know, Ty. This Riley bird's motion for a change of venue. Don't see the need."

Tyree pretended relief. "Glad to hear it."

"I'll formally rule from the bench tomorrow. These Yankees come down here, think they got to teach us how to try cases."

Tyree remembered the lady lawyer. She had taught him some-thing, all right. At least confirmed what he believed—that no mat-ter what they looked liked, you couldn't trust'em.

"I tell you what's a fact, Ty." Judge Reeves's high, rather ag-grieved voice, a little loud and slurred, slipped into the country accent natural to him. "A defendant don't get a fair trial in my courtroom, I don't care where it's at, he ain't likely to get one nowhere."

"Course not, Judge."

Tyree glanced at the slender Movado on his left wrist. Not yet six o'clock and the old soak was already hitting the sauce.

MEG

SHEP AND MEG HAD DINNER TOGETHER AT THE PURITY CAFE BUT
not to celebrate their return to Waitsfield. Far from it, Meg
thought. Returning to what all too recently had been the black-belt
South? Dinner in a greasy-spoon restaurant on a nearly deserted
"downtown" street? Being back in harness with Shep Riley? If it
hadn't been for her encouraging meetings with Jase Allman and
Flushing—Meg caught herself quickly—Fielding Johns, she'd have
wished to be almost anywhere else. Like at home with Alton and
the children.

They ate in rarely broken silence. A few remarks about the forth-
coming trial. Meg's account of her talk with Jase. They wondered
doubtfully if he'd *really* testify. Shep said Easter Lilly was rock-
steady for self-defense. Meg suggested that she might have found a
pigeon for the jury. Then Shep put his fork down beside his obviously gristly steak, leaned across the Purity's tattletale-gray table-
cloth and said with an air of resolution, "Listen . . . when we left
here last spring—"

Meg lifted a silencing hand. "I don't want to talk about that."

"But I need to explain . . ."

"Don't bother."

She was determined not to pay attention to any more of his

blarney. Shep Riley could talk the moon out of the sky. Or a woman into bed—especially, she thought, if a faithless bitch like me already wants to make love . . .

Impatiently, she broke off her own thought. *Love had nothing to do with it* she told herself. *I just wanted a good fuck.*

She still was disturbed, in spite of this admission, by the comparison of herself with Ida Sue Allman that had occurred to her at the Dinette. Before that, Meg had not felt overly guilty about sleeping with Shep. It had been, she'd told herself, only that one night. And the first time since her marriage to Alton that she'd done it with another man. She'd missed what she knew it would be like with Shep and probably never would be with Alton. A woman, she believed, had as much right as a man to the pleasures of sex. Especially since it was she who would bear the possible consequence nine months later.

That day, however, as she thought she recognized the face of betrayal on Ida Sue Allman, she had feared at once that she wore it, too. Since that moment, Alton's adoring eyes and trusting face had seemed to follow her like a shadow. Slowly, inexorably, face and eyes had become accusing, and Meg knew exactly why she could neither evade nor ignore them: because she had come back to Waitsfield eager to sleep with Shep Riley again.

Fuck his eyes out.

"Just let me tell you this one thing," Shep insisted. "I did some checking up on that guy at the motel desk. The one with the cigarette in his mouth? A few years ago he passed some rubber checks. Bounced'em like the Chicago Bulls. I made another phone call and found out that Best Western doesn't hire anybody with a criminal record. They said they'd fire anybody with a record that managed to sneak on their payroll anyway."

"That's positively medieval!"

"Which is exactly what this joker did—sneak on their payroll. And don't get too liberal over Carl Hoover till you know the worst."

Meg already was having second thoughts. "Jase told me Hoover's in Tyree Neely's pocket."

"Bet your sweet ass. Or was. Tyree pulled some wires on that bad-check rap and Hoover only got probation. Plus he's still got his job with Best Western. Five will get you ten he owes that to Tyree, too.''

"So to all your other sins," Meg said—relieved to be diverted from thoughts of her own—"you can now add blackmail?"

Shep grinned broadly and drank iced tea, looking at her happily over the rim of the glass.

"Let's just say, my dear, that Mister Carl Hoover—if he wants to keep that job—will never again call up Tyree Neely to tell him that you and I have had a little party in your room."

Meg turned scarlet but focused immediately on what Carl Hoover had done rather than on what she and Shep had done.

"That prick did *that?*"

"I'd admire your language," Shep said, "if it weren't so mild. That prick did exactly that. Which is what I was trying to explain."

Meg was angered and embarrassed. Bad enough to have done what she'd done. The world certainly would think so. But to be spied on by a check bouncer in a one-towel motel! To have to sit in court with Tyree Neely leering at her! And it was small consolation to realize that Shep hadn't been as crude and dismissive as she'd thought.

"So that's why you hustled us out of town after . . .'' Meg paused. Somehow it seemed more improper to talk about than to have done. "After what you call a party."

"You surely wouldn't want me to call it a *funeral*." His smile was insinuating. "Even if you did almost put me in the grave that night. Positively Amazonian, you were."

Meg was further infuriated. "So you just ran away. The very next day."

"From the New South Motel," Shep said, "and Carl Hoover. Not from your delightful bag of tricks . . ."

"*Damn* you!" Meg found herself shaking her fork at Shep, as if to jab it in his face. "*You're* the one that—"

"But I left too abruptly, I concede. I've been feeling bad about that all summer."

"I'll bet," Meg said. "Sitting up there in Vermont with the crocodile tears streaming down your face."

"No, really, I felt terrible. I knew you didn't understand."

She was in no mood to accept lame and tardy apologies, or any

243

excuses at all. It was hard to face her own transgressions; but it was easy—made her feel better—to attack Shep Riley.

"Did it even occur to you while you were feeling so terrible that you could have told me what it was all about? But you were probably too busy fly-fishing with all those Vermont sexpots?"

"Sure, I thought about telling you," Shep said. "But when I found out Hoover was squealing, I just wanted to get us out of here before Tyree put the black spot on us all over town. Then I just wanted to find a way to fix Hoover."

Meg looked him in the eye, determined that he should feel as bad as she did. Worse, if possible.

"Bullshit, Riley. As soon as you found out it wouldn't be smart to come tomcatting into my room anytime you felt like it"—Meg was feeling better with each word—"you hit the road. Chickened out."

Shep looked hurt. She had seen him do it many times. As often before, it softened her anger. *But not enough.* Like all men when it came to sex, Shep Riley was as transparent as a pane of glass.

She went on with relish, "What you really wanted was to make sure nobody would be spying on you the next time you came to get your piece of ass."

Shep tried harder to look hurt. Then, as if in surrender, he smiled the smile of a teenager caught reading *Hustler*. And with a return of male bravado announced, "What a way to die!"

"Trouble is"—Meg meant every word, gloried in them, in their repeated punches to his shocked face—"there's not ever going to be another party."

On the way back to the New South/Best Western in the Beeline Cab, she felt almost clean again. They did not speak.

But Quentin Hodges, hack license number 2, was apparently oblivious to the chill of silence in the backseat. "Too bad y'all won't be in town long nuff to see the SCCH op'ner. They got a hell of a team this year, them Stonies."

To be polite, Meg asked, "Don't they usually?"

"Yeah, pretty good most years. Not always. This season, I hear they really gonna kick some butt."

Neither Meg nor Shep replied. Quentin Hodges seemed to rush to explain himself.

"I figger Tyree'll finish off your case in a day or so. Open-and-shut like it is."

Shep apparently decided not to let this pass. "You mean that Easter Lilly killed Tyree's brother?"

"She don't deny it, does she?" The Beeline Cab turned into the motel driveway. "Says in the paper she don't."

"But what if it was self-defense?"

"And what if I'm the Sultan of Swat?"

"It *was* self-defense," Meg said. "And we'll prove it."

Shep paid and tipped, and they got out of the cab into the breezeless night. A nearly full moon lit the clear skies. The motel swimming pool glittered in its lawnlike setting. A sudden silence of traffic allowed the harsh rattle of cicadas and bullbats to be heard, and through the highway smells of gasoline and rubber tires, Meg thought she detected a valiant scent of pine needles.

"Good luck, then," Quentin Hodges said. "Y'all still here for that op'ner, tickets're on me."

He drove off. Shep Riley, not looking at Meg, gazed over the pool toward the highway busy with passing cars. Tires whistled on the heat-softened pavement. Beyond a screen door, Meg saw Carl Hoover and his dangling cigarette materialize as if by magic behind the reception desk. But his presence was no longer a problem. And anyway . . .

There's not ever going to be another party.

For a moment, astounded, aghast, she wished there would be. Now, tonight.

A shudder ran through her body—a convulsion of desire, she knew, overriding the guilt she had felt, the remorse, even the fleeting cleanliness of her denial. Saddened, exhilirated too, she understood she wanted Shep Riley . . . in bed, on the floor, wherever. He could make her see the colored lights.

"When did *you* decide it was self-defense?" Shep said.

His quiet words, calling her back to the case, the trial, were like cold water on her face in the morning.

"It took a while. Especially after I paid some doctor to examine her and he found no evidence of penetration."

"But he couldn't have seen her until several days after it happened."

"Shep . . . there's *no* evidence of actual rape except her unsupported word."

"If he had the knife at her throat," Shep said, "it's still assault with intent. Which justifies self-defense."

"Right. And the more I thought about that knife of Ben's, the more something bothered me about it."

Shep laughed and said sarcastically, "Bothered the hell out of Ben, too. Killed him, in fact."

Meg ignored his macabre joke. "That knife wasn't a switchblade, you know. I kept wondering about that."

Beneath the brilliant southern moon and in the light spilling from the motel office, she saw Shep staring at her and sensed that she had caught his interest. Shep always had been quick on the uptake. One of the things that made him so attractive.

"So I went to the hardware and bought a knife just like Ben's. Then I went home and practiced with Alton."

Shep laughed again. "He can't be *that* bad."

"Not that kind of practice."

He's not bad at all she thought. *Just not* . . . she groped through her vocabulary for the right word. *Not thrilling*.

"I mean I put the knife in Alton's back pocket, where Ben carried his, to see if I could take it away from him."

"And of course you could." Shep sounded impatient. "That night in the jail, if Easter got him back to her cell the way Tyree claims she did, Ben would have been half out of his mind. Crazy for her. She could have easily grabbed his knife."

Shep's voice had thickened. He said slowly, reluctantly, "Maybe all the way out of his mind. Over a woman like that."

Meg saw a strange look cross her face, but she was eager to tell what she had learned in practice with Alton. She touched Shep's arm, asking urgently, "What then, Shep? What would have happened *after* she got hold of the knife? *That's* when Tyree will claim she killed him."

Book Five

THE SEATS OF THE THEATER-STYLE CHAIRS ON THE MAIN FLOOR OF the Stonewall County courtroom had been cushioned, if ungenerously, as far back as the days of populism and segregation. Inevitably, the padding had been packed as thin as cheap carpeting by the applied bottoms of generations watching what passed for justice in that jurisdiction.

In the late twentieth century, upon the ascent to power of Tyree Neely, succeeding his father John Bell in dominance of Stonewall County, the main-floor seats had been recushioned. And by Tyree's time, the enlightened concern for voters that had moved him to this reform necessarily had to be biracial. So, to what would have been the consternation of his father, Tyree had ordered the seats in the balcony cushioned, too.

For uncounted decades before segregation was outlawed and voting rights promised, the balcony had been reserved for what even in the Clinton era much of Stonewall County persisted in calling "the colored." Tyree Neely therefore was challenging custom and tradition when he had the balcony seats cushioned to make the new black voters as comfortable as the white, while both watched the mills of the law grind exceedingly small.

After the various triumphs of the civil rights movement, however—perversely, as it seemed, and perhaps unfortunately—"the colored" would no longer climb to the balcony or confine themselves to places formerly designated for them. They sat in the orchestra seats, they ate at the lunch counters and cafés, they relieved themselves in the rest rooms, they drank at the water fountains, and they slept in the hotel beds once as closed to them as had been Waitsfield High and the championship eleven on which Tug Johnson had played left guard.

Nor would white people lower themselves to occupy seats they had been taught for a lifetime were for colored only. So the balcony of the Stonewall County courtroom, even with newly cushioned seats and no matter what exciting criminal was on trial, usually was as empty as the Cinemaplex Plaza after midnight.

When Superior Court Judge Ottis P. Reeves of the state's Eastern District convened the trial of Easter Lilly Odum early one hot Monday morning, with Sheriff Johnson standing by the bench as massive as a haystack, his tentlike uniform trousers upheld by his prized buckle on a size 48 belt girdling his middle, the crack of the judge's gavel echoed from the ceiling and the balcony's vacant seats. The main floor was crowded, however, perhaps a few more of the colored than the white occupying its recushioned seats, the races mingling in random fashion never seen in the good old days of John Bell Neely.

Daisy Thorpe sat uncomfortably in a front-row seat, between—on her left—Dr. Fred Worthington, whom she knew was one of the numerous lovers of Easter Lilly Odum and believed to be a dope dealer (a black doctor from some one-room medical school with no cadavers naturally would sell tons of morphine and speed, Daisy reasoned, and probably shot himself up, too); and—on her right—Good Jelly Cass, proprietress of the only eating place in Cognac, a Stonewall community few noncoloreds anymore dared to call "niggertown," and through which Daisy never drove without locking her car doors. Daisy never had actually *stopped* in Cognac.

She had no idea why Good Jelly Cass was called Good Jelly, but she did know that Tyree Neely—though he suspected—never had been able to prove that the woman bootlegged liquor and permitted dice games in the back rooms of her place, which the Sanitary Department once had had to close. Daisy had never heard of a white restaurant in Stonewall County being closed for sanitary reasons.

As court convened that morning, Good Jelly Cass smelled powerfully of body powder. Daisy hoped that as the day wore on and
the air-conditioned but crowded courtroom inevitably grew
warmer, the powder sprinkled on Good Jelly's ample form could
hold its own. Bad enough to have her right armrest usurped by
Good Jelly's fat left arm, the elbow of which seemed aggressively
to keep nudging Daisy. She did not need BO to make things worse.

"Oyez, oyez," Lancey Gregg, a skinny man in a bow tie,
crooned up front. Then Lancey shouted something about this honorable court. If he meant Ot Reeves, Daisy thought, as the be-
robed judge entered and took his seat—looking as if he suffered
from gas on his stomach—the fact was that the man was a
drinker, a pincher, and on the bench only by Tyree Neely's suf-
ferance. Tyree therefore would handle this honorable court, she
was sure, like silly putty.

"Honey . . ." Good Jelly Cass's froggy voice apparently was
meant as a whisper but could be heard over several rows of seats.
"Yuh man gonna ax the chambuh?"

Daisy shifted as far to the left as she could without touching Dr.
Worthington's white suit, which she was uncomfortably wary of
smudging. Heads turned along the front row and Tug Johnson
frowned in their direction. Hoping Good Jelly would be hushed,
Daisy murmured, "No idea"—though if Good Jelly was referring
to the *gas* chamber, Daisy knew Tyree was indeed going to demand
it. Tyree had no sympathy whatever for Easter Lilly as a woman,
and why should he? Hadn't she murdered Tyree's brother?

It flustered Daisy, however, that a fat old auntie knew she
worked for Tyree Neely and had called him "yuh man." Probably
thought there was plenty going on between them. Daisy hated the
idea of the colored poking their broad noses into her business.

"He do," Good Jelly rasped, "bruthas say this town ain't got
enuff fire hose." Her powdered arm moved sharply into Daisy's
ribs, as if to nudge a sleeper awake.

Dr. Worthington, who could not have helped overhearing,
leaned an inch toward Daisy, raised a white-clad arm, and whispered
behind his hand, "Big talk. Nobody gonna need fire hose."

His words frightened Daisy further, since she could not be sure
which message was meant for Tyree, or if either was. So she huddled between the two coloreds, hunching her shoulders, nervously

pulling her skirt down over her tightly clasped knees. Why hadn't Tyree put her in a more secluded seat?

Not fair she thought, remembering the empty cushioned seats in the balcony. White people didn't treat *them* that way anymore.

Daisy did not usually attend trials, knowing Tyree preferred that she keep the office going while he was in court. He had no need of her in the courtroom, other than occasionally asking her to bring down some papers or a volume of the code. She had come to the Odum trial mostly because she knew Tyree aimed to get Easter Lilly convicted in short order and she wanted a chance to show her admiration for him. Smooth out any remaining edges of the Jase Allman screwup.

Besides, "I'm really going to *love* seeing you put that Riley person in his place," she had said to Tyree just before they left the office together. *The skinny lady, too.* But Tyree had not seemed to be listening.

"You sure that answering machine is on?" he said.

Now, inside the railing that divided the court proper from those attending, Tyree sat alone—as Daisy knew he preferred—almost in front of her, at a table he kept as clear of books and papers as he did his office desk. Tyree was so organized, he was scary.

"Won't be a long trial," he'd told her. "Just a few witnesses. My summation and Riley's. Jury'll be out maybe an hour. Then . . ." He opened a desk drawer and took out the bird book Daisy hated, since he never had allowed her access to it. "Then the fat lady sings."

Peering around Good Jelly Cass's bulk in its gaily flowered organdy dress, Daisy saw on her right, on the other side of the gate at the end of the middle aisle, Shep Riley's red hair bent over a table somewhat more cluttered than Tyree's. Easter Lilly Odum sat beside him. Even wearing jailhouse denim, Easter Lilly seemed the same sexual creature Daisy had always—well, not exactly envied, since Easter was colored—*noticed*.

Daisy was more interested in the woman lawyer at the end of the defense table. What Riley could see in such a string bean was a mystery. No figure to speak of. But of course, as boys used to say about a certain kind of girl in high school, she would put out. Which explained a lot.

Easter Lilly whispered something in Riley's ear just then, her lips so close it might almost have been a kiss. One well-shaped brown arm fell familiarly across his shoulders. Beyond them, Daisy saw the woman lawyer stiffen. Probably realizing, Daisy thought, that Easter Lilly would put out, too. Even back in high school.

Daisy had been paying more attention to the characters than to the courtroom drama, so she was surprised when Lancey Gregg opened a door and a group of men and women marched past him— sort of in ranks if not exactly in step. The jury, Daisy supposed. Five blacks, seven whites. Four women, only one black.

She knew all of the whites. And not a single one, she knew from Tyree's correspondence and office dealings, plus calls she'd overheard, could afford to cross him. Like Lena Covington, Cooter's mother. Cooter had been a temp but now was a regular jailer with a fat county paycheck.

Or Alvin Levine, Waitsfield's only Jewish merchant. Tyree single-handedly had forced Alvin, against solid resistance, into the Longleaf Country Club, which had the only golf course in Stonewall County. Daisy herself had inherited a membership among the few assets Randolph Thorpe had left her, and since had worked her handicap down to 14 off the women's tees. Once, no other partner being available, Daisy priding herself on her lack of prejudice, she had even played a mixed twosome with Alvin Levine, finding him not at all kikey and almost pathetically grateful to Tyree. As well he might be.

Then there was the Reverend Clarence Patch. On pain of exposure in the *News-Messenger,* Tyree had warned the Rev. Patch not to contribute again to Save Stonewall's Soul (SSS), a committee run by bootleggers but financed mostly from church funds. SSS tried and failed every election year to get state liquor stores voted out of the county. Tyree himself drank only a frozen daiquiri now and then, but he detested bootleggers as moral lepers and tax-evaders, and he welcomed the Stonewall County School Board's share of legal state liquor stores' substantial profits.

And so on. Even had Daisy Thorpe harbored a keener sense of the supposed purity of the criminal justice system than she had absorbed from the "social science" course at SCCH, she would have thought Tyree Neely clever to arrange things—as she assumed—so favorably for himself. Daisy had learned early that the race was to the swift; and she was herself adept at improving her lie on the back nine at Longleaf.

She was a little puzzled to see Flushing Johns in the back row of the jury box, because nobody really knew anything much about him. People said his wife drank but Daisy knew one or two other wives who drank—who wouldn't with husbands like theirs?—and still managed to get supper on the table. Of course, Flushing Johns owed his job to Tyree (Daisy had overheard Watt Lang, the dry cleaner, ask on the telephone if it wasn't "kind of a shitty job"), and she was confident that Tyree would have kept the man off the jury if he'd been worried about having him on it.

Good Jelly's elbow nudged Daisy again. Another swampy whisper carried far enough to evoke another Tug Johnson frown: "All Toms up theah, honey."

Daisy had not lived a lifetime in the South without knowing what a Tom was. So Good Jelly's disapproval of the blacks on the jury only reassured her. They would all be anxious to do what Tyree Neely expected of them.

The gravel cracked, followed by Ot Reeves's high-pitched and reproachful voice. "Awduh! Awduh in the coteroom."

Everyone seemed to be staring at Good Jelly, hence at Daisy in the next seat. Ordinarily, Daisy liked to be looked at, but not *stared* at. Even Riley and Easter Lilly turned from their table and the unspeakable Riley, seeing Daisy, winked insolently. Dr. Worthington crossed his legs, careful of his white creases; Lancey Gregg, openmouthed, gaped; Tug Johnson shifted as massively as a bus pulling out of the Greyhound station; and it seemed to Daisy that Tyree Neely, alone at the prosecution table, was the only person in the courtroom whose eyes were not on her. Not, she thought resentfully, that they ever *really* had been.

Ot Reeves's gavel cracked again. "Mistuh Neely," he said, with perhaps excessive politeness, "you may begin."

Tyree stood and walked in front of the table where he had been sitting. Daisy thought him trim and neat in his light green poplin suit, his striped white and orange button-down shirt, the nubby tie that nicely picked up the orange stripes. The cuffs of the shirt extended a proper inch below the ends of his coat sleeves. Of course, if *she* were dressing him, she'd manage somehow not to let him wear two-tone shoes even in the summertime. Oxblood Wee-juns looked better on his small feet and would be perfect with the poplin suit.

Tyree spoke without notes or ostentation—needing neither, Daisy felt sure, in a simple case like this one.

"Your Honor, the State believes this is a clear case of murder. Premeditated murder, if you please, and under the laws not only of this State but of humanity, deserving of the ultimate penalty."

"Uh-uh," Good Jelly rumbled, and Dr. Worthington, as if he had been holding his breath, let it out in a sigh.

In a flat and unexcited voice, Tyree explained that on the night in question, the accused, Easter Lilly Odum, was the only prisoner in Stonewall County jail. She had been incarcerated on a charge of truck theft brought on good and sufficient evidence by Southland Power and Light Company. The jailer on duty had been a deputy sheriff of good reputation named Benjamin T. Neely, aged thirty-one.

"Now the State will show, Your Honor, that—"

"Objection." Riley had risen to his feet. To Daisy, it seemed impolite of him to interrupt when Tyree was just getting started. But she would have expected little else. "The prosecutor has passed over the important fact that the deputy, Benjamin T. Neely, was his own brother. Or that the deputy's reputation—"

Ot Reeves cut him off with a sharp gavel. "Irrelevant," he said. "Deceased's iden'ty and reppatation not at issue here."

"—was anything but good," Riley finished—even though Daisy and everybody else had plainly heard the judge tell him to shut up. He sat down, looking satisfied.

"Lemme infawm counsel," Judge Reeves said, looking severe, "that in my cote, when he's ovuhruled, he's ovuhruled. Peer-yud."

"Yes, Your Honor."

Counsel looked smug, anyway. Redheaded jerk, Daisy thought. His skinny doxy was positively smirking.

Tyree resumed, Daisy glad that he didn't rant and rave—though she knew he had been greatly affected by his brother's murder. But Tyree was always in control of his emotions—as she knew all too well.

"We don't know exactly how she did it, Your Honor, but that night the accused managed to get the deceased to come into her cell. If I may now direct yours and the jury's attention to the accused . . ." Tyree half turned toward the defense table. "It will be seen that a woman of such striking appearance would be easily able to accomplish such a thing. She—"

The rude redhead jumped to his feet. "Your Honor, my client's appearance is not an issue here. And if the State doesn't even know—"

Judge Reeves's gavel cracked again. "Op'nin statement, counsel. Evi-dence will come later."

It went on that way, Tyree explaining what had happened in the jail, depicting just enough of Easter Lilly's life to suggest how round her heels were. Unruffled, unexcited, he went steadily on until he reached the climactic moment in Easter Lilly's cell:

"And then, Your Honor—ladies and gentlemen of the jury— can there be any doubt"—he swung again toward the defense table and this time pointed at Easter Lilly—"that this known temptress with her known history of carnal interracial relations, with her demonstrated hatred of white people . . . can there be the slightest doubt that, having seized Ben Neely's pocketknife while distract-ing—"

The obnoxious Riley was quickly on his feet: "Your Honor, to call the weapon in question a pocketknife is like calling a Colt forty-five a peashooter."

Ot Reeves, as well he might, sounded exasperated: "They'll be able to see fuh themselves, Counsel."

Tyree seemed undistracted:

"Who can doubt that after seizing Deputy Neely's pocketknife while distracting him with wanton acts and displays of sexual aban-don . . . isn't it plain that the accused deliberately and with malice aforethought struck him to the heart with the blade of his own knife?"

Redheaded Riley held his tongue and kept his seat, though Easter Lilly Odum was shaking her handsome head vigorously. The court-room silence was significant, Daisy thought. Tyree had made his statement quietly, without theatrics, and therefore the more elo-quently and effectively. She scanned the faces of the jurors; they looked either impressed or impassive; and she was sure that Tyree had convinced them, as she herself was convinced.

"Shee-it," Good Jelly Cass said out loud, in two syllables, break-ing the silence Tyree had wrought. This time, as if to silence heresy, Tug Johnson—one hand caressing his championship belt buckle—moved menacingly toward the railing that separated court and spec-tators.

SHEP

AFTER SHEP RILEY FOLLOWED TYREE'S STATEMENT WITH HIS OWN
opening speech for the defense, he sat down and listened as the
prosecutor called his first witness—an elderly white woman, so fat
she overflowed the witness stand, her jowly face framed by green-
rimmed spectacles lifted to a pair of gimlet eyes by underslung
earpieces.

Easter Lilly whispered in recognition, "The old sow!"

Shep knew from the prosecution's witness list what under Tyree's first questions the old sow confirmed in aggrieved tones—that
she was Miss Lila Tillett, for many years a full-time, later a substitute, teacher at Waitsfield High, then at SCCH. Her piled silvery
hair and porcine face quivered indignantly as she added, "Now I'm
over seventy, they got no use for me."

Tyree offered no sympathy. "Did there come a time at SCCH,"
he asked, "when you were called upon to substitute for one Elmore
Timmons, a social science teacher?"

"Yes, sir, there sure did."

"What year was that, if you remember?"

She told him. "Remember it like yesterday."

"And do you remember why at that time you had to take over
his classes?"

"He got run out of town for carryin on with one of the colored girls. That'un over there." She pointed at Easter Lilly.

Even as Shep was jumping up to shout, "Objection!" Judge Reeves cracked down the gavel.

"Just ansuh the question, ma'am. Jury will ignoah the rest of the witness statement."

The judge sounded as apologetic as if he might formerly have been one of the old sow's students, and Shep wondered if he had been. But he did not bother to cross-examine, since Easter Lilly already had been pointed out to the jury as having "carried on" with a white teacher. Not that everyone in Stonewall County, including the jurors, didn't know it anyway.

Tyree politely excused Miss Tillett and called F. Gardner Crump. Mr. Crump, walking with a stoop and a cane, took the witness stand to identify himself as the first principal, now retired, of the new, integrated SCCH.

"I mean desegregated," he corrected himself.

"Do you remember a social science teacher named Elmore Timmons?"

"Not likely to forget *him*."

Did Mr. Crump's pinched face and the eyes that glittered behind his granny glasses, Shep amused himself by wondering, resemble one of the birds the prosecutor liked to chase? Maybe a flycatcher? Or a coot? Shep had no idea what either looked like, but their names seemed right for F. Gardner Crump.

"Elmore Timmons was white, wasn't he?"

"Sure was," Mr. Crump chirped. "Graduated Em'ry'n Henry."

"Did you ever have occasion to . . . ah . . . caution him about his conduct at SCCH?"

"Was my duty. Couldn't have a faculty member contrib'tin to the delinquency of a minor."

"And that minor—do you see that person in this courtroom?"

"Her." Mr. Crump pointed at Easter Lilly, sitting quietly at Shep's side. "An A-student back then."

Mr. Crump was not loath, under Tyree's questioning, to explain how he and other "responsible community leaders" finally had given Elmore Timmons the choice of leaving his job and quitting Waitsfield permanently, or being prosecuted.

"'Cept if you ask me," Mr. Crump volunteered brightly, "it was *her* that did most of the contrib'tin.'"

"Your Honor!" Shep erupted, even though it was too late to wipe the words out of the jurors' minds. "Nobody *did* ask him." But again he waived cross-examination as useless.

"Lawyer," Easter Lilly whispered when he stayed in his chair. "I thought you were gonna win me this case. Why aren't you makin more speeches? Kickin some ass?"

He shivered at the touch of her lips on his earlobe and jotted on a legal pad to show her: "Give me time."

He underlined "time" twice, and stared at the blank, seemingly uninterested face of juror number 8, trying to read his expression. There was none; the face told him nothing. But if Meg was right . . .

When Judge Reeves had summoned the panelists to voir dire in the week just past, Shep had made little effort to block many of the candidates. Having gone over the list with Meg, who with the help of Jase Allman had canvassed most of those picked from the tax and voter rolls, he realized that knocking off even as many as he could would not do him much good. Too many of the rest still would owe or fear Tyree Neely.

He had managed to strike a few, like former Corporal Jed Peters, who had reported for jury duty wearing a VFW cap festooned with patriotic badges and medals. Tyree had been willing to seat Peters, but Shep approached the man warily.

"You're obviously proud of your country, Mister Peters."

"I was," Peters said, "until all this crime."

Shep used a peremptory to dismiss him. He perhaps wasted, but did not regret, another used on Gaither Franklin, the local Ford dealer, who twisted impatiently under questioning and kept looking at his watch.

"You in a hurry?" Shep inquired at last.

"Well, I'm a busy man, you know."

So busy, Shep guessed, that he would want to vote guilty at once and get it over with.

On the whole, however, Shep reasoned that if he didn't make the voir dire a long, acrimonious fight, arguing over every name, contesting every seat, perhaps Tyree wouldn't either. The prosecutor had no real reason to, anyway, since the list was so favorable to him.

After F. Gardner Crump hobbled off the witness stand, Tyree called Deputy Rob Moore, who seemed not as eager to testify as the retired principal had been. In his starched uniform, shiny gunbelt, and creaking boots, Deputy Moore still looked apologetic when he took the oath.

"Tell the court what your duties are, Deputy Moore."

"Right now, I'm day jailer. Seven to three."

"Right now?"

"Transferred from nighttime. Use to work three to leven peeyem."

"And at that time, who would relieve you for the later shift?"

"Ben Neely. He'd work leven to seven."

"And did there come a time when the accused, Easter Lilly Odum, was your only prisoner?"

"Yeah," Rob Moore said.

"Did you notice anything in particular about her?"

"Well . . . she wan't what you'd call easy to get on with. Had a tongue on her like a razor blade and she din't mind usin it. Always complainin bout the food. Stuff like that."

"Recall anything else about her that seemed out of line?"

"Other than that tongue of hers?" Rob Moore glanced at Easter Lilly, then quickly away. "Seem to me she kind of took a shine to Ben Neely."

"Lyin cracker," Easter Lilly whispered in Shep's ear.

"What's that mean, Deputy Moore? What exactly did you see?"

Rob Moore shifted in the witness chair, and stared at the floor.

"One night I stayed on awhile after Ben come in, so I could watch Jay Leno. I notice Ben was back in the cellblock kind of a long time, so when Jay Leno went off I stuck my head past the door there to tell Ben I was leavin. An he's back there yackin it up with her." He nodded in Easter Lilly's direction, not looking up.

"Was she fully dressed? At that hour of the night."

"Well . . . kind of partway."

"Explain that, Deputy. And would you mind talking to me or the jury instead of the floor?"

Rob Moore looked up then, looked at the jury, looked at Easter Lilly, then at Tyree Neely.

"I mean she was kind of open down to here." He touched himself midway between chest and stomach. "Not all the way but . . . you know. Ben could get an eyeful."

Easter Lilly muttered something angry, and shifted in her chair. Her knee nudged Shep's thigh, and at what seemed to him an almost electric touch he jerked his leg aside. Christ, he thought, thinking of the eyeful Ben Neely supposedly had got. Look down at those long enough, a man'd never look up. Or back.

Deputy Moore went on to say—almost sorrowfully, Shep thought—that several times, late in his shift or early in Ben Neely's, he had seen conversations between the deceased and the accused. Not exactly secret, of course, couldn't be no secrets in the cell-block. But kind of playful. Friendly-like.

"Touching?" Tyree asked.

"Not that I ever seen, Mister Neely."

"But of course, Deputy, every night after you left, there'd be maybe seven or eight hours, wouldn't you say, when you weren't *there* to see whether these playful chats, these friendly little talks, wound up with them touching each other. Maybe kissing?"

"Objection," Shep called. "Putting things in the eyes of the witness that counsel himself says the witness couldn't have seen."

"Now, Mistuh Neely," Judge Reeves said amiably. "You know bettuh'n that."

This time, and not just to reassure Easter Lilly, Shep did not waive cross-examination. He stood close to the witness stand and tried to fix Deputy Moore's evasive eyes with his.

"Now, Deputy, that night you stayed to watch Jay Leno, you say you saw Ben Neely and the defendant yacking it up in the cellblock. How do you know Ben could get what you called an eyeful?"

"Well, see," Rob Moore said. "Her dress was sort of open way down to here." The deputy's meaty hands waved in vague circles in front of his chest.

Visualizing himself the eyeful in question, Shep glanced at the defense table. Easter's denim dress was buttoned primly to her slender neck but swelled out beautifully above her waist. Shaking her head, she was looking at Meg. *Men* the shaking head seemed to say of Rob Moore's testimony. *Hopeless.*

"Well, could *you* get an eyeful?" Shep asked Deputy Moore.

"Not that far away."

"Then you don't actually know that Ben did, either?"

Rob Moore met his eyes almost happily. "Ben Neely," he said, "never missed that kind of a sight'n'is whole life."

Tyree objected, of course, and Judge Reeves sustained, but Shep sat down encouraged. Not for long.

"What kind of a sight do you mean?" Tyree asked in reexamination.

Deputy Moore was looking at the floor again. His hands rose in front of his chest.

"What it look like to me she was showin'im."

"Witness excused," Tyree said quickly. Shep was able to get the deputy's obvious conclusion expunged from the trial record, but not, he knew, from the jury's ears.

Easter whispered, "Must of told that cracker his ass is fired he don't say all that lying shit."

Shep did not doubt that Rob Moore had been told something like that. Whether it was lying shit, he was not so sure. Easter Lilly knew very well the effect she had on men; he, Shep Riley, was Exhibit 1. It was not impossible that she'd given Ben Neely an occasional "eyeful" or whispered something promising in his ear. But that didn't mean she'd necessarily lured him into her cell, like a black widow to her web, and murdered him.

Shep hoped the jury had seen that Rob Moore was not an impressive prosecution witness—reluctant to speak, not wanting to look at Easter Lilly when he did. Shep tried in vain to read such a reaction in the blank face of juror number 8. *Nothing*. Maybe Tyree knew something Meg had overlooked.

Then Tyree surprised Shep and, obviously, Judge Reeves: "Your Honor, the State rests."

The judge recovered quickly enough to call a recess. When he left the courtroom, Meg came around the defense table to lean on her elbows facing Shep and Easter Lilly.

"Your opening statement was terrific," she told Shep.

"Just like it happened," Easter Lilly said. "Was the *truth* you told, Lawyer."

Shep was pleased, particularly, to feel again the warm touch of her knee against his thigh.

"But what's Neely up to," Meg said, "resting so soon?" As always in court, Shep thought, she was all business.

"Cause that cracker's got no case." Easter Lilly thumped the table lightly. "Nobody knows what happen that night cept me."

"Maybe not. But he *has* got a case," Shep said. "It's already made. You had an affair with one white man and took a shine to another one, so . . ."

"I wouldn't give doodly-squat to that Klucker Ben Neely!"

"But because Tyree doesn't have an eyewitness," Shep went on, "he's suggested you and Ben were getting it on." The thought was painful to him. "He's rested on that, to leave it foremost in the jurors' minds. And he expects to kill us on summation."

"So he had to go and drag in Mister Timmons." Anger edged Easter Lilly's voice. "After all these years they just can't leave'im alone."

And neither can you, Shep thought jealously. He was tired of hearing about Elmore Timmons, tired of thinking about Easter Lilly and Elmore Timmons.

"Well, we don't have a witness, either," Meg said, "since you decided not to put Easter on the stand."

Just then, a black man in a white suit leaned on the railing and spoke to Easter Lilly. She turned to reply. Shep heard her call the visitor "Fred, honey," and was annoyed again.

Under the table he could feel Easter's knee, still touching his thigh. With the boyfriend standing there in his white goddam suit, Shep suddenly resented the excitement her mere touch caused him. He resented Easter Lilly, too, and most of all his own foolish predicament. He had known for months, certainly after he'd received her note, that Easter Lilly had him on her string, like a wet, flopping trout. When he'd heard her words in the cellblock—*But what I need is a* lawyer—he'd realized she knew it, too. She could touch him and he'd jerk; speak and he'd react. He was astounded, after his many amours, to be so susceptible to a woman, any woman. He was accustomed to control, certainly of himself. Of Penny. Even of Meg—most of the time, anyway.

He resented thinking as constantly as he did, even sometimes dreaming, about Easter Lilly Odum. Not because she was black—though he'd never been involved with a black woman, he knew it was just a good-ol-boy myth that they were more sexually exotic than white women. Meg, for instance, might be mannerly, reserved; she might not flaunt or even seem to be aware of herself. In bed, however, she gave herself up completely to passion, yielding and consuming at once. Meg's demanding mouth had more than once reduced him to idiocy, and when on that spring night at the New South/Best Western she had mounted him like an Indian on a pony, her eyes blazed down as if to light brush at the feet of a human sacrifice.

"That Rob Moore lied like a sailor, didn't he?" he heard Meg saying to Easter Lilly. All business in the courtroom; but in the bedroom . . . which was the difference. He had made love to Meg dozens of times and probably would again, when she got down off her high horse. As he believed she would, sooner or later.

"You got that right," Easter said. "Ben Neely tried but he *never* saw down my dress."

Easter Lilly, however, was forbidden fruit—twice forbidden. No code of ethics permitted a lawyer to make love to his client, and Shep Riley would not be—*could* not be—like those white males who for hundreds of years had exploited black women's bodies.

He had come to Waitsfield—before he'd ever even seen Easter Lilly Odum or heard of Elmore Timmons or J. Preston Cadieux—because he was convinced that Easter Lilly was a victim. His intuition, his lifelong conviction that the big fish eat the little fish, had guided his belief and behavior and he had seen nothing in Stonewall County to contradict his belief. He might be obsessed by a woman—Shep painfully conceded—but he was defending Easter Lilly for a more honorable reason: because she *was* a victim of the injustice that seemed to him so nearly to rule the world.

Therefore, he thought—wanting to believe it—I've got her on the string, too. They needed each other. But Easter Lilly—he had to admit—conceivably could get another lawyer. Shep was not sure how and when he could get himself back. Here, now, in the courtroom, Meg watching—at the mere thought of Easter Lilly, his desire rose in him like a river nearing the top of a levee.

Just then, a black hand, extending from a white-clad arm, touched Shep's shoulder. He looked up. Fred Worthington said, "You're doing good. We're counting on you."

Shep wanted to slap the man's face, hating the proprietary tone of the boyfriend's words, despising his own unwanted jealousy. But before he could say or do anything, Lancey Gregg sang out, "Oyez!" again, Worthington moved hurriedly toward his front-row seat, and Judge Reeves returned, his face a little flushed and his eyes brighter.

From the bench, he pointed the shaft of his gavel at the defense table.

"May begin, Mistuh Counsel."

Shep stood up, relieved to be free of the intolerable, deceptively promising touch of Easter's leg against his.

"Your Honor," he said. "Defense calls Jason Allman."

MEG

MEG RESUMED HER SEAT AT THE END OF THE DEFENSE TABLE AND watched Jase stride down the aisle. He still displayed the purposeful appearance of law enforcement, if not its official uniform. He had put aside his ill-fitting security guard's outfit and wore a shiny gray suit, its jacket marginally too tight across his broad shoulders. Off the rack at the Kmart, Meg guessed.

Ida Sue had fitted Jase out for court in a green necktie with horizontal bands that clashed against his vertically striped blue shirt. The tie appeared to be choking him and its knot was askew, as if he had loosened, then tightened it without looking into a mirror.

Meg decided in faint amusement that Jase was the picture of solid manliness, right down to his aura of dressed-up discomfort. Who could doubt the rectitude of a man who looked so ready and able to do his duty, despite a tight collar?

Jase passed through the gate at the end of the aisle and went quickly to the witness stand, looking neither at Shep nor Tyree Neely. Meg was glad he was *their* witness, showing none of Rob Moore's furtive reluctance.

Jase's loud response to the oath rang through the courtroom and echoed from the empty balcony: "I do!" Unnecessarily he bent to kiss—with an audible smack—Lancey Gregg's proffered Bible.

Then he settled himself firmly in the witness chair, a ramrod picture of determination.

Shep, as Meg had seen him do many times, quickly disposed of the preliminaries and got down to business.

"Mister Allman, did you hear Deputy Rob Moore's testimony?"

Something, however, was different about Shep—something more than the missing sideburns or the neatly cropped red hair. He had, as always, an advocate's air of confidence, a brisk way of asserting in body language that he knew his business. But as Jase replied that he certainly did hear Rob Moore's testimony, Meg sensed something new and strange about Shep Riley—something she already had noticed and wondered at, during his opening statement.

"Well, do you have of your own knowledge anything to add to his . . . ah . . . perception that the defendant and Ben Neely became friendly?"

Shep had turned his back on the witness stand and was strolling casually toward the jury box.

"I never saw nuthin like that," Jase said.

As he spoke, Meg was looking at Shep Riley, who was looking at Easter Lilly. At Jase's words, Meg saw, or thought she saw, a look of genuine relief touch Shep's face. It triggered in her a quick memory of standing outside the New South/Best Western, hearing Shep's voice thicken . . . *out of his mind . . . a woman like that . . .*

Before Shep turned back to the witness stand, he smiled at Easter Lilly, and Meg knew—as always, trusting her instinct—that he had heard something that he desperately wanted to hear, said by someone he could believe.

"You mean when you were the daytime jailer?"

"See, she wa'nt friendly to *any* of us," Jase said. "I told my wife oncet, it was like havin a rattlesnake coiled up back there."

"Mighty right," Easter Lilly murmured, the words audible to Meg at the end of the table. "Ready to strike."

Still reflecting on the relief she'd seen on Shep's face, Meg looked across the table at their client and sensed for the first time what Easter Lilly's customary antagonism had blinded her to—what Elmore Timmons had seen in the teenage schoolgirl, what even Ben Neely must somehow have glimpsed in the black woman jailbird: *beauty unreachable as truth.*

Mr. Timmons had risked and lost his white identity—who in

America had anything more precious?—in the need to touch that beauty. To Ben Neely it must have seemed so remote from his grasp, his distance from it so unbridgeable, that only by violence could he come near . . . *a woman like that* . . .

Meg was sure Shep Riley had seen it, too—that Easter Lilly Odum was not merely an angry person trapped in a beautiful shell, a pretty black girl with a hard edge of resentment. That her physical beauty sheltered a harsh spirit, even nourished it in a world indifferent to beauty, would not much have troubled a man able, as Shep Riley was, to sense Easter Lilly's rarity.

"Now, then, Mister Allman," Shep was saying to the witness, "it was you, was it not, who on the morning in question found Deputy Neely's body in the defendant's cell?"

"I never seen a worse sight."

"So just tell the court in your own words what you saw that morning."

Jase gave a terse description of the morning scene in Easter Lilly's deserted cell, and concluded, "Strangest thing to me was how all that blood seem to run straight into the drain-hole."

Shep let this gory image hang in the courtroom atmosphere, while he paced to the jury box and back, seemingly in thought— part of his practiced courtroom manner. Meg knew him so well she believed she could read his mind—and, knowing him like that, realized that if Shep Riley, too, was fantasizing about Easter Lilly Odum, his fantasy would be sexual. But what could his fantasy be *but* sexual? What was the passion of the artist—the sculptor at his marble, the painter at his canvas? And most men could neither shape marble nor paint canvas. They had only their maleness by which to express or even recognize their passions.

"Now what, if anything," Shep said, "did you notice about the deceased's hand?"

"They was blood on it, kind of dried up. Not like comin out of where the knife was stuck in his chest. Like a separate cut."

For once, however, Shep couldn't tumble a woman into bed, take what he wanted, and go his way. Not *that* woman. Easter Lilly was black and a client—but far more than that. She was unobtainable, like a vision of an oasis in the desert, never quite to be reached. In this case, Shep Riley's fantasy could never be his reality. And he would know it.

"Where was this cut?"

Jase drew a line across his palm with his forefinger. "Like that," he said.

"And do you remember which hand was cut like that?"

Jase leaned back in the witness stand, rolled up his eyes in the effort to recall, to envision again that morning's scene.

"Left hand. I was standin bout where you're standin, lookin down. Was his left hand, all right."

"Now, to your knowledge, was Ben Neely left-handed?"

Jase pondered the question briefly. "Any time I seen'im writin or eatin or anything like that, maybe usin his keys, it was always with his right."

Shep quickly entered into evidence the lines from the coroner's report that corroborated Jase's description of a cut on Ben Neely's bloody left hand.

"Now, Mister Allman," he asked, "when Ben Neely first came on as a jailer, is it true that you acted as his mentor?"

"Tried to show'im what to do, if that's what you mean."

"Was that your own idea? Or did somebody ask you to do that?"

Jase jerked his head toward the prosecution table. "Mister Neely there, he ast me to kind of keep an eye on'is brother."

Shep feigned surprise. Meg was sure he fooled no one, least of all the jury.

"The prosecutor?"

"Called'im Benjy. Said he was'nt really such a bad kid." Jase's voice conveyed ample doubt about this judgment.

"So what kind of advice did you give . . . ah . . . Benjy?"

"Lemme think a minute." Jase did, then went on. "Always be on time so's somebody fresh is on guard. Always be in uniform so's in the cells they's no doubt who's in charge. Don't answer nobody that whines about the food, cause they all whine about the food, an you can't do nuthin about it, anyway."

"What, if anything, about weapons?"

"Never take one back in the cells. This druggie we had back there one time? Tripped out on some kind-a stuff? Tried to grab my piece outta my holster. Taught me the hard way not to carry it in the cellblock."

"And did you pass that on to Deputy Neely?"

"Well, see, I seen'im come outta there oncet with that big ol

Swiss knife stickin outta his hip pocket. Ben, I says, you dern fool, you just askin for it, takin that knife back there. Far's I know, he never took it in the cellblock again. Not stickin outta his hip pocket, anyway.''

Shep had gone again into his pacing, man-in-thought routine. Watching this familiar performance—his head bowed, his hands clasped behind him—Meg wondered if even as he questioned Jase Allman, his thoughts actually were on Easter Lilly Odum.

''But the prosecutor says that's exactly what Deputy Neely must have done the night he was stabbed,'' Shep said. ''He must've taken the knife into her cell.''

Jase Allman glanced at Tyree, settled himself more firmly in the witness chair, lifted his chin, and said, ''Maybe the prosecutor knows better, but I'd be mighty surprised Ben was fool enough to do what he knew better'n to do.''

''But you said yourself that you saw that same knife sticking out of Ben Neely's chest that morning? Didn't you?''

''I sure-God did.''

''So how would you account for that? Since you don't believe he would have carried his knife into the cellblock that night?''

Jase cleared his throat, ran a long finger inside his tight collar, and glanced nervously at Tyree Neely before he answered, ''What I said was . . . I said not in'is pocket. I said I didn't b'leeve Ben carried'is knife in there in'is pocket.''

JASE

AFTER SHEP RILEY FINISHED HIS QUESTIONS AND SAT DOWN, JASE watched with apprehension as Tyree Neely advanced toward the witness stand. Jase was not worried for himself. He'd already answered the toughest questions, and had to give up the deputy's job and the prospects that Ida Sue had treasured. Her displeasure was the worst personal penalty he could imagine. But Jase also dreaded the possibility that Tyree might spread public dirt on Ida Sue. He hadn't done it so far, but Jase had gone up against him in open court, and Tyree Neely was not a man to turn the other cheek.

"Jase." Tyree did not look outraged. But he still reminded Jase of a cat stalking a bird in the weeds. "If I understand what you've just told the court, Jase, you believe . . . but you weren't there when it happened, were you?"

"Nossir. Nobody there but him and her."

If Ida Sue had come to the trial, sight of her might buck him up. Except she wouldn't love it that he'd gone against Tyree.

"Could of had your old job back," Jase could hear her saying. "Got a house in town." Which was maybe true.

"But your personal reasoning," Tyree said, "is that Deputy Ben Neely went back to the accused's cell with his knife out and open in his hand. Is that right?"

"Way I figger it, yessir." Might's well be hung for a sheep as a goat.

"With intent to do her bodily harm?"

"Well . . . maybe just kind of scare'er a little."

"*Threaten* bodily harm, then?"

Jase took a deep breath. Ida Sue might not understand but he had sworn a long time ago to uphold the law, and he didn't aim to lie under oath. Or back off from Tyree Neely anymore. Not even for a job on the county payroll or a house in town.

"Can't see no other reason," he said.

Tyree turned to Judge Reeves and spread his arms wide.

"Your Honor, I'm going to make the objection my colleague at the defense table would be making if this testimony weren't favorable to the false and malicious case he's trying so hard to make. This witness has just stated a personal conclusion for which there is no evidence but his unsupported opinion. Not an iota. Not a smidgen. Not a jot nor tittle of evidence. The entire testimony of this witness is just a tissue of supposition based only on his deductive reasoning—maybe flawed, maybe imaginary. Who knows?"

Jase was not subtle or sensitive to nuances. But he could tell that Tyree's tone suggested that *he* knew and therefore Judge Reeves surely did, and probably the jurors. And if they didn't, they should. Jase was infuriated to have his word doubted, and Shep Riley was on his feet before Tyree finished speaking.

"Whose case is false and malicious," Shep declared forcefully, "is for the jury to decide, Your Honor. We have here a question about a violent death to which everyone agrees there were no witnesses. Now I ask you to remember, Your Honor . . ."

Shep swung toward the jury box. "Ladies and gentlemen also, I ask you to recall Deputy Rob Moore's testimony. When he took the stand, it was the State that started this business of having Deputy Neely's former colleagues suggest what *might* have happened in the jail that night. Now, when the defense gets its turn, the State wants to call off the game. I don't think—"

Judge Reeves tapped his gavel and said, "Proach the bench, please."

Jase on the witness stand was near enough to hear, even with the lawyers' backs to him, their arguments repeated in murmurs.

He heard the judge's reply, too, "Seem like to me what's good for the goose oughtta be good for the ganduh."

Tyree Neely's back stiffened and Jase heard his unbelieving whisper. "Judge . . . you're gonna let all this moonshine stand?"

"Gonna let yoah jury figguh it out, Ty."

Jase thought Ot Reeves had subtly emphasized *yoah*. And the judge should have known Tyree hated to be called Ty.

"I'm wrong, you can get me revuhsed." Judge Reeves sat back in his high swivel chair. "Bout ready to retiah, anyway."

Tyree Neely was not smiling when he turned back to the witness stand. Jase had seen him mad before, and he felt his innards begin to churn. Tyree could be a mean sonovagun when crossed.

"Now, Jase," the prosecutor began, mildly enough. Then he abruptly switched his line of questioning. "Tell the court how come you quit the sheriff's department."

Here we go.

For a moment, Jase wished he were safely back on the county payroll, in uniform, in Tyree's good graces. But then all that bullshit about Ida Sue would be lying in the gutter for anybody to step in. He'd still be working for fat-ass Johnson. And he'd be in hell with his back broke before he'd do that again.

Tyree prompted, "Jase?"

Jase had never once thought that Tug's story could be true. Ida Sue might be kind of eager to live in town and all, but that was only womanlike. She was no more capable of cheating on him than he was of cheating on her. They'd taken solemn vows before the Good Lord, hadn't they? And the closest he'd ever come to violating those vows was looking at bare boobs in the movies. On the other hand, Jase thought it genuinely low-down for any man to put a dirty mouth on a woman's name. Like that lard-bucket done to Suedy. It would be downright dishonorable, Jase believed, to have any truck at all, let alone work with scum that'd be so indecent.

"Why'd you resign as a deputy sheriff?" Tyree demanded.

Jase thought fast. "Other opportunities."

"As a security guard? Out at the mall?"

Jase followed with a line picked up from some Harvard type on *McNeil-Lehrer,* which he occasionally watched after Peter Jennings. He had recognized the idea as useful to deflect Ida Sue's complaints about his mall job.

"In the private sector," he intoned, trying to sound like the Harvard, "anybody willin to work and take a risk can get ahead."

Tyree looked startled. "You mean at the mall?"

"Ain't that the Merican Way?" From the corner of his eye, Jase saw the lady lawyer clap a hand over her mouth.

"But Jase . . ." Tyree's voice sharpened. "Isn't it true you had a personal falling out with Sheriff Johnson?"

"Immaterial," Shep Riley sang out. "Irrelevant."

Tyree looked at Judge Reeves as if they both understood they were dealing with a stranger unaccustomed to local ways.

"I'm trying to get at this witness's motives, Your Honor. For impugning the character of a fellow officer who can no longer defend himself against false accusations."

"Go on then," Ot Reeves said, with the decisive air of a man in charge.

Tyree turned back to the witness chair. Jase flinched a little from the hard light in the prosecutor's eyes.

"Isn't it true, Jase, that after Sheriff Johnson made certain representations to me, you turned in your badge? Threw it down on Daisy Thorpe's desk, as a matter of fact?"

Certain representations. Maybe he won't say what they were, Jase thought. Which didn't mean they hadn't been said. Or that Tyree Neely hadn't listened. Maybe he'd be ashamed to repeat them. As he should be.

"You wasn't there at the time."

"But it's true, isn't it, that you quit in protest?"

"Them things he tole you, *they* wasn't true. He——"

"But it *is* true, isn't it, that you still bear a grudge against Sheriff Johnson?"

"Dern right. But——"

"And against me, because I listened to him?"

What did Jase Allman ever do to Tyree Neely, Jase asked himself, to deserve a charge like that from a man he'd trusted? Hadn't he tried to look after Tyree's asshole brother? Done ever'thing else he was told? Even paid sky-high rent on a rust-bucket trailer Ida Sue was ashamed to live in?

"You ought to've kicked that lyin fathead"—as he spoke, Jase looked Tyree Neely in the eye—"right outten your office."

"So now, just to get back at me"—Tyree's voice had risen and he pointed a long finger into Jase's face—"you sit right here in this court and straight-out *lie* about my brother that's dead and buried out beside our old daddy that did more for this county than any man that ever lived! Didn't you just plain lie about a poor dead boy that can't answer back?"

Jase was stunned and outraged. He and Ida Sue were the *real* victims of lies. And *his* word was good as gold. But he still shied from the possibility of provoking Tyree into repeating Tug Johnson's shitbird "representations." So, before Jase could think what to say, Tyree and Shep Riley were simultaneously shouting:

Shep (at Judge Reeves): "Counsel's bullying this witness!"

Tyree (at Jase): "Didn't you lie about Benjy to get back at me?"

The lawyers, glaring at each other, fell silent at the same moment. The courtroom was still as the aftermath of a storm, except for a hoarse mutter from a large black woman in a flowered dress sitting in the front row. "Barnyard cats!" she said.

Jase recognized Good Jelly Cass, who seemed to have been addressing Daisy Thorpe, huddled between Good Jelly and Easter Lilly's medical boyfriend in the ice cream suit. Tug Johnson was looking at Good Jelly like he thought he was man enough to shut up a woman. Which Jase doubted. Not one that near his own size, anyway.

"Awduh!" Judge Reeves shouted, slamming down his gavel and glaring at Good Jelly. "Ain't gonna have these outbreaks!" He glared around the courtroom before saying in a quieter voice:

"Lunchtime, anyway. Y'all come back in at two. Counsel, see me in my chambuhs. All-a you."

TYREE

IN JOHN BELL NEELY'S DAY, THE STONEWALL COUNTY COURTHOUSE judges' chambers had not been impressive. The old man had disdained convenience, even for himself, particularly if it cost taxpayers money, therefore probably votes.

When Tyree Neely succeeded his father, kicked Ottis P. Reeves upstairs, and cleared the prosecutor's office for himself, he made a real effort to upgrade the judges' chambers. Unlike his father, Tyree appreciated the uses of convenience. He had an eye not only to the gratitude Ot Reeves and other circuit judges presumably would feel, but to a valuable future consideration—that Tyree Neely might one day want to elevate himself to the bench.

So at the time of Easter Lilly Odum's trial, Ot Reeves's chambers were carpeted, fluorescent, and air-conditioned. They were replastered every year or so, and high windows provided a Norman Rockwell view of old men sleeping on the benches under the courthouse trees. The decor was completed by a hotel-style minibar, a private bathroom, a desk the size of a Ping-Pong table, and a black leather sofa for midday naps.

Judge Reeves was not napping when Tyree, Shep Riley, and Meg Whitman knocked, then entered at his call. He was sitting behind the broad expanse of desk, on which he pretended—Tyree suspected—to be reading a thick legal tome that had left a gap like a missing tooth along the shelves of lawbooks that covered an entire wall.

"Sit down, folks." The judge did not bother to look up. They seated themselves on the leather sofa, the woman between the two men. Ducks in a row, Tyree thought.

Judge Reeves closed the volume before him with a slap not unlike that of a banging gavel. From a drawer he produced a nearly full bottle of Maker's Mark and set it with solicitude on the desktop.

"Goes a long way to cool tempuhs," he said. "Y'all care to indulge?"

Three heads shook almost in unison. Judge Reeves took a glass, a spoon, and a sugar bowl from another drawer. He put a spoonful of sugar in the glass and two carefully measured fingers of Maker's Mark on top of the sugar—all of which caused Tyree Neely to feel as if he were in a time warp.

In an age of vodka, beer, and white wine—in Stonewall County, the last was always called Shablee—he had not seen anyone mix a cold-water toddy for years. Not since John Bell Neely had made it a nightly ritual to be completed before his wife Gladys was allowed to put the family supper on the table. In the old man's last years, Benjy sometimes had been permitted to pour the bourbon.

Without leaving his desk, Judge Reeves spun in his chair to the minibar behind him, extricated half a glassful of ice cubes, rose, and carried his glass into the bathroom. Running water was briefly heard. When he returned, his glass was wrapped neatly in a paper towel. He sank into his chair, took a long drink, and said without preamble, "Y'all givin me a hod time."

Neither Shep nor Tyree Neely replied. But after a moment, Meg said, "I don't think anybody means to, Your Honor."

The inevitable female urge, Tyree thought, to ease tensions. A nice-seeming lady. Too bad she was immoral.

Once Meg had spoken, Judge Reeves took note of her crossed legs, and stared rather blatantly. Ot Reeves still had his taste for women as well as for booze, Tyree noted.

"I been hearin cases a long time." The judge continued to contemplate the woman lawyer's legs, as if they reminded him of long-ago trials. Tyree could feel her hands move down to tug at her skirt. "Too long maybe. Anyways, long enough I know what's goin on heah."

He took a pull at his toddy, lowered it, and gazed at its icy surface with approval. "Both you boys say they wan't no witnesses. I can see for myself they ain't much evidence, either. So it don't take Earl Warren to see you both aim to talk the jury into thinkin what you want'em to think. Am I right, honey . . . I mean ma'am?"

Meg nodded, and pulled at her skirt again. Legs on the skinny side, Tyree thought, though he did not consider himself a good judge. But Ot Reeves was not one to quibble about details, either.

"So what I aimed to tell y'all," the judge said, "let's cut out all this 'irrelevant, immaterial' crap. Beggin yoah pahdon, ma'am. All this objectin, I mean."

No doubt about it, Tyree thought. About time to turn Ot out to pasture. He'd even said he was willing.

"You rested the State, Ty. How bout you, Couns'lor?"

"If the State's finished with cross," Shep said, "I just have a few questions on redirect."

"Then you'll rest, too?"

"Well . . . depends, Your Honor." Riley was properly evasive, Tyree thought. The judge's job was not to set speed laws. Ot definitely had slipped a little over the hill. Sometimes even forgot his friends, like with that goose and gander bit.

Judge Reeves drank a third time from his toddy and put down the paper-wrapped glass, empty.

"Fuh lunch," he said, his eyes still on Meg's legs, "there's the Purity down the street aways. Fraid I can't recommend it." He took a sandwich in a plastic bag from still another desk drawer. "Last time I et there, had the runs for two days. Beggin yoah pahdon again, honey."

When court reconvened in the drowsy afternoon, Jase Allman was still on the stand, looking somewhat rumpled and uneasy. So far, Tyree was sure, the State had the edge. Rob Moore had planted the seeds of victory in ground already plowed by Elmore Timmons. And though he'd hated to do it, Tyree believed he'd sufficiently tainted Jase Allman's credibility with that grudge charge.

Besides which, he thought, Riley had been a surprising pushover in voir dire. In defense's shoes, he'd have challenged half the jurors Riley had seated without a fight. But Tyree listened carefully as Riley began his redirect.

"Now Jase . . . counsel for the State says you lied when you suggested Deputy Neely went to the defendant's cell with an open knife in his hand to threaten her with bodily harm. Why would you lie about a thing like that?"

"I didn't."

"To get revenge on Deputy Neely's brother?" Shep gestured at the prosecution table. "The prosecutor, I mean?"

"I ain't lookin for revenge."

He probably wasn't. Tyree was suddenly depressed. He hated having had to go after Jase Allman. The man would have made a good sheriff someday. A better head than Tug Johnson, which wasn't saying much. But still dumb enough not to question orders and loyal enough to take any heat that came along.

"In fact, Jase, you'd have been better off to try to *protect* Ben Neely, wouldn't you?"

"I ain't sure."

"You think you might even have got your deputy job back if you'd done that?"

Tyree started to object, then remembered that Ot Reeves wanted to get the whole thing into the jury room. Fix himself another toddy.

"I don't want that job back." Jase stared across the courtroom at Tug Johnson. "I wouldn't take it if it was offered."

For a moment, Tyree thought Shep Riley had committed the cardinal courtroom sin: asking a witness a question without knowing what the answer would be.

"So the fact is, isn't it," Shep said, "that lying about Ben Neely, protecting him, accepting the State's version of events, wouldn't have done you any good? Even if you'd been offered your old job back, you wouldn't have lied to get it."

"I wouldn't cross the street for that job."

The man had natural credibility, Tyree thought sadly. He *looked* manly. He *sounded* square.

"So you *didn't* lie, did you? You just told the truth?"

"Like I always try to do."

"And let the chips fall where they may?"

Jase grunted a sort of assent.

"The repotuh can't put that noise in the recud," Judge Reeves said, indicating a woman working at a shorthand machine. "Ansuh yes or no."

"Yes, sir!" Jase said loudly.

Tyree prided himself on his realism. He knew at once that whatever he had done before lunch to make Jase Allman look like a vindictive liar had been wasted in the afternoon. Nobody was likely to believe that open-faced, plainspoken Jase Allman would lie under oath—especially a jury full of people who thought him a straightshooter. Tyree was oddly proud of the man. He'd stood up. But Tyree saw no reason to despair of his own case.

As Shep Riley rested for the defense, Tyree jotted a few notes for his summation. He would still nail down the lid on Easter Lilly Odum's coffin. Just because a big-shot out-of-town lawyer had conned thickheaded Jase Allman into turning his coat against a man who had always helped him was no reason to back off. John Bell Neely had never backed off from anything. And he hadn't raised his oldest son to be a quitter.

Tyree was eager to get at the jury, but the defense summation had to come first. Riley began while standing right before the jury box, his hands planted on the railing in front of it, his eyes roving directly over the jurors' faces.

Showboat, Tyree thought. Ought to be a darkie somewhere, singing "Ol' Man River."

"Ladies and gentlemen. You're here in the great tradition on which our criminal justice system rests—the tradition of good men and true coming to honest judgment. And, at long last, long overdue"—Shep beamed, Tyree thought fatuously, at Callie Igoe in the front row of the jury box—"good women and true. You're here because counsel for the State and I determined that you were willing and able to make honest, honorable, independent judgments."

Much good that kind of back scratching would do him with this jury, Tyree thought. Which if it came in with any verdict except the one *he* would demand, all those good folks and true had better start watching their hides. Maybe in some other county.

"Judgments free of preconceived notions. Free of prejudice because of gossip you might have heard or headlines in the media. Whatever you've seen on TV."

Even as a lawyer, Tyree Neely felt no more guilt or compunction that the jury was biased in his favor than a ballplayer would feel if the star of the opposing team had a broken leg and couldn't play. Tyree did what he could for Stonewall County—guarded its morals, stimulated its prosperity, maintained law and order—and everybody knew it. If he also turned an honest dollar for himself, he'd earned it. And it was no more than his due from a grateful county that he should have his way in the courtroom. Quits on Saturday night, John Bell used to say.

"You're here because we have confidence in your ability to make a considered judgment on just what you've heard in this courtroom. And nothing else."

Not, Tyree cynically noted, a "considered judgment on the facts presented in this trial." No wonder, "facts" having been scarce as hen's teeth. Other than the unassailable facts that Ben Neely had been knifed to death in Easter Lilly Odum's cell, by Easter Lilly Odum. It hadn't happened anywhere else. And Easter Lilly didn't deny that she'd wielded the knife.

It had been an open-and-shut case until Riley and his kept woman (Tyree hated to think the last two words but what else could he call her?)—until the two of them drummed up this self-defense malarkey. Which came down to the outrageous and unbelievable accusation that John Bell Neely's son had tried to rape a nigger (again, Tyree flinched at having thought the word).

"Now I'd like you to pay close attention," Riley was saying, "to a demonstration my associate and I believe will be enlightening."

Meg stood and crossed the courtroom. Definitely too thin, Tyree thought. Still . . . the fact was, even knowing what he did, he liked to look at her. And she didn't have her woman's hooks out for him.

Meg handed Riley State's Exhibit 1—the red-handled Swiss Army knife—which he held up for the jurors to see.

"This is the knife, ladies and gentlemen, that killed Ben Neely. Now the State would have you believe that Deputy Neely went into the defendant's cell with this deadly weapon in his back pocket. Like this."

Ostentatiously, Shep took off his jacket, put the Swiss knife in a back pocket of his trousers, and piroutted like a model so the jury could see the red haft extending plainly into view. Meg draped his jacket over the back of a chair at the defense table, and returned to Riley's side.

"Now if you give the State's scenario any credit at all . . ."

Shep paused and appeared to fix his eyes on a juror in the back row. Flushing Johns, Tyree thought, and immediately told himself again that he was getting entirely too careless, even in his mind. He did not want to think that nickname, any more than the N-word, lest he forget and use it orally. Maybe even in front of *Fielding* Johns, one of the real assets he'd managed to bring to Stonewall County.

"Though we don't believe that scenario has even a particle of validity. The State claims that Deputy Neely with the knife in his back pocket and this defendant"—he gestured behind him at Easter Lilly—"must have embraced right there in her jail cell. Like this." Riley put his arms around Meg, and she hugged him, too, but their bodies scarcely touched—looking, Tyree thought, deceptively like teenagers after a round of spin-the-bottle. Careful not to set off any suspicion in some juror's imagination.

"Now you may think a jail cell is a strange place for a man and a woman to be . . . ah . . . playing around," Riley said, "and I certainly think so, too."

He winked rather elaborately at Callie Igoe in the front row. Mistake, Tyree thought, knowing Callie was the kind who waited outside the door of Neely Methodist every Sunday morning. Callie's hair was in the usual tight bun, and she pursed her lips as Riley talked on and on. Tyree noted her disapproval for future reference.

"Different races, at that," Riley said. "To you and me all this might sound farfetched. But still—that's what the State wants you to think. And the prosecution further believes—anyway, they want *you* to believe—that even while Deputy Neely and the defendant were loving it up . . ."

Downright criminal to hear the Neely name used in any such context. But the fat was in the fire and there might be worse to come.

". . . she reaches around him"—Meg did so—"and steals the knife out of his pocket."

Meg held it up behind Riley's back. He half turned, and she moved with him, like a dancer following his lead. That gave the jurors a profile view of their loosely linked bodies.

"Now, of course, she *could* have done that," Riley said. "You've just seen how. But then what, ladies and gentlemen?" He released Meg and turned squarely to the jury box, his voice rising. "Then what?"

Only footlights were missing, Tyree thought, doubting that these playacting tactics were going over. Stonewall folks tended to be matter-of-fact. No weeping, wailing, or gnashing of teeth. Even when Mayor Gordon Allbright, a real vote-getter, dropped dead on Main Street in front of Two Guys Appliance Repair, some people stepped right over the corpse.

Tyree could not be sure, however. In his memory, no Stonewall jury ever had seen a spectacle quite like this. Maybe Riley and the woman were scoring more points than he knew. Tyree watched rather sourly as the two lawyers pantomimed a struggle for the knife, the woman trying at the same time to get its blade open. But in less than a minute, Riley had snatched the knife away from her.

Unopened.

Meg returned to the defense table and Riley faced the jury box, waving the big red knife like a trophy.

"So you see, ladies and gentlemen, the State's scenario just won't wash, will it? She could steal the knife but *she couldn't get it open.* Not if Deputy Neely was trying to take it back from her, as I was. As he surely would have been trying to do. And let me call your attention to something else—something crucial."

He put the knife, still unopened, on the railing of the jury box and raised both hands above his head, palms out, looking from Tyree Neely's seat at the prosecution table like a Holy Roller shouting *Hallelujah!*

"No cuts, ladies and gentlemen. No cuts! The knife was never opened. If she got hold of the knife as the State in its desperation for a conviction insists she did, she still couldn't get it open! Not against Deputy Neely's resistance. So it *couldn't* have cut his left hand *across the palm.*"

He paused dramatically, slowly lowering his hands. He picked up the knife and strolled along the railing, looking at the jurors.

The man should be put up for an Oscar, Tyree thought.

"But we know—don't we, ladies and gentlemen?—we know that Deputy Neely *did* suffer a cut on his left palm. Former Deputy Allman told us so. The coroner's report tells us so. Which means that there's something wrong with the State's scenario, *something terribly wrong.*"

Riley stopped, leaned on the rail, and looked fixedly in the direction of juror number 8. Or was it number 9—Howell Bancroft, a plumbing and heating contractor who depended heavily on county contracts. Tyree could not be absolutely certain.

Then, after a pause that seemed to Tyree longer than the Book of Genesis, Riley spoke again, slowly and dramatically. "So wrong, ladies and gentlemen, that nothing remotely like the State's ludicrous scenario—nothing like that *could* have happened and nothing like that actually *did* happen in the defendant's cell that terrible night."

EASTER LILLY

EASTER LILLY LISTENED WITH ABSORBED INTEREST AS SHEP RILEY summed up—thinking that he made what had happened in her cell a good deal clearer to the jury than she ever had made it to herself. She was gripped particularly by Riley's dramatic account of Ben Neely waking her up with the point of a knife at her throat.

Too bad, she thought, that it hadn't happened quite as Riley so graphically described.

". . . there she was, ladies and gentlemen, alone in that cell-block, a man's weight holding her down on her bed, that cold and heartless steel touching her throat. There she was, less than an inch . . . less than a hairsbreadth . . . from death." His voice dropped to a dramatic whisper. "Or worse than death."

Man talk, Easter thought. Thinking *that's* worse than death. *Nothing's* worse than death.

Riley cleverly fuzzed over, she was relieved to hear, the question whether Ben Neely actually had got his whang into her before she started to fight for the knife. Some white-ass doctor the lady lawyer sent to the jail had messed that one up. But to hear Riley tell it, it didn't make all that much difference.

"Because with the knife at her throat, Deputy Neely clearly *intended* to rape her." Riley banged his fist on the railing between him and the jurors. "The defendant clearly *believed* he was trying to rape her. And that establishes just what we claim—that Easter Lilly Odum acted that night *not* with premeditation but in terror and self-defense."

Self-defense, anyway. I never once aimed to *kill* that cracker.

Only when Ben snatched at the knife and cut his hand on the open blade, he'd yelled like a baby, grabbed his cut hand with the other one, and hopped off the cot and around the cell like a kid playing hopscotch. What was *that* to be in terror of? A cracker with his britches down, jumping around like a chicken with its head cut off? His business flopping up and down like a wet sock?

The memory raised another question in her mind. How *had* she got possession of the knife, so that Ben'd cut his hand trying to grab it back from her? Not the way Riley and his snooty sidekick had playacted. Easter Lilly was sure there'd been no such fight. Nor did it seem to her that she could ever have stolen the knife out of Ben's pants pocket. Surely she'd remember risking anything like that, or actually doing it.

So how had she got hold of the knife?

"Your Honor . . . ladies and gentlemen of the jury," Riley was saying, obviously moving toward a climax, "we therefore submit our case to your sound judgment, believing as we do that you can come to *no* other conclusion . . . that neither the evidence nor basic common sense will support *any* other conclusion . . ."

She'd been surprised to find Ben Neely on top of her—his whiskey breath in her face. Ben trying to squirm between her legs, begging all the time, "Lemme have it, baby . . . you know you want it, too . . ."

Which made her furious all over again, just to think of that dirty cracker telling *her* she wanted what *he* wanted. When all she wanted was him off of her.

"Any other conclusion than the truth that this defendant acted as any woman would have, in response to that profound female instinct that no man can fully comprehend . . . an instinct to fight by any desperate means available a savage and abominable attack not just on her person"—again the dramatic whisper—"but on her very woman's self."

Man talk again. That a woman's pussy was a woman's very self. When all it actually was, was what *they* thought was her very self.

Riley paused in front of the jury box, letting his final words sink in. Easter Lilly's gaze fell on the red Swiss Army knife lying tagged on the railing of the jury box. Memory lit her mind with nightmare clarity. She saw like a splash of blood that red-handled knife lying on the dingy jailhouse sheet. Must have fallen from Ben's pocket, Ben struggling to get his hips out of his pants and underpants— unclean Jockeys, she recalled irrelevantly—so he could stick his swollen cock, thick as a cucumber, between her thighs. She saw the knife lying there, seized it, opened it, as his hands clawed at her panties.

"You want it too . . . baby . . . you know you want it!"

Riley was coming back to the defense table, his summation ended, his hands in his pockets, his face exhausted with effort. He slumped into the chair beside her. Seizing the moment, Easter Lilly put her hand on his leg and squeezed. She touched her lips to his ear.

"Told it like it was," she lied. "Made'em *see* it."

She hoped he had. She felt at that moment, more passionately than ever before, how much she wanted to walk. Now maybe she would. Maybe escape the chamber. Escape Tyree Neely. He was just then standing up at the prosecution table.

Riley's leg trembled under her hand, she heard his breath suck in, and for a fleeting moment she felt sorry for him, and faintly ashamed of having let him build up his man's silly woman-crazed fantasy. Like poor fool Ben Neely, who'd really believed she wanted what he wanted. Believed it right to the end.

The moment of sympathy passed quickly. After all, that red head—a good lawyer's head for the courtroom, that was clear and she was grateful, but for ordinary life not much wiser than Ben Neely's—that red head had conjured its own folly. Hadn't he told her plainly *I'm not in it for money?*

"Mistuh Neely," Judge Reeves said, with a gentle—Easter Lilly thought deferential—tap of his gavel. She watched Tyree, cool looking in his poplin suit, stroll to the jury box, confidence showing in his every movement.

"The show," he said softly, "is over. From here on, ladies and gentlemen, no more theatrics."

Easter Lilly found herself wishing, as she often had before, that it had been this quiet devil into whose heart she had plunged the red-handled knife. But it was hard to picture Tyree Neely hopping like a chicken with his pants down around his ankles. It was hard to picture Tyree with his pants down.

"No more theatrics," Tyree said again. "Just facts that bear on the case at hand." He swung around suddenly, pointed at Easter Lilly, and let his voice rise. "And one indisputable fact is that this black Jezebel has a history of seducing white men!"

He turned back to the jury box, his voice falling again to a level just barely audible at the defense table.

"Of course I say that with no racial intent, ladies and gentlemen, as I'm sure you understand. Indeed, the time for racial disrespect and discrimination is long over here in our beloved Southland— here, certainly, in Stonewall County."

Shit you say. Easter Lilly shrank a little in her chair, but she knew she could not escape what was coming. *You can run* Joe Louis said *but you can't hide.* Joe had been speaking of a white opponent, she knew, but his words ought to be on the gravestone of every black in America.

"But in this case, two unimpeachable witnesses, rightly honored for their long service to the youth of Stonewall—"

That old sow?

"—have confirmed, and I believe I may say, Your Honor"— Tyree looked apologetically at the bench—"that it's well-known in this community that the accused had a long-standing, notorious, and illicit relationship with one Elmore Timmons. Up to that time he was a respected teacher at SCCH—a *white* teacher."

That you ran out of town. And what was illicit about it? Easter Lilly wanted to stand up and ask. *And how would you know, anyway?*

"And since that happened within the memory of the witnesses y'all heard here today, the State believes, ladies and gentlemen, that the accused—"

Once again, Tyree swung around and pointed at Easter Lilly. *No more theatrics,* she thought bitterly.

"—this admittedly beautiful woman . . . now, I say that in all sincerity . . ."

He could shove his sincerity. Easter Lilly didn't want to be beautiful. Being beautiful had caused most of her trouble. Being beautiful had never got her what she really wanted, which was just to be free and accepted in the world around her.

". . . and even though counsel for the defense claims that her beauty is irrelevant to this case. The State believes that this beautiful but deceiving woman, with all the wiles learned in a lifetime of luring decent men into her web . . ."

Decent? The only truly decent man, white, black or any other color, she'd ever known, had been Mr. Timmons—the same Mr. Timmons that Tyree Neely, in supposed defense of racial purity, had banished from "decent" society.

". . . this woman was able to persuade another impressionable white man that *he* was someone special . . . particularly and fatally, that he was special to *her.*"

Fred Worthington. With a sudden pang of remorse, she remembered that Fred had been a loyal friend, too. But decent? What Fred really wanted, what they all wanted—Ben Neely just more openly—was her body. A piece of ass. Even Fred.

"Now let me deal briefly with that Academy Award scene in which defense counsel"—Tyree waved dismissively behind him— "*both* defense counsel abandoned legal argument for show biz. They tried to demonstrate that even if the defendant stole the knife from Deputy Neely's pocket, she still couldn't have opened that deadly blade. So, these amateur thespians wanted you to believe, she couldn't have stabbed"—Tyree's voice seemed to quaver—"that naive and trusting young man . . . in the heart."

Shep Riley whispered to Easter Lilly, "Talk about amateur thespians!"

Tyree struck the palm of his hand on the jury box railing.

"Nonsense! I say nonsense! And I know this jury is too smart to believe nonsense—whatever defense counsel may think of your intelligence. That scene out of a grade B movie was utter . . . absolute . . . unmitigated . . . speculation!"

Easter Lilly had the sinking feeling that Tyree was scoring points. Nothing like that fight scene had happened. Tyree had spotted it for a fake. Surely the jury—some of them anyway—had spotted it, too.

"And even as speculation, that melodramatic scene depended entirely on Jezebel there being in Deputy Neely's arms . . . and remaining in his arms . . . while she stole the knife out of his pocket and tried to open it. But the State doesn't accuse her of being as dumb as defense counsel wants you to believe she was. The fact is that she could have had any number of opportunities to grab that knife and open it. Any number, ladies and gentlemen! From the moment she lured him into that death cell of hers—like a spider lures a fly!''

Easter Lilly was enraged. Death cell! When she'd been rotting in there like a melon dumped in the trash. When the mothafucka himself had started it—Ben coming back every night with a wet leer on his cracker face, grabbing his crotch, grinning like a baboon in heat, looking her over like she was some kind of a chorus girl in a G-string. Until she'd have had to be deaf, dumb, blind, and crippled not to know he was climbing up the bars to get into her.

"They say it couldn't have happened . . .'' Tyree's voice was heavy with sarcasm. "Not the way they're trying to tell it, maybe.''

She'd have been the fool, she'd have been *really* dumb, not to notice the way Ben was practically waving his dick at her. Not to take advantage of the idiot state he was in. Play him for little favors. Because who could know what she might get out of him? For nothing except a little kissy-coo and maybe a quick hand job.

Tyree had paused, then walked slowly and silently along the railing, gazing at the jurors, finally speaking. "But you and I know, ladies and gentlemen, it *could* have happened a dozen other ways. And I think you know it *did*.''

He turned to the defense table and took a step or two toward it. "And where, I ask defense counsel . . .'' He paused again for effect, and in the silence, all the way across the courtroom, Easter Lilly heard Tug Johnson's stomach rumbling. Or maybe it was the clerk's.

". . . where are the panties?'' Tyree demanded.

Before anyone could have answered, even if the prosecutor had expected an answer, he turned back to the jury and shouted, "The *torn* panties! That she wanted people to believe this bloodthirsty rapist ripped off of her the night he died in her cell.''

Which was exactly the way it happened. Only not in the course of a rape, since Ben Neely was still begging her for "a little piece,'' slobbering like an idiot while he tore at her clothes.

"Why haven't they introduced those panties, ladies and gentlemen? She showed'em to *me* the day the state police brought her back to jail. Why haven't they put those panties in evidence?''

Again, too quickly for intervention, he thundered an answer to his own question. ''Because they know those panties wouldn't fool an idiot! Much less you smart folks on this jury. Because they knew I'd be ready to show she had plenty of time to tear'em herself. Time *and* motive, ladies and gentlemen! To tear those panties herself, then blame it on a dead man that can't defend himself. You *bet* I'd've been ready to show both time *and* motive.''

The euphoria that had briefly seized Easter Lilly during Riley's summation faded. She knew nothing about trials and the law, but she could tell from the jurors' faces that Tyree was making an impression. Especially the old prune female in the front row with lips like matchsticks and hair as tight on her skull as a shower cap. The battle-ax that kept staring at her like she'd been found under a rock.

''And now, members of the jury, I want you to think back carefully to the testimony of Deputy Rob Moore. Vital testimony, ladies and gentlemen. Crucial testimony. The key to this case.''

Easter Lilly frantically tried to recall what Rob Moore had said. Something about her and Ben Neely. Sounding like it happened in a whorehouse.

Tyree with his unfailing courtesy spoke across the courtroom to the woman at the recording machine, ''Read to the jury, please, ma'am, what Deputy Moore said when I asked him if there was anything about the defendant that seemed out of line.''

The woman shuffled through lengths of tape before finding the passage:

''Seem to me like she kind of took a shine to Ben Neely.''

Which was not just a lie, Easter thought, but a *damn* lie.

Tyree, however, told the woman to read on, and things got rapidly worse.

''I mean she was kind of open down to here . . . Ben could get an eyeful.''

Easter Lilly remembered then the suggestive way in which Rob Moore, on the stand, had waved his hands in front of his chest. Suggesting what kind of an eyeful Ben Neely got. But even when she'd tried to work Ben up a little—not hard to do—she'd never opened but one button farther down than she usually did in that stinking and airless cellblock. Some eyeful!

"So there you have it, ladies and gentlemen. Deputy Moore actually saw Jezebel flaunting her body at Deputy Neely."

"My name's Easter!" Her fierce whisper might have burned Shep Riley's ear.

"He can call you that," he whispered back. "Biblical term. Make'em think you're a shameless woman."

"But Rob was *lying*. I ain't flaunted nothing!"

Riley stared at her, eyes wide with incredulity. But she knew he believed her. As clearly as if he had spoken, she read the message plain on his face:

You don't have to flaunt much to flaunt it all.

Even in her fear of Tyree and the gas chamber she realized it was true. True but unfair. Riley had seen in her what Ben Neely saw. It made no difference, none at all, that she knew it was only what they thought they saw—what they wanted to see.

Wishful men, pleasing themselves in fantasy! Seeing in her something in which, after Mr. Timmons, she had no interest. As if it were owed to them. Ol Massa claiming his rights!

For a moment, her rage was so hot, her hatred so deep, that she wished she had the knife in her hand again. Such men had brought her to this. Because Ben Neely had seen in her, or thought he saw, wished he saw, the lurid satisfaction of his wildest cravings, Easter Lilly Odum sat in Stonewall County court no better than a dead woman. Labeled Jezebel to the world. The only real acceptance in her life, as well as the one man who had given it, sneered at and scorned.

"So we know, don't we, ladies and gentlemen . . ." Tyree was speaking now directly to the old prune in the front row, leaning on the rail in front of her. "We know how she lured him into her cell that night. The way loose and shameless women—"

I am not! Easter Lilly wanted to scream. Your brother was the loose and shameless one. Not me!

"—have always worked their wiles on gullible men. Since Eve offered the apple."

Tyree seemed now to be in intimate conversation with the old prune, whose face glowed with the pleasure of disapproval.

"And even if it hurts me to say it, even if my great old daddy were still alive it would kill him to hear it, I have to admit, ladies and gentlemen—"

Were tears actually trembling, Easter Lilly wondered, in the prune's gimlet eyes?

"—that my foolish little brother was gullible about women. Since he was at SCCH, they could twist him around their little fingers." Tyree straightened, shrugged. "A look in the eye, a motion of the hand—that's all it took with Benjy."

He began to walk back and forth again. Stalking, Easter Lilly thought. Stalking *me.*

"So there they were, alone in the jail, middle of the night. No one to see, no one to hear, no one to tell. After what she'd been doing to him, she'd only have had to call his name. Probably only once. He'd have been back there in a second. Eager. Trusting. Naive, no doubt about that. A fool, I guess."

Tyree stopped pacing and turned to face the jury.

"But not a rapist! My brother was *not* a rapist. No Neely was ever a rapist. No! She got him back there—Rob Moore told us how. She got him back there, got hold of his knife, and then . . . this . . . this . . ."

Tyree turned again and pointed once more at Easter Lilly Odum. He paused, his arm out, and seemed to search for a word.

Going to call me a name, Easter thought. Worse than Jezebel this time. He's going to . . .

"Bitch!" Ben Neely had yelled at her across the cell, still hopping up and down, still clutching his bleeding hand. "You *cut* me, you stinkin nigger bitch!"

She had taken it too often—the curses, the names, the groping hands, the insults. The degradation. She had taken it too often. In the red-stained darkness of the cell, Ben Neely was no longer a comic schoolyard figure howling and hopscotching in pain, tripping over his fallen pants, his suddenly limp maleness flopping and swinging like a puppy dog's tail. Ben was Men. And he was White.

"Stinkin bitch!" he yelled again.

She had suffered them too often, taken their abuse too long. But now she had the knife open in her hand. She had the knife and she had taken enough.

"This woman," Tyree said quietly, "this beautiful and deceiving woman murdered Deputy Ben Neely. In cold blood. With malice aforethought. Just the way she'd planned, from the first time she gave him an eyeful and let him think what he naturally thought, what any man would have thought . . . what she knew he would think. She planned it, ladies and gentlemen. Just the way it happened.''

Easter Lilly believed she was hearing her death warrant. She heard it quietly. She could see it, too, in the faces of the jury— that of the old prune in the front row positively triumphant. Tyree Neely had spoken her death warrant, and it did not matter that in the dim red light of truth nothing had happened as he said.

They would drop the pellets and put her down. This time there would be no knife in her hand. It would make no difference that once again they had seen what they wanted to see and thought what they wanted to think.

MEG

MEG TAPPED ON THE DOOR TO JUDGE REEVES'S CHAMBERS. WHEN she heard him call, she opened the door a foot or two, looked around it and said, "You wanted to see me?"

The judge was at his desk, on which was spread a copy of the *Capital Times*. A single glass wrapped in a paper towel and the bottle of Maker's Mark—now half empty—stood beside the newspaper.

"Come in. Ready for a toddy now?"

Meg advanced into the room, reluctant to let the door close behind her. The strong smell of old goat was tangible in the mechanically cooled and circulated air of the judge's chambers.

"Thank you, Judge, but I pass."

"Set a spell, anyway." Judge Reeves indicated a chair pulled close beside his desk.

Meg could hardly refuse the invitation, but she could not reach the chair by the desk without letting the door close. And she had heard all she needed to know about Ot Reeves.

"I won't bite," he said. "Whatevuh you hud."

She could only smile good-naturedly and let the door close. But when she sat in the designated chair, she was careful to keep her knees and ankles together, her feet flat on the floor. Meg had been before the bar long enough to know that in the eyes of judges and lawyers, a woman lawyer was still a woman. And as such, unless a veritable crone, fair game.

The jury had been out for an hour when Judge Reeves's note summoning Meg to his chambers had been handed to her at the defense table. Shep Riley had gone to the men's room and Easter Lilly was deep in conversation with Dr. Worthington. Meg had no one to tell where she was going, but she was not too worried. What could happen in a public courthouse?

"You won'drin why I ask you back heah?" Ot Reeves inquired.

Not really, Meg thought. She said pleasantly, "It's nice of you to offer me a drink."

"Bettuh if you'd take it. Lighten up a little."

She shook her head, smiling, determined.

"But what I really had in mind," the judge said, "was tell you a secret."

The hairs began to tingle on the back of Meg's neck. She was not afraid of Ot Reeves's liver-spotted hands—he looked old and frail and kind of pathetic—but she shrank from any kind of a scene. In a judge's chambers, of all places.

"See," he said, "I ain't been home in more'n a week. Won't get theah tonight, eithuh."

"Maybe you shouldn't tell me the secret, then. Maybe you ought to save it for Miz Reeves."

Judge Reeves drank off his toddy and poured more Maker's Mark into his wrapped glass. Then he spoke: "She knows a'ready. This heah was my last case."

"You're really retiring?"

He tapped the middle desk drawer. "Papuhs all filled out."

Flattery was in order. "But you're too young to retire, Judge."

"Shit," Ot Reeves said. "If I was, you'd be ovuh on that couch on yoah back sted of lookin at me like I was a hunnud yeahs old. Which I ain't, not quite."

"Why, Judge, I'm not sure what you mean . . ." Though it was perfectly clear.

"Hell, you don't," the judge said again. "But you won't file no complaint on me. Since I ain't laid a glove on you and I'm quittin, anyway."

Meg, who in her years in professional life had become a veteran of sexual innuendo and harassment, was amused. She had half ex-

297

pected to be propositioned and supposed she had been. But the usual wrestling match had not developed, and clearly wouldn't—not with this tipsy old man who seemed more nearly to be amusing himself than stoking elderly fires.

Meg reached for his glass and took a sip of Maker's Mark, although she hated bourbon.

"I wasn't thinking of a complaint, Judge." She held up the glass in a toasting gesture, concealing her distaste for the sweetened liquor, and put it back on his desk. "I'm not the complaining kind."

"I nevuh thought you were. S'why I offuh'd you a toddy. But nowadays"—he shrugged and picked up the glass—"a man acts like a man, he maybe winds up in the slammuh. I don't mean no offense."

"None taken."

Meg genuinely felt none, though by contemporary standards she supposed she should have. It made her faintly uneasy that she felt rather flattered instead. Vindicated as a woman, which was ridiculous. By the interest of a goaty old man looking back with rheumy eyes at long-ago adventures!

"You a married lady?" For a moment, Meg thought the judge had said "a mad lady." Then she deciphered the accent and held up her left hand, with its gold band on her ring finger.

"Happily."

"Then don't go messin round with that redhead."

As coquettishly as a schoolgirl denying an obvious interest in the football captain, Meg started to protest. Then she understood—she should have guessed before—that Carl Hoover's tale-telling probably had reached Judge Reeves's ears. Via Tyree, no doubt. She wanted to reply angrily because what she did was none of Ot Reeves's business. Nor Tyree's. They had no right . . .

"Sides," the judge said, "I'd make you a bet Riley's got it up for the blackbird."

Meg shrank within herself, at first at the racial slur. Her mind quickly concentrated itself, however, on the judge's assertion, its meaning for Meg Whitman. Ot Reeves had said only what she herself had thought was the case, but his remark was painful in a way her own perception had not been—as an accusation may be more arresting than self-reproach. The judge had seen that Easter Lilly was the one who consumed Shep's thoughts.

When it used to be me.

How could it have been otherwise? Easter Lilly, Meg recognized in the courtroom, must have been touched by a random finger. Of God? Meg was neither religious nor mystical, but from what other source—she wondered in something near awe—could beauty like Easter's, timeless, untouchable, of no race or age or color, have sprung? Meg *knew* she was not born of the same clay.

"Judge," she managed to lie, "I've got better sense than to mess around with Shep Riley." The southern euphemism, she thought, did not in fact describe what she *had* been doing.

For as if by an uncontrolled chain reaction of recognition, she had seen, too, that if Easter Lilly was Shep's unreality, Shep himself had been her own. All those years, however obscured by marriage and family and security, Shep Riley had been *her* fantasy. And not just the swirling bright lights—Shep in bed, inside her, their bodies one, the ecstatic pleasures of man and woman she had found with no one but him. Though she lived in a more rational universe than the unafraid Shep, his faith, his forays into the lion's den for his conviction that the powerful always preyed on the powerless—*that* Shep, too, had been her ideal, the hidden root of her dissatisfaction with an unchallenging life. But like all ideals, it was unreachable.

"Then you ain't the cheatin kind?"

She did not know how to answer. But whatever she did or didn't do in the future, she was determined to face herself squarely—and the world, too.

She said, "You thought I *was,* didn't you?"

The judge grinned sheepishly. "Tyree kind of hinted. But I ought to've known bettuh."

Should he have? If Tyree had been smarmy, he'd also been dead on, and his hint might have led a randy old-timer like Ot Reeves to think she'd be willing. If a man thought a woman *would,* Meg had learned long before, he always believed she would with *him.*

"I *was* the cheatin kind," Judge Reeves said rather dreamily. "What the wuld calls cheatin."

Too much Maker's Mark, Meg thought. Like a dutiful daughter, she warned, "Don't say anything you'll regret tomorrow."

"I just called it livin, though. Which a man's got to figguh out how to do fuh hisself."

Or a woman. Meg made to herself no virtuous promises, lest

they prove only another kind of fantasy. Shep, even lost in his own hopeless dream of Easter Lilly, had caused Meg to recognize that she was a sensual woman, to understand the glory of *being* a woman.

"I miss it," Judge Reeves said. "Livin, I mean."

For a moment, in the strange mutual comfort they seemed to share, despite differences in age and outlook, she almost wanted to give that back to him. But she knew without asking that he, too, had only been fantasizing, about things as they used to be.

Then another tap at the door caused Judge Reeves to call out grumpily, "What is it?"

Lancey Gregg came in with a note in his hand. Meg stood up to leave but the judge stopped her. "Prob'ly from the jury," he said.

He opened the note and read. His eyes widened. He put the note facedown on his desk, took a pen from a holder, scribbled a few words on its back, and returned it to Lancey. "Hand this note to the fohman."

"Yessir." Lancey hurried out of the room.

Meg could not contain her lawyer's curiosity.

"Judge, does that mean the jury can't agree?"

Ot Reeves grinned thinly, not looking quite so old and harmless as he had a moment before.

"You was to have dinnuh with me, I might break the rules and tell you."

Meg smiled, too. "And if I didn't know I could find out anyway, I might go along." At the door, she turned and added, still smiling, "To dinner, I mean."

"Fuh no moah'n that," Judge Reeves said, "I doubt I'd pay off."

JASE

HOPING TO AVOID FURTHER CONFRONTATION WITH TYREE NEELY, Jase Allman drove straight to Green Oaks as soon as the trial was over and the jury left the courtroom. He had stuck his neck out for Easter Lilly Odum and what he believed was the truth, and he was glad he'd done it—more or less. But enough was enough. It was one thing to do what was right. It was something else to go an extra mile. He didn't need no more hoo-haw with Tyree Neely.

Ida Sue's Bronco was already parked in the drive, when he stopped his Toyota beside it. He went up the rickety steps of their mobile home reluctantly, sure that Dinette chatter would have informed her of what he'd done in court. Burned his bridges with Tyree. Pissed away the house in town.

So he was surprised when Ida Sue practically leaped—a little heavily—into his arms. He caught her somehow, staggering back in the cramped living room with its mostly built-in furniture.

She ain't heard yet, he thought.

"Jase!" she cried. "You got it!"

He let her slide through his arms to the floor, her skirt bunching up a little in his hands.

"I knew you would," she cried. "I knew it!"

He held her close, squeezing her soft bottom through the skirt, and looked down into her flushed and smiling face.

"Knew what?"

"You'd get the appointment!"

Jase could guess what that meant, but he was enjoying the feel of her bottom in his hands and her boobs against his chest. Ida Sue had not been what you'd call loving since he'd quit the county. So first things first, he thought.

"What appointment is that?"

For answer, she jumped again and as his arms closed more tightly around her, holding her off her feet, she planted a wet kiss on his mouth. Jase seized the opportunity for some deep French. Ida Sue, tasting of Life Savers, responded hotly.

When he put her down, her upturned face was lit with joy.

"You'll be *so* handsome, Jase! In your uniform."

That could mean only one thing.

"I must of got the academy," he said.

Ida Sue broke away from him and pranced to the folding table in the dining room. She picked up a brown envelope and hurried back.

"October term."

As calmly as he could, he took the letter from her and read that he had passed the exam with a score of 612 points out of a possible 1,000—squeaked by, he thought—and should report to the state police academy for six weeks' training beginning at 9 A.M. September 15.

"It just *had* to be good news," Ida Sue said. "After all the bad. Minute I seen it in the mailbox, I *knew* it was good news."

Jase had not been so confident. Not the math so much, but all that English on the exam. They were under court order to take black guys, too. And it was always possible somebody would check with Tyree. Then the shit might've hit the fan. Even now—Jase studied the letter closely for fine print—they still could take it away. They could always take anything away.

"I'm *so* proud." Ida Sue looked up at him slyly and began to fiddle with his belt buckle.

Never look a gift horse in the mouth, Jase's mother had taught him. He began unbuttoning Ida Sue's blouse.

"Ah, Suedy," he said, "I gotta be the luckiest man in the whole damn world."

DAISY

WHEN LANCEY GREGG CALLED, THE JURY HAD BEEN OUT ONLY AN hour or two. Daisy and Tyree had returned to Tyree's third-floor courthouse office, Tyree urging Daisy to call it a day and go home. But she said she'd be on pins and needles anyway until she knew how it all came out. Not that there was any doubt. Let me stay, she begged prettily, till we know for sure. Tyree had acquiesced without enthusiasm.

When Lancey's call came, Daisy immediately put it through to Tyree. Naturally, she kept her own extension open.

"You won't b'leeve this," Lancey told Tyree. "Those fuckin assholes are hung up."

Daisy never blinked at the language she sometimes heard when listening to Tyree's calls. This time, she was so dumbfounded by the news that she hardly noticed the words. How could anyone who had heard Tyree explain so clearly what had happened doubt that it *had* happened, just that way?

Tyree let a little silence hang on the line—in reproof of the language, Daisy supposed, as much as anger at the information.

"They can't agree?" he finally asked.

Tyree had put Lancey in as clerk of the court and co-signed a second mortgage for him at the Bright Leaf Bank. Tyree trusted Lancey—as much, to Daisy's knowledge, as he trusted anyone.

"That's the word they sent out."

"So what did Ot do?"

"Sent back word to keep trying," Lancey said. "They're still at it."

Daisy could hardly believe Tyree remained calm—particularly when she knew how strongly he felt about Easter Lilly.

"Well, keep me posted." Tyree actually sounded as if he were talking about one of his real estate deals instead of his brother's murderer.

Later, Daisy made an excuse to carry a file into the inner office. She found Tyree working on his bird book. His bird book! With the jury still out.

"An hour and a half now," she ventured. "You think they'll be coming back soon?"

"Soon enough." Tyree held up a photo he was about to paste into the bird book. "Ever seen one of these?"

Daisy was so excited to be admitted, for once, to his inner sanctum, that she momentarily forgot the jury. She looked closely at the photo, in which some fat bird appeared to be paddling on water.

"Some kind of a duck?"

"Not bad, Daisy." Tyree glanced at the photo. "Actually a pied-bill grebe. Maybe you'll make a birder yet."

These words caused Daisy to float back to her own desk, where she passed another hour buffing her nails, reading the Help Wanted ads in the *Capital Times*—a habit she had developed in self-defense after the Jase Allman mess—and studying a paperback Roget's The-saurus to improve her word power.

When Lancey Gregg called again, she did not even have to put it through to the inner office. "Tell Tyree he better get on down here. They're comin in."

Tyree quickly closed the bird book and put on his jacket after she passed on this message. Maybe, Daisy decided, he was not quite as calm as he wanted her to think.

"No need for you to come down," he said.

But Daisy was not about to be dismissed as usual. "Don't be

silly." She was a little frightened by her own temerity. "I wouldn't miss this for the world."

They went along the third-floor corridor in silence. In the elevator, emboldened by Tyree's apparent acceptance of her defiant last words, she mustered the nerve to adjust his nubby tie. It didn't need it—Tyree's tie never needed adjusting—but the act gave her an excuse to stand close enough to give him a whiff of her perfume and a sense of her presence. Close enough to be kissed.

She did not let her body touch his and certainly didn't expect him to kiss her, and of course Tyree didn't. But as she gave his necktie a last tug, she looked up into his face, confident of the perfume, and said, "You were wonderful in court today."

He grunted. "So was the other guy."

"Why . . . I thought you tore him to *shreds.*"

The elevator stopped, and the doors clanked open. As they emerged into the ground-floor corridor, she was amazed to feel Tyree actually take her arm. His hand, just above her elbow, felt strong and protective. She gave thanks for the perfume.

"Let's see what the jury thinks," he said.

Daisy was not sure whether this meant he was uncertain, or that he was being characteristically modest. Modest, she decided as they went along the center aisle of the courtroom. She had seldom known Tyree to be uncertain about anything.

At the gate, she started to pull away toward her front-row seat. But Tyree held on to her arm.

"Daisy . . . when this is over . . ." She could barely hear him above the mutter of the spectators, some of whom were drifting back in. Others had held on to their courtroom seats, so that the auditorium was nearly as full as it had been during the trial itself. "Come back up to the office."

Releasing her arm, he turned away to the prosecution table. Thrilled to the bone, Daisy took her seat between Good Jelly Cass and Dr. Worthington in his white suit. Why would Tyree tell her to come back to the office? Unless . . . but that couldn't be. No perfume was *that* effective.

"Way I figgers it," Good Jelly gruffed across her to Dr. Worthington, "they gonna take out a nigguh, they'd-a done it in fi'minutes."

The doctor looked skeptical and crossed his legs. The creases in his white trousers were long gone.

"Think they'll turn *that* gal loose, Jelly, you better think again."

Daisy agreed, even though she knew from Lancey Gregg that there'd been some kind of trouble in the jury room. But she couldn't believe they'd actually decide Easter Lilly was not guilty. If they did, they'd have to just *ignore* Tyree's arguments. That was hardly likely since his arguments had been so powerful. And besides, nobody on that jury would lightly cross Tyree Neely. She squirmed with pride in what she dared, finally, to hope was just maybe about to become her man.

To her right, at the defense table, Shep Riley was slumped in his chair, looking, she thought, like a man who had been torn to shreds. But Easter Lilly sat up straight beside him, her handsome head held high on her graceful neck. You had to hand it to Easter Lilly, Daisy thought reluctantly. Easter had never been afraid of anything. But then she'd never faced what she was facing now.

Beyond them, the beanpole female lawyer sat looking over the courtroom. As Daisy watched, the woman's gaze turned slowly back to Shep Riley, and a serenity settled on her face, even a kind of sadness, that Daisy had not noticed before. Or maybe it hadn't been there. It was not anything in the structure of the head, or the combination of eyes and hair, or the suggestion of the mouth— certainly not in the makeup, which Daisy thought inadequate for a woman who needed all the help she could get.

Before she could further define what she saw in the woman lawyer's face, Lancey Gregg began to do his oyez thing. Ot Reeves entered—a little unsteadily, it appeared to Daisy—and took his elevated seat. In a minute or two, the jury came filing in. Looking a little solemn, which was only fitting since they were about to send a woman to the gas chamber.

A classmate, Daisy thought incredulously—remembering Easter Lilly that way for the first time in years. Who'd ever think a classmate would be going to the gas chamber? Even one forced on you by the Supreme Court.

When the jury had settled into its seats, Judge Reeves tapped his gavel and asked, "Ladies and gentlemen of the jury, have you reached a verdict?"

The foreman, Mr. Goodwrench from the Buick agency—actually

Walter Thornberry, but everybody called him Mr. Goodwrench, after the TV ad—stood up, looking nervous.

"No, Your Honor."

"Still?" Judge Reeves said.

Mr. Goodwrench was practically a genius with carburetors and valves. But his own garage businss had bankrupted him in the recession of '92.

"Still, Your Honor."

Daisy was aghast. She could not imagine what was happening, especially with Tyree sitting as quietly at the prosecution table as if the judge and Mr. Goodwrench were discussing their golf swings. No verdict! The idea seemed impossible.

"I could send you back to try some moah," Judge Reeves said. "I got plenty of time, and I reckon the defendant does, too."

Mr. Goodwrench shook his head. "Wouldn't do any good, Your Honor. I satisfied myself about that."

Tyree, an incorporator at Owens Buick, had got Walter Thornberry his chief mechanic's job after the bankruptcy. So there must be some kind of a mistake. How could Walter possibly . . .

"Deadlocked that bad, Mistuh Foahman?"

"Hopeless," Mr. Goodwrench said.

"No use to try again?"

"None a-tall. We'd be here till after New Year's, Your Honor."

Loud talk and chatter erupted in the courtroom. Judge Reeves banged his gavel.

"Awduh!" he shouted.

Daisy had heard the phrase "hung jury" but she was not sure exactly what it meant. She only knew that her man had been prevented from getting the conviction and the victory he deserved. And that smart-ass redhead Riley with all his interruptions was somehow responsible. Daisy looked quickly at the defense table and saw Easter Lilly throw her arms around Riley's goddamned neck.

"Awduh!" Ot Reeves shouted again. His gavel sounded to Daisy Thorpe like a popgun.

Dr. Worthington, his broad black face beaming, leaned across her to give a loud high-five to Good Jelly Cass.

"Din't I tell you?" Jelly said. "Ain't take this long to gas no nigguh!"

Bewildered, wanting to run to Tyree's side, console what must

307

be his anguish, Daisy looked up to see him slowly rise to his feet. Judge Reeves was banging and shouting but Tyree's authoritative voice cut through the noise more effectively. When Tyree Neely spoke in Stonewall County, Daisy thought defiantly, he didn't need a gavel.

"Your Honor . . ." The courtroom quieted at Tyree's words. "The State requests the jury be polled."

"So awduhed." Judge Reeves banged the gavel one more time. "Clerk will poll the jury. Jurors will answer when called."

Lancey Gregg took over. "Mister Good—Mister Foreman, how do you vote?"

"Guilty, Your Honor."

"Juror number two, how do you vote?"

"Guilty as sin, Your Honor."

"Don't need no editoyals," Judge Reeves said. "Just yoah vote."

"Number three?"

"Guilty!"

And so it went. The guilty votes responded to Lancey Gregg without hesitation, one after another, piling up. Lena Covington, Alvin Levine, Callie Igoe, the Reverend Clarence Patch—all voted guilty. As they'd better, Daisy thought. But then who . . . it seemed like they were all voting guilty.

"Juror number eight?"

Fielding D. Johns stood up and in a clear, resonant voice declared himself. "*Not* guilty, Your Honor!"

Flushing Johns! Daisy looked quickly at Tyree. He was sitting with his head down, making notes, as if he hadn't even noticed that that idiot Johns . . .

"Stepped in his own shit," Daisy muttered.

Good Jelly Cass leaned heavily against her. "Wha'd you say, honey?"

"I said . . ." Daisy began boldly, but even to an African American she could not repeat her reflexive words. "He's in real trouble."

"Ass-deep," Jelly said.

A silence had fallen on the courtroom. Fielding D. Johns sat down, staring straight ahead. Lancey Gregg demanded, "Juror number nine?"

Howell Bancroft, seeming to lean as far as possible away from juror number eight, rose to his feet. "Guilty!" he boomed.

Ten, eleven, and twelve echoed him. In the end, only Flushing Johns had voted "not guilty."

So the total was 11 to 1 guilty, which in Daisy's opinion certainly ought to have been good enough. Not just a clear but an overwhelming vote for guilty. Daisy was stunned to think that one vote—from an outsider, practically a stranger—could negate all Tyree's hard work, thwart his grief for his brother and his family name.

She watched in sheer disbelief as Tyree walked stiffly to the defense table and took Shep Riley's outstretched hand. She was relieved, however, that not even the suggestion of a smile touched Tyree's face in response to Riley's hateful grin. Tyree almost literally turned his back, and for a moment Daisy could believe he'd do *something*, put a stop to this incredible business, take command somehow. Remind them that eleven jurors—eleven!—had voted guilty.

The jubilation at the defense table, joined by the doctor in his white suit, and the collapse into blubbery tears of Good Jelly Cass told Daisy, however, that eleven to one had not been enough.

Tyree had lost.

Easter Lilly Odum had got away with murder.

TYREE

AS THE ELEVATOR TOOK DAISY AND TYREE FROM THE FIRST TO THE third floor of the county courthouse, she balled up a small fist and struck a poster mounted on the wall of the car. Stonewall Planned Parenthood, the poster proclaimed, was prepared to advise on a variety of reproductive problems without regard to race.

"It's so unfair!" Daisy cried, grasping her bruised fist in her other hand, in anger as well as pain. "You *proved* she did it. Only that one stupid—"

"That one was enough," Tyree said. "I lost that jury in voir dire. Let me see that hand."

"It's nothing. You lost it where?"

"When I let Riley seat Flushing Johns. When Riley was summing up, I saw him speaking right straight to the guy. I should have known right then it was all over. Is it bleeding?"

Daisy held out her exquisite white hand. Its knuckles were red but not bleeding.

"Why didn't you complain to the judge?"

"About what? It's my job to keep the other guy's pigeons off the jury. I had plenty on there myself." Tyree examined her hand closely, turning it gently in both of his. "Does it still hurt?"

"Not so much."

He couldn't remember ever having held Daisy's hand before.

"Not with you holding it."

Daisy's hand was soft and warm, and he could not help imagining it stroking his hair, his face . . . He cut off that line of thought immediately. Weakness.

"You could have broken a knuckle. And if it swells up . . ."

He had meant to say the hand would turn purple and ugly, but he realized that Daisy would twist that into a compliment to her pretty hands. So he finished lamely, "You probably couldn't type."

Daisy let her hand linger in his, anyway. She squared her shoulders in something like determination, raised her face toward his, and let her tongue appear briefly, beautifully, between her scarlet lips. "When I was a little girl and hurt myself somewhere," she whispered, "Mother would kiss it and make it well."

The elevator stopped, the doors opened, and their clang echoed along the empty corridor in front of them. Tyree knew a come-on when he heard one, but he was a little pent-up after the hung jury and upset with himself about his handpicked sanitation engineer. Stressed, he thought—a plight that, if extreme, usually sent him off to the woods in search of birds. As it was, right there in the elevator in plain view of any passing voters, he raised Daisy's hand to his lips and kissed her knuckles.

"I'm not your mother," he said, "but I like the remedy."

Bad mistake.

He saw it at once. On top of the Flushing Johns foul-up, too many for his own good.

Daisy appeared about to burst with joy. If he'd *really* kissed her, he thought, she'd have melted like a burning candle. An awful thought. Even as it was, she looked as if he had just placed a ring on her third finger, left hand—even if it actually was the right with which she'd socked the Planned Parenthood poster, and like a crazy fool he'd kissed.

Never too late, Tyree thought. "Good thing I told you to come back." He took her by the arm and pulled her out of the elevator. "I had a sort of premonition there'd be work to do. First thing you do, Daisy, get out all the correspondence from when I hired Johns. See what I promised him and what he promised me."

Cut the kidding and get back to business. Get her busy again. Mind off wedding bells and back to the office.

"Then tomorrow"—Tyree propelled Daisy rapidly along the corridor—"check with the liquor store. Claude Connally, the manager there, Claude owes me a coupla favors. Find out from Claude *exactly* how much booze Johns or his wife or both buy every week. I hear she's crocked and falling down every night."

He took his keys from his pants pocket, opened the office door, and all but shoved Daisy inside. Being in the office was like being in charge again.

"And get me their kid's college address. Just in case I need to get in touch with him."

He turned toward his inner office. "Bring me that Johns correspondence right away."

"It really did stop hurting," Daisy said. "After you kissed it."

Tyree cursed himself. But it was always good policy to focus on the lesser of two evils.

"I should have seen it coming," he said. "With Johns, I mean. The way everybody's been riding the guy, with his education and all, he was bound to take it out on somebody."

He had ignored Daisy's plain hint and saw the disappointment in her face. Encouraged, he delivered a clincher. "After all, I was the one brought the guy to Stonewall. At a fat salary, too. And never cracked a single joke about his name. I just never thought it'd be *me* he'd dump on."

Scratch one mistake.

Daisy lifted her chin, her saddened face. "I don't see why you blame yourself. After all you did for him, what would have made anybody think he'd sell you out?"

He realized, then, that Daisy Thorpe could roll with the punch. Daisy was all right. But Daisy was for the long haul, and Tyree had decided long ago that the long haul was not for him. Besides, she was spoiled goods, and no Neely would ever take some TV creep's wet deck.

The idea, as much as the phrase, made Tyree flinch. Getting entirely too careless, he thought, and reverted quickly to his higher self.

"They'll all sell you out," he said, "if they've got a reason. If I'd realized Johns hated me and this whole county so much, I'd've never let him on that jury."

SHEP

AS TYREE NEELY, UNSMILING, TURNED AWAY FROM SHEP RILEY, DR.
Worthington extended a long, white-clad arm past Easter Lilly
Odum. Grinning, he pumped Shep Riley's hand.

"Got to shake the hand of a man that pulled off a miracle," he
said. "Right under Tyree Neely's nose."

Shep took the proffered hand. Beyond the railing, spectators
milled about, pushing their way into the aisle and the corridor
beyond. Blacks were laughing, slapping backs. A few shouted jovially to Easter Lilly. The whites were grim and silent.

"I don't know if it was a miracle, Doctor. But whatever it was,
Meg did it, not me."

Meg had come to stand beside Shep, and said, "No . . . you
argued brilliantly."

Shep was excited, exuberant. He watched with satisfaction as
Tyree Neely and Daisy Thorpe slowly struggled up the center aisle,
the throng of departing spectators clogging their way. He had forgotten in his torpid New York and Vermont years the thrill of
pulling off a big one. Sticking it in their eye.

"You were always the best," Meg said. "Nobody can persuade
a jury like you."

The remark brought Shep back to reality. "Not *this* jury. If you hadn't found the pigeon, Meg . . . if you hadn't told me to get Flushing Johns on that jury . . .''

"Fielding," Meg said.

"Fielding Johns." He looked at Easter Lilly talking to acquaintances across the railing. "She'd be eating jail food tonight."

Sheriff Tug Johnson, fingering his belt buckle, arrived at Shep's side in time to hear this remark.

"Too good for her," he said. "Tell'er to come pick up'er damn stuff." He turned to Easter Lilly and said, over her head, not looking her in the eye, "Glad to be shut of you, Killer."

Shep and Dr. Worthington protested as if in one voice:

"Now listen, Sheriff . . ."

"You got no right . . ."

Easter Lilly interrupted both to ask the sheriff: "You're glad I'm getting out, are you?"

"I'd be gladder, you were going where you belong."

Ignoring all further protestations, Sheriff Johnson walked away, his massive body ponderous as a circus elephant's.

"You see?" Fred Worthington shook Shep's hand again, fervently. "It *was* a miracle, what you did."

"Miracle is right." Easter Lilly's voice could barely be heard above the murmur of talk from the spectators still in the courtroom. "But what's this pigeon shit?"

Shep sat down beside her. "We didn't tell you because we couldn't be sure how it would turn out. But that one not-guilty vote that hung the jury? Meg was pretty sure Fielding Johns would vote that way."

"How come?" Easter said. "I never even met the man."

Meg sat down, too. "Twenty years ago in Massachusetts his sister was raped. When she brought charges, nobody believed her. They threw the case out. What they usually did in those days."

"So we got our pigeon on the jury," Shep said. "Somebody we felt sure would listen to our case and probably vote our way."

Easter Lilly nodded. "So what he did, he got even for his sister?"

"You could put it that way. Or"—Shep remembered Meg saying that Fielding Johns was passionate about the law's indifference to women who'd been raped—"you could say he wanted to see justice done in your case. Unlike hers."

"Bullshit," Easter Lilly said. "He didn't give a damn about me any more than the rest of you crackers."

Wondering if he'd heard right, Shep thought *She can't mean me.*

"Now, Easter." Fred Worthington, still standing, spoke as if to an unruly child. "No need for——"

"Nor you, either!" Easter Lilly's voice rose, turned harsh. "Least that pigeon didn't want my ass, like you do." She turned hot, dark eyes on Shep Riley. "Like my lawyer. Both of you horny as Ben Neely."

Shep felt as if he had been caught masturbating in bed. Of course she'd known, seen from the start, that he was obsessed, wanting her, even dreaming of her. But he'd never touched her and never would have. So for her now to accuse him . . .

"Easter!" Fred Worthington, tall in his rumpled white suit, put a quieting hand on her shoulder. "You're excited, you're——"

"Fred, dammit! I'll say what I want." Easter Lilly shook away his hand and seared him with a contemptuous glance.

"Then I will, too," Shep said. "I may deserve to be called horny. But not like Ben Neely. I never tried to rape you."

Easter Lilly spoke deliberately and into his face. "Neither did he."

"What?" The stupidity of his single word echoed in Shep's head, but could not blot out the shock of hers. For a moment, as if he had suffered a blow to his stomach, he thought he could not breathe. Then, in the sudden silence of the courtroom, he heard a strangled sound in his throat and felt a hot, knifelike pain in his lungs. He stared at Easter Lilly, wanting to protest, knowing somehow that . . .

"Ben Neely didn't try to rape me," she said, softly, clearly, her words and her eyes leaving no doubt.

Shep saw then, hating what he saw, the truth he had resisted. *Blinded* he thought *as if I'd put out my own eyes.* By the beauty within which——he saw at last——Easter's anger and animosity boiled like volcanic lava in a majestic peak.

Fred Worthington sat down suddenly, as if his legs had crumpled beneath him.

"Of course it wasn't rape," Meg said. "She's been lying from the start. She fooled all of you macho men."

Easter Lilly's head turned slowly, her eyes malevolent, seeming to see Meg at the table for the first time.

"But not you." It was an admission, not a question.

"Not from the first time I saw you. When you got your kicks telling me how he got it in and how big it was. I thought that was kind of strange for a woman to brag about."

"Then for God's sake, Meg . . ." Shep felt himself in a sort of kaleidoscope of whirling and elusive words. He could catch hold of none of them. "Why'd you help . . . if you knew . . ."

"She didn't give a damn about me, either." Easter's words crackled like lightning. "She just wanted you to win your case."

"Then it *was* murder!" Fred Worthington said. Most of the spectators had departed and Fred's words rang harshly in the empty courtroom. Two men at the door into the corridor turned briefly to look back, then went on out.

After a while, Easter spoke with no more fire in her voice. "He wouldn't let me alone. Night after night, after me this way, after me that. Didn't take three guesses what he wanted."

Her anger, Shep saw, had been momentarily expended in accusation, confession. Now she wanted the justification he did not wish to grant. He felt betrayed—not so much by Easter Lilly as by the faith in which he had lived.

"And you let Ben think he could get what he wanted, didn't you?" Meg said.

Easter Lilly flared wearily. "You sound like'is brother. All I let that cracker think, he was already thinking."

Like me. Shep saw himself with terrible clarity. She let me think what I was already thinking, too.

Counting on you to get me off.

"Then that night I wake up and he's on top of me."

Fred Worthington tried desperately to salvage something from the wreckage. "With the knife at your throat?"

"No, just begging. Kind of crying, too. He wanted pussy so bad." She stared at Fred, then at Shep. "How come you dudes want that thing so bad?"

Shep could think of no answer. How come indeed? He listened in silence as Easter Lilly told the rest of it without tears or dramatics, her voice echoing hollowly in the empty courtroom. How she'd picked up the knife from the bed where it must have fallen from Ben's pocket while he was getting his britches off. How she'd opened a blade before Ben even knew she had the knife, held on when he swiped at it to take it away, and cut his hand. Pictured him hopping and screeching around the cell, his hand bleeding and his pecker flopping, tripping on the pants down around his ankles, until in his pain and outrage he'd called her a stinking bitch for cutting him.

"Up till then, I didn't mean'im no harm. Just wanted'im off of me. Never thought about *killing*'im." Then, in a final whisper, "Till after I did."

A black man wearing a Lawn Boy cap and a Dallas Cowboys T-shirt came in and began to sweep between the rows, the cushioned bottom of each seat thudding up as he worked his broom under it. Fred Worthington sat with his head in his hands. Voices spoke loudly in the courthouse hallway. The sounds of traffic moving around the courthouse square seemed far off, from another world.

Meg broke the silence. "I guess that wraps it up for now," she said. "I'm going back to the motel. Get a good night's sleep."

It *can't* be wrapped up, Shep thought desperately. Had to be more to say. Something to be done. But he could think of nothing.

"I'll go with you." He felt empty, defeated, directionless—as if he'd lost his way in a desert and could find no landmarks.

They stood up. Across the table, Fred Worthington's face was a study in pain. But Easter Lilly held herself like a queen on the way to the guillotine, Shep thought, erect, unyielding, disdaining the crowd gathered for the beheading. He had never seen her so beautiful.

"Lawyer," she said, "I thank you for what you did."

"Thank Meg. Thank the pigeon."

"I mean . . . you believed me. That's what I thank you for."

"I did," Shep said. "I really did believe you." He wondered, momentarily, dramatically, if he would ever believe anyone again.

"I'm sorry about the rest, too. But you never understood . . ." For a moment, a look so bereft crossed Easter's classic face that Shep, even in his own disillusionment, sensed genuine pain in her. "Nobody understands. The only man I ever cared about, they ran'im out of town."

Fred Worthington bent his face to the tabletop.

"Cause he cared about me." Easter Lilly put her hand gently on the back of Fred's head. She did not look again at Shep Riley, and he followed Meg up the center aisle and out of the courtroom.

From a public telephone in a downstairs corridor, Shep called for the Beeline Cab. Then he and Meg waited on the baked sidewalk in the fierce late afternoon heat. The limed Confederate soldier gazed down at them from his eternal charge into defeat. Cars went by, their drivers seeing nothing but the street. A horn blew. Over a nearby intersection, a traffic light blinked yellowly.

"If there's another trial . . ." Meg began, but Shep interrupted almost angrily.

"Then she'll have to get along without me. I've got fish to catch in Vermont." He suddenly longed for a dry doughnut at the snack bar of the Little Giant. At least, those doughnuts were never deceptive. "But I doubt if there'll be another trial. Tyree won't want to have his brother accused of rape again. That precious Neely name smudged up in public."

"Maybe not." Meg hesitated, then appeared to plunge ahead. "You thought you were in love with her, didn't you? No wonder . . . a woman like that."

Shep shrugged. "Love? All I know is, the first time I saw her . . . seemed like I went out of my head."

"So you slept with me that same night."

He protested vainly, hearing the falsity of his words, remembering with shame that he'd been thinking mostly of Easter Lilly while he and Meg drained each other.

She took hold of his arm, gently. "I confess"—she squeezed lightly—"I wanted to have a party, too. That night."

"Not anymore, I guess."

"Nolo contendere, Counselor. We were always pretty good together, but now I've got kids and a husband. That I want to keep."

"Does he know how lucky he is?"

"Not entirely," Meg said. "But I hope enough."

He felt like a halfback after a hard tackle, getting up from the ground to resume the game. He said, "If not, give me a call sometime."

Meg laughed and let go his arm. "I'm afraid I wouldn't be much of a substitute for Easter Lilly. Even in a wet dream."

He smiled ruefully. "She really is beautiful, isn't she?"

"I'm not exactly ugly," Meg said, "but I'm not in her league."

He could not help but ask, "And you really knew she was lying all the time?"

"*Thought* she was. But like she said . . . I wanted to help you win the case. I was just being a lawyer until it dawned on me you were in love with her. Then——"

"Obsessed." Shep was determined to see things clear. He had lived in fantasy for too long.

"Then I wanted to shake you loose from whatever it was. Now I guess I don't need to, after"——Meg looked up at the courthouse——"all that."

Shep nodded. "I'm shook enough. But Meg . . . listen . . . I didn't believe her just because I was obsessed or in love or whatever I was. I believed her . . . I fought for her because I wanted to. Because I really did see her as a *victim*."

He wondered, however, as they stood there on the sidewalk, the late-day sun beating down like hatred, the blistering air redolent of asphalt and tires and gasoline, how he ever could know the truth. Had he been under a woman's spell rather than—at least as much as—a passion for justice? He did not want to believe it—either that his desire for Easter Lilly had contaminated his faith, or that his faith had been vulnerable to illusion.

"You're a believer," Meg said. "Which is why I believe in you."

He was relieved. He wanted Meg to believe in him. If she did, he might still be able to believe in himself. He began to clutch at the straws of faith.

"Because you see," he said, "if it wasn't literally true that Ben Neely tried to rape her in the cell that night, there was this bigger truth I never lost sight of. That she *had been raped*, anyway."

The Beeline Cab pulled up to the curb just then. Quentin Hodges seemed to be craning his neck, looking at the upper floors of the courthouse.

"They've all been raped," Shep said. "I believed that when I came down here, and nothing's happened to change my mind."

Suddenly he felt no regret at the trial's outcome. That strangely appealing woman—so much anger trapped inside so much beauty—had deceived him, but the deceit, he told himself, had been tactical, trivial. He had been a dupe, but he had not been *wrong*.

"I don't much believe in bigger truths," Meg said. "It's hard enough to know the little ones."

Shep followed her into the backseat. He glanced back at the courthouse, wishing involuntarily that he could see Easter Lilly one more time. But in his head he heard her voice:

The only man I ever cared about.

He put aside forever the wish to see Easter Lilly again. That was trivial, too, and triviality could not change the way of the world.

The cab began to move. "Big or little," Shep said, "I'm damn glad you told me to get Flushing Johns on that jury."

He had meant the remark as due tribute to Meg's work. But the irony of his words struck him with the force of the summer sun:

I came down here to seek justice. And instead, we fixed the fight.

"Did you notice," Quentin Hodges, slowing for the blinking yellow signal, spoke over his shoulder, "Tyree's light still burnin on the third floor? That sonovagun never stops workin."

DAISY

DAISY HAD FOUND IT DIFFICULT TO TRACK DOWN THE JOHNS BOY'S college address. When she finally took it into Tyree's inner office, Waitsfield Avenue was barely visible in the slowly falling summer dusk outside his window. In his shirtsleeves, Tyree was reviewing the Fielding Johns correspondence.

Daisy was angry still at his insensitivity. She placed the typewritten address slip on his desk. Her hand hurt. It was going to swell up, she feared, and he'd hardly even seemed to care, after that one moment in the elevator.

Tyree had been sweet then, the way he could be. And she liked seeing him go right back to work, despite what must have been crushing disappointment at his failure to win court vindication of the Neely name. It came to her as she stood above him that he'd taught by example—still was teaching—a more useful lesson than any she'd learned from Vic Buckley or Randolph Thorpe or even dirty old Dr. Huntington.

Never give up.

Looking down at his bent head, Daisy decided that, like Tyree himself, she never would.

He glanced carelessly at the address slip, then at her. As if I'm part of the furniture, she thought. But I won't be just furniture forever.

"Thanks, Daisy. You better get on home, late as it is."

"So what're *you* going to do now?"

Tyree's face hardened. "Find a new sanitation engineer."

Daisy had no doubt he would. Fielding Johns had owed him and failed to pay the debt. Tyree Neely did not like to be disappointed in those he had counted on.

"I meant about Easter Lilly," she said.

Looking surprised, as if he didn't know why she'd bothered to ask, Tyree said without hesitation, "Try her again. Soon as I can draw up a new murder charge."

DATE DUE

JAN 1 3 '99 S			
JAN 1 3 1999			